HE STRUGGLED TO HIS HANDS AND KNEES JUST AS SHE REACHED HIM, HER BARE FEET COVERED IN WET GRASS

She paused, fear nearly swallowing her. Was he okay? She could return to the house.

His head hung down, his wet hair obscuring his face. This close, the violence done to his body was even more evident. A large surgical scar wound around his left thigh, and another healed knife wound showed on his left hip.

"Malcolm?" she whispered, her voice stolen by the storm. She reached out and touched his shoulder.

He jumped up so quickly, she screamed. Pivoting, he turned to face her, his legs braced and his fists clenched. Fire lanced in his green eyes. Terror and fury sharpened the rugged angles of his hard face. Blood mingled with rain on his right temple.

Her feet froze. Her legs shook. She couldn't move. He was so much taller, so much bigger, than anybody she'd ever met. If he attacked her, she didn't have a chance.

But she still couldn't run.

Recognition slowly filled his eyes, making him look more human than animal. "Pippa."

Also by Rebecca Zanetti

HIDDEN

REBECCA ZANETTI

ZEBRA BOOKS
KENSINGTON PUBLISHING CORP.

http://www.kensingtonbooks.com

ZEBRA BOOKS are published by

Kensington Publishing Corp.
119 West 40th Street
New York, NY 10018

All Kensington titles, imprints, and distributed lines are available at special quantity discounts for bulk purchases for sales promotion, premiums, fund-raising, educational, or institutional use.

Special book excerpts or customized printings can also be created to fit specific needs. For details, write or phone the office of the Kensington Sales Manager: Attn.: Sales Department. Kensington Publishing Corp., 119 West 40th Street, New York, NY 10018. Phone: 1-800-221-2647.

Zebra and the Z logo Reg. U.S. Pat. & TM Off.

First Printing: October 2018
ISBN-13: 978-1-4201-4581-6
ISBN-10: 1-4201-4581-9

eISBN-13: 978-1-4201-4582-3
eISBN-10: 1-4201-4582-7

10 9 8 7 6 5 4 3 2 1

Printed in the United States of America

This one's for Big Tone.
I like you and I love you. Always.

ACKNOWLEDGMENTS

I'm so excited about this new Requisition Force series! I have many people to thank for getting this book to readers, and I sincerely apologize to anyone I've forgotten.

Thank you to Gabe and Karlina for being such awesome kids. Being your mom is my biggest blessing. I can't belie how much you've both grown, and I'm excited to see w you do next.

Thank you to my hardworking editor, Alicia Cond

Thank you to the rest of the Kensington gang: Ale Nicolajsen, Steven Zacharius, Adam Zacharius, Ross/ Lynn Cully, Vida Engstrand, Jane Nutter, Lauren Lauren Jernigan, Kimberly Richardson, and Rebec monese.

Thank you to my wonderful agent, Caitlin Bl to Liza Dawson and the entire Dawson group, very hard for me.

Thank you to Jillian Stein for the abs work and for being such an amazing frie

Thanks to my fantastic street team, P their creative and hardworking leade

Thanks also to my constant supp English, Debbie and Travis Smit Jessica and Jonah Namson, ar

Chapter One

The day he moved in next door, dark clouds covered the sky with the promise of a powerful storm. Pippa watched from her window, the one over the kitchen sink, partially hidden by the cheerful polka-dotted curtains. Yellow dots over crisp white background—what she figured happy people would use.

He moved box after box after box through the two-stall garage, all by himself, cut muscles bunching in his arms.

Angles and shadows made up his face, more shadows than angles. He didn't smile, and although he didn't frown, his expression had settled into harsh lines.

A guy like him, dangerously handsome, should probably have friends helping.

Yet he didn't. His black truck, dusty yet seemingly well kept, sat alone in the driveway as he removed the crates.

She swallowed several times, instinctively knowing he wasn't a man to cross, even if she had been a person who crossed others. She was not.

For a while, she tried to amuse herself with counting the boxes, and then guessing the weight, and then just studying the man. He appeared to be in his early thirties, maybe just a few years older than her.

Thick black hair fell to his collar in unruly waves, giving him an unkempt appearance that hinted nobody took care of him. His shoulders were tense yet his body language fluid. She couldn't see his eyes.

The question, the damn wondering, would keep her up at night.

But no way, there was absolutely *no way*, she would venture outside to appease the beast of curiosity.

The new neighbor stood well over six feet tall, his shoulders broad, his long legs encased in worn and frayed jeans. If a man could be hard all over, head to toe, even in movement, then he was.

A scar curved in a half-moon shape over his left eye, and some sort of tattoo, a crest or something, decorated his muscled left bicep. She tilted her head, reaching for the curtains to push them aside a little more.

He paused and turned, much like an animal going on alert, an overlarge box held easily in his arms. Green. Those eyes, narrow and suspicious, alert and dangerous, focused directly on her.

She gasped. Her heart thundered. She fell to the floor below the counter. Not to the side, not even in a crouch, she fell flat on her butt on the well-scrubbed tiles. Her heart ticking, she wrapped her arms around her shins and rested her chin on her knees.

She bit her lip and held her breath, shutting her eyes.

Nothing.

No sound, no hint of an approaching person, no rap on the door. Her throat closed, making it nearly impossible to breathe.

After about ten minutes of holding perfectly still, she lifted her head. Another five and she released her legs. Then she rolled up onto her knees and reached for the counter, her fingers curling over.

Chapter One

The day he moved in next door, dark clouds covered the sky with the promise of a powerful storm. Pippa watched from her window, the one over the kitchen sink, partially hidden by the cheerful polka-dotted curtains. Yellow dots over crisp white background—what she figured happy people would use.

He moved box after box after box through the two-stall garage, all by himself, cut muscles bunching in his arms.

Angles and shadows made up his face, more shadows than angles. He didn't smile, and although he didn't frown, his expression had settled into harsh lines.

A guy like him, dangerously handsome, should probably have friends helping.

Yet he didn't. His black truck, dusty yet seemingly well kept, sat alone in the driveway as he removed the crates.

She swallowed several times, instinctively knowing he wasn't a man to cross, even if she had been a person who crossed others. She was not.

For a while, she tried to amuse herself with counting the boxes, and then guessing the weight, and then just studying the man. He appeared to be in his early thirties, maybe just a few years older than her.

Thick black hair fell to his collar in unruly waves, giving him an unkempt appearance that hinted nobody took care of him. His shoulders were tense yet his body language fluid. She couldn't see his eyes.

The question, the damn wondering, would keep her up at night.

But no way, there was absolutely *no way*, she would venture outside to appease the beast of curiosity.

The new neighbor stood well over six feet tall, his shoulders broad, his long legs encased in worn and frayed jeans. If a man could be hard all over, head to toe, even in movement, then he was.

A scar curved in a half-moon shape over his left eye, and some sort of tattoo, a crest or something, decorated his muscled left bicep. She tilted her head, reaching for the curtains to push them aside a little more.

He paused and turned, much like an animal going on alert, an overlarge box held easily in his arms. Green. Those eyes, narrow and suspicious, alert and dangerous, focused directly on her.

She gasped. Her heart thundered. She fell to the floor below the counter. Not to the side, not even in a crouch, she fell flat on her butt on the well-scrubbed tiles. Her heart ticking, she wrapped her arms around her shins and rested her chin on her knees.

She bit her lip and held her breath, shutting her eyes.

Nothing.

No sound, no hint of an approaching person, no rap on the door. Her throat closed, making it nearly impossible to breathe.

After about ten minutes of holding perfectly still, she lifted her head. Another five and she released her legs. Then she rolled up onto her knees and reached for the counter, her fingers curling over.

This one's for Big Tone.
I like you and I love you. Always.

ACKNOWLEDGMENTS

I'm so excited about this new Requisition Force series! I have many people to thank for getting this book to readers, and I sincerely apologize to anyone I've forgotten.

Thank you to Gabe and Karlina for being such awesome kids. Being your mom is my biggest blessing. I can't believe how much you've both grown, and I'm excited to see what you do next.

Thank you to my hardworking editor, Alicia Condon.

Thank you to the rest of the Kensington gang: Alexandra Nicolajsen, Steven Zacharius, Adam Zacharius, Ross Plotkin, Lynn Cully, Vida Engstrand, Jane Nutter, Lauren Vasallo, Lauren Jernigan, Kimberly Richardson, and Rebecca Cremonese.

Thank you to my wonderful agent, Caitlin Blasdell, and to Liza Dawson and the entire Dawson group, who work so very hard for me.

Thank you to Jillian Stein for the absolutely fantastic work and for being such an amazing friend.

Thanks to my fantastic street team, Rebecca's Rebels, and their creative and hardworking leader, Minga Portillo.

Thanks also to my constant support system: Gail and Jim English, Debbie and Travis Smith, Stephanie and Don West, Jessica and Jonah Namson, and Kathy and Herb Zanetti.

Taking a deep breath, she pulled herself to stand, angling to the side of the counter.

He stood at the window, facing her, his chest taking up most of the panes.

Her heart exploded. She screamed, turned, and ran. She cleared the kitchen in three steps and plowed through the living room, smashing into an antique table that had sat in the same place since the day she'd moved in.

Pain ratcheted up her leg, and she dropped, making panicked grunting noises as she crawled past the sofa toward her bedroom. Her hands slapped the polished wooden floor, and she sobbed out, reaching the room and slamming the door.

She yanked her legs up to her chest again, her back to the door, and reached up to engage the lock. She rocked back and forth, careful not to make a sound.

The doorbell rang.

Her chest tightened, and her vision fuzzed. Tremors started from her shoulders down to her waist and back up. *Not now. Not now. God, not now.* She took several deep breaths and acknowledged the oncoming panic attack much as Dr. Valentine had taught her. Sometimes letting the panic in actually abated it.

Not this time.

The attack took her full force, pricking sweat along her body. Her arms shook and her legs went numb. Her breathing panted out, her vision fuzzed, and her heart blasted into motion.

Maybe it really was a heart attack this time.

No. It was only a panic attack.

But it could be a heart attack. Maybe the doctors had missed something in her tests. Or perhaps it was a stroke.

She couldn't make it to the phone to dial for help.

Her heart hurt. Her chest really ached. Glancing up at the lock, a flimsy golden thing, she inched away from the door to the bed table on her hands and knees. Jerking open the drawer, she fumbled for a Xanax.

She popped the pill beneath her tongue, letting it quickly absorb. The bitter chalkiness made her gag, but she didn't move until it had dissolved.

A hard, rapping sound echoed from the living room.

No, no, no. He was knocking on the door. Was it locked? Of course it was locked. She always kept it locked. But would a lock, even a really good one, keep a guy like that out?

Definitely no.

She'd been watching him, and he knew it. Maybe he wasn't a guy who wanted to be watched, which was why he was moving his stuff all alone. Worse yet, had he been sent to find her? He had looked so furious. Was he angry?

If so, what could she do?

The online martial arts lessons she'd taken lately ran through her head, but once again, she wondered if one could really learn self-defense by watching videos. Something told her that all the self-defense lessons in the world wouldn't help against that guy.

Oh, why had Mrs. Maloni moved to Florida? Sure, the elderly lady wanted to be closer to her grandchildren, but Cottage Grove was a much better place to live.

Her house had sold in less than a week.

Pippa had hoped to watch young children play and frolic in the large treed backyard, but this guy didn't seem to have a family.

Perhaps he'd bring one in, yet there was something chillingly solitary about him.

Of course, she rarely set foot outside her house, so maybe family men had changed.

Probably not, though.

He knocked again, the sound stronger and more insistent this time.

She opened the bedroom door and peered around the corner. The front door was visible above the sofa.

He knocked again. "Lady?" Deep and rich, his voice easily carried into her home.

She might have squawked.

"Listen, lady. I, ah, saw you fall and just wanna make sure you're all right. You don't have to answer the door." His tone didn't rise and remained perfectly calm.

She sucked in a deep breath and tried to answer him, but only air came out. Man, she was pathetic. She tapped her head against the doorframe in a sad attempt to self-soothe.

"Um, are you okay?" he asked, hidden by the big front door. "I can call for help."

No. Oh, no. She swallowed several times. "I'm all right." Finally, her voice worked. "Honest. It's okay. Don't call for anybody." If she didn't let them in, the authorities would probably break down the door, right? She couldn't have that.

Silence came from the front porch, but no steps echoed. He remained in place.

Her heart continued to thunder against her ribs. She wiped her sweaty palms down her yoga pants. Why wasn't he leaving? "Okay?" she whispered.

"You sure you don't need help?" he called, his voice rich and deep. Definitely sexy, with a whole male edge that went with that spectacular body. "I promise I can be all sorts of helpful to damsels in distress."

Was that a line? Was he trying to flirt with her or put her at ease? What could she say back? Something equally flirty so he'd be at ease and not curious about her? Nothing came to her fuzzing mind. "I'm sure." *Go away.* Please, he had to go away.

"Okay." Heavy bootsteps clomped across her front porch, and then silence.

He was gone.

* * *

Hours later, Malcolm West kept moving boxes into his house, wondering about the pretty lady next door. She hadn't reappeared in the window for hours.

He knew the sound of terror, and he knew it well. The woman, whoever she was, had been beyond frightened at seeing him in the window. Damn it. What the hell had he been thinking to approach her house like that?

A fence enclosed their backyards together, and he'd wondered why. Had a family once shared the two homes?

He grabbed the last box of stuff from the truck and hefted it toward the house. Maybe this had been a mistake. He'd purchased the little one-story home sight unseen because of the white clapboard siding, the blue shutters, and the damn name of the town—Cottage Grove. It sounded peaceful.

He'd never truly see peace again, and he knew it.

All the homes the real estate agent had emailed him about had been sad and run-down . . . until this one. It had been on the market only a few days, and the agent had insisted it wouldn't be for long. After a month of searching desperately for a place to call home, he'd jumped on the sale.

It had been so convenient, it seemed like a stroke of fate.

If he believed in fate, which he did not.

He walked through the simple one-story home and dropped another box in the kitchen, looking out at the pine trees beyond the wooden fence. The area had been subdivided into twenty-acre lots, with tons and tons of trees, so he'd figured he wouldn't see any other houses, which had suited him just fine.

Yet his house was next to another, and one fence enclosed their backyards together.

No other homes were even visible.

He sighed and started to turn for the living room when a

sound caught his attention. His body automatically went on full alert, and he reached for the SIG hidden at the back of his waist. Had they found him? Somebody had just come in the front door.

"Detective West? Don't shoot. I'm a friendly," came a deep male voice.

Malcolm pulled the gun free, the weight of it in his hand more familiar than his own voice. "Friendlies don't show up uninvited," he said calmly, eyeing the two main exits from the room in case he needed to run.

A guy strode into the kitchen, hands loose at his sides. Probably in his thirties, he had bloodshot eyes, short, mussed-up brown hair, and graceful movements. His gaze showed he'd seen some shit, and there was a slight tremble in his right arm. Trying to kick a habit, was he?

Malcolm pointed the weapon at the guy's head. "Two seconds."

The man looked at the few boxes set around the room, not seeming to notice the gun. Even with the tremor, he moved like he could fight. "There's nowhere to sit."

"You're not staying." Malcolm could get to the vehicle hidden a mile away within minutes and then take off again. The pretty cottage was a useless dream, and he'd known it the second he'd signed the papers. "I'd hate to ruin the minty-green wallpaper." It had flowers on it, and he'd planned to change it anyway.

"Then don't." The guy leaned against the wall and shook out his arm.

"What are you kicking?" Malcolm asked, his voice going low.

The guy winced. "I'm losing some friends."

"Jack, Jose, and Bud?" Mal guessed easily.

"Mainly Jack Daniel's." Now he eyed the weapon. "Mind putting that down?"

Mal didn't flinch. "Who are you?"

Broad shoulders heaved in an exaggerated sigh. "My name is Angus Force, and I'm here to offer you an opportunity."

"Is that a fact? I don't need a new toaster." Mal slid the gun back into place. "Go away."

"Detective—"

"I'm not a detective any longer. Get out of my house." Mal could use a good fight, and he was about to give himself what he needed.

"Whoa." Force held up a hand. "Just hear me out. I'm with a new unit attached to the Homeland Defense Department, and we need a guy with your skills."

Heat rushed up Mal's chest. His main skill these days was keeping himself from going ballistic on assholes, and he was about to fail in that. "I'm not interested. Now get the hell out of my house."

Force shook his head. "I understand you're struggling with the aftereffects of a difficult assignment, but you won. You got the bad guys."

Yeah, but how many people had died? In front of him? Mal's vision started to narrow with darkness from the corners of his eyes. "You don't want to be here any longer, Force."

"You think you're the only one with PTSD, dickhead?" Force spat, losing his casual façade.

"No, but I ain't lookin' to bond over it." Sweat rolled down Mal's back. "How'd you find me anyway?"

Force visibly settled himself. "It's not exactly a coincidence that you bought this house. The only one that came close to what you were searching for." He looked around the old-lady cheerful kitchen. "Though it is sweet."

Mal's fingers closed into a fist. "You set me up."

"Yeah, we did. We need you here." Force gestured around. Mal's lungs compressed. "Why?"

"Because you're the best undercover cop we've ever seen, and we need that right now. Bad." Force ran a shaking hand through his hair.

"Why?" Mal asked, already fearing the answer.

"The shut-in next door. She's the key to one of the biggest homegrown threats to our entire country. And here you are." Force's eyes gleamed with the hit.

Well, fuck.

Chapter Two

The smell of comfort and sugar filled Pippa's kitchen in the form of freshly baked banana bread, chocolate chip cookies, and homemade apple pie. By the time the pie had started to cool, her heart rate had returned to normal. Almost.

How much of a dork had she made of herself hours before? She tried to keep from peeking through her kitchen window like some creepy stalker, but her neighbor had a visitor. So the guy *did* have friends.

Tough guy, kind of sexy, dangerous-looking friends.

Well, one friend anyway. She'd seen him stride up the walkway and go right into the house without knocking. He was tall, like the neighbor. Messy dark hair and muscly arms beneath a ratty T-shirt. Who were these guys?

Giving up the fight, she dusted off her hands and walked at a sedate pace, just like a normal person, through her living room to the wide window facing the street. The visitor had a clean black truck. A big one.

Maybe the two guys were some sort of black truck club. She grinned at the thought. You could tell a lot about people from their vehicles.

Take her. She had a fifteen-year-old, sturdy Subaru she'd purchased five years ago. It sat quietly in the garage and was only used about once a month. Just growing old and dusty. Like her.

Movement in the truck caught her eye.

She sidled closer to the window. Somebody was in the driver's side of the truck. Even though it was chilly outside, a sign of the early spring season, the window was down. Her sofa sat under her window, so she perched on her knees and squinted.

A furry head turned, and sharp brown eyes caught hers. A dog. She gasped. How did the dog know she was looking?

His tongue lolled out. She chuckled. Adorable. The pooch had a huge head with darker fur across his eyes and nose in a kind of a mask. She'd seen German shepherds on television, and they always looked so dangerous. This one looked furry and bored. Somehow, his expression appeared as if he was put out by something—maybe by being left in the truck.

She slowly lifted her hand and waved. Man, she was totally losing it. Maybe it was time to venture outside again to the real world. Visit a mall or something.

The dog's left ear lifted higher. His powerful shoulders bunched, and he leaped through the window, landing gracefully on the asphalt.

She jerked back.

As if on a mission, he cleared the clean row of shrubs between the two driveways and prowled up hers, sleek muscles moving beneath his thick brown fur. He paused at the sidewalk and sniffed the shoots of her tulips, which were just beginning to sprout.

Turning his head, he gave a mighty sneeze.

She laughed.

He lifted his head and continued on, reaching her porch. Then he barked. Once.

She blinked. This was a little nutty. Catching her breath, she looked outside in every direction. Nothing. The two houses were located at the end of a cul-de-sac, across from forested land. The nearest house was more than twenty miles down the quiet road.

The dog barked again.

Okay. A normal person wouldn't just go and open her door to a barking German shepherd. She pushed herself off the comfortable denim sofa and turned for the door. Since when had she been normal?

It took several seconds to disengage the multiple locks, and then she opened the door, keeping a tight grip on the edge in case she needed to slam it shut. "Um, hello."

The dog remained sitting and cocked his head to the side.

She knew better than to crouch and put her face close to his teeth. So she held out a hand.

He moved forward, sniffed her hand, and then gave it a giant lick. A slight whine escaped him, and he pushed toward her, trying to lick all her fingers up to the wrist.

She laughed and shoved him back. Apparently, she hadn't wiped the sugar from the pie off her hand.

"Roscoe!" A sharp voice snapped from the other porch.

She yelped, and the dog sprang into action, his shoulders striking her knees. He turned and bounded back toward the truck, leaping smoothly through the open window. She teetered and then fell flat on her butt. For the second time that day.

The neighbor and his visitor both visibly blanched from across the way.

"Damn." Her new neighbor cleared the shrubs in one leap, striding toward her, his chin down. When had they come outside? "Lady, I'm sorry." He reached her in seconds, holding out a hand large enough to wrap around her entire neck. He was so . . . big.

She couldn't breathe. Her hands remained frozen on the porch.

He studied her with those startling green eyes and then dropped to his haunches so they were eye to eye. "You're all right." His voice, dark and deep and rumbly, was somehow soothing. And he smelled . . . good. Masculine and foresty. "Did the dog frighten you?" He turned his head to look over his shoulder at his friend. The man was standing at the driver's door of his truck, watching them.

"No," she whispered, her voice trembling.

Her neighbor turned back, his full focus on her again. "Did I?"

She swallowed. Considering she was trembling, she'd look even more like a moron if she lied. "No." What the heck. Lie anyway.

His lips twitched and he almost grinned. The slight action lightened his eyes enough to make them even more fascinating.

The guy at the truck opened his door, shoved the dog to the other side, and jumped in. "I'll be in touch, West," he called out, igniting the engine and whipping around in the street. He reached the edge of Pippa's drive and rolled down the dog's window. The dog seemed to be smiling somehow. "Remember what I said."

The neighbor called West didn't look at the other guy again. "I said no," he said, loud enough for his voice to carry. "Don't come back." The darkness in his tone was backed up by the clear threat.

Pippa's eyes widened. So . . . not friends. Any words she might have had dried up in her throat.

The truck sped off.

West watched her for two seconds and then seemed to make a decision. He dropped from his haunches to his butt on her porch, wincing as he forced his jean-clad legs into a crossed position. "You're scared, and I'm trying not to tower over you, but you're a little thing, aren't you?"

Even sitting, he did tower. But there was a sweetness in his actions that had her shoulders slowly relaxing. "Are you hurt?" She found her voice again.

His dark eyebrows lifted. "Left thigh. Injury that's getting better."

Okay. Time to stop being such a wimp. If he could act normal just sitting on the hard planks of her front porch, so could she. She held out her hand. "Pippa Smith."

His arm lifted slowly, as if he was trying really hard not to spook her. "Malcolm West."

The second his hand enfolded hers, warmth and a jolt of awareness shot up her arm. Her breath caught again, and this time fear had nothing to do with it. She was acting like some Victorian damsel meeting a man for the first time. "I'm not a virgin or anything," she blurted out.

Oh God. Heat flushed into her face. Had she just said that?

His chin lowered just a bit, giving him almost a predatory look, although amusement glimmered in his eyes. "Is that an invitation?"

The bright pink blush across the woman's high cheek-bones made her seem even more delicate somehow. She had shoulder-length brown hair and deep ocean-blue eyes. Even if fear didn't seem to hover around her, there was a fragility to her that brought out an awareness in him he sure as hell didn't need. "Why do I scare you?" he asked before he could stop his damn mouth from working.

She withdrew her soft hand. "Who says you scare me?"

It was so obvious he couldn't even respond. So he let his gaze drop to her neck and the vein pulsing there.

The desire to dive right into her head, into her secrets, slashed into him with a too-familiar feeling. There was a reason he'd been a cop. But that reason was gone. "Is it me or all men?" Why was he still asking questions?

Thunder rolled in the distance, and she angled her head

to better see the gathering cloud cover. "Why was there a man at your house who you told to never return?"

Well. Apparently, he wasn't the only nosy one. "I was a cop, things went bad, and that guy wants me to be a cop again."

Her gaze snapped back to him, the movement like a startled bird. Her mouth formed a small *o*.

Ah, hell. "Is there some reason you don't like cops?" This shivering woman couldn't be a threat to anybody. Angus Force had been full of crap. Without question. "Pippa?" Her name was pert. Cute. But she was deeper than that. He could already tell.

She slowly shook her head. "No. I'm not afraid of police officers."

Lie. Surprisingly, she wasn't bad at lying. Not great, though. He was still breathing because of his ability to play a part and detect deceit. So he decided to play along. "So, men."

Her head tilted just enough to be intriguing. She sighed. "No. People." Her face scrunched up, making her look younger than what had to be late twenties.

Ah. "You're agoraphobic." How odd to be having this conversation on a porch with rain about to arrive. But he didn't want to move. If he moved, she'd go back inside. He'd never met a mystery he didn't want to unravel.

Maybe some things never changed.

She shook her head, sending that long mass of hair tumbling. "No. Not agoraphobic." She sighed. "Close enough, though. When you don't do something for a long time, then it's hard to do it again, you know?"

Not really. But at least she was talking.

He opened his mouth to speak, and the scent of sweetness caught him. He turned his head to her slightly open door. "What in the world is that?" He lifted his nose and sniffed. That was better than anything he'd smelled in ages.

She stiffened, as if brought back into the real world. Then she scrambled, using the door to reach her feet. "I, ah, bake sometimes." The flush intensified as she looked down at him from not much height. "A lot. I bake a lot."

It smelled like what heaven should smell like. He'd probably never know. Was it rude to beg? It probably was. Would she let him buy whatever it was that smelled so good? It was probably also rude to offer money to a new neighbor for baked goods. He'd never learned much in the manners department. Manipulation, hell yeah. But something in him, something he definitely didn't want to examine, balked at manipulating her. "I can microwave," he offered. "Good noodles."

"Oh." She slid the door open and edged halfway inside. Indecision crossed her face; she looked almost pained. She probably had great manners and was now fighting them.

He rolled to his feet and shook out his left leg, which had cramped. The ache from his thigh was a constant companion, but at least the bullet had missed an artery. When he could, he took several steps back to give her space.

The skies opened, and rain began to drop.

"Um, I could give you a couple of cookies, if you'd like." Her knuckles were white as she clutched the door.

Damn, he wanted those cookies. But her body language, even if he wasn't an expert, showed she didn't want him inside. In fact, she was barring the way. "My boots are dirty," he lied easily. "I'd love a couple of cookies, but do you mind if I stay on the porch? My socks have holes, and I'd rather not remove my boots. Too much ego, you know."

She blinked, self-derision mixing with relief in her stunning eyes. They were clearer than a July sky in Montana. He'd been on a case there years ago. "Sure. I'll be right back." She disappeared.

He didn't move. Not an inch. With her hyperawareness, she'd hear the creak of a porch board, and she'd be scared again. So he barely breathed. There wasn't much he wouldn't do for a homemade cookie that smelled like it'd melt the second you tasted it.

She reappeared again with a large basket in her hands. "Here." She thrust it over.

He took it, leaning down. The fragrance nearly dropped him to his knees. "What is all of this?"

She shuffled back. "Cookies, some banana bread, and an apple pie." Her shrug lifted slim shoulders. "I can't eat it all."

"I can't take all of this." But he was already backing away before she could change her mind.

She smiled. "Sure you can. Welcome to the neighborhood." Then she glanced around at the completely deserted vicinity. "Well. Welcome to the end of nowhere anyway." Then she shut the door in his face.

He lowered his nose and inhaled deeply. The pie. He'd definitely start with the pie. His mind spinning, he turned and walked easily through the rain to his front door, already dialing and then lifting his phone to his ear.

"Miss me?" Angus Force said by way of greeting, with the sound of light traffic around him.

Mal kicked his door shut. "I want the records on her. Not agreeing to help you, but I want the files." He clicked off before Force could piss him off.

Then he leaned back against the door, the basket of goodies in his hands and curiosity in his head. He should repack his stuff and hit the road. Get the hell out of there.

But she'd given him a pie.

Chapter Three

Pippa woke with a startled gasp, bolting upright in bed. Her heart thundered and her stomach cramped. "It was just a dream," she whispered into the darkness. Just a dream. It wasn't real. This was real. She pinched her arm to make sure.

Ouch.

Okay. Even though a nightlight near the door illuminated the room, she fumbled for a brighter light on the antique bed table. Used to the routine, she took several deep breaths and studied her pretty room. She'd painted her tables and dresser a very bright green. Her bedspread was a cheerful yellow, and her rug a soothing combination of the two. The exact opposite of muted and proper colors.

She reached for the glass of water near her, noticing it was empty. Her throat hurt.

Maneuvering out of the bed, she slid her feet into slippers and moved toward the bedroom door, taking seconds to disengage the three locks.

Pausing out of habit, she closed her eyes and listened. Quiet, the peaceful kind, filled her house. No odd signatures of anything or anyone who shouldn't be there. So she padded down the hallway into the kitchen and filled her glass at the sink.

Rain pattered against the window, and the wind had picked up to a low roar. It sounded ominous. But enough of a moon shone through the clouds that she could see the trees swaying past the grass in the backyard, fresh pine needles whipping around in a frenzy.

Then she saw him.

Malcolm West stood with his back to her in the center of the yard, wearing only boxers, his head up and his body shuddering. Rain sluiced over him, showing the hard ridges and planes of his body. Which was shaking almost violently.

The hair stood up on her arms. Silently, she moved to the sliding glass door, almost pressing her nose to it.

The light was dim enough that she could make him out, but the entire scene was a little hazy. His fists were clenched. The muscles in his arms and back bunched—impossibly so. His chest heaved, moving his entire torso.

Oh. If that wasn't a panic attack, she didn't know what was. A part of her, the good and righteous part, knew she should run out there and offer help. Give comfort.

The much stronger part of her remained stiffly in place, unable to move.

He howled something, the sound pained and lost in the wind. Yet anger rode it, almost visible.

She stepped back from the glass.

Lightning cracked, and she jumped. For a second, the entire yard was lit up. He was all male, full of power. Almost animalistic in the middle of that storm. His wet hair curled to his shoulders, and there was damage on that magnificent body. Three healed bullet holes near his right shoulder blade, and what looked like knife wounds down his left rib cage.

Her breath sped up, and she pressed her hand to the glass.

How could something so dangerous, somebody so dangerous, draw her? Maybe she really did have that evil core she'd been accused of.

He was wounded, and he was deadly. She knew that as well as she knew her own soul.

The yearning inside her to join him, to touch him, shocked her. But still, her hand released one of the door locks.

Another large crack, and something spun through the air. That tree branch she'd meant to have removed. He partially turned, probably out of instinct, just in time to get hit in the head.

He went down fast and hard.

She gasped. *Get up. Get up. Get up.*

He didn't move. Facedown in the wet grass, pine needles already falling on his bare back, he remained still. Too still.

She swallowed, her heart beating so fast it was hard to breathe as she finished unlocking the door. Was this the heart attack she'd been waiting for? She had to put all her weight into moving the heavy door, but she got it open.

The rain and wind attacked her instantly.

What if he was dead? A hit to the temple could kill somebody. Everyone knew that.

She blinked and looked in the direction the branch had come from. The tree had cracked and was swaying crazily. She'd been meaning to have somebody cut it down. It was definitely going to fall.

Right on the downed ex-cop.

This was her fault. She hadn't called a forester because she hadn't wanted to talk to anybody on the phone. Her weakness had created danger.

There was no choice. She had to help him.

Her breath came out in a rush, and she launched into motion, ignoring fear. She ran across her brick patio and onto the grass, the wild wind competing with the ringing between her ears. The rain smashed against her pink tank top and shorts, molding the soft material to her body. Her hair whipped around in the wind, getting soaked, and she shoved tendrils out of her eyes, having to squint.

He struggled to his hands and knees just as she reached him, her bare feet covered in wet grass.

She paused, fear nearly swallowing her. Was he okay? She could return to the house.

His head hung down, his wet hair obscuring his face. This close, the violence done to his body was even more evident. A large surgical scar wound around his left thigh, and another healed knife wound showed on his left hip.

"Malcolm?" she whispered, her voice stolen by the storm. She reached out and touched his shoulder.

He jumped up so quickly, she screamed. Pivoting, he turned to face her, his legs braced and his fists clenched. Fire lanced in his green eyes. Terror and fury sharpened the rugged angles of his hard face. Blood mingled with rain on his right temple.

Her feet froze. Her legs shook. She couldn't move. He was so much taller, so much bigger, than anybody she'd ever met. If he attacked her, she didn't have a chance.

But she still couldn't run.

Recognition slowly filled his eyes, making him look more human than animal. "Pippa." His chest heaved. He dropped to one knee, and water splashed up.

She grasped his arm, his skin slippery from the rain but still heated. "Don't pass out again. I can't get you inside by myself." Going on instinct, swallowing her fear, she shoved her body beneath his arm. "Muscle weighs more than fat." Babbling now, she lifted up and helped him stumble to his feet. "You don't have any fat." Not an ounce. Even his abdomen, now that she could see it, was ripped. "So you're heavy. I can't drag you inside." He outweighed her by at least a hundred pounds. Probably more.

"I'm okay," he slurred, staggering by her side toward the patio.

"Right." She kept going until they reached the sliding glass door, feeling small and defenseless so close to him.

With his free hand, he carelessly slid the heavy door the rest of the way open. His easy strength rippled tension through her abdomen. Awareness and something else. Something heated and needy that she'd worry about later.

Then they were inside her cheery yellow-patterned kitchen. She helped him sit at the quaint round table, and the antique wooden chair groaned under his weight.

She took a step back.

He overwhelmed the chair. His wet hair and the blood on his face gave him a primitive, dangerous look.

And she'd brought him into her safe haven.

Mal's chest ached, probably because his heart had rammed against his rib cage in a way that had to be unhealthy. Certainly unnecessary. He often awoke in the dead middle of a panic attack, and fresh air always seemed to help, so he usually ran outside like a wild animal.

He hadn't considered he'd get beaned in the head this time.

Everything hurt. His head, his face, his hip, his damn leg. But warmth and the smell of freshly baked cookies wafted around, somehow calming him.

He blinked water out of his eyes and focused.

Pippa hovered near the open sliding door, her hair a wet mass around her head, rain on her angled face. Her tiny tank top and shorts were soaking wet and plastered to a surprisingly curvy body. Her nipples were diamond hard against the flimsy cotton, and even though she was short, her bare legs were plenty long for her body.

That quickly, his cock joined the cacophony of pain. Hard and needy.

Her eyes widened.

He sprawled in the flimsy chair and didn't look down. In only boxer briefs—wet ones—there was probably no doubt where his mind had gone. "I won't hurt you, Pippa." The name didn't feel right on his tongue. Why not?

She swallowed, her throat moving with the effort. "I'm sorry about your head. It was my fault."

Unless she'd walked out and hit him with a bat, he didn't see how. "It was a tree branch from our shared backyard. It's my fault as much as yours." He tried to wipe blood away from his temple. "Let's blame Mother Nature. She's always been a total witch to me."

Pippa's laugh was strained.

The room still spun a bit around his head or he'd stand up and get out of there. "Give me a minute to get my bearings and I'll leave you alone." Even though she was scared as hell of him, she'd rushed out into that storm when he'd been injured. Then she'd brought him into her home. He'd bet his last twenty dollars she'd never brought another person in here. The woman had a kindness to her. "Okay?"

His promise seemed to galvanize her. She rushed for a kitchen towel and moved toward him, pressing it to his head. "You might need to see a doctor."

He placed his hand over hers, even though the pressure hurt his head more. "I've been harmed worse, sweetheart." Her hand was wet and smooth beneath his. Small and delicate—so damn breakable.

This close, her scent of sugar cookies and something unique, something all her and surprisingly sultry, filled his head. If he just turned his head a couple of inches, his mouth would be near those enticing breasts. His groan had nothing to do with the gash in his temple.

She lightened her hold. "I have aspirin."

He had the hard-on of an eighteen-year-old kid. He also had Glenlivet back home. A shot or five would help.

Even with the outside door open, intimacy hushed through the small room. His body wanted to explore it while his brain fired out a *hell no*. He ignored her breasts and lifted his head, meeting her gaze.

Ah.

Awareness, warning, fear, curiosity, need. Maybe it was the night, or maybe it was the scare outside, but the woman's expression was completely unguarded. He wasn't the only one in the room having a fight between his body and his brain.

Her sapphire gaze dropped to his bare chest. And then lower.

His dick jumped in response, as if having its own conversation with her.

A fascinating—truly fascinating—blush spread from her chest, up her neck, and over her still wet face. "Well." Her pretty pink lips barely moved with the word.

He held his breath. Would she make a move? If she did, he'd be all in. Even though it'd be a mistake of torrential proportions, he'd have those shorts off her in a second. But she had to make the move. A guy like him, one who outsized her so completely, couldn't make the move. He wouldn't. But if she offered, he'd probably be able to die happy. Or at least content. Definitely grateful.

She removed her hand and retreated several steps, her gaze lifting to a place beyond his left shoulder.

The disappointment was like a hammer to the gut.

She cleared her throat. "I'm not good with people. With being around people."

Was she telling him to leave? "I understand." He could probably stand without keeling over now.

"Mrs. Maloni lived in your house before you, and we were friends. We talked and spent time together," Pippa said, her voice soft. "She was a good neighbor."

Was she asking him to be a friend? "I don't have friends," he admitted, his headache diminishing enough that he could breathe. "At least, I haven't in a long time."

Her gaze returned to his. "Why not?"

He couldn't sit there with a full-on erection in his wet underwear and bond with her. For one thing, her plastered and very thin clothes revealed every smooth line and curve of her body, and his mouth was watering with the need to explore every inch. So he planted a hand on the table and forced himself to stand. "Pippa? I'm happy to be your neighbor, and I can try to be your friend. But we're going to have to start tomorrow, or rather, later today, when we're both fully dressed."

A small smile played on her lips. "This is rather ridiculous."

That wasn't the word he'd choose, but he returned her smile. It had been so long since he'd actually been honest with somebody, he wasn't sure how to do it. "If you'd asked me into the bedroom, I would've said yes."

She tilted her head to the side. "I know." Then she moved out of the way so he could go back outside. "Were you serious about being friends?"

"Sure. Why not?" Every bit of him knew he wasn't leaving Cottage Grove now. How could he?

"Okay." Her voice was tentative. "Tomorrow, late afternoon, after I finish my work for the day. We'll walk the property and maybe get to know each other. We can look for any threats."

An odd word to choose, really. Not damaged trees or

property problems, but threats. "Okay. I'm running errands most of the day but will make it a point to be here by early afternoon." He kept her towel and headed out to the patio before striding back into the storm.

One of many coming his way, if history had taught him anything.

Chapter Four

Parking the truck in a half-full parking lot, Mal double-checked the address he'd scrawled on a sticky note. "Odd," he murmured, looking around. The building in front of him definitely had been built in the seventies. Square, beige-colored, three stories high.

The morning drive from Cottage Grove in Virginia to this oddly placed building outside DC had taken him more than an hour, and he'd questioned his wisdom with every mile.

A deserted grassy area with worn picnic tables sat to the left, while a row of similar buildings extended to the right. Behind him was the interstate. The area was quiet—eerily so.

He hesitated to lock his SIG in the glove compartment, but without credentials, he couldn't very well walk into a government building armed. If this *was* a government building. Chances were, it was one of those satellite offices for overflow, but that was close enough.

Jumping out, his boots hit wet pavement. The rain had softened, barely falling, but it still dampened his hair as he strode around parked vehicles to pull open the glass front door.

The interior hadn't been updated. Worn yellow tiles, a

marquis on the wall with mismatched letters, dingy white paint. No security and complete silence. An elevator bank of two faux wood elevators was over to the right. He moved toward the marquis, not surprised that the HDD wasn't listed. Had he gotten the address wrong?

An ancient elevator opened, and Angus Force stepped out. He wore a full suit and looked like a fed from years back. While shorter than before, his hair was still messy; he'd tamed it back with some sort of gel, and his tie was neatly knotted. "West."

Mal looked around the deadly silent floor. All the doors to the offices were closed. "Nice place you've got here."

"The gym is on the ground floor at the end of the building." Force flashed a quick smile. "You think this is nice? Wait till you see your office." He stepped back into the elevator.

Mal shook his head and followed. The elevator hitched when he stepped inside. "I'm not joining your team." Especially in this hellhole. "You said if I came in you'd give me the records you supposedly have on Pippa."

"So, it's Pippa now, is it?" Force murmured, pressing the far-left button. "First name basis already? You *are* good."

Mal didn't rise to the bait as the elevator began to descend. "We're heading down."

"Yep. Nothing gets by you, Detective," Force said cheerfully, tugging on his tie.

"What's a Homeland Defense unit doing in this place?" Curiosity was a bitch.

They descended two floors, and the doors slid open to a small alcove with a flickering light. An old door to the right looked like it led to a closet, and a smaller one to the left had a restroom sign above it, old and tilted. "We're kind of a dirty secret nobody wants around," Force said, striding through the alcove. "And I lied."

Mal followed him to see a bullpen of sorts with several

scratched old desks scattered around, a few piled high with dusty boxes. Garbage and discarded computers lined one wall. "About what?"

"You don't have an office." Force pointed to four open doorways across the wide room. "From left to right: my office, case room one, case room two, and computer center." He gestured around the room. "You can have first choice of desks. I was thinking of arranging them in a circle or something Zenlike. What do you think?"

Mal cut him a look. "I don't give a damn how you decorate." The paint on the walls was peeling, and the yellowish lights from the ceiling buzzed. The floor was dirty cement. "Just give me the files."

The elevator dinged and opened.

Mal turned slightly to face the elevator. The guy who stepped off looked like he belonged in one of those superhero movies.

As the bad guy.

The huge, scary, psychotic bad guy.

Force smiled. "Right on time. Lieutenant Commander Clarence Wolfe, meet Detective Malcolm West."

"I'm not a detective any longer," Mal said at the same time Wolfe muttered, "I'm not a lieutenant commander."

"Right," Force said, turning and moving farther into the room. "I keep forgetting. In fact, I'd like to swear you both in as agents with the HDD."

Wolfe looked around and sighed. He wore ripped jeans, a torn shirt, and a worn leather jacket. His hair was cut short, his eyes brown, and his jaw solid rock. A scar slashed from his left temple down to his jugular. He had to be at least six-six, if not taller. "This place is worse than I thought yesterday."

What was going on? Mal's gaze drifted to the case rooms. "When you said this was a new unit, you weren't exaggerating."

"No." Force strode through the desks and entered case room two.

Mal looked sideways at Wolfe, who returned the look.

"Why aren't you a detective any longer?" Wolfe asked, his voice low and hoarse.

"Why aren't you a lieutenant commander?" Mal returned.

"Rumor has it, I'm insane." Wolfe turned and followed Force into the case room, oddly graceful for a man his size.

The guy looked insane. Rumors were often true. Mal looked around again and then made his way through the desks to the doorway, where he glanced inside. A long conference table faced a huge whiteboard set up like a murder board. His gaze instantly caught Pippa's picture lined up with several other women to the right. The designation "An Teaghlaigh" was scrawled across the top of the entire board.

Force caught his focus. "Means *family* in Gaelic."

Wolfe yanked out a chair and dropped his muscled bulk into it. "Is this my case? The one that'll get me back into the Teams?"

"No. On this one, West will be primary," Force said, gesturing for Malcolm to sit. "If he stays."

Mal slowly drew out a chair, weights settling on his chest. "You have two minutes to tell me what's going on. Then I'm out of here." Why would Force want a guy with his skill set on this?

The huge dog from yesterday padded inside, looked around, and then found a corner to flop into.

"That's Roscoe," Force said easily. "He's a good dog but has a few quirks."

Quirks? A hundred-pound German shepherd with quirks? That sounded just freaking great. Malcolm returned his attention to the board, where a man's picture was on the left side, clearly labeled. He had intense brown eyes, angular features, and longish brown hair. A young Johnny Depp before the eyeliner. "Who's Isaac Leon, and why are the Greek signs alpha and omega below his name?"

Force leaned against the left wall. "Leon is a cult leader, and he claims to be *the* Alpha and Omega. His people call him the One."

"Only Christ is the Alpha and Omega," Wolfe said softly, eyeing the dog in the corner. "Your puppy looks hungry."

"Don't bite him and he won't bite you," Force said easily.

So, the hulking ex-soldier knew his Bible a little. Mal nodded toward the pictures of four women. "I'm taking it they're members of this little cult?" All four women were beautiful, but Pippa had something special about her. Must be those eyes.

Force nodded. "Yes. Those are the ones we've been able to identify so far. They've all left the cult and have been leading lives off the grid since. We've only found Pippa and a woman now named Trixie."

"Could be innocent," Mal murmured, his gaze on the picture of Pippa. It had been taken at least five years earlier, if not more. Her hair was longer, her face fuller.

"Right." Force reached into one of the many boxes dumped around the room and brought out a picture he taped beneath Pippa's. "We're still getting organized. This is her mother, Janice. We believe she's still in the cult."

"Why?" Mal asked, studying the picture. Unlike her daughter, the woman was a blonde, but Pippa had her eyes.

"We have more pictures," Force said.

Mal exhaled. "All right. There are tons of cults in the country. Why the interest in this one?"

Force tapped a pencil. "First, I did an analysis of where the cult has been located and compared it to runaway rates and deaths. There's a strong correlation."

"Okay. Normal cult stuff," Mal said. "Runaways and deaths can be covered by state or local cops. What else?"

"Second, I conducted a linguistic analysis, or rather had

a friend do it, and the results reveal a trend toward violence and action. We have intel that the group has been planning an attack for years. Putting these women in place has been part of the plan. Unfortunately, the pictures are from years ago, and Pippa is one of only two we've found so far. We think her real name is Mary, by the way."

Her name hadn't seemed right. Mal kept his face impassive. "How do you know about the rest of the women if you haven't found them yet?"

"My third step was to get to somebody inside. That's how we got the pictures," Force said, shaking his head. "But she's a woman, and with the hierarchy of the cult, she can't get into the inner circle. She's good, but nobody is that good."

Mal leaned back. "So you want me to get to know Pippa and pump her for information." Other ways he could pump her filled his mind, and he shoved them away.

"For a start," Force agreed.

"What kind of a threat are we looking at?" Wolfe asked, his gaze not leaving the dog.

Roscoe kept his focus on Clarence Wolfe, not wavering.

Were they having some weird staring contest?

Force cleared his throat. "The dog won't blink."

"Neither will I," Wolfe murmured, not moving.

Yep. Crazy. Malcolm studied Angus Force. "You didn't answer his question."

Force looked back. "Our intel from our source indicates a mass attack with suicide explosives. Don't know where, but our source thinks it'll happen very soon. The cult has relocated to West Virginia . . . rather close to here, actually. So we think the attack will take place in DC, but as you know . . ."

"New York is close. As are several other cities," Mal said. None of this was making a lot of sense, and he didn't like the way the hair was rising on his arms. "Why are we in the basement of a shithole office building if there's an imminent terrorist attack? What is this unit? Who are you?"

Force grinned, the sight oddly and suddenly familiar. "At the moment, I'm the only one who thinks the cult is going to make an attack, so I've created case room two to find out."

Angus squinted and imagined Force with a clean-shaven face and FBI-issue hair. Realization kicked him in the balls. "I know you. The FBI special agent who took down the Surgeon. The media only caught a couple of pictures of you, and they never got your name. I thought you looked familiar."

Force frowned. "Those damn pictures. Journalists. Hate 'em."

Mal slowly shook his head. "What's an FBI profiler, *the* FBI profiler, doing creating an HDD unit in a basement? What the hell, man?" And why was the guy still shaking from alcohol withdrawal?

Force rubbed the scruff across his jaw. "What do you know about the Lassiter case?"

Mal sat back. He'd been deep under cover in the mob at the time, but he remembered some details from the news. "Henry Wayne Lassiter was a serial killer who did some sick shit with women. Kidnapped and killed at least, what, ten?"

"Twelve that we know of," Force said, his eyes darkening.

Right. "You tracked him down and put him away." Mal cocked his head to the side. "They called him the Surgeon because of his ritual and what he did to the bodies. And here's the interesting part: He was a lowly analyst for the HDD." When the world found out that an employee, even just an office drone, at the Homeland Defense Department had been a serial killer, the agency had taken a huge hit. "You killed him when you arrested him. There was a shoot-out."

Force crossed his arms. "So they tell me."

Mal let his chin drop. "You . . . disagree?"

"Yeah. I shot him, but he wasn't dead on-site," Force said, his voice low. "Everyone thinks I'm nuts, but I don't think he's dead. The HDD owes me one big-time, so we have this crappy little office to investigate. It also keeps me from going to the press."

Mal's back teeth began to ache. "Do you or do you not have proof Lassiter is alive?"

"I have no proof." Force's voice went dead flat. "I left the FBI after the case and was just fine never going back to that world, but an informant I used to have at HDD left me a couple of messages on my phone—cryptic ones—about the case not being over. Then the messages disappeared, as did my informant."

"Well, that's not creepy at all," Mal murmured. Sometimes cops just couldn't let go of a case. Was that Angus's problem? "And this?" He swept his hand toward the board.

"The deal I made with the HDD," Force said, his gaze turning to the picture of the man on the board. "If I keep my mouth shut about Lassiter, they'll throw us a case or two. I've weeded out the ones that have merit, and this one does. That's based on my gut instinct. Evidence is sorely lacking."

Yet he already had somebody undercover in the cult. "So, your informant. You turned her." Somehow.

Force nodded. "Yeah. There's something going on with the group."

Now that didn't sound ominous at all. Mal frowned, his leg aching. He gingerly rubbed the side of his thigh. "I get why you're here." Either Force's instincts were right, or he was letting ghosts rule his life. "I even think I understand why you're here," Mal said to the soldier still staring at the dog. He'd mentioned getting back to the Teams, and no doubt Force had promised him help if they succeeded in their job. "Why am I here?"

"Like I said," Force said easily, "you're the best undercover cop I've ever seen."

Mal breathed out, the air oddly hot. "As flattering as that is, getting close to a lonely woman, or even a sociopathic one, if you're right about her, doesn't require much undercover skill."

"I'm aware." Force turned back toward Mal to face him head-on. "There's more to your assignment than just getting close to Pippa Smith."

"You want me to seduce her," Mal muttered, his head starting to pound.

Force snorted. "You wish. Man. Why did you go there?"

Mal blinked. Because he'd wanted to go there, obviously. "Explain."

Amusement glimmered in Force's eyes for the briefest of seconds. "Hey. You can do that part of your job any way you want. Become her confidant. If that takes multiple orgasms, I'm sure you're up to the task."

Mal's chin lowered as his anger stirred. If he told Force to stop talking about Pippa that way, then Force would know he had him. "If you can't provide three orgasms at a time, why bother?" he drawled. "What's the second part of my so-called assignment?"

Force's amusement disappeared. "We want you to infiltrate the cult, of course."

Mal stiffened. "What?"

"Yeah. As yourself." Force glanced at the still silent staring war going on between soldier and canine and then focused back on Mal. "An ex-detective drunk who's fighting demons every night and drinking them away every day. You're the perfect mark for a cult. Especially one with a terrorist bent."

Mal's lungs seized, but he kept his expression placid. "You want me to join a cult and also get close to a former cult member without letting those two worlds collide."

Force nodded. "Like I said, you're the best. If anybody can do it, you can."

Mal stared at the man, no longer curious. About anything. His last assignment had nearly killed him. This one, this one would take everything he had. "Nobody is that good."

"Well, then. I guess we're about to find out," Force said. "Right?"

Chapter Five

Pippa smoothed her hair for the tenth time and waited by the back door. Wait. That was too eager. She studied her sparkling-clean kitchen. There was nothing to do. Should she go outside to meet Malcolm? Or should she wait for him to knock on the door?

Geez. This wasn't a date, for goodness' sake.

Sure, she'd put on lip gloss and a bright purple sweater. That didn't mean anything. Except that her very handsome neighbor was about to show up and walk their property with her. What if he asked her questions again?

He wasn't a cop any longer, but surely he could tell if somebody was lying. She'd gotten pretty good at it, but she was no expert.

His sharp rap on the back door made her jump. She turned and strode over to pull the heavy sliding glass open. "Hi."

"Hi." He smiled, but his deep green eyes remained serious. A small cut was surrounded by a purple bruise on his temple from the night before. Today he wore a faded black leather jacket over a white shirt and worn jeans. "You might need a coat."

She shook her head and moved toward him. "This is a

warm sweater." She'd paired it with dark jeans and her rain boots. "I'll be fine." Though it was nice to have somebody worry about whether she'd be cold or not. Why had she stopped dating so long ago?

Oh yeah.

But this was different. He was her neighbor, and he seemed to have no interest in exploring the world out there. She smiled at him and moved outside, turning to shut the door.

He beat her to it, easily sliding it closed again with one hand.

Once again, his strength gave her the flutters. Those green eyes didn't hurt either. "How's your head?" she asked, peering way up into his face.

"Tough as ever." He grinned. His lips were firm and curved just right. He looked like a guy who could kiss.

She ducked her head to hide a blush and turned to start walking. It had been way too long since she'd flirted, and she was probably looking like a complete dork. The good news was that she'd investigated him online during the day, and he really was an ex-cop. So he wasn't here to find her. She was still safe. Should she tell him she'd read the newspaper articles about his bravery? About how he'd brought down an entire mob family? Or was that something he wanted to forget?

"What are you thinking?" he asked, gently taking her arm as they crossed from the wet grass to the forested land.

"I read about you today." She followed a barely there hiking trail, heading straight away from their properties. "The online article didn't mention you'd quit being a cop." Which was lucky for her.

"I was still in the hospital when the news moved on to better stories." He reached in front of her and held a tree branch out of the way so she could pass. "Are there any news articles about you? I feel like I'm behind in the getting-to-know-you phase of this friendship," he said.

Was he flirting with her? Her body heated in a way she'd all but forgotten. She glanced back and had to look up. "No. I'm pretty boring." It hit her, then. She was in the woods, completely isolated, with a man she'd just met. Away from her home and out and exposed. But she'd read about him, and there had even been a picture, so he had to be all right. Didn't he? "So . . ."

He grasped her arm and turned her to face him. Trees bracketed them on both sides and clouds had started rolling in. "Your breathing just changed and you've gone pale. Why?" Those dark emerald eyes seemed to look right through her.

"I'm fine." Her lungs seized, but she looked him in the eye.

He released her and took a step back. Slowly, he turned his head and looked at the trees all around them. "What's your deal, Pippa?"

Oh boy, that was a question. "I don't know what you mean."

"Yes, you do." His voice was a low rumble. "Yesterday I thought you were a terrified shut-in who couldn't even answer the door. Then you let me inside your house last night. Now you're walking outside, away from the house, with somebody you barely know. Oh, you just registered that, and it freaked you out. But you still came outside with me."

It figured an ex-cop would be so observant. "I'm not agoraphobic. I just don't like crowds. Cities and big groups of people bother me." As well as cameras. They were everywhere. "It's not so much that I have to stay in my home. I just don't like going anywhere else." As an explanation, it was the best she could do.

"Why?" he asked, his tone soft. Inviting. Coaxing.

Her heart sped up and adrenaline flooded through her. A fight-or-flight reaction. Instinctive. His tone, the trust-me tone. She heard that in her nightmares. A manipulation that could be felt, if not defined. She couldn't outrun him, and she more than likely couldn't outfight him. So she smiled her prettiest smile and lightly kicked the ground. "I'm just a serious introvert. Really shy, too."

His eyes narrowed.

She fell back on looking innocent and clueless. It had saved her life more than once.

Then, that quickly, his expression cleared. "Fair enough. Sorry if I made you uncomfortable. It's the detective in me. Always trying to solve puzzles."

Oh. She swallowed. Had she totally misinterpreted him? Her past just wouldn't leave her alone. "Okay." Scrambling, she tried to think of something, anything, to say. "How did you get the scar over your eye?"

He gingerly rubbed the moon shape. "Still looks bad, huh?"

"No," she blurted out. "Makes you look tough. Dangerous and kind of sexy." Why wouldn't her mouth work *with* her brain instead of against it? She hunched her shoulders.

He snorted. "That's sweet of you."

Darn it. The guy probably didn't want to talk about it. Scars were personal. Very. "I'm sorry to pry," she said.

He shook his head. "No, it's all right. I got hit with a golf ball while undercover a long time ago. Just thought the scar was fading."

"A golf ball," she murmured.

His smile invited shared amusement. "Sorry to disappoint you, but that's the truth. I suck at golf, for the record."

Her smile matched his, grounding her in the moment. With him. "I'm more of a gin rummy player myself." Especially via the computer. The seconds drew out, tying them in a way she couldn't decipher.

He blinked. Then he sighed. "It was a bottle to the head. From my grandfather." His eyes darkened. "I tell most people the golf ball story."

Her heart warmed. Hot and bright. "Oh."

He shrugged. "I don't like the sad, pitying look."

Yet he'd told her the truth. The real truth. Without even meaning to, he'd made her feel special. "I think you're brave," she whispered.

He cocked his head to the side, studying her.

Okay. Back to business. She turned and pointed at a large rock. "That rock is the far end of our properties. Your twenty acres go to the south and mine go to the north from here." She wasn't walking forty acres with him.

Thunder ripped closer than she'd expected. The air charged.

He winced. "We'd better get back to shelter." Taking her arm again, he let his hand slide down her wrist to grasp her hand. "Let's hurry."

Awareness shot up her arm and zinged through her body. Surely he'd taken her hand just to get them moving. But his touch awakened all sorts of feelings in her. Aroused sensations she'd lost. She felt warm and safe and protected. She'd forgotten this feeling of her hand in a man's. His hand was bigger than any she'd held before.

Was the old saying true about men's hands?

She stumbled.

He slowed down. "You okay?"

She nodded, biting her lip. Why did her brain keep going to raunchy land with him? He might be a flowers-and-poetry type of guy, not a shove-a-girl-up-against-a-wall-and-go-at-it one. Her secret fantasy that she'd never shared with anybody. Hard and fast and kind of scary—overcome by passion. But that took trust, and she didn't know how to do that. Either way, he looked like he could really kiss.

What in the world was wrong with her? "Do you have anybody, Malcolm?" she asked, trooping along behind him.

"Anybody?" He held another branch for her, keeping her hand in his.

"Yes. Family, girlfriend, cop buddies." While he'd said he didn't have friends, that couldn't be true.

A gentle rain started to fall, and he lengthened his strides, keeping her with him. "No. No family, no girlfriend, no friends. Even as a cop, I was undercover for a long time. I had a handler, but we weren't close. So I don't have anybody."

"Me either," she whispered, which was almost the absolute truth.

Now she just had to keep it that way, no matter how warm his hand or how sexy his lips. Forget fantasies of hot and wild passionate encounters with a strong man. She'd learned the hard way that to survive, she had to remain alone.

Period.

Her hand felt tiny in his. Right. A police shrink had described him once as having overly protective instincts toward delicate women, probably because he'd never had one in his life and wasn't sure what to do with them. Even his one serious girlfriend had been a badass cop. The shrink had defined his instincts as a weakness.

But he was also a cop, and Pippa was lying. Was it possible she was a brainwashed cult member? When it had come down to it, Angus Force had refused to hand over her file for twenty-four hours. Just long enough for Mal to decide whether he wanted in or not.

He didn't.

But he was curious about Pippa. Was she crazy? Or did she need help?

He led her out of the forest and onto their mutual lawn. "I'm having trouble organizing the kitchen," he said, letting his shoulders slump.

She moved up to his side, not pulling her hand away. "Trouble?"

He'd noticed her house was perfectly organized, so he

nodded and gave her his best helpless-guy look. "Yeah. I'm sure there's a right drawer for utensils and stuff like that, but what goes where, you know?"

"Oh." She looked at the back of his small white clapboard house and then at hers. While hers had a brick patio and his stone, they were basically identical. "Well, I could help, if you'd like."

That was the idea. He let his eyes widen just a fraction. "Would you? That would be great. I can offer you lunch."

Her brow wrinkled, making her look cute. Very. "You said you can't cook."

"No, but I can order pizza." That quickly, he was back on the job and leading her to his house. "Do you think organizational skills are inherited or taught?"

"Probably taught," she said, just as the rain started to fall in earnest.

Interesting. "Who taught you, beautiful?" he asked, sliding open his back door.

Her stride hitched as she followed him into the house. "Probably my mom?" Her voice had been slightly tentative, so he needed to open up before she did.

"I always wanted a mom." He shrugged out of his jacket and tossed it over a kitchen chair. The house had come furnished, and the kitchen set was wooden and comfortable. "Never got one."

Sympathy flashed in her blue eyes. "I'm sorry."

He shrugged. "My folks died in a fire right after I was born, and I was raised by my grandpa. A drinker. A total bastard. He's long dead." The words were true and saying them still hurt a little. But that was how you got into somebody else's head. "Is your mom around?"

Pippa tried to retreat; he could see it in her eyes. But he'd shared, so she'd be obligated. Yeah, he was good at his job and could be a total dick. "No. My mother is gone."

"I'm sorry." Mal turned to study her. There was a ring of

truth to her words, but something was off. Plus, Force had told him her mother was still in the cult. "How did she die?" he asked, leaning back against the peach Formica counter and trying to look relaxed.

Pippa's mouth opened and then closed. "Car wreck. Destroyed her quickly."

Interesting. Again, some truth with the lie. "Where is she buried? Can you visit the grave?"

Pippa blinked. "Enough sad talk. Really." She looked at the white-painted drawers to the right of the sink. "That's where Mrs. Maloni kept her utensils."

He nodded and tried to remember which box held the utensils he'd bought at Target. His gaze caught on the furniture in the living room. All floral and old ladyish. He couldn't afford new stuff, and he bit back a wince.

Pippa caught his focus. "You could get slipcovers."

He paused. "Slipcovers?"

"Yeah. They cover the sofa and chairs. There are tons to choose from. If you have a computer, I can show you sites." She moved to the nearest box and opened it. "These are socks."

"Oh." He loped toward her, not missing the widening of her pupils. She was as aware of him as he was of her. He crouched and slid another box toward her, opening it slowly. The new utensils. "Do you shop a lot online?"

She nodded and reached for the box of forks. "Sure. I work online, too."

"Doing what?" It was getting easier to question her.

She took the forks over to the drawer by the sink. "I'm a virtual assistant to several self-employed people. A couple of business owners, an artist, two dentists, an art dealer, three stockbrokers, and an author. I do their accounting, make their travel plans, or assist in whatever they need."

Sounded like an ideal job for a shut-in. It also sounded perfectly innocent. "What kind of businesses do the owners have?"

"One is a small construction business and the other is an antiques store. He travels a lot." She struggled to open the box and then started putting forks in a slot. Mrs. Maloni had left the divider thingy in the drawer.

"What kind of construction?" Mal asked casually.

Pippa shrugged. "Everything from demolition to renovation. It's profitable."

Demolition. Interesting. So, she had an easy way to get her hands on explosives. Mal grabbed the boxes holding knives and spoons and slid them to her across the counter. "Sounds like a good living."

"It's okay." She took the knives. "You were gone earlier today. Where were you?"

His mind finally shoved away all the external noise. All the excuses. It was time to decide, so he did. "I took a new job."

Her eyebrows lifted. "You have a job already?"

"Yeah." That was that, then. He was in.

Chapter Six

Special Agent Angus Force enjoyed early mornings in the office. He always had. When the coffee was fresh, the quiet still there, and nobody had informed him of a dead body. Oh, that always came. But at the moment, alone in the crappy basement, he sipped his warm drink and studied his murder board in case room one.

The elevator dinged outside, but he didn't move. West was a detective. He could find Angus.

The man's heavy steps echoed through the empty bull pen, and then movement came at the door. "I'll take the job."

Angus didn't bother turning around. "I know."

Silence ticked for two beats, and West walked into the room, yanking out a chair at the conference table. He set down an entire platter of what looked like cookies and banana bread. "How did you know?"

Angus slowly turned. "You baked for me? How sweet."

"No." Apparently, the decision hadn't been an easy one. West's green eyes were bloodshot, his jaw scruff heavier than usual. White lines fanned out from his eyes, and it looked like he had a hell of a headache. "These are from Pippa. How did you know I'd take the job?"

"I'm a profiler. The best." It wasn't bragging if it was the truth.

"Ah." West's chin dropped. "Profile me, then."

Angus sighed. Why did they always ask that? Curiosity? The need to be understood? The desire to prove him wrong? "You became a cop because you wanted to protect people who couldn't protect themselves. Because you had a guardian who beat the shit out of you until you were old enough to leave."

West snorted. "You could get that from my personnel file."

From his psychiatric file, actually. Angus nodded. "You were good at undercover because to survive, you learned how to manipulate other people. How to say the right thing, do the right thing, become the right thing."

"Again, not impressed." West turned his attention to the murder board, studying the pictures of the Surgeon's victims. What was left of them anyway. His jaw tightened.

"What you didn't expect on your last assignment was that you'd get close to the marks. That you'd like the criminal family and form bonds. When you broke those bonds, something broke in you." Force turned back to the murder board as well.

Tension emanated from West. "Fair enough." He sighed. "So, I'm taking this job now because I want to, what? Redeem myself? Be a hero? What?"

Angus's lips twitched, but he didn't smile. "No. That's not why you're taking on a cult."

"Then why?" Challenge and curiosity lowered West's voice.

Angus exhaled. "You like the girl, Mal. That's why you're taking the job." Sometimes it really was that simple.

West mulled it over. "She's sweet. I don't see her wanting to kill a bunch of people."

Yeah, the guy had a hero complex. Wanted to save people

because he'd never been saved. "You can be sweet and also be a sociopath. Or a brainwashed victim who's trying to find the kingdom of heaven," Angus returned.

West frowned. "I don't know."

"You want to save her, get into her head. Possibly her bed." Angus turned, waiting until Mal met his gaze. "I've got your back. No matter what happens, in this unit you're protected. Remember that."

West sat back, surprise flashing across his hard face for the briefest of moments. "Ditto."

It was important. Angus had been out there, on his own, falling from a limb too many times. This was his unit, and he'd created it the way he wanted. Mainly. "We need a name."

West blanched. "I told her last night that I'd taken a job. She asked doing what, and I told her it was with the government."

"Smart. Stick as close to the truth as possible," Angus said. There was a reason West was the best at this. "What's the problem?"

"She asked which agency, and I said it was in requisitions."

Angus barked out a laugh. "A paper pusher? That wouldn't concern her. Smart." Then he mulled it over. "In fact, I kind of like it. Requisitions."

"Nah, we need more than just that. Another word," West murmured.

Angus twisted his lip. "Okay. Requisition Unit. Yeah."

West chuckled. "No. I've got it. The Requisition Force."

Angus leaned back. "We're not using my last name."

"Yeah, we are. The Requisition Force. It carries the connotation of us being harmless, or not. The ambiguity works in our favor either way."

That seemed a little too much. "You're kidding." Angus frowned.

"Nope."

Angus shrugged. "Nope. Just requisitions." At least West was getting involved. But they'd keep it simple.

West looked back at the board. "Where are we on this case?"

"Nowhere," Angus said, his gut starting to churn. "I can't even prove he's not dead." He pointed to the stack of letters that spouted philosophical bullshit and challenge. "Feel free to get caught up. But for now, we've got nothing until he makes another move." That was the sad part.

"He sent you letters?" Mal glanced at the stack. "That's personal."

"It was a sick game between the two of us," Angus said.

West eyed him, the letters, and then the board. "I'd read that—"

Angus nodded. "Yeah. He got my sister first. Don't want to talk about it." There was still a hole in him that would never be filled. No matter what. "Your first duty is the cult case. My source says they're gearing up for something, but I don't know what or when."

West nodded. Then he glanced at the empty doorway. "Before I forget, who won the staring contest yesterday? Wolfe or the dog?"

"They both finally fell asleep," Angus said, tilting his head to see the board differently. To find a clue.

West snorted. "Is Clarence Wolfe crazy?"

"No more than you or me," Angus returned.

"So, yes." Malcolm drummed his fingers on the table. "It's time you gave me the records on Pippa and the family cult. I want to know everything."

The elevator dinged in the other room. Angus's calmness started to dissipate.

"Must be Wolfe," Mal said.

"No. I wish." Angus pushed his chair back. "We're saddled with a shrink for the unit, so I asked her to meet you this morning for her take on the cult and Pippa Smith. She's also shrinking your head—never forget it."

West stood up. "You didn't know I'd be here this morning."

Angus straightened his shoulders. "Yeah. I did."

Malcolm followed Force out of the room, his thoughts jumbled. Was Force a freaking mind reader or what? No wonder the guy had been able to bring down one of the most brilliant serial killers in history. What had it cost Force to get into the Surgeon's head?

Two men dressed in suits and a petite woman in a pencil skirt and a white blouse waited on the other side of the bull pen.

Tension rolled off Angus with a heat Mal could feel. This was interesting. He stood shoulder to shoulder with Angus, letting the three walk to them.

Angus nodded at the woman. "Dr. Nari Zhang, this is Special Agent Malcolm West."

Mal hadn't been sworn in yet, but he still held out a hand. "Hi."

"Hello." Zhang had long black hair and intelligent dark eyes. Her three-inch heels still only made her about five-foot-four. "It's nice to meet you. Angus has been so forthcoming with your information that I've been . . . curious." Amusement tipped up her full lips.

Angus huffed out what could only be a suffering sigh. "The doctor is here to help, and also to report back to our handlers—these guys—if we're fit for duty or not."

No tension there. What had the doctor done to be relegated to the office from hell? Malcolm released her hand. "Wonderful." He turned his attention to the two men.

Angus jerked his head at the younger guy. "Special Agent Tom Rutherford." The derisive tone said it all.

Rutherford held out a hand. He was sleek with blond hair, wore a suit that had to cost as much as a small car, and had perfectly manicured hands. "Hello."

Mal disliked him immediately. He shook hands, surprised by the strong grip. "Yeah. Hi."

Angus's voice mellowed just a little at the next introduction. "Special Agent Kurt Fields."

Fields held out a gnarled hand. He was older, with world-wise brown eyes and a salt-and-pepper beard. "Hi." He glanced around. "This is a shithole." His shake was firm and quick. His ill-fitting suit showed a wiry body and his stained brown tie probably was purchased in the early eighties.

Dr. Zhang set down a large laptop bag. "Where's my office?"

Angus stiffened. "You'll have to choose a desk here in the middle. There isn't another office."

Her smile was perfectly polite. "That won't do. I need to speak privately as the . . . shrink, as you put it. I'll require an office."

Angus's smile was a bit feral. He sure didn't like shrinks, now did he? He looked around and then pointed at the one closed door on the south wall. "That's the best I can do. We've been using it as a storage closet."

Zhang's eyes tightened a fraction, and then her smile widened. "That would be lovely. Thank you so much, Special Agent Force." She turned to Malcolm. "For now, how about we chat in one of the conference rooms?"

Getting between these two would be a total mistake. Zhang and Force were oil and water, without question. But Malcolm nodded and gestured ahead of him, reaching down to pick up her laptop bag. It was every bit as heavy as it had looked. "After you."

Rutherford turned to leave.

Angus cleared his throat to stop him. "When is my computer expert getting here?"

It was Fields who answered. "We're having a little trouble with the prison transfer. Give us another day."

Mal paused. "Our computer expert is in prison?"

"Not for long," Rutherford said, sarcasm lacing his tone. "Why leave the criminals in prison? What's the good in that?"

Mal didn't have time for this crap. Force could deal with the bureaucracy. Mal turned and followed the sharp clicks of Dr. Zhang's heels into case room two and set her laptop bag on the table. "Dr. Zhang, I'm sensing a lot of tension."

She shut the door and then pulled out a seat. "We're going to be working together for a while. How about you call me Nari?"

He narrowed his gaze and also drew out a chair at the head of the table. "I think I should keep your title in mind when we speak." The last thing he wanted was to be kicked from the unit because of PTSD or any of his other issues. Once he was in, he wanted it to be his decision to leave.

She sighed. "I'm not here to judge you. I'm here to help."

"Uh-huh," Malcolm said, kicking out his boots. "Right."

She rolled her eyes, looking very undoctorlike. "Really. I'm here to provide insight into individual cases, and also act as a counselor for the team. I'm trained, and I'm good at this. The only time I'll go outside the unit is if you're going to hurt yourself or anybody else. That's it. I promise."

The woman was beautiful and earnest. He couldn't sense any falsehood in her. But she was trained by the HDD, so that might not mean much. In addition, she must've screwed up somewhere to be here right now. "What did you do wrong?"

She blinked. "Nothing."

Okay. She sucked at lying. Mal shook his head. "You expect honesty but won't give it?"

Her lips tightened. "It's none of your business. How's that?"

Fair enough. At least it was the truth. "All right, Nari. What do you know about my case?"

"I'm the resident expert at the moment," she said, no arrogance in her tone.

"Have you met Pippa?" he asked.

"No."

"I have. She's sweet and kind." He tilted his head. "Very."

Nari nodded. "I understand. Tell me how the family you infiltrated felt about you. What was their name? The Bodoni family?"

Just the name was like a punch to the gut. "They liked me. Thought I was a stand-up guy."

"Right. Because you are." She smiled. "You were good and kind with them, but you had a reason. A higher reason for manipulating them. For getting to know them and bond with them. Doesn't make you a bad person."

Didn't it? He'd taken down the biggest drug dealer in the states, and he still felt shitty about it. His gut felt its usual punch. "Makes me an asshole."

"No. My point is, you were doing your job. Something you believed in. It didn't change who you were inside. Not really."

Sure it did. "So you're saying that Pippa can actually be sweet and kind . . . and still want to kill a bunch of people."

"If she's doing it for the right reasons, or what she's been brainwashed to think are the right reasons, then yes. If she truly believes that Isaac Leon is God, or is from God, and that she's doing God's work by fire and destruction, then she could still appear sweet and be planning to kill."

Mal shook his head.

"Isn't that how you did it?" Nari asked quietly. "How you

justified being part of the Bodoni brotherhood while also reporting back on their activities?"

"Yes." Man, he hated that the shrink was making sense.

She took out several pictures and laid them on the conference table. "Pippa Smith came into being almost seven years ago. She was eighteen years old and suddenly had a driver's license and a social security card."

He picked up a picture of her license taken years ago. "The cult has connections?"

"I'm not sure." Nari handed over several faded photos. "Our source found these in some old boxes at the cult when they were moving. I think that's Pippa as a child." She pointed.

Malcolm squinted at a pretty ten-year-old with blue eyes and pigtails. "Could be." He started reading through the documents. "She cut ties with them seven years ago?"

"Yes. She seemed to have left around the age of eighteen, the same time as another member named Tulip. Then, five years ago, at least three other women did the same." Nari pointed to a chart with dates and names but no locations.

"Maybe they got free," Malcolm said quietly. "Escaped."

"Perhaps, but our source has been snooping and eavesdropping as much as possible and has found schematics for bombs. She thinks a mass attack is coming soon," Nari said.

Malcolm turned to face Nari, his instincts flaring to life. "Is that why your inside source flipped?"

"No. She flipped because Isaac Leon raped her cousin, and the cousin then overdosed on heroin. The girl was just eighteen."

Mal wanted this guy taken down. Now. "How did you find Pippa?"

"The pictures." Nari handed over two of Pippa as an adult. She had to be around eighteen years old. "We put her face into the system and got a hit at a veterinarian's office six months ago. Tracked her down from there."

"A vet's?"

Nari nodded. "Sick cat, apparently. We were lucky."

Maybe the woman wanted to be left alone and was escaping a bad past, just like him. Shouldn't she be given the benefit of the doubt? She baked cookies for strangers, for goodness' sake. "Pippa lives by herself and hasn't infiltrated anybody."

"Hasn't she?" Nari handed over a file. "Her list of clients is interesting. Start with the construction company." She took out another picture and slid it toward Mal.

"What's this?" He lifted it to see a current photo of Pippa, her long hair up in a ball cap, sitting at a table with another woman who was also slightly disguised by a hat and nondescript clothing.

"That's Tulip, who was also a member of the cult. She's now called Trixie. We have pictures of them together as young adults. Now they meet once a month in a little diner in the middle of nowhere. Place called Pine's, outside of Minuteville. A good two hours from where Pippa lives." Nari glanced at her phone. "They meet on the first of every month. Which is tomorrow."

Chapter Seven

Pippa eyed the thick casserole cooling on her counter. Malcolm had returned home from work about an hour before and disappeared into his house. The kitchen light was on, as was one in the living room. But he hadn't knocked on her door.

Why would he? It wasn't like they were dating or anything.

But the guy had to eat something, right? Wouldn't it be neighborly for her to take over a casserole? Especially because he'd had a tree service show up earlier to cut down the dangerous tree. She could take the food over as a thank-you.

Who was she kidding? She just wanted to see him again. While she had to keep her past private, they could still be friends. She'd been friends with Mrs. Maloni.

Making up her mind, she gathered the casserole dish into a holder and moved toward the front door before she could talk sense into herself. It had finally stopped raining, and the air was fresh and clean outside. She breathed deep and strode across her driveway, over the shrubs, and up to his front door. She had to use her elbow to press the doorbell.

He opened the door wearing only unbuttoned jeans, a

towel in his hand as he rubbed water out of his shaggy hair. The bruise at his temple had already faded to a light purple.

Her mouth went dry. Completely.

His chest was broad and muscled, and this was the first time she'd been this close to it. Wow. Even his bare feet looked tough somehow.

"I made you a casserole," she blurted out, shoving the holder toward him. "As a thank-you. For the tree. You were in the shower. I'm sorry."

He took the food, his green gaze inscrutable. "I'm out of the shower now. Come on in."

She blinked. Was he going to put on a shirt? Even though she'd yanked on boots with two-inch heels, he towered over her. "How tall are you, anyway?"

He shrugged a very bare shoulder and moved aside to let her in. "Six-four, last time I checked."

Yeah. That's what she thought. This close, she could make out the tattoo. It was a black and windy series of symbols that combined into something both beautiful and oddly dangerous, as if meant as a warning.

He glanced down. "Got it at eighteen while drunk on a beach in the middle of nowhere. Means 'always survive.'" He smiled. "Come on in."

Taking a deep breath of his masculine soap, she moved past him into the living room. The floral sofa, chairs, and end tables remained, but Mrs. Maloni had taken all her knickknacks, paintings, and decorations. "You need a picture or two on the wall."

"Yeah." He shut the door, heat from his body washing over her back. "It was nice of you to bring me food."

Her body started to tingle, so she launched herself at the kitchen through the archway. "It was nice of you to take care of that tree I should've dealt with months ago." The boxes were gone. He'd put everything away the previous night.

Maybe he didn't sleep much either. She turned around. "How was work today?"

"Illuminating," he said, setting the food on the counter.

She tilted her head. "How so?"

His gaze ran over her bold red sweater, dark jeans, new brown boots and then back up. "You look pretty."

Heat climbed into her face. "Thank you." He looked . . . hungry. Very. "Um, I didn't mean to disturb you. Just wanted to bring over the food." She should probably leave. There was something off about him. An alertness, or even a hint of anger. What was going on?

"You can't let me eat it alone." He opened a cupboard and brought out plain white plates. New ones with no chips. "Will you join me?" The muscles in his back moved nicely, but those scars showed so much violence.

He set everything on the table.

Her knees felt a little weak, so she took a seat and accepted the big spoon he handed over. "You seem tense. Was it a bad day?" She had no right to ask.

"No." He drew a bottle of Chardonnay out of the fridge. It was already open. "Would you like a glass of wine?"

"Sure." The casserole was beef and cheese, and it did smell delicious. When he returned with two full glasses of the deep golden liquid, she forced a smile. "You seem more like a beer man. Were you expecting somebody else?"

"I was expecting you." He set his bulk into the chair across from her.

She blinked. Was her little crush that obvious? She pushed the plate away. "I'm sorry. I should really—"

He grasped her arm. "No, I'm sorry." He sighed. "I'm being a dick, and there's no reason. Please sit back down." His eyes lightened to the color of a spring meadow. "Work was weird, and I don't like being unsettled."

She sat back down, and he released her. Even when he'd

stopped her, his touch had been gentle. There was something so careful about him. As if he was afraid he'd scare or hurt her. "What's weird about requisitions? Isn't it a bunch of paperwork?"

He took a long swallow of his wine. "Yeah, but I also have to go interview a jackass who we think took a bunch of official request forms. I have to go tomorrow, which is a freaking Saturday."

Her eyebrows lifted. "Sounds like a dangerous animal." Her lips twitched.

He met her gaze and finally smiled. "Exactly. I've gone from fighting the mob to dealing with a nerd with a form fetish." Mal dug into the casserole, sighing with pleasure as he chewed.

Her shoulders relaxed and she reached for her wine. "That's funny." She took a sip, letting the crisp flavor cool down her throat.

They ate in silence for a while, and she continued drinking wine, not really caring when he refilled her glass. Finally, she was stuffed. "Do you miss your old job?" It had to be difficult to go from being a hero to pushing paper. Didn't it?

He paused. "No. It was hard pretending to be somebody I wasn't." His gaze returned to her face. "Know what I mean?"

Her stomach turned over. "I guess we all play parts for different people. Everyone does." Would that answer suffice? How much did he see?

He nodded. "Yeah. I guess that's true."

"The article I read said you'd been undercover for more than two years with the actual mob." How had he survived?

He nodded, taking a drink of his wine. "I went in as a slightly crazy enforcer and befriended the only son of Mario Bodini. He'd lost two other sons. One to drugs and the other to violence. They needed somebody trustworthy who could help with the drug business." Mal's voice remained flat, as if he were giving an official report.

She grasped his hand, trying to give comfort. "The paper said Bodini had killed more than twenty people through the years."

"Yeah, but his son hadn't." Guilt flashed across Mal's face. "Junior could've been a decent guy if he'd had a different family. If he hadn't wanted to please his father so badly."

"Did he die in that raid?" she asked quietly, feeling for the suffering ex-cop. Why did the past have to haunt them all so persistently?

Mal shook his body, his gaze becoming veiled. "Yeah. A lot of people died." His smile didn't crease his cheeks. "And now I've become a guy who argues about how many pencils a receptionist should get. Not to mention getting to talk to dorks who steal papers."

That was probably her cue to leave. Seeing him in pain made her want to comfort him, and with his still bare chest, her ideas for doing so were leading her into thoughts she couldn't have with him. They had to remain friends. "So. Thank you for the wine."

"This was delicious." He sighed, his body visibly relaxing. "I had hoped to work on the house tomorrow instead of tracking down that idiot. It's at least a two-hour drive. Somewhere outside of a place called Minuteville."

She choked, coughing. What? Minuteville? Tomorrow?

"Hey." He set down his wineglass and reached around to pat her on the back, watching her carefully. "Are you okay?"

"Wrong tube," she gasped, trying to get herself under control. This was disastrous. He was going to be around Minuteville the next day? She'd call off her meeting, but surely Trixie needed money. She cleared her throat. "I'm okay now."

"Good." He smiled. "Anyway, I'd hoped to maybe get this place in order tomorrow, and I had been planning on begging for your help. My grand plan was to bribe you with this wine."

She forced a smile. "I am that easy. Good wine will get me every time." She stood and placed her plate in the sink. Whoa. Too much wine. The entire world fuzzed, and she forgot all about tomorrow's problems as she turned around to face him. "Though I should, ah, get going." She had to get out of there. Now.

He stood and set his plate on top of hers, having to lean around her to do it. His body bracketed her against the sink. So warm and big and enticing. "Are you sure you're all right?" He tucked his knuckle beneath her chin and slowly lifted her face.

The wine fizzed through her, mixing with the panic. Then there was her reaction to him. Scary and fluttery. "I'm fine." Her gaze dropped to his lips. They were just so kissable. And he'd seemed vulnerable when he'd been talking about the mob. He'd opened up to her. She stopped breathing.

"Good." His thumb ran along the bottom of her jawline, an odd strength in the movement.

Without thinking, she levered up and set her mouth against his. Ah. Those lips were firm and yummy.

He paused for a second and then he kissed her back, taking over. One arm snaked around her waist, and he pressed her against the counter, going deep.

The soft sound of need she made should've embarrassed her. But her body went from relaxed to full-on aroused in less than a second. Plastered against him, she could feel muscles and hardness everywhere. Her hands flattened against his bare chest.

Then she curled her nails into all that smooth strength. The small sting must've shocked him, because he somehow moved in even closer, grasping her hips and lifting her onto the cool counter. Her butt hit and she gave a slight bounce.

His hand slid into her hair, tugging her head back, his hips spreading her thighs.

It was the most vulnerable and erotic position she'd ever been in. One she'd fantasized about. He held her in place, providing balance and taking control. His tongue swept inside her mouth, enticing her.

Heat rushed through her veins, lighting her nerves, pinpointing in a desperate throb between her legs.

He kept one hand in her hair and one at her hip, and she wanted him touching her everywhere. Her breasts ached, needy. Desire grabbed her as he pressed closer. She moaned. So close. There were too many clothes between them. God, she was curious. She caressed her way down his chest and over the hard ridges of his abdomen.

He gave a low grunt and lifted his head, letting her catch her breath.

His eyes were the color of a wild, tumultuous river. Primitive and filled with a hunger that promised to consume her. Then, slowly, she could see him come back into himself. His expression cleared. "Pippa."

The one word. The way he said the name she'd chosen and not the one she'd been born with. This was more than just sex. He was more than just sex. How could she do this, with him, and lie? He was a hero, a man who'd saved countless lives at the expense of his own safety. He deserved the truth, which was more than she could give. She blinked. Her hands dropped. Letting herself get tipsy was no excuse.

What had she just done?

Chapter Eight

Mal recognized the panic in Pippa's eyes. Jesus. What the hell was he doing, putting her on the counter?

Gently, he grasped her hips, lifted her, and set her on her feet.

She swayed and then caught her balance, so he released her and took several steps back. His heart beat as if he'd just run from a gang of drug dealers, and his cock was harder than he remembered it ever being. Which, considering he was doing nothing but manipulating her right now, showed what a deviant bastard he'd really become. "I'm sorry," he murmured. "Did I hurt you?"

She blinked, her eyes an unfathomable blue. "No. I liked it." Her feet shuffled. "I mean, the whole getting carried away." Her chin lifted. "I'm not breakable, and I like that you didn't treat me as such." Her voice cracked at the end.

His chest ached. "It's okay, Pippa." But it wasn't. Not at all.

She nodded, her chest panting out air. "I know."

The nearly invisible earbud in his left ear crackled. "I'm clear from her house," Clarence Wolfe said. "Will come approach your house from the rear. When you turn off the kitchen light, I'll enter."

Fuck. Wolfe had heard everything. Mal fought to keep his expression unreadable.

Pippa sidled by him, pressing her back to the counter. "I have an early morning tomorrow to meet one of my, um, clients. Thank you for dinner. I mean, for the wine."

A meeting? But she wasn't going to mention the town. Probably didn't think he'd find that same diner. He tried to smile and took her arm, wondering what she'd say tomorrow when they accidentally ran into each other. "I may not have had a mama to teach me manners, but even I know to escort a lady home after plying her with wine." He clicked off the kitchen light.

She stumbled, and he righted her, helping her out the front door. The woman was a lightweight because they still had half a bottle of the wine left, and she was definitely buzzed. A light rain was barely noticeable but did help cool his libido a little. When he got her to her door, he helped her unlock all the locks, set her inside, and waited for the locks to reengage.

Then he took a deep breath. One and then another. Hopefully, Wolfe was as good as promised and hadn't left a trace in her house.

Setting his hands in his pockets, Mal whistled as he walked back to his place in his bare feet, just in case she was watching. Yeah, he felt like shit for keeping her busy while Wolfe tossed her place.

Once back inside his house, he double-checked that the blinds were closed. "Well?"

Wolfe had settled his large bulk on the sofa. His short dark hair was damp, and the outline of a knife sheath could be seen on his left calf. "She likes bright clothing, silk underwear, and spicy novels. Is trying to learn how to knit but sucks at it."

Mal dropped into a floral chair, attempting not to be intrigued by the underwear. "What else?"

"I copied her hard drive and will get it to our computer guru as soon as we have one." Wolfe's brown eyes revealed nothing. For his breaking-and-entering escapade, he wore the same jeans and ripped shirt as he'd had on earlier beneath a leather jacket that no doubt hid a gun. Or two. Wet grass now covered his boots. "I did notice that she plays online games. Is pretty good at War Monger Two."

Most introverts or shut-ins did the same. "So I'm just an asshole," Mal muttered.

Wolfe leaned toward him, no expression in those dark eyes. "You didn't do anything wrong. I heard your entire night. She kissed you, man."

Yeah, but he'd kissed her back. And if she hadn't looked scared, he wasn't entirely sure he wouldn't have taken it farther. "I've worn a wire or an earbud so many times, I actually forgot it was there," he murmured, looking down at his hands. "That can't be good."

"Doesn't hurt in this kind of situation," Wolfe said. "I took a bite of the casserole on my way through. The woman can cook."

Mal nodded. She'd cooked for him out of kindness, and he'd only kept her occupied so Wolfe could go through her underwear drawer. "Basically, this was a waste of time."

"I didn't say that."

Mal stiffened. He looked up. "What do you mean?"

Wolfe tossed his phone over. "Found her go-bag. In a false bottom under the kitchen sink."

Pippa had a go-bag. Mal's gut churned, but he clicked on the photos Wolfe had taken. The bag held a gun, cash, a burner phone, and passports. "How many?" He flicked through the pictures, the investigator in him taking over.

"Two other complete identities," Wolfe said easily. "And about twenty thousand in cash. If she needs to rabbit, she can do it quick."

Mal tossed the phone back. A sharp pain pierced behind

his left eye, promising a migraine. Not many innocent people had go-bags. "Make copies for the files and have the computer person research both of the other identities. See if Pippa has used them, and if so, when and for how long. And we need to find out where she got them."

"Copy that," Wolfe said, shoving the phone in his battered jacket pocket. "I didn't find any evidence of explosives, but I wasn't expecting to. Can I have some of the casserole?"

Mal stood, his chest feeling like he'd been kicked by a horse. This sucked. "Have it all. I'm going to bed. At least, I'm gonna try." He felt as if there were weights on his shoulders, and he moved around the furniture like he was eighty years old.

"You have nightmares?" Wolfe asked, not moving, his voice hoarse.

Mal paused and faced the former soldier. "Yeah. You?"

Wolfe studied him. "Yeah. I have nightmares." He jerked his head toward the wine bottle on the kitchen table. "Drinkin' doesn't help."

"I know," Mal said softly. He didn't have the energy to share war stories. Not right now.

Wolfe opened his mouth and then closed it, obviously deciding not to say whatever he had in mind. He cleared his throat. "You focused on the plan tomorrow?"

"Affirmative," Mal muttered. "If nothing else, I always get the job done." His phone buzzed in his back pocket and he paused. There was nobody in the world who should be calling him. He took it out and read the number. He swore. "There is no reason for you to call me," he said, answering it.

"Sorry, buddy," Lieutenant Jack Montego muttered, his voice as cranky as ever. "I'm getting pushback from the effin' DA about the case against the two Bodini henchmen who survived the shoot-out."

"No." Mal barely kept from snapping his phone in two. "I was told they'd pled out. No trial. No testimony." He was done with that life. "Aren't you supposed to be retiring?" Montego had been Mal's handler on the Bodini case, and he'd been inching toward the end of his gig the whole time, staying in only to finish up.

"Next month. Heading right to Florida." Montego cleared his throat. "Don't get your panties in a bunch. The DA just wants to meet with you once, and he thinks he can get the two to plea."

"It's Comstock, isn't it?" Mal shook his head. The ambitious young DA was a total pain in the ass. But the guy got the job done. Almost every time. "I can't head to New York right now."

"Comstock said he'd come to you. Just say where and when."

Mal cut his gaze at Wolfe, who had no trouble eavesdropping in plain sight. "I think I just found a legitimate reason to be in that diner." Smiling for the first time that night, he returned his attention to the phone. "Fine. Tell Comstock he can have thirty minutes. Tomorrow at eleven-fifteen a.m. at a diner called Pine's in Minuteville. If he's late, even five minutes, I'm gone." He clicked off.

"Aren't you a multitasker?" Wolfe asked dryly. "The guy you're meeting? He look like a DA?"

Mal slowly nodded. "Yeah. Let's see just how spooked Pippa gets." It was time to push her a little. The woman had a go-bag.

Why?

Chapter Nine

Pippa knew the route by heart. Back roads, long strips of deserted countryside except for a couple of old thrift stores without surveillance cameras. That was the key. No cameras.

She'd had to take two Xanax and meditate for an hour before leaving home. It was getting harder and harder to do so, and she only made the journey once a month. Her fear had grown to a degree that couldn't be healthy. Not a fear of crowds or groups, like she'd told Malcolm. It was a fear of being spotted. Of being found.

She drove the familiar two hours listening to country music, her mind on Malcolm West. His kiss had stayed with her all night, making her skin feel too tight and her heart beat too quickly. She'd taken her usual sleeping pill, but even that hadn't helped.

A part of her, the self-destructive part that knew better, wished she'd just yanked off her top and offered him everything.

But she couldn't do that. Everything included truth, and hers had holes.

The colored contacts she wore made her eyes water beneath the thick glasses that were all glass. No prescription. She'd temporarily darkened her hair and had the end of her ponytail coming out of a ball cap, which also shielded her face. If she was ever caught on camera, hopefully she wouldn't be recognizable.

She pulled into the dirt parking area of Pine's diner and cautiously looked around.

The place was a couple of miles off the interstate with no hotel, gas station, or other businesses around. A bunch of long-haul trucks were parked over by the trees. As far as she could tell, only truckers knew of the place. There wasn't even a sign on the interstate about food nearby.

She cut her engine and stepped into the crisp spring air. The second she moved into the open, her body chilled. Her heart stuttered. It was okay. She could do this. At least it had stopped raining. She'd worn her baggiest jeans and sweat-shirt, hoping to add pounds to her frame. Her nails were short and unpainted, and she wore no makeup.

If anybody needed to describe her, they'd have a hard time.

Taking a deep breath, she looked around again, and then walked casually in nondescript black boots to the front door.

The outside of Pine's was clapboard and peeling paint. The inside smelled like comfort food. Worn red booths lined two walls with a wide counter and seats along the middle. She walked past the counter and went to the last booth in the back.

Trixie looked up from a book and smiled. "Hello, Sister."

Warmth rushed into Pippa as she hugged her friend. "I've missed you."

Trixie set the book to the side, her eyes sparkling beneath her hat brim. "I've missed you more." She'd filled out a little in the last month and didn't look so sickly.

"You finally got over that cold." Relief washed through Pippa, even though she could feel people all around them. So many people. She wished she could be back in her quiet office at home.

Trixie nodded. "Turns out it was bronchitis. Thanks for the extra money. I needed it for medication."

"Any time." Trixie was Pippa's age but had never lived a normal life, whereas Pippa could claim one until she had turned ten. "That's what friends are for." She studied her friend, who'd dyed her naturally dark brown hair a pretty red. "The color suits you."

Trixie grinned as the waitress showed up and took their order. Neither one of them needed to look at the menu. It was memorized by now. When the waitress had taken off after scribbling their order, she leaned closer, nearly across the table. "I thought somebody was following me the other day, but then nothing happened."

Pippa reached for her hand. "It's okay to be paranoid. But they can't find us. Our documents are too good." She hoped. Man, she hoped.

"Yeah. I didn't know if it was cops or the family."

Wasn't that always the question? "How's work going?"

Trixie rolled her eyes. "Bad tips last month. The economy is making everyone cranky." Then she brightened. "But I was bumped up to the dinner shift, so things should get better soon."

"Good." Pippa's heart lightened a little. She reached for a Visa cash card from her purse and pushed it across the table. "I had a good month and wanted to share." It was easy to transfer money from her bank account to the check card and have it shipped to her at home. No ATMs, no cash, and definitely no cameras.

Trixie eyed the money. "I can't take that."

"Sure you can." Pippa took a sip of her water. "I don't need it. Please, Trixie. You're all the family I have left."

Trixie took the card and slipped it into her pocket, her eyes lightening. "I'll pay you back someday. I promise."

Unlikely and unnecessary. "So, you dating anybody?" Pippa asked.

Trixie shrugged. "Not really. One of the line cooks has asked me out, but I don't know. It's hard to be me, you know?"

"I know exactly," Pippa murmured. "I kissed a guy last night. A man. A tough man."

Trixie's mouth dropped open. "You did not. You? I thought after Miami you'd never date anybody ever again."

James in Miami had been a good guy until her family had found her. Then he was freaked out. And she'd had to run again. "This guy is different. I don't think anybody would scare him, but I also don't think he'd forgive being lied to." She chewed on her lip. "And he's an ex-cop."

Trixie's eyes widened. "No. You can't date a cop. You know what we've done."

Pippa tried to breathe. "He's an ex-cop. Not one any longer." But he still had followed the law. Enforced it. Would he turn her in if he knew the truth? Did she even know the truth? "I like him."

Trixie shook her head. "It's probably a bad idea. Maybe. Or perhaps it's time to get busy with a hot guy?"

Pippa leaned forward. "He kissed like the guys on television. All hot and wild."

Trixie chuckled. "Why did you stop him? Why not have crazy sex with him?"

Pippa sighed. "You know why. Lying has become second nature to me. This man definitely deserves better."

"There is no better than you, but I get what you're saying," Trixie said, her smile disappearing. "We're going to be old cat ladies. Speaking of which, did you get a cat yet?"

Pippa rubbed her chest. "No." Einstein had died nearly five months before, and she didn't feel ready to get another cat. Oddly enough, it felt like cheating on the cranky old tabby. "Not yet."

"I bought a fish." Trixie snorted. "He's a Betta, and I named him Alpha."

Pippa chuckled, feeling much better than she had in weeks.

A shadow crossed the table, and she looked up, already smiling for the waitress. Then she stopped breathing. "Malcolm," she croaked.

He smiled, his green eyes twinkling. "This is a surprise. Are you following me, gorgeous?"

She blinked and quickly turned her head to look around. Just normal people eating greasy diner food. "How did you find this place?" she whispered, her body tensing to flee. If she could even get past him.

His eyebrows went down, and he placed a hand on her shoulder. "Hey. Are you all right?"

No. Hell no. This didn't make sense. "Why are you here?" she asked, looking at Trixie and then back at him.

Trixie had tensed and paled, and her hand was already on the table to shove herself up and start running.

Mal took a step back. He looked different in dress slacks and a blazer over a crisp white shirt. Unbuttoned at the top, however. "I have a meeting here in ten minutes. It's the only place outside of Minuteville to eat lunch this early. I told you I was heading here for an interview. Remember?" He studied her, concern in his tone.

"I remember," she said, looking around again.

He cocked his head to the side. "Did you dye your hair darker?"

God. That had to seem weird. She licked her lips. "I was just trying something new. But I didn't like it, so I tossed on the hat." She gave the last excuse before he could ask. Hopefully, he wouldn't notice her different eye color behind the thick glasses and under the brim of the hat. "It was a mistake."

"Hmm." In the suit, he looked like a government agent. One she'd been taught to fear so long ago. "Why didn't you tell me your meeting was here? I mean, after I said I was heading to Minuteville?"

She swallowed and plastered on her practiced smile. A quick glance at Trixie showed an identical expression. "This was a last-minute change."

Trixie nodded dutifully. "Right. We usually meet closer to DC. Better restaurants, you know. But I had a date out here last night and ended up staying the night. So this was better."

Pippa barely kept from shooting her a pathetically grateful look. Great cover. They had to get out of there before Mal asked more questions. But she'd seem rude and suspicious if she didn't introduce them. "Sally Peterson, please meet my new neighbor, Malcolm West."

Trixie held out a hand. "It's so very nice to meet you."

Mal took her hand. "You too, Sally." He glanced toward the door and nodded. "My guy is here."

Pippa reached for her purse to leave just as the waitress brought their lunches. Damn.

Mal moved out of the way. "Oh, good. You're just starting to eat." He moved back in and tugged her ponytail almost playfully. "I'd love to see the darker hair. How about you and I grab dessert after our lunches? I have a couple of things I'd like to run past you."

Trixie's eyebrows rose, and amusement danced in her eyes. "You were saying you'd like to try the apple pie."

Pippa barely tightened her lips. Now her friend was trying to matchmake? Pippa was a baker—she didn't try diner pie. Ever. For Pete's sake. "Oh, I'm not sure."

"Please?" Mal said, his voice low and coaxing. "It'd be nice to share a piece of that pie."

She was stuck. There was no way to refuse without creating more suspicion. She looked over her shoulder at a man who'd just slid into a booth. "All right." She jerked her head. "Is that the person you're meeting?"

"Yes." Mal's jaw visibly tightened. "That's him."

"The paper pusher?" she asked. The guy had a snazzy suit and a power tie, smoothed-back dark hair, dark eyes, and a nicely trimmed beard. He looked more like a stockbroker than an office drone.

Mal shook his head. "No. I met with him already, earlier. This guy's a DA from New York who has a cabin nearby for fishing. Jerk probably wants to combine his vacation with work, so he can write it off."

She stiffened.

Mal chuckled. "Don't like lawyers? Me either." He released her hair. "Or are you worried about the law?" His voice was teasing, but his eyes were alert. Like always.

She coughed out a laugh. "Funny. No, it's the suit. Never liked a guy in a suit." Her gaze went pointedly to Mal's blazer.

He winked. "I'll take off the jacket for dessert, then. Sally, it was nice to meet you." He grinned at Trixie. "And Miss Smith? I'm greatly looking forward to our dessert date. If you're really good, I'll spring for ice cream, too." With that, he turned and loped gracefully toward the booth closer to the door.

Pippa let out air she hadn't realized she'd been holding.

Trixie mouthed the word *wow*.

Pippa tried to control her breathing and prevent herself from running out of the diner like a crazy woman.

"He's hot," Trixie said thoughtfully, digging into her salad. "Looks like a cop, though."

Pippa jolted. "How so?"

"His eyes. Reminds me of that cop outside of, where was it? Milwaukee. Except not so furious. Well, maybe a little angry." Trixie chewed for a few moments, her gaze over Pippa's shoulder. "Yeah. He has a nice smile, but there's boiling emotion in him. Right?"

Pippa nodded. "I think so. He's an ex-cop, by the way." She leaned over and swiped the brown contacts out of her eyes. If she tried to keep them in while having ice cream with Malcolm, he'd definitely notice.

Trixie sighed. "Once a cop, always a cop. You know if they ever catch us, we're done for. They have our fingerprints."

"Maybe." She could feel Malcolm's presence in the diner. "Maybe the family lied to us. Maybe nobody has our fingerprints. We were just kids, Trix."

Trixie nodded. "That's true. But are you going to take the chance?"

Pippa bit her lip again. She was tired of *not* taking chances. At some point, didn't she have to start living? If not, what had she been fighting for?

Chapter Ten

Malcolm sat across from the lawyer and ran his gaze down his expensive suit. "You couldn't dress down for a diner in the middle of nowhere?" he drawled.

Comstock set down the stained menu with a long-suffering sigh. "I was in court, flew my ass down here, am meeting with you, and then flying back to effin' court." When the waitress appeared, he gave her a thousand-dollar smile and asked for the special.

"I'll have the same," Mal said, not giving a crap what the special was.

His earbud crackled. "Talked to a couple of truckers. They said to order the pastrami," Angus Force said easily.

Wolfe snorted, and Malcolm cut him a hard look across the diner. The soldier was sitting in a booth by himself, facing the door. They'd left Angus outside because Pippa had seen him the other day. "I ordered the pastrami," Wolfe said, tucking in his chin. "I've gotten several pictures of the woman with Pippa. Who's following her after lunch?"

"I am," Angus said.

Malcolm tuned back in to whatever the lawyer was saying. "I'm not testifying," he said, just in case that was where the conversation had turned.

"You don't have to. God. Don't you listen?" Comstock muttered, wiping off his utensils on the napkin. "I just need you to run me through the evidence specifically against these two guys. The file is a little light, and I'm sure it's just because they weren't high up in the organization."

Jesus. The last thing in the world Mal wanted to remember was those morons. But he recounted every detail, more than once, while the attorney made notes. They finished their sandwiches.

Thankfully, both Force and Wolfe mainly stayed silent through the earpiece.

Finally, Comstock sat back. "That's enough. They'll have to plea out. Thank you, Detective."

"I'm not a detective." Mal wanted to get back to Pippa. Why the hell did she have a go-bag?

His earbud crackled. "We have movement out here," Angus said tersely, the wind whistling through the line.

Mal stiffened and angled more to the side so he could ask, "How many?"

"How many what?" Comstock asked, counting out bills for lunch.

"Two cars. One going out back," Angus said. "Shit! Get down, get down, get down!"

Mal launched himself into motion, grabbing Comstock by the neck and tossing him to the floor. He was halfway back to Pippa when the front windows exploded with gunfire. "Get down!" he yelled. He reached her as she was trying to run from the booth. He smashed into both her and Trixie, forcing them beneath the table. "Stay right there." Yanking his SIG from the back of his waist, he crouched down, covering them.

More bullets sprayed through the window. Several people were screaming, and the scent of blood, hot and coppery, filled the day. Pie pans exploded, spitting bits of apple and crust into the air.

Wolfe maneuvered gracefully besides the booths, heading for the front door. "How many?" he asked into his comm.

Three quick shots echoed from the front of the building, all in rapid succession. "Three in front . . . down," Angus said, his voice flat. "They weren't looking behind themselves. Watch the back door. I'll head around. Looked like two unfriendlies in the truck as it drove by, but I can't be sure."

High-pitched screams and the patter of gunfire flashed into Malcolm's brain, mixing with the last time he'd been shot. The two moments combined, fuzzing his thoughts. His body froze. His heart rate accelerated and his lungs solidified.

God. Not now.

Two gunshots pinged from the kitchen. He shook himself out of it. Now. Stay in the now.

Pippa whimpered next to him, and that sound, that one small sound, brought him entirely back to the present. He lifted his gun and waited.

Groans of pain and the crunch of glass came from behind him. Then muscled shoulders rested against his. Wolfe. "Are we clear out front?" the soldier asked.

"Affirmative," Angus said through the comms. "I'm almost at the rear of the building."

Smooth as a panther, Wolfe pivoted and put his shoulder next to Malcolm's, pointing his weapon at the swinging kitchen door, and then he slid sideways, settling against the opposing booth to view both the front and back. The guy was definitely well trained.

Sobbing came from somewhere behind the counter.

"Everyone stay in place." Malcolm barely raised his voice. "Keep your heads down."

The kitchen door was kicked open, and a gunman wearing a ski mask moved in, AK-47 spraying toward the floor. Tiles chipped and exploded. Mal aimed for center mass and squeezed the trigger. The bastard fell back, his gun still firing, now up toward the ceiling. Then he went down.

Quiet, the unnatural kind, came from the kitchen. Mal sprang up. "Go," he ordered.

Wolfe reached the door first, angling to the side. "You kick."

Mal's arm started to shake. Fucking panic attack. Not now. He nodded. "You want high?"

"Low. I go low and to the right," Wolfe whispered, his legs tense but his tone clear.

Mal counted. "One. Two. Three." He kicked open the swinging door. Wolfe instantly went through and went low, his gun pointed right. Mal was on his heels, high and left.

Two quick shots from Wolfe's gun, and the last shooter went down to the right of a food cart.

Mal moved in, going to the left and sweeping the rest of the kitchen. "Clear."

"Clear," Wolfe said, jogging up. He reached the first gunman and ripped off the guy's face mask. Brown hair, dead eyes. "Know him?"

"No." Mal took off the other guy's mask. "This guy either." Mal flipped him over and searched for identification. Nothing.

Angus Force came silently from the far side of the kitchen, his gun still in his hand. He set it at his waist and took out a phone, snapping pictures of the two dead guys. "We'll find out who hired them."

The swinging door opened, and Mal pivoted, pulling his gun out at the same time as Wolfe and Force.

"Whoa." DA Comstock had blood all over one shoulder and splashed over his face. His left hand covered a wound on his arm, and his fingers were already coated. He looked down at the guy by Wolfe and swore.

"You know this guy?" Force asked.

Comstock nodded. "Yeah. Lowlife thug for hire. I put

him away three years ago on a weapons charge. Didn't know he was out."

Mal's gut rolled over. "This is about you?"

"And probably you," Comstock said thoughtfully, his face unnaturally pale. "That guy"—he nodded toward the other body—"did some low-level work for the Bodinis years ago. Looks like the two guys I'm prosecuting still have a little juice."

The room started to waver, and Mal shoved the panic attack back. The shots echoed in his head. He shook it, trying to get clear. "We set up this meet last night. Who did you tell?"

"Just your lieutenant." Comstock grimaced. "That's it. I made my own travel arrangements."

It would've taken eight hours for the shooters to drive from New York, but there had been time. "Have him checked out, but I'd bet my life it wasn't Montego." Mal read people too well. The lieutenant might be about to retire, but his blood ran blue.

"Give me your cell phones," Force said. "If it wasn't Montego—and we'll find out—one of you has a bug."

Fuck. If they knew where Mal's house was, he'd have to move. Even if they took down the two henchmen in New York, there was always another lowlife who'd like to make a name for himself. Show some weird allegiance to a family that basically no longer existed.

Screaming came from the other room. They all turned and hurried into the diner.

Mal reached Pippa just as sirens trilled in the distance. She was leaning over a woman on the shattered ground, pressing her hands against a leg wound. She looked up, her blue eyes already wide and in shock.

Relief slashed him that she was all right. Everything inside him wanted to pick her up and hold her.

The sirens got louder.

Panic replaced the shock across her face.

Pippa sat next to Trixie in the back of a parked ambulance, a blanket over her shoulders and her legs swinging. The diner parking lot was awash in the swirl of blue and red lights. Local cops, ATF, even FBI agents had already arrived.

The wounded had been taken to hospitals and the dead had been put into body bags.

"We should've run the second they let us outside," Trixie said again.

"That would've raised more suspicion," Pippa countered, watching Malcolm finish talking to a couple of guys with big yellow FBI letters across their jackets. She needed to know he was near. "Just remember who you are now." Her shoulders trembled, and she tried to stop it. She might never get warm again.

"When they first started shooting, I thought . . ." Trixie stared at the lights across the lot.

"Me too," Pippa whispered. "But they don't want us dead. If they find us, they're taking us back." Especially her. She was special in *his* eyes, after all. For now, she couldn't stop watching Malcolm. He worked the scene methodically, his gaze returning to her often. He'd protected her and taken down that gunman like some hero in a television show. Her body heated. Finally.

Then an agent of about fifty started walking their way.

Trixie tensed.

"We're covered," Pippa whispered in reminder. "Just be you."

The agent wore long gray slacks and a crisp white shirt beneath her FBI jacket. Her black hair was thick and curly, her brown eyes sharp and intelligent. "I'm sorry about the wait, ladies. We wanted to talk to as many of the wounded as we could before they were taken to the hospital." Her accent was South Georgia and sultry smooth.

"We were under a table," Trixie blurted out.

The agent nodded. "That was smart. My name is Special Agent Mykisha Jackson, and if you're up to it, I'd like to get your statements." The agent's tone recommended that they be up to it.

Pippa cleared her throat. "We arrived at eleven this morning for lunch."

"Let's start with your names and your addresses," Jackson said easily, taking out a battered notepad. "Your name?"

"Pippa Smith," Pippa said, watching Malcolm approach from the corner of her eye. A part of her heated and flushed, and the other part felt pathetically grateful. Could he stop the questioning? She gave her address.

The agent arched her eyebrows. "That's quite a drive for lunch." She waited expectantly.

"We like to go antique shopping," Pippa said, her voice trembling. She'd memorized the speech in case they were ever questioned, but she hadn't imagined a scene like this. "So we meet here for lunch and hit the antique shops in the area. It's our hobby."

Malcolm reached them, his gaze intense. "Are you sure you're both all right?"

Pippa nodded, while Trixie remained frozen in place.

Jackson eyed Malcolm. "Have you finished giving your statement?"

Mal nodded. "Yes. I've turned over my gun and phone as well. My guess is that they'd bugged Comstock's phone. I've been off the grid."

"Damn lawyers," Jackson grumbled, turning back to her notepad.

Mal nodded, his gaze raking Pippa. "Are you sure you're all right?"

"No," she murmured honestly. "When the shooting started, we tried to run out of the booth and would've just been killed." Her instincts had been terrible. "If you hadn't shoved us under the table, we'd be dead." Her entire body hurt all of a sudden.

Jackson reached out and patted her shoulder. "Most people aren't trained to deal with gunfire. Your instincts told you to run, so you did. You're going to want to talk to a professional after this. It can help."

A professional. Yeah. A shrink would have a field day with her mind. Pippa tried to smile for the agent. "Thanks." Another guy, the one kind of in charge of the scene, caught her eye. It was the same guy who'd been at Malcolm's house with the dog, which was now following the guy around, sniffing the ground once in a while. The man Mal had told to go away. "Why is he here?" She frowned and focused on Malcolm.

"He's my boss," Mal said, looking big and strong in the swirling lights. Heroic, even. "He was late meeting me and the lawyer."

His boss? That guy didn't look like a government paper pusher. "What's his name?" Pippa asked, before she could stop herself.

Agent Jackson looked over her shoulder. "That there is Angus Force. Special Agent Angus Force. Former FBI and currently with . . . somebody. Not sure who." She glanced over at Malcolm. "I'd heard you'd retired from active duty."

"I have," Malcolm said, his expression earnest. Too earnest?

The agent glanced at Angus Force where he stood talking quietly to a guy who had ATF across his jacket. "I heard he retired as well. Got lost in the middle of nowhere and in a bottle."

"He's just finishing up some business," Mal said quietly, leaning his shoulder against the side of the ambulance. His green eyes cut through the chaos of the day. "Neither of us is active. I'm basically pushing papers just to build up a pension."

"Hmm. Neither of you are coming across particularly retired." Jackson looked him over and then returned her attention to Pippa. "What kind of antiques do you like?"

Pippa blinked. "Pink and green Depression ware."

"I like Belleek," Trixie piped up, her eyes still haunted. "Always wished I was from Ireland."

"Where are you from?" the agent asked.

Pippa lowered her chin and tried to focus. This woman was smart. They had to be on their game. "I'm from Seattle," she said. "So is Trixie. We met right after high school." God, she hoped Trixie remembered their story.

This one anyway.

Chapter Eleven

Mal kept impatience at bay as he parked his truck and strode up the sidewalk to his house. Angus Force parked his truck and stepped out with his dog, while Clarence Wolfe lumbered out of the passenger side. They had insisted on following him home.

He glanced over to see Pippa's kitchen light on. Though he'd wanted to drive her home hours before, she'd been released from the scene long before he had.

Because he was most likely the target. Or the secondary target, if Comstock was primary.

It had started raining again, and darkness was beginning to fall. He could still smell the blood and hear the screams. It'd be a lousy night. He unlocked his door and shoved his way inside. "You guys don't need to babysit me." His right arm trembled, and his vision kept going gray. This was going to be a bad one.

Both men ignored him, following him inside. He waited for the dog and then was unable to stop himself from locking the door. Yep. Hypervigilance. One of the classic signs of PTSD.

Force dropped onto the floral sofa and wiped a hand across his forehead. "What a screwed-up day. We're trying to stay under the radar, and here we are in the middle of a goddamn shoot-out." He leaned back, strain clear on his face. "Got the report. The bug was on Comstock's phone."

Thank God.

Wolfe kept going through the archway to the kitchen. "Where's the booze?" he asked.

"Bottom shelf of the pantry," Mal said wearily, sitting in the matching flowered chair. His head hurt, his hip ached, and his damaged leg felt like it was on fire. "The FBI guys did a good job of keeping the press away."

Force opened his eyes. "Did you see your girl? How she kept herself angled away from any cameras?"

"Yeah," Mal said, energy popping throughout his exhausted body like a shaken-up soda ready to explode. "I also noticed that she stayed in character. True to the Pippa Smith identity the entire time. Didn't slip up once."

Wolfe strode in with three glasses—full glasses—of Jack Daniel's in his hands.

"Wait—" Force started to sit up, but before he could get far, the dog had leaped up and swiped one of the glasses between sharp teeth. "Damn it, Roscoe."

Roscoe set down the glass almost gently and slurped up half the contents in one big gulp.

Wolfe looked down at the rapidly drinking dog. "What the hell?"

Force shook his head. "He likes whiskey. As a dog, it should totally destroy his liver. But I've had him checked out several times at the vet's after he's snuck into the booze, and it doesn't."

Roscoe emptied the tumbler and sat, looking up at the remaining glasses in Wolfe's hands with big eyes. He whined, the sound mournful.

"He also doesn't know when to stop," Force muttered. "No more, Roscoe."

The dog cut Force a truly dirty look, then lumbered over to the corner and lay down.

"Huh." Wolfe handed a glass to Malcolm and one to Force. "Is that why he's retired?"

"One of the many reasons." Force took the glass, looking at the liquid as if he knew better but, at the moment, didn't give a shit.

Wolfe returned to the kitchen for another glass and this time brought the bottle with him.

The dog perked up.

"No," Force snapped.

The dog sighed and lowered his head onto his paws. But his gaze remained on the bottle.

Malcolm knew how he felt.

Wolfe took the one remaining chair, his glass now full.

Force held up his glass. "For surviving the day."

"Surviving," Malcolm answered, taking a deep drink. The liquid exploded in his gut and spread out, giving warmth and a little calm. He looked at the two men who might've saved his life that day. "Thank you for being there."

"Always, Brother," Wolfe said, his gaze only slightly less crazy than normal. "I miss my team. It's good to have one again."

Yeah. A team. "Nothing quite bonds you like gunfire and blood," Mal murmured, taking another drink. The room started to mellow, the flowers on the couch seeming to fade. Ah. He loved this feeling. "I'm sorry I might've compromised our op."

"We're fine," Force said, taking another drink. "It probably didn't hurt for your girl to see you save her life. Maybe she'll trust you. Tell you some truths."

His girl. Pippa was so far from being Mal's girl, it wasn't funny. "Maybe. Or the fact that she saw me shoot a guy will push her away." Mal glanced down. His glass was empty. That was fast. Before he could reach for the bottle, Wolfe was there, refilling him. Now that was a buddy. He smiled. "You as crazy as you seem?"

Wolfe shrugged. "Maybe. Got a head injury, but I wasn't a straight arrow before, you know. Was across the world and an op went bad. Lost four guys. Good guys."

Wolfe had lost brothers, Force had lost his sister to a serial killer, and Mal had lost . . . what? He'd been the one to kill the closest thing he'd ever had to a brother. So what had he lost? "My soul," he murmured. Yeah. That sounded right.

Force's eyes sharpened even as he poured himself another glass. "Who needs it?"

Wolfe paused with his glass halfway to his mouth. "We all do. Souls are important, man."

Were they? Why? Souls made shooting people hurt. Made seducing pretty women with stunning blue eyes a bad idea. Why couldn't that be a good idea? "I don't know. It seems like we're always trying to ignore the damage," Mal said, his voice slurring only a little. "Do you think she has a soul?"

Wolfe gave Force a look and then took a deep drink. "Yeah. I think the blue-eyed chick has a soul. I also think she's a good liar. Watched her at the crime scene. She was scared shitless but managed to keep her story straight. That's talent, man."

Talent. Just great. "Right," Mal muttered.

Angus West straightened up. "Could just be a finely honed survival instinct. She looks innocent, but she's good under pressure. Maybe it's a necessity?"

Maybe. Who the hell knew? Mal sighed. "Hey. Who followed her friend home?"

"Didn't need to. Got her address at the scene," Force said. His phone buzzed, and he brought it to his face. "We have an update on the Lassiter case. A possible sighting, which is probably bull. But we need to check it out." He stood, looked at the bottle, and quickly poured three more shots. "I can leave Wolfe and Roscoe here with you."

Ah, man. The guys were worried about him. Mal stood and lifted his glass. "It's not my first shooting. It probably won't be my last. You can't cuddle and spoon me every time."

Wolfe snorted as he stood, lifting his glass as well. "Fair enough. Here's to brotherhood. We're gonna need it."

"Nothing like a shoot-out to create it," Force said, tipping back his entire glass. "Call if you need us." Then he glanced around. "Wait a minute. You don't have a phone." He sighed and scratched his head. "Take mine."

"I've got two burner phones," Mal said.

Force set down his glass. "Of course you do. Roscoe, let's go."

The dog bounded up and moved for the door. At the last second, he spun around and tackled the bottle to the ground. Sucking the neck of the bottle into his mouth, he sat up and tipped his head back with the bottle in the air. The remaining liquid quickly disappeared down his throat.

Mal watched him, frozen. "Wow."

The dog returned the bottle to the table, setting it upright. His tail wagged happily.

Wolfe nodded. "That's impressive."

Force snarled at his dog. "Roscoe, I'm going to send you back to rehab if you do that again." Then he followed the dog to the door and unlocked it, quickly stepping out into the rain. "It's going to be a rough night, West. Sure you don't want company?"

"I'm sure." Mal gestured Wolfe out as well. The walls were closing in, and he needed to be alone. Whatever happened, he could handle it. "But thanks." He meant it. Truly.

Wolfe clapped him on the back hard enough to bruise. "You've got it. See you at the office."

Mal shut the door, locked it, and leaned back against it.

His body had gone nicely numb from the booze. It had been so long since he'd gotten buzzed with buddies that he'd forgotten the sense of comfort. Of knowing somebody had his back. The last guy who'd had his back had been a mark.

Thunder ripped across the sky outside, and he jumped.

Almost in a daze, he retrieved another quart of Jack from the kitchen and returned to the sofa, drinking directly from the bottle. He wasn't as smooth as the dog, but he could get the job done. He downed half the bottle, trying to pass out. Holding the glass against his chest, he put his head back and closed his eyes. That quickly, he was back in the nightmare.

"I think the redhead had the hots for you." Junior Bodini flicked his lighter in a nervous habit as they drove away from the curb.

Mal shot the kid a grimace and took a sharp left turn. "Rumor has it she has the hots for everyone."

Junior shrugged, and the streetlights played over the rough angles of his face. He was broad if not tall, sharp if not brilliant. His face was round, his eyes brown, and his muscles well deserved. "Why don't you ever take one of them home?" They'd been partying at one of the Bodini bars, and women were plentiful.

Mal tried to concentrate on the conversation. The raid was happening in twenty minutes. "I like to chase for a while. Those? Those chicks were easy catches." He kept his Brooklyn voice in place. "Saw you give a fifty to the bum on the street. Your dad told you to stop doing that." The senior Bodini was all about tough-guy image in thousand-dollar suits.

Junior shrugged. "Guy needed money. I have a lot. Why not give it to him?"

Mal had gotten close to the twenty-two-year-old kid while

working as his bodyguard the last three months, and he still hadn't quite figured him out. "You helped one guy get through the week. And yet you run drugs that kill kids."

"We don't deal to kids," Junior snapped, sitting all the way up in the seat.

Mal cut him a look. "Your dealers do. No judgment, man. Just that pieces of you don't make sense."

"You're my body man," Junior retorted, his shoulders slumping. "Not your job to analyze me."

True enough. And the assignment had been a serious step up in the organization after spending nearly two years running drugs and busting heads. Taking money. Now he was on the inside, where he'd gotten enough information to plan the raid. The one he was leading Junior into. "Sorry. None of my business," Mal said.

Junior flicked the lighter and shuffled his shoulders in the dark leather jacket. "Nah. I'm sorry." He sighed. "You know? Before my brothers died, I wanted to be a doctor. One that studied the brain."

Mal nodded. He'd seen the anatomy books in Junior's suite, and once he'd realized it wasn't for figuring out how to kill people, he'd done some digging. Junior had even taken the MCAT and done fairly well. "Why don't you, Junior?" Urgency swept him, and he had to fight to keep his voice normal. "You could still be a doctor. Get out of drugs." He was taking a huge risk just saying those words.

Junior looked out the window. "Family is the beginning and the end, Mal. It just is." His voice was low. Sad. "You're like a brother to me. I hope you know that."

It was like a kick to the balls. Mal swallowed as he pulled through the gates and drove over the rough cobblestones to the mansion. The night was eerily quiet.

Junior stepped out and walked up to the door. He opened it, and the entire world lit up. Police cars, spotlights, even a helicopter. "Fuck." *He bolted inside the house, and the sound of breaking glass came from every direction as SWAT breached the building.*

Mal stayed on his six as Bodini henchmen poured from the dining room, all packing weapons. "Six unfriendlies," he said quietly into the mic at his wrist.

SWAT teams came from every hallway. A couple of the Bodini men fired and were quickly taken down. Mario Bodini came around the corner, already firing wildly.

Mal shoved Junior out of the way and took a bullet to the thigh. Pain exploded inside him, and he bellowed. Three more impacted his upper·back, and he fell to one knee. Then he turned just as one of the SWAT guys took the elder Bodini out with a kill shot between the eyes. The portly mob boss flew back onto the dining room table, sending food sliding in every direction.

The other three dropped their weapons.

"Dad!" Junior yelled. He stumbled to his feet, halfway into the dining room. Then he yanked up a cowering maid, pressing his gun to her head. "Everyone get back. Get fucking back." His voice was a high shriek.

Barely standing, Mal managed to whip out his gun, pointing it at Junior. "Let her go, J. You have to. Now."

The maid was around twenty and petite. Her huge blue eyes tracked Mal, but she didn't make a sound.

Junior held her close, his gun to her temple. His eyes widened. Betrayal flashed hot and bright across his face. "Malcolm." The sound was pained.

Mal nodded as dizziness threatened to take him. "Yeah. NYPD. Let me help you, Junior. Get you out of here. Maybe get you that chance to study the brain." His heart was thundering, but he kept his voice level. "Please. Let her go."

Junior's gaze moved from his dead father to all the SWAT

members with guns trained on him and then back to Malcolm.
"Fuck you." His body tensed.
Mal fired.

Months later, he sat bolt upright on the floral sofa, gasping as his heart tried to stop. God. He set the bottle down. Heat flashed down his arms. His lungs stuttered.

He'd killed Junior. One shot between the eyes.

Hot. It was too fucking hot. He stumbled through the archway to the kitchen and ripped open the back door, running out into the dark night and the rain. He lifted his head. God. This hurt so bad. His head spun and his body ached.

For about ten minutes, he gulped in rain and air, trying to control the panic.

"Malcolm?"

He spun to see Pippa just behind him, her hair wet against her face. Even through the darkness, her blue eyes caught him. Warmed him. He put out a hand. "Go away, Pippa. Not now."

She moved to him, running her hands down his chilled arms. "It's okay." She turned him. "I wondered about the gunfire today. If it would hurt you. Take you back to a bad time and place." Her voice was a low hum as she walked him toward his back door. "I have panic attacks, too. It's okay. Take a deep breath."

He didn't want a deep breath. He paused on the patio, looking down at her. "You were waiting for me?" The entire world was fuzzy.

She nodded and reached up to smooth rain off his face. "You saved me, Malcolm. Let me save you now."

Her T-shirt and yoga pants had molded to her curves. That quickly, he went from fuzzy to ravenous. This was too good to be true. Was he still dreaming?

His body sprang to life and his brain went to one place. Maybe to avoid every other place. His hand trembled with the need to touch her. "Go back to your house, Pippa." His voice was strained.

Her face softened. "No." Then she leaned up on her toes and pressed her lips to his.

With that one soft touch, he broke.

Chapter Twelve

Pippa didn't stop to think. She'd been scared, and he'd been there for her. And now, he needed her. Right or wrong, she could take the demons away for the night.

And she wanted him. With everything she had and most things she'd never admit, she wanted Malcolm West in a way that she couldn't explain. He was like a furious, wounded animal, and while she wanted to soothe him, she was also drawn to that primitive side of him.

Why fight it? She'd be running again soon. Why not have this night? It was time to at least live a little bit. There was nothing to lose. So she kissed him.

His anger vibrated around them, pushing her on.

He held back for a heartbeat, and then his control snapped. He was so close to her, she could feel the change in him. He grasped her hips and lifted her off the ground, putting her back to the sliding glass door.

Just like she'd imagined.

She curled around him, her legs spread by his hips. Her thighs instinctively tightened against his rib cage, and the flip-flops she'd worn to run outside dropped to the patio.

He kissed her, his tongue stealing her control, his body taking over. Hard and strong and male. She could do nothing but kiss him back, letting the feelings he created wash through her. Completely take her over.

Her most sensitive places swelled and ached. Her nipples hardened against her wet shirt, pushing against his chest, needing relief. So much need. Hunger and desire.

His wet hair dripped onto her face, and she didn't care.

He pushed against her, forcing her to ride the hard ridge of his erection. His jeans were barely holding him back. His mouth was destroying her, and she had never felt so good. So free. He tasted of whiskey and the night. She shot her hands through his wet hair, tangling her fingers.

He planted a hand on the glass door and lifted his head. His chest panted, and his eyes had turned the deep green of an out-of-control gas flame. "This is a mistake. Hold on a minute."

"Life is full of mistakes." She rubbed against him, and electricity crackled inside her. "You saved my life," she whispered, tugging lightly on his hair. "Doesn't that make me yours? For the night?" The wine she'd drunk warmed her, spurring her on. She was leaving. For one night, just one, she could be with a hero like him. And maybe ease him in the process.

His eyes flared at her words. "You were probably in danger because of me."

"Don't let facts get in the way of a good fantasy of one night," she murmured, her lips still tingling from the force of his. What would he be like? Totally letting loose? A shiver took her. The part of her that was bad, probably born bad, wanted to know. Wanted to go dark with him and find out. Before she had to become somebody else again.

His lids half-lowered, giving him the look of a predator pinning his prey. His body holding her to the glass, he reached out with his free hand and ran his finger along her jawline. "One night?"

She nodded, her skin sensitized by his gentle touch. "Just

one. You and me and none of the other stuff. No jobs, no pasts, no bullets flying by. No panic attacks." Could they escape? Just for a few hours?

"Your hair is normal again. I like your natural color." His dick jumped between her legs, really trying to escape his jeans.

"I washed out the darker dye. Decided it just wasn't me." She shimmied her butt on the glass, rubbing against him. The guy felt huge. She swallowed. Warning tried to pierce her intent, but she shoved it way.

He continued his exploration, running his finger down her neck and over her clavicle. She held her breath, wondering.

Keeping her gaze, holding her eyes captive, he moved his finger down her chest and over one hard nipple. Then he pinched.

She gasped, her nostrils flaring. Sensations streaked through her, hitting every needy nerve.

"I ain't sweet or gentle, baby," he murmured, twisting lightly, infusing the pleasure with pain.

Her head knocked back on the glass. God. "I don't want either," she said, giving him the truth. Sweet and gentle were lies. This? This hot and dangerous passion was real.

He released her nipple and palmed her breast, rubbing the pain away. Only pleasure remained. "You've gone from too scared to open the door for me to offering me the night. I find that interesting." His hand flattened over her abdomen, his fingers extending across her entire front.

"Strangers scare me," she said, sucking in her stomach and wanting his touch lower. Much lower. "You're not a stranger any longer."

He blinked. That green darkened in those wild eyes. "You don't know me."

"Show me, then. Show me who you are," she whispered, cupping his face. "I don't care who you've been or what you've done. Just show me now." Reaching up, she sank her teeth into his bottom lip.

A part of her, the elements that had survived the last eight years, yelled at her to stop. To run and get away. Now. But she was tired of hiding. Tired of not living and not feeling.

The obvious struggle in him, the one that clenched his biceps into ripped muscle, spurred her on. Could she make him lose that control? For her? It'd be worth the cost. Soon she'd be alone again, and probably even more secluded than now. This night, she wanted. Just a piece of him to take with her. This hero who'd jumped in front of bullets for her. This wounded male who had a darkness in him she could almost taste.

His chest hitched.

She released his bottom lip and licked it. The whiskey tasted good, but he tasted better. Then she reached down and caressed his length, trying to grip him.

He growled. Low and deep.

She shivered at the sound.

He opened the sliding door and walked inside carrying her. One broad hand flattened across her butt to hold her in place as he shut the door and locked it. "How long has it been for you?" Long strides had them down the hallway and into the master bedroom. He had a big bed with a dark comforter and a couple of bed tables.

This wasn't about talk. She grabbed his face and kissed him, her tongue darting inside his warm mouth.

His fist tangled in her hair and he jerked her head back, the movement rough. Tingles exploded along her scalp. "I asked you a question." His voice was dark and hoarse.

Oh, the need to challenge him, to see how far he'd go, shocked her in its intensity. Not once in her life had she explored this side of herself. With him, she couldn't seem to stop. "Who cares?"

He leaned in. "You want me?"

She nodded. Hadn't she made that perfectly clear?

"All of me?" His voice had lowered even more somehow.

A warning tingled through her. "Yes."

"Then when I ask a question, you answer it." His eyebrows rose when she remained silent. "No. Hmmm. All right. I'll find out myself." He gripped the back of her yoga pants and stripped them off, along with her panties. Then he yanked her shirt over her head.

Cool air brushed her naked body. He was fully clothed, his jeans and shirt wet, and a sense of vulnerability speared through her. He kept her aloft and against him. Her thighs trembled against his flanks.

"Want to tell me now?" he rumbled.

She blinked and slowly shook her head. The ache in her was deep—so deep.

"All right." Capturing her gaze, he tilted her body and slid his middle finger inside her. "Baby, you're wet."

Mini explosions rocketed through her, and she widened her eyes, her body going rigid. Shock mixed with pleasure. He drew a circle inside her, and she arched against him, crying out. It felt too good. Her body tightened like a bow.

What had she done? Even though he still felt in control of himself, there was a tension with him. One that whispered she'd pushed him too far. "Malcolm."

"Feels like a while. You're tight." He continued to explore, his touch firm. "How long, Pippa? Last time you pushed me, I pinched you."

"Almost five years," she blurted out in a rush of self-protection.

His jaw hardened. "That's a long time."

Yeah. It was. She tried to keep her eyes open, but his finger was killing her. She was so close. And she'd never felt like this. The other two guys, the ones she'd become intimate with so long ago, faded into nothingness. Probably forever.

He removed his hand, and she gave a small groan of protest as he set her on the bed. The need in her body was starting to really hurt. Then he removed his shirt and kicked out of his boots and jeans.

Whoa. He was long and hard. Thick too. She pressed her mouth together. Was it possible to be too big?

He pressed a hand to her upper chest and pushed. She fell back, and before she could laugh, he spread her legs and settled his mouth on her. The second his lips touched her, she went off. The orgasm shook her, and she barely noticed he'd slipped two fingers inside her. He forced her to ride the waves, and she completely lost herself in the moment.

Bliss took her, and she finally relaxed, going soft.

He licked her. Once and again.

She reached for his hair to pull him up.

"Not yet. You have to be ready." His mouth was on her sex as he spoke, and vibrations careened through her lower body. He licked her again, his fingers doing their magic, driving her up. Higher and higher. When she broke this time, she bit her lip to keep from crying out his name.

Then he stood up.

With the light from the kitchen behind him, his face was in shadow. But his form was all muscle. Grasping her hips, he pushed her further up the bed. His big body climbed up her, and he balanced on one arm as he reached for the drawer of the end table. The condom crinkled, and then he was sheathed.

Her body felt both satiated and empty. She reached for his shoulders, curling her fingers over. The way he was poised over her—it was protective somehow. She'd never felt protected by a man before. He hesitated, and she widened her legs. "Malcolm, I need you." The words were probably the truest she'd ever spoken.

He pushed inside her, stretching her to the point of pain. She stiffened, and he paused, waiting several beats. Then he pushed more. "God, you're big," she murmured, trying to relax her lower half.

He chuckled, the sound pained. Then he put his forehead to hers.

She ran her palms down the hard ridges of his arms and back up. So much strength. Then she caressed his back, going over every bullet and knife wound. He was a survivor. Like her. Finally, he was fully embedded in her.

Pain and pleasure and fullness swept her along with a hunger that hadn't abated. He slowly pulled out and then pushed back in. "I don't want to hurt you," he murmured, his arms rigid.

"You won't." She lifted her thighs to the sides of his hips, taking him deeper. They both groaned at the sensation. "Just don't hold back." He hadn't let her hold anything back all night, and she wanted the same freedom for him. "Please."

His body shuddered. "All right." He went slow a couple more times, and then one strong hand grabbed her butt, partially lifting her from the bed. He tangled his other hand in her hair, holding her in place for his mouth.

This kiss wasn't seeking. It wasn't even challenging. This was claiming. Deep and sure, dark and unforgiving.

Then he started to move. Hard and fast, his muscles bunching along his body, he powered into her. Deep. All of him taking all of her. It wasn't gentle or sweet, touching or inspiring. It was a hard-out, full-on possession.

And she felt closer to him than anybody in her entire life. Tension built inside her with a hot edge, and she rode it, digging her nails into his back. The orgasm took her, shuddering through her, sending her somewhere else.

He sank his teeth into her shoulder and came, his hard body tightening impossibly.

Her arms dropped to the bed and her body relaxed. With

him still inside her, his powerful body above hers, she finally found peace.

Lifting one exhausted arm, she brushed wet hair away from his warrior's face. She smiled.

His green eyes burned through the darkness, although most of his face was still in shadow. Then he started to move again, his dick hardening inside her once more. "You're mine for the night, remember? We're not done."

Chapter Thirteen

Alone in case room one, Angus Force dry swallowed three aspirin and watched the video of the so-called sighting of Henry Lassiter, taken at an ATM the day before in New Orleans. It wasn't him. So much for facial recognition software he wasn't even supposed to have access to. He needed a computer expert. Now.

Roscoe whined from the corner, where he lay near a bowl of water. Sighing, Angus drew two more aspirin from the bottle. "Open."

The dog opened his mouth, and Angus neatly threw the pills in. "I told you not to drink so much, damn it." Even the vet was stumped by how Roscoe kept surviving his bouts with alcohol. He had a better liver than most hard-drinking cops.

Roscoe swallowed the pills, gave him a dirty look, and set his furry chin on his paws. He sniffed a few times, closed his eyes, and started snoring.

The elevator dinged, and Angus lifted his head. The boot-steps were heavy, with a slight emphasis on the left leg. Interesting. It was early for West to show up. Very.

West crossed into the room and tossed a fast-food bag on the counter. "Thought you might need food."

Roscoe snorted and opened his eyes.

West looked at the dog, drew out a sausage patty, and tossed it at him.

The dog snatched it out of the air, and his tail wagged for the first time that morning.

"Don't encourage him," Angus said, his gaze on the screen. Nope. Definitely wasn't Lassiter. "He deserves the hangover." Angus looked at West. "Your eyes are clear and your shoulders more relaxed than I've ever seen them." Holy shit. West had slept with the mark. Yep. That was guilt in those eyes and irritation in that expression. Would he deny it?

West dropped into a chair. "I think you're wrong about her."

Ah, man. "Is that your head or your dick talking?"

West studied him, intelligence in his gaze. "I'm not sure."

Fair enough. "Please tell me it wasn't us getting you sloshed that made you go knock on her door." Then he'd feel guilty, too.

West shook his still-damp hair. "No." He kicked back, truly looking better than he had since the case had begun. Maybe Angus should get laid. "In fact, I kinda got the feeling she was considering bolting today. A last-night kind of thing. Have sex with the crazy guy next door and then make a run for it."

Might make sense after the shoot-out. "Think you changed her mind with your magic touch?"

West reached for a breakfast burrito from the bag. "Possibly. I was pretty good, I think. Although the Jack Daniel's might've given me more of a hero complex than I deserve." He took a bite, chewing thoughtfully. "To make sure, I disabled her car before I left today, so we're covered."

Angus grinned. Yeah. The guy was good. "If she notices, she'll probably ask her new lover to take a look at the car." In which case, they'd know for sure she was rabbiting.

West grimaced. "Felt like a dick doing it."

That's because West was a good guy. Whether he knew it or liked it or not.

West looked at the evidence across the table. Sighing, he grasped a piece of paper in a clear envelope, a letter from a case six years ago, and read the script out loud.

Dearest Angus,
I am so enjoying our game together. The women . . .
they are so lovely. Like a flock seeking the light, like
a moon filling the night, they are bright. Their hearts
will always be mine. Until we meet again.

Yours,
Henry

Malcolm looked up. "*Dearest*? What's up with the corny poem?"

Angus rubbed his chest. "It's from an old philosophy text written by a guy named Llewellyn. He's long dead."

Mal grimaced. "And the hearts? Lassiter ate those, if I remember right. That's just creepy."

"No kidding." Angus tugged the bag of food closer. "He liked to spend time with the women he kidnapped before killing them. He could be anywhere now." Tension crawled, along Angus's shoulders until his head hurt even worse. The doubt in West's eyes wasn't helping. "He's alive, Malcolm. And somehow, he's out there."

West studied him for a moment and then nodded. "Okay."

"You'll see." Frustration burned bile through Angus's stomach. Was he getting another ulcer?

"What can I do?" West asked quietly.

Angus shook his head. "You're primary on the cult case. Keep on it. In fact, you're about to go undercover again. I was going to give you a day, but if you're up to it, we could make contact later this afternoon."

"I'm up to it," West said, his shoulders straightening.

Crap. The man was going to try to save the girl. It was in every mini expression on his face. Angus mulled over what to say and decided silence was best. For now.

The old elevator dinged, and soon heels clipped across the room.

Angus's tension intensified, making even his toes hurt.

The shrink poked her head in, her brown eyes sparkling. A box of stuff, including a plant, was clutched in her slender hands. Apparently, she was making the most out of her dreaded assignment. Angus had to respect that.

She shifted the box in her hands. "I need a few minutes to get my office set up, and then I'd like to talk to you both about the shoot-out yesterday."

Angus raked her with his gaze. Silk blouse, gray skirt, black heels. "We usually dress down here on the weekend," he drawled, knowing he was being an asshole but not quite ready to hold it back.

Her smile brightened her already pretty face. "I had a morning meeting in DC. Otherwise, I assure you, I'd be in comfy clothes to decorate."

Guilt slashed him. "Do you need help moving boxes?"

Amusement lit West's eyes, but he wisely stayed silent.

Nari shook her head. "Nope. I've got it. Thanks." Then she clip-clopped her way out of sight.

West cleared his throat. "Is it all shrinks or just that one who make you grind your teeth?"

"All of 'em," Angus said, reaching for another burrito. "One got my sister killed."

West grimaced. "Sorry."

The elevator dinged again, and then Clarence Wolfe's boots clumped swiftly across the bull pen and into the room. He set down a carrier full of coffees. "Lattes, gentlemen. The special was a springtime spice."

Angus frowned, glaring at the drinks. "Is that whipped cream?"

"Yep." Wolfe took a chair at the head of the table, his latte already half gone. "With sprinkles on top."

West eyed the soldier and then took a coffee, sipped. He grimaced. "Jesus. Sugar."

Wolfe nodded happily. He was wearing ripped jeans, a torn shirt, and the same leather jacket. Was that the same outfit as yesterday? Or did he have that many pairs of ripped and torn clothing? A mangled ear above his left jacket pocket caught Angus's eye.

He cleared his throat. "Wolfe? What's in your pocket?"

"Oh." Wolfe set down his coffee and took a cracker from his other pocket. He held it up. Slowly, a dirty kitten with bright blue eyes lifted up its head, took the cracker, and dropped back down. "That's Kat," Wolfe said.

"I know it's a cat," Angus said. Sure, the guy's personnel file had gone into his PTSD, paranoia, and anger issues. But the soldier didn't really seem nuts. "Why is there a kitten in your pocket?" Now those were words he'd never thought he'd say.

"Where else am I gonna put him?" Wolfe asked, reaching for his coffee again.

Angus turned to West, who was studying Wolfe, speculation in his green eyes. West shrugged.

Angus took one of the coffees. As a profiler, he had been one of the best before his meltdown. Had he made a mistake putting Wolfe on the team? They'd needed an Ops specialist as well as a guy who had no trouble breaking down doors—with his head, if necessary. "Where did you get the cat?"

"Kat. *Kat*. His name is Kat." Wolfe polished off his coffee. "I found him over in the park. Looked for a mama or any littermates, but nothing. So either somebody dropped him off, or something out there got his family."

"He'll need shots." West finally spoke up.

Angus shook his head. "You can't make a kitten part of the team here."

"You have a dog," Wolfe said reasonably.

Well. That was true. "All right. But if he shows a penchant for booze, he's out. One alcoholic animal around here is enough," Angus said.

Wolfe nodded. "Fair enough. Besides, he likes goldfish." Wolfe gave the cat another yellow treat. "Crackers. Goldfish Crackers. I haven't given him a real goldfish. Yet."

Angus watched the soldier. Very fine lines around his mouth. Oh, he was good, but he was joking. Probably. Besides degrees in psychology and criminology, Angus had extensively studied microexpressions. He'd been called a human lie detector, and it was almost true. Of course, most rules were tossed out the door when it came to sociopaths or the insane.

Roscoe perked up from the corner. Lumbering to his feet, he padded around the table and went straight for Wolfe.

Wolfe held still. "He won't try to eat Kat, will he?"

"Roscoe, no bite," Angus said easily. He could control the dog when it came to other animals. So long as they weren't carrying whiskey somewhere.

Roscoe reached Wolfe and sniffed his pocket. Kat lifted his head up. One of his ears was slightly mangled, but his eyes were bright. He batted at Roscoe's nose with one little paw. Roscoe turned and gave Angus a long-suffering look. Sighing, he moved back to his corner, lay down, and went back to sleep.

"Gentlemen?" Dr. Nari Zhang appeared at the door.

Angus jumped. "Jesus." He looked down at the thick socks on her feet, which were intriguingly dainty. The new doc was way too appealing for him to be this irritated with her. Which only pissed him off more. "New rule. You keep the loud shoes on all day. No changing into socks."

She rolled her eyes. "I had hoped to talk to all three of you about the shooting yesterday. It had to have brought up difficult memories. How did everyone sleep?"

"Fantastic," West said smoothly.

"Never better," Wolfe agreed.

"Like a baby," Angus said.

Nari sighed. "You're all morons. You can take that as my professional opinion."

That quickly, she went from being a pain in the ass to being somewhat cute. Human, at least. Angus reminded himself that he liked big-boned women. Ones who could go all night and then go some more. Not some brilliant, delicate, fine-boned smart aleck. Nope. Not for him. "How about we talk about the cult case first?" he asked.

She blew out air as if thinking over an argument. Finally, she shrugged. "All right. You profile, me analyze." As a Tarzan/Jane imitation, it sucked.

Angus bit back a grin. Now that was completely cute. Not just kind of. Then he frowned. "Let's go, then. West is going undercover in about five hours. Let's get him up to speed. If there's time afterward, you can have sessions with both Wolfe and West." He ignored their irritated looks.

Wolfe grabbed the coffees and moved past the shrink with West on his heels carrying the rest of the food.

Nari tapped her foot, waiting until the two men had loudly settled in the other case room. She moved toward him, her hips way too graceful. "What about you? When do you want to talk?"

He stood, towering over her with at least twelve inches of height advantage. "Never."

She tilted her head, those fine features not looking intimidated in the slightest. "I'm afraid that's not the deal."

He breathed in slowly. She was cute and small and smart—and she wanted to help. More importantly, part of his deal with the HDD was that he'd allow their shrink to make sure his team wasn't going off the rails. They needed a shrink, even one who'd gotten in trouble, although they wouldn't tell him what she'd done. He'd argued, but they hadn't budged on that requirement. "You can talk to my team, Dr. Zhang. But my brain is off-limits."

"Why? I'd only need about three minutes." Her grin lit up those glimmering brown eyes.

He barked out a laugh before he could help himself. While she'd only met the team the day before, he'd been dealing with her for weeks now. And the more he was around her, the more he wanted to know about her.

That wouldn't do.

So he gave her a polite nod. "Let's get to work."

"Fine, but I'm not giving up," she whispered in his wake.

Chapter Fourteen

Malcolm settled into a chair and tried to drink the sugary coffee Wolfe had brought. "Listen, I really appreciate the coffee."

Wolfe nodded, pleasure curving his lips. He patted his pocket. "Good. Wanted to be friends."

Mal tossed the rest of his sentence—where he told Wolfe that he preferred plain coffee with just milk and no syrup, whipped cream, or sprinkles—away. Maybe he could order a coffee the way he wanted at some point and Wolfe would notice.

Jesus. He was turning into a wimp.

Angus Force and Nari Zhang moved into the room. The tension between them was interesting to watch, but it couldn't become a distraction. They chose seats at opposite sides of the table.

Wolfe barely rolled his eyes, but West caught it and threw back an almost smile.

Force grabbed a remote, and a screen dropped down in front of the murder board. He pointed the remote at the lights, and they slowly dimmed.

"Cool," Wolfe said. A plaintive meow came from his pocket. "Oh. Kat doesn't like the dark."

Force muttered something that didn't sound polite and ignited a screen. "There. Light."

"Perfect," Wolfe said, his tone satisfied.

Force hit another button, and a picture came up on the screen. "This is our CI. She's living with the cult but wants out the second we bust them." The picture was of a fiftysomething woman with dark brown hair liberally sprinkled with gray. "Her name is Orchid, and she's to be covered."

Mal memorized her face. "Got it."

Another picture flashed across the screen. Force's jaw hardened. "Meet Isaac Leon, also known as the One, the Alpha and Omega, and the Prophet."

The guy had intense brown eyes, a trimmed goatee, and thick brown hair that curled beneath his jaw. In the picture, he wore a white tank top, a silver necklace, and a gray bandanna across his forehead.

Nari whistled. "Most guys can't carry off the bandanna look. He can."

Force cleared his throat. "Isaac was born John Landers in Iowa. Lived with his single mom until he was sixteen, when he moved to Los Angeles to make his fortune in movies. Changed his name to Emanuel Jordan."

Guy looked like he could be an actor. Even in a still shot, he seemed charismatic.

Force clicked another slide, and Isaac appeared with very nice arrest numbers across his chest. "Has priors for fraud and burglary. Served two years in a California minor-security facility." More slides clicked across. "Moved to Dallas when he was twenty-five, changed his name to Isaac Leon, and created An Teaghlaigh."

"The Family," Mal murmured, reading the time line below the pictures. "They moved from Dallas to Atlanta to Milwaukee to Boise and then outside of Boston. Now they're in West Virginia. Finding more members, I guess."

"Yes," Nari murmured. "The original cult was based on

a sense of family and community. A place to get clean, be yourself, and live a simple life." She drummed pink nails on the table. "As well as worship him. We've interviewed a couple of members who've left. Apparently, sex with the good Prophet is a way to heaven."

Malcolm's chest ached.

Force nodded. "I'd profile him as narcissistic and probably sociopathic."

"So what's changed?" Malcolm asked, trying not to think of Pippa with this guy. If she'd left the cult years ago, she would've been eighteen to Isaac's thirty-five. Old enough for consent.

"He's nuts. Started believing his own hype, is my guess," Nari said quietly. "Persecution complex, and then digging into the Bible and misinterpreting it. Getting carried away with fire and brimstone, I think."

"Plus—" Force clicked the button and pictures started accumulating across the screen. "It's important to note that we believe any attack will have women sacrificing themselves. As far as we know right now, good ol' Isaac doesn't intend to self-harm."

What a dick. Malcolm wiped a hand across his eyes. "All right. How does the cult work?"

"Cults create a sense of community. If you're thinking thoughts adverse to the leader or the cult, you're being disloyal. It's a grave sin," Nari said.

"We're looking at peer pressure to a crazy degree," Force agreed. "The individual has no meaning."

Sounded like hell. Mal sighed. "Give me my cover."

Force slid a manila file across the battered conference table. "Meet Malcolm West. He has PTSD, alcohol issues, anger issues, and battles self-hatred."

Mal opened the file folder to see his face, battered and bruised, right after he'd been admitted to the hospital with bullet holes in his body. "The self-hatred is a little harsh."

Speaking of which, he'd love a shot of Jack Daniel's right then.

"You're suffering and you're looking for enlightenment. Something to believe in," Force said quietly, his jaw tightening.

"What?" Mal asked, his chest heating. "You look concerned. I'm a master at undercover work." The last was said with enough self-derision that he had to double-check his thinking on the self-hatred. Yeah. He was okay.

Force clicked another button. "I know you are, but have you ever gone under and back repeatedly? You have to be you in the cult and then be you with Pippa. And they're each slightly different yous."

The fact that Force's sentence made sense might be a sign that things were getting seriously messed up. "No problem," Mal said. "It's all me, right? Anyway, it's the same Op. I'll have to pump Pippa for information." He tried to keep his voice nonchalant, but by the narrowing of Force's eyes, he'd failed.

"It's okay to want to save the girl," Force murmured. "I promise we'll do our best for her when this is done. You have my word."

"I wasn't asking," Mal returned.

"Yes, you were," Force said, looking at the screen again. "These are copies of pictures from cult archives our CI has gotten out to us. The earliest one we have of Pippa shows her around nine or ten. This one is Pippa at seventeen—about a year before she left. The woman on her right is allegedly her mother."

Pippa stared right at the camera, her gaze serious, her face calm and unanimated. The woman next to her had blond hair and similar blue eyes. But she looked deliriously happy.

Mal swallowed. "Was Pippa abused?"

"Don't know," Force said. "From what I understand, it's possible. But I really don't know."

Mal exhaled slowly. He'd taken her like a wild animal the previous night. Then he'd left her sleeping quietly in his bed while he'd sabotaged her car and come in to figure out how to dig into her past and maybe ruin her future. "I'm such an asshole."

"It's a job," Wolfe said, feeding his cat. "You have to remember that this is just a job."

Force arched both eyebrows. "He's right. Tell me now if you want out."

If he got out, who would protect Pippa? Even if she was brainwashed, which he didn't believe, he wanted to save her. The go-bag was a concern, as was the fact that her name wasn't really her name. "I'm good," Mal said. "Give me what you have on Pippa after she left the cult."

Force clicked more buttons, and three licenses with Pippa's picture and different names came up—the ones Wolfe had found in the go-bag. "These are good. Phenomenally good," he said. "We know the cult has money, and a lot of it. Members give everything they have, and from what we've traced, they invest well also. If the cult didn't acquire the identities for her, I don't understand where she'd get the money to buy such high-end aliases. Her bank accounts don't reflect much accumulation."

Mal rubbed his aching thigh. "Can you trace her movements after the cult?"

More buttons and more pictures. "She headed for Seattle first and then to Miami," Force said. Pictures of her from different security cameras showed up. "Then she disappeared five years ago and started using the Pippa identity. Holed herself up in Cottage Grove and hasn't looked back."

Mal nodded, studying the IDs. "Pippa, Patty, and Polly. What were the names she used in Washington and Florida?"

"Paige and Pamela," Nari said. "It could be a smart move, just so she remembers to turn around if somebody new says her name."

Force frowned. "I don't think so."

"Me either actually," Nari murmured. "You say her name is Mary?"

"That's only what our CI said. That her name was Mary in the cult," Force said.

Mal leaned forward. "Do we have a birth certificate?"

"No," Force said. "Can't find it."

"Her name, her real name, started with a P," Mal said, knowing it deep down. "Before they joined the cult. She's not letting go of that." Maybe there was hope for her. "I could just ask her."

Nari turned suddenly toward him. "I don't think we're there yet. If you ask her, she's no longer a source. What if you get into the cult and need information from her?"

"Agreed," Force said. "You don't broach the truth until after you're under. She fits the profile, Mal. She has fake identities there's no way she could buy, and she has contacts in construction. We have *pictures* of her at the cult."

"She uses a false name and only goes places where cameras can't catch her," Wolfe said. "I watched her after the shoot-out. She purposely put herself and her friend in a position the news cameras couldn't see. And when she finally moved, she kept the blanket on as well as the hat—and the dyed hair was a nice touch."

Force clicked off the screen and turned on the lights before the cat could complain. "If you want, I could meet with her. Profile her for you."

Mal studied the unit leader. It was time to trust or not. "Okay. I'll arrange something. Maybe a dinner?"

The click of heels kind of scraped the cement outside the door. Mal and Wolfe instantly sat at attention. The elevator hadn't dinged, and everyone in the basement right now sat inside case room two.

"Oh, man," Force said, his chin dropping to his chest. "Did you leave your door open, Nari?"

The shrink looked over, blinking. "Well, yes. Why?"

Roscoe clopped into the room, his front paws in her high heels. His tongue lolled out and he doggy grinned.

Wolfe's jaw dropped open.

Malcolm looked, shook his head, and looked again. "The German shepherd is wearing high heels."

Nari angled her neck. "He's a cross-dresser?"

"No," Angus said. "He has a complex because of another, bigger dog. I've told him he's really big, and he is, but any chance he gets to use heels or boots, the bastard puts them on his front legs."

The dog overturned a shoe, and it scraped against the concrete.

Nari winced. "Dude. Those are Jimmy Choos."

The dog flipped the pump over and slid his left paw back into it. His tail wagged enthusiastically.

Mal glanced sideways at Angus. He wasn't sure whether to be amused or bemused. "You said he had a few quirks. Any chance you'll hit us with the rest of them right now?"

"No," Force said shortly. "Hopefully, we'll have worked the other ones out before they become an issue. This one, this one is okay." He winced. "Except he gets bored with the shoes and eventually chews them up."

Nari's gasp only made Roscoe's tail wag harder and faster.

Wolfe shot Force a look. "And you said I couldn't have a cat."

Malcolm looked around the room. "Just so we have this straight. I'm going undercover in a cult that might be planning to use explosives to harm a lot of people in the name of the Bible." He tried to quiet the rioting in his head. "I've slept with the mark, who we all know I want to save. The new shrink wants to get into my head, and I don't want that."

"I really do want inside your head," Nari said, her eyes lighting up.

Mal ignored her and looked at Wolfe. "You're a little nuts and now have a kitten in your pocket."

Wolfe nodded.

"And you, our leader." Mal focused on Angus. "Not only are you obsessed with a serial killer case that might just exist in your mind and splits your focus, but you have a high-heel-loving dog that's also an alcoholic."

"What's your point?" Force asked, his dark eyebrows slashing down.

His point? What the hell was his point? He scrubbed both hands down his whiskered jaw. "I'm not going to ask what could go wrong. You know why? I just want to know what's going to go right."

"Probably not much," Wolfe said cheerfully. Then he fed another Goldfish Cracker to his kitten while the dog clip-clopped around the room and scratched up something called Jimmy Choos.

Chapter Fifteen

Pippa rolled over in the big bed, the scent of Malcolm West all over her. She blinked. The house was quiet—peacefully so. A note by the bed caught her eye, and she lifted it.

Hey, Beautiful,
*   I had to go in to work for a little while to deal with the shooting yesterday. Again, I'm sorry I brought my past to your door and almost got you shot. Last night was amazing. I'll bring you a treat from town.*

> *Yours,*
> *M*

Oddly enough, she'd never received a love note before. Of course, she hadn't spent much time dating either. She stretched again and winced as all sorts of aches and pains flared to life in all sorts of interesting places. Last night had been amazing. Not mellow either.

She hadn't realized she could feel like that. Wild and free. Totally taken.

Her eyelids fluttered, and she snuggled down in surprisingly soft sheets. Malcolm West. Would he still like her if he knew the truth? Sometimes her doubts threatened to drown her. But she had to believe in herself. If she didn't, who would?

Rain pattered quietly against the window, and she let herself fall back to sleep.

The dream was a comfortable one compared to some of the others. They were regular, whether or not she took a sleeping pill.

She was nine years old again—almost ten. "But I don't want to leave my friends," she'd protested to her mother as they walked into the entryway of the big house outside town. People in light-colored clothing smiled and nodded as they moved around, all working on something. Dusting, vacuuming, carrying food.

Her mama held her hand and looked down, a new smile on her face. It had been hard the last four years, after her daddy died. He'd been a hero. A real one in the army. But then Mama had gone to work, a lot of work, and she always had tired lines around her eyes.

The lines were gone today.

"You'll like it here, sweetheart," her mama said. "I promise. I found us a new family."

She didn't want a new family.

"Come. You have to meet him." Her mama pulled her past wicker furniture and down a long hallway. Some people sat along the way, their eyes closed, their legs crossed. It was weird, and she had to be careful not to step on them.

They reached a room at the end, and her mama knocked.

"Enter." It was a man's voice, but it sounded funny.

Her mama moved inside, her step almost a hop. "Prophet. I'd like you to meet my daughter."

The man looked a little bit like a movie star. He wore

white pants and a tank top, and his hair curled to his shoulders. His eyes were a light brown, almost gold, and they looked her up and down. His expression went from a small smile to total concentration. "Hello, Mary."

She looked up at her mama. "My name isn't Mary."

Her mom tightened her hold, and it hurt a little bit. "We all get new names here. It's a new start, sweetheart."

A new name? She liked her old name. "Daddy gave me my name." She didn't remember him much except that he was a hero and he loved her. A lot.

The Prophet guy walked around his big desk and reached her, crouching down so they were at eye level. He smelled funny. Like he had rubbed fruity lotion on his arms. "Your father was a great man in history, and he was a friend of mine. You can be grateful you came from him. We are grateful for every blessing in our lives."

"You knew my daddy?" she blurted out.

His smile showed very white teeth. "Yes. We graduated high school together, along with your mother. All of us."

"We were close friends." Her mother made a small sound of approval. A twittering of sorts. "But we lost touch somehow."

Now her mama sounded sad again.

The guy looked up at her mama and smiled. "Often things come full circle, Angel."

Angel? Her mama's new name was Angel? Was this really happening? "Why can't I keep my old name?" Her voice trembled a little this time.

The man ran a hand down her hair, and she barely kept from stepping back. But Mama wouldn't like that. Somehow, she knew it. "Because you're special. When your mother contacted me, and I saw pictures of you, I knew. I just knew you were the special one. Those blue eyes and brown hair were made for a godly woman. I've been looking for you for a long time. Mary is a special name," he said.

So was Jennifer. She liked being called Jennifer. Of

course, her dad had called her Pipsqueak. She remembered his voice, and she had a video of him talking to her at the beach. But she wasn't going to tell the Prophet guy that. "Why is Mary special?" she asked, when he kept looking at her. Was she supposed to say something?

He leaned in. "Because it can be a pure name or a whore's name. A saint or a sinner. Which do you want to be?"

She blinked. "What's a whore?"

"Ah. I can see we need to study our Bible." His smile got wider, and he looked at her in a way that made her stomach feel funny. "For now, we have to make sure others know you're the special one. You may call me Isaac."

Her mother gasped. "Oh, Mary. What an honor."

She slowly nodded. All right. To make her mama happy, she'd let them call her Mary. But in her head, in her heart, she'd be Pipsqueak. That would make it okay. Maybe they wouldn't stay at this place very long.

Isaac stood up and moved to the side, in front of Mama. "It is a great honor to have you here among An Teaghlaigh, my sweet Angel." He cupped her face and leaned in until their foreheads touched.

This was weird. Super weird.

Her mother let go of her hand. "I'm so glad I found you again." Her eyes closed, and she swayed. "It is my honor to serve you. To serve the family. Always."

Isaac reached behind himself and took a bell off the desk. He rang it, and the sound was tinkly.

A woman instantly opened the door. She was older, maybe about eighteen, with curly brown hair and even darker eyes. "How may I serve?" she asked, her eyes remaining down.

"Juliet. Wonderful. Please take little Mary to the other children. I think they're studying the Bible," Isaac said. "Angel and I require a cleansing."

Juliet nodded and reached out a hand. "Mary. Come with me."

Jennifer, or Mary, looked up at her mama. But Mama was looking at Isaac with her eyes shining and her mouth partly open. "Mama?"

"Go, sweetheart," Mama said. "My duty is here."

Another weird feeling lumped in Mary's tummy, and her ears burned. She took the Juliet lady's hand and followed her out of the room. At the last second, she looked back to see Isaac kissing Mama, his hand on her bum.

His eyes opened, and he looked right at her. Then he squeezed Mama closer to him.

Mary turned around and tried not to run. Where would she go?

Years later, she awoke in the big bed, letting Malcolm's scent soothe her. Through the years, as she grew up, she'd slowly begun to know her destiny. Or rather, what Isaac believed to be her destiny. She was supposed to have been his special bride when she turned eighteen, but in one night, one moment really, she'd tossed that fate away. What she'd done to survive, she could never take back.

To answer Isaac's first question of her, she'd definitely chosen the path of a sinner and not a saint.

It was too late to change that now.

Mal settled in the passenger side of the truck with Force driving while the dog snored contentedly in the backseat as they drove toward rural West Virginia.

"The dive apartment we rented for you is only a couple of blocks from the bar," Force said, his hands relaxed on the steering wheel. "It'll be an easy trace for the cult if they decide to try to recruit you. Our intel says they will. They're seeking anybody with law enforcement or military experience."

Yet another reason it looked like things were heating up. "How long have I been renting the dive?"

"Two months," Force said.

Mal stiffened. "Seriously? Two months ago you knew I'd take on this assignment?"

"I profiled you and figured if you made it out of the hospital, you'd need to do something that mattered. This does." Force glanced in his rearview mirror and switched lanes on the interstate. "The apartment is on the bottom floor—basement, really—with its own access from the alley. Nobody will have expected to see you come and go."

It felt good to be part of an Op again. Mal surveyed Force. He was a decent guy. Smart. And, more importantly, he'd have Mal's back. "This bar. You're sure I'll make contact?"

"Yes. Our source will make sure they're at Blue's to recruit today. She'll be with at least two other members, and she'll try not to be the one to make contact. You saw her picture. Name is Orchid." Force exited the interstate into rolling hills and sparse trees.

"This Orchid. What's her story?" They hadn't had time to get into it with all the other information to go over in such a short time.

"Boyfriend dumped her in her forties and she joined the cult. Thought it was fun at first and had that great feeling. Then realized she was being drugged sometimes, and a friend of hers was raped and then overdosed on heroine." Force took a left turn onto a quiet street. "Orchid called the ex-boyfriend, who happened to be a buddy of mine and a retired agent at the FBI. Went a little nutty and had to retire, so doesn't have much pull. We took it from there about four months ago. She's tough, man. Smart and determined."

It was now Mal's job to keep her alive.

"You sure you're ready for this?" Force slowed down at a small gas station that needed fresh paint and faced him, his gaze intense.

"Yes." Mal checked his earbud. With his hair longer, it was easy to keep it hidden. "I'll be in touch." Jumping out of the truck, he tucked his hands in his ripped jeans and ducked his head against the wind. The walk to the bar took ten minutes.

Blue's had a pothole-riddled dirt parking lot, a few dented trucks scattered around, and bullet holes in the door. Nice. He opened it and moved inside the dark interior.

The smell of old beer and worn leather smashed into him. This was a bar made for drinking. Two guys sat on barstools at different sides of the bar, one with his head down and the other looking straight ahead. Low-lying tables were scattered throughout, and dartboards hung haphazardly from a far wall. The walls looked like cheap velvet wallpaper that had been ripped in several places.

Mal chose a damaged stool in the middle.

The bartender, a mammoth of a man with a bald head and a gold tooth, sauntered his way. "Drink?"

"Jack with ice. Triple," Mal said, avoiding eye contact.

The bartender grabbed a glass and poured. "Want to run a tab?"

Mal nodded and tipped back the drink, taking it all. He shoved the glass forward. "Another."

The bartender poured.

This time Mal rolled the liquid around in the glass, staring at it. His insides had already warmed, and his limbs felt looser. He sipped for a while as a crowd started to make its way in. A surprising number of people started drinking early. Construction workers, loners, a couple of guys in suits. After his second repour, he caught sight of Orchid.

She was with two other women and a man, all dressed in

white or beige linen. They sat at a table and ordered blended drinks. Then they started working the crowd.

It was impressive. Flirting and chatting, they managed to get a bead on people quickly. They moved with apparent ease from the ones he would've guessed weren't interested to those who looked down on their luck.

The guy was the first to approach him. He ordered a drink next to Mal.

"Hi," the guy said.

Mal nodded, staring at the remainder of his drink.

"I'm Tree," the guy said.

Mal looked up as if in surprise. "Tree? Your name is Tree?"

The guy had blue eyes, longish blond hair, and capped teeth. Had to be about twenty. Smelled like money even in the plain clothing. "Yeah. I have a natural affinity with the elements. Tree fits."

All righty. Tree also had dilated pupils and was high on something other than just life. "Mal. Name is Mal." He focused back on the tempting liquid.

"You look like a guy who needs a friend," Tree said, accepting his beer.

Mal snorted. "I had to shoot the last guy I called a friend." He shifted his weight enough that his jacket opened and revealed his gun, this one a Ruger. "You want to leave me alone, Tree." He downed the rest of his drink and gestured for the bartender to refill him.

The bartender poured and then paused. His hand went below the counter. "You can't have a gun in a bar."

Mal stiffened. "I'm licensed. Ex-cop." He kept his hand away from his gun and drew out his wallet to flash the permit to carry he'd created that morning. "See?"

The bartender relaxed but still frowned. "Even so. Keep that thing hidden."

Tree cleared his throat.

Mal turned only his head. "Go away, Tree."

The kid nodded and moved on, heading over to a woman in her fifties downing Fireball like her life had just ended. Her pink suit was disheveled and her mascara had run.

Mal sipped his drink.

Ten minutes later, a perky blonde sat on the stool next to him. "Excuse me. I can't find my friend, Leslie. Have you seen a pretty redhead? She has my wallet, and I'd like a drink."

Mal slowly turned. The woman had to be around twenty, with big blue eyes and a nearly see-through shirt. He let himself blink a couple of times. "I haven't seen a redhead named Leslie. Now or ever." His gaze ran over what had to be considered very nice breasts. "But I could buy you a drink."

Her eyes widened. "You could?" She touched his arm, sliding her hand down in a caress. "That would be so nice."

Wouldn't it, though? He nodded to the bartender and turned back to the blonde. That quickly, he was in.

Chapter Sixteen

Pippa sat at her computer and finished organizing the travel plans for one of her clients. What would it be like to go anywhere she wanted? To not worry about airport security, cameras, and whether her license would hold up to TSA standards?

The rain had continued all day, and she'd gotten a lot done, trying not to think about Malcolm. When would he get home?

She had never had a night like that and wasn't sure how to act.

Her phone buzzed, and she lifted it to her ear upon recognizing the number. "Trixie. How are you?"

"Okay. A couple of flashbacks and a nightmare. What about you?" Trixie whispered.

Four orgasms and a flashback actually. "I'm okay. Wondering if it's time to move on again." The idea made her chest hurt. There was no future with Malcolm or anybody else, but that didn't mean she could just up and leave. What if there was a slice in time for them more than just last night? He definitely deserved somebody whole and not nutty for his future. The guy was a hero. But she could be his present. "I'm not sure what to do."

"I've been thinking the same thing." Trixie lived an hour outside of Minuteville in the other direction. "We stayed away from the cameras, and I'm sure our identities held up. But still, I feel like they're getting close. You know?"

Pippa bit her lip. She was feeling the same thing, but a good part of her unease was caused by Malcolm. "Yeah. I think we're safe, though."

Trixie sighed. "Anything new with the sexy cop?"

"Ex-cop," Pippa corrected, her body flushing at just the mention. "No." She wasn't ready to share.

"I think it's great you're able to, well, you know. See a guy and not freak out." Pain tinged Trixie's voice.

Ice slid into Pippa's veins. "Isaac didn't rape me, Trixie. I was spared." Tears pricked her eyes. "You have a case against him if you ever want it. I'll testify on your behalf." The statute of limitations wasn't up.

Trixie scoffed. "Like anybody would believe us. And we'd end up in jail, too."

Pippa dropped her head. "I know." She pushed her keyboard toward the computer so she could rest her elbows on the desk. "I sent you a good list of counselors near you. Please tell me you looked one up."

"Have you?" Trixie asked. "You weren't raped, but I think it might've been worse for you. You can't be okay after all that."

Bile rose in Pippa's throat. "I still have online appointments with Dr. Valentine. He's fantastic, and I wish you'd call him." Three emails dinged about the travel plans. "I have to go. If you need me, call me. I'll be right there, Sister."

"Ditto." Trixie hung up.

Pippa buried herself in work, forgetting all about the past. Night had arrived by the time Malcolm's truck pulled into his driveway.

Her heartbeat quickened. She smoothed back her hair and looked down. Blue T-shirt and plain yoga pants. But she'd painted her toenails an electric pink, so she looked somewhat put together. Even so, when his soft rap came on the door, she jumped.

She almost yelled for him to come in and then remembered she had triple locks on each door. Oh yeah. Okay. Get a grip. Steeling her shoulders, she moved to the door and opened it. "Hi."

He held Chinese food in his hands and intensity in his gaze. "Hi. I brought dinner."

All of a sudden, she realized she was starving. "I forgot to eat." Anything actually.

His dark eyebrows arched. "Then we should fix that." Cool, crisp air washed in with him. At least it had stopped raining.

Butterflies wound almost leisurely through her abdomen. A low pull tightened her muscles. She moved aside to let him pass. Why was she so nervous? Oh yeah. Four orgasms in one night.

He walked past her, paused, and turned. "Are you all right?"

"Yes," she breathed.

"Was I too rough last night?" His eyes darkened.

She shook her head. "No. Just the right amount of rough."

His grin lightened something inside her. Something she hadn't realized was heavy. "I hope I wasn't too rough on you," she teased, shutting the door.

He chuckled and strode with long lengths into the kitchen to deposit the bags of food. "I do have a couple of interesting scratches along my ass."

She stopped. "Seriously?"

"Yep." He unpacked the cartons and looked around before finding dishes.

Heat infused her face and she hustled for the counter and an open bottle of Cabernet. "Wine?"

He glanced at the bottle. "Feel free. I'd better stick to water. Had my fill of booze today."

She blinked and poured one glass. "I thought you were at work."

"I was. Had to meet a guy in a bar and get information from him. Hence a bunch of alcohol I didn't need." Mal grabbed utensils and dropped into a chair.

She took a seat and eyed the food. Unease filtered into her pleasure at having his company. "Are you undercover again?" If he'd gone active, she'd have to leave. It was just too risky to date a detective. She wasn't that good.

"No." He dished out rice and noodles. "Still with requisitions. But I'm working on that form-stealing case." Tiny lines fanned out from his eyes. Was he tense? Stressed?

"Oh." She put a couple of pot stickers on her plate. "I didn't know forms were so important."

He chewed thoughtfully. "Well, just imagine what you can do with forms. Think of the items you can order and then return for money. It can be quite profitable."

She swallowed some of the wine, letting it warm her. "You don't seem like a guy who'd be happy on the sidelines like that," she murmured. "I saw you in action. You were good." Really good, or a lot more people would be dead. The thought both intrigued and threatened her.

He tipped back his water. "Says the enticing woman hiding in a cottage at the end of a long lane."

Good point.

"Speaking of which, how is it you were okay being in that diner?" he asked.

She finished chewing some spicy chicken. "The restaurant is out of the way and hardly ever very busy. I don't feel hemmed in, and there's never a crowd." Though it had been getting harder and harder to force herself to be around people. She needed to work on that.

He reached out and lifted her chin with one knuckle.

"I should've asked. Are you all right? Seeing a shoot-out like that is terrifying, and that wasn't my first by a long shot, pardon the pun." His warm finger was gentle, his eyes seeking.

She took a moment, absurdly touched by his concern. "I was scared, but everything happened so quickly that it was over almost as soon as it started." Truth be told, her biggest concern had been to keep hidden.

"I won't let anything happen to you, Pippa. I promise." He removed his hand, but an intensity remained in his expression. A look that took her breath away.

This was temporary, and she couldn't rely on that kind of protection. "You don't need to make me promises." She probably didn't deserve them. Those kinds of vows required honesty in exchange.

"Yet I just did." He tilted his head. "You can trust me. You know that, right?"

For the first time in years, she was tempted to tell the full truth. To give him all of herself. But what would that accomplish? The past was in the past, and it had to stay there. "I know."

A veil dropped over his eyes and he returned to his food.

She had the oddest sense that she'd disappointed him, so she struggled to find something to talk about. Anything. "Do you miss being undercover?"

He paused in the middle of eating. "Not really. I mean, it's hard to meld your real life with a new, fictional life and then remember it's not true." He looked up. "Know what I mean?"

She shook her head, the movement shaky even to her. "Not really. I'm just me."

His smile was smooth and reassuring. "I find you fascinating, and I haven't gotten in the front door yet. Tell me about your family."

She'd forgotten this part about dating, if what they were doing could be called dating. "Oh. Well. My dad was in the army. Died somewhere across the world from here when I was around six years old, and we never really found out how or why." How different would her life had been if he had lived?

Mal leaned back. "I'm sorry." His eyes turned liquid.

She shrugged. "I don't remember much about him, to be honest. My mom and I moved around a lot after that, but we didn't much get along. When I was eighteen, I went out on my own and haven't looked back." That was about as truthful as she could get.

Malcolm frowned. "I thought you said she died in a car accident."

Oh God. They'd talked about her mom already. In all the craziness, Pippa had forgotten. "Yeah, she did. After I left home at eighteen."

He set down his napkin. "I'm sorry. Can you visit her grave?"

"No." Who even knew where her mother was these days? The family liked to move around to find new money and new marks. "I don't think about her much." She wished it were possible they weren't looking for her any longer. "Um, now I remember you saying your folks were deceased and your grandpa raised you."

"Yeah. He was an ass." Mal took another drink of his water. "I had a shrink tell me once that I have abandonment issues. That I push people away." He shrugged. "But being alone made it possible for me to go undercover several times, and the last time it was for two years."

Abandonment issues? Kind of made sense. "You seem like a hero to me. The type to eventually settle down with the right woman and be a badass dad."

One eyebrow arched. He kicked his legs out under the table and patted his very flat belly. "Boy, do you have me pegged wrong. Can you imagine how screwed up a woman would have to be to end up with me?"

She coughed out a laugh. Many adjectives described her, and screwup was apt. But now she was just fantasizing. He'd never end up with a liar. "You're selling yourself short."

"No." He tugged his T-shirt down and scratched his neck. "I'm always investigating. Don't know how to trust anybody. And if I had someone who was actually mine—I mean really mine—I'm sure I'd be a complete possessive dick."

There was something sweet about his admission. Or perhaps that was just a dream she couldn't have. "I see you as more protective than possessive."

"Not much of a difference, blue eyes." He glanced at the clock on the microwave. "Now, I have a proposition for you."

Her breath sped up, but her body was so tired. Or maybe her brain was just exhausted. The talk with Trixie, although short, had taken a toll. The past often did. Even so, curiosity made her ask, "What's your proposition?"

"I'm tired, and by the look of you, you're exhausted." He stood and tossed all the garbage away. "Do you have a television in your bedroom?"

She stilled. "Yes. Why?"

He barked out a laugh, the muscles in his chest moving nicely. "Nothing salacious, I promise you. How about we cuddle down, watch a dumb movie, and fall asleep?"

Her little heart rolled right over and sighed. The hottest guy she'd ever met wanted to snuggle with her? No sex but comfort? He was turning out to be way too good to be true. "Who are you?" she murmured.

His head lifted. An unidentifiable light entered his eyes. "That's always the question, now isn't it?"

Chapter Seventeen

Even the snuggly woman in Malcolm's arms couldn't keep the flashback images at bay. Junior with a hole in his head. Other victims drowning in blood. The dead people at the diner. Finally, at around three in the morning, he gently extricated himself from the warm bed.

He checked the locks on the back door and the one to the garage. Then he moved to the front door and stopped. Shaking his head, he returned to double-check the back-door locks. Hypervigilance sucked. Then he went out the front door, made sure it locked behind him, and jogged quietly toward the street. Wolfe's truck was parked several yards up the road.

Mal jumped in. "Mornin.'"

"You too." Wolfe handed over a bottle of Jack Daniel's. "Do what you've gotta do." He started the engine and began driving down the deserted road. Kat peeked out from his pocket and gave a welcoming meow.

Well, at least the kitten was still alive. Malcolm took the bottle and drank several swallows before spilling some on his T-shirt and jeans. Then he rubbed some into his hair. "Good?"

"You stink. It's good." Wolfe took the bottle and drank a couple of shots.

"Hey. You're my driver," Mal said, not really caring.

Wolfe handed it back. "Lid."

Mal took another swig to the gut, then twisted the lid back into place.

Wolfe reached into the glove box and handed over a cheap-looking pen and a burner phone. "The pen is actually a camera. Get as many faces as you can. Call in an hour if they don't pick you up."

"Oh, they'll pick me up." Mal messed up his hair more. "I told the sweet blonde that I often return to the back of the bar in the early morning hours and try to find any leftover booze. That sometimes they throw bottles out that aren't quite done."

"That's just sad, man." Wolfe sped up.

"That's the whole point." Mal studied the soldier. "Where do you live anyway?"

Wolfe reached the interstate and pulled on. "I found an apartment complex just off the exit where the offices are. It's okay. Came furnished."

"Where were you before that?"

Wolfe twisted on the heater. His voice remained level. Perfectly so. "Syria."

Ah. "Do you miss the Teams?"

"Yes." Wolfe pressed the accelerator. "I disobeyed orders. Probably can't go back."

Mal rolled his neck. "I thought your deal with Force was to get you back."

Wolfe shrugged. "Force might have the juice, but I doubt it. It'll be interesting when he tries and fails and then owes me."

"He's a profiler. You sure he hasn't profiled you just right?" Mal asked.

Wolfe cut him a look. "Maybe. He sure got you right."

Yeah. Mal had noticed. "Want to talk about your last mission? When you disobeyed orders?"

"No."

Fair enough. They drove the rest of the way in companionable silence as the dawn began to break through the cloudy sky. Mal relaxed, enjoying the quiet tone and camaraderie. He hadn't realized how much he'd missed such moments until right now. Just as they reached the block of Blue's bar, the skies opened. "Ah, shit."

Wolfe pulled over in a deserted lot. "Take the phone."

"No." Mal slid it over the console. "If I go with them, and if they search me, they won't understand why I have a burner phone. Just meet me here around six tonight."

Wolfe frowned and looked even deadlier than usual. "I'm not sending you in there alone. We're a team now."

The guy obviously took that very seriously. "No choice. This is undercover." Mal clapped him on the arm. "And ditto." He jumped out of the truck and into the rain, quickly jogging away before Wolfe could try to stop him. Rain smashed down and mixed with the alcohol in his hair, making him smell even worse.

Before he knew it, he was behind Blue's, going through a huge green metal garbage dumpster. Holy crap. There really was a bottle of tequila with booze still in it. He took it out, found a nice place slightly sheltered from the rain, and waited.

By the time they arrived, he'd finished the alcohol and was soaking wet.

Tree ran across the mud puddles. "Hey, Mal. How's it going?"

Mal let his head loll on his shoulders. "Pine? Wait. No. Tree. Dude, what are you doing here?" His voice slurred just the right amount.

"We were driving by and saw you." Tree shoved a surprisingly strong shoulder beneath Mal's arm. "How about breakfast? You need some food."

Mal let the empty bottle crash to the pavement. There was no way Tree had seen him while driving by. But considering he was supposed to be drunk, he let himself be herded toward a sleek black van.

The door opened, and the blonde was there. She'd said her name was April because good things arrived in the spring. Today she had on very short white shorts and a tube top, again with no bra. "Malcolm," she said, reaching out toned arms to help him into the van. "How fortunate we found you. The storm is just getting worse."

Tree smoothly removed Mal's gun as April pushed back his hair. "Such a handsome face."

Right.

Tree shut the door and ran around to jump into the driver's seat, leaving Mal alone with April.

"I want my gun back, Tree," Mal slurred, letting April put his head on her shoulder and caress his leg.

"No problem. After breakfast." Tree pressed the accelerator, and they zoomed out of the lot.

About an hour passed before they drove beneath an imposing archway toward a colonial-style mansion. Green grass and rolling hills led to surrounding mountains. The place was beautiful. Even though it was raining, kids played out front and slid over wet grass, laughing merrily.

"The gardens are out back," April said, her hand at the very top of Mal's thigh.

They parked, and Tree jumped out to open the door. "We'll get you some food and then take you wherever you want to go." He held out a hand to help a now dry Malcolm.

Mal stepped out and made a show of trying to straighten his torn and dirty shirt. "I'm not exactly fit for company."

April trilled a laugh and slid her arm through his. "Don't be silly. We'd never think of judging on looks here." She escorted him up the wide steps and between massive columns into a wide foyer with shiny wood furniture beneath a sparkling chandelier. "Welcome to our home."

Mal stumbled and looked around. "This place is beautiful." He looked down at the small blonde. "Who are you people?"

She laughed again and drew him down the hallway to the left. "Let's get you some food and we'll talk about that."

Tree headed in the opposite direction.

With Mal's gun.

After a truly excellent meal of beef and rice, Mal found himself alone in a thick stone shower with steam rising all around him. He'd kept it cool during lunch while meeting several long-standing members of the family. Nobody asked him for anything, and everyone seemed relaxed and happy.

The steam made him feel secure. Damn, he felt good. For the first time since he'd been shot, his leg didn't hurt. Before he could contemplate that, the door opened, and April walked inside, completely nude.

He moved away from the spray, his mind oddly fuzzy. "Whoa. Um, no."

She smiled, her body nubile and tight. Intriguing triangles around her breasts showed she'd worn a bikini recently. "I just came to help you." Her slim hands reached for the soap on the ledge.

His heart rate picked up while his body seemed to somehow relax.

They'd drugged him. The realization helped his brain to kick in even as his body remained way too content. "Listen, April. I don't need help." His tongue felt thick. The sense of euphoria was interesting. A small dose of meth? It could've been a hundred different things.

April set the bar of soap against his chest and began massaging him.

He grabbed her wrist and set her to the side, turning back into the spray. "How old are you anyway?"

"I can be any age you want." She moved into him, pressing her breasts against his back.

An image of Pippa flashed through his head, and he shut off the water. "Sorry, sweetheart. My guess is you're around eighteen, and that's way too young." He shoved wet hair away from his face and turned around to face her. "Why did you come in here?"

"To help you," she said, her face earnest.

"Why?" He studied her eyes. Clear and probably not drugged? He wasn't sure.

She reached out and ran her hands over his chest. "Because that's what we do here. We help people. And I thought you could use a release."

The wrong woman had her hands on him. He grasped her wrists and pulled them away from his body. "Is that what happens here? Everyone has sex and finds release?" A part of him wanted to disappear back into the steam by himself. Just get lost in the steam and not have to do this job. Stupid drugs. "April?"

She shook her now-wet hair. "No. We're encouraged to find our own paths. Our own bliss."

His bliss at the moment would be putting his fist through the face of whoever had taught this kid to use her body to manipulate men. "Where are the towels?"

For the first time, her expression changed. Fear and then hurt filled her eyes, and tears started spilling over. "You don't think I'm pretty. I'm fat. I know it."

Now that manipulation he recognized. "You're perfect the way you are." He released her and moved out of the shower, finding towels and quickly wrapping one around himself. He handed one over to her, and she took it, holding it to the side.

"Do you have a girlfriend?" she asked, dripping water onto the expensive tiles.

Trying to find out about his life, was she? Man, she was good. "No. No girlfriend, no family, no more friends." His jaw hardened, because it might be the truth. "I was a cop, and when you're undercover, you have nobody."

"You can have me." She shook back her thick hair.

His heart broke a little. There was a sweetness to her, and he didn't want to hurt her feelings. Yeah. That's what they counted on. But he had a part to play. "Like I said, you're too young for me. Too cute and bouncy. That's a good thing, April."

"I'm not a virgin or anything." She pouted out her bottom lip.

Yeah, he got that. He looked around. "My clothes are gone." Instead, neatly folded linen pants and a white shirt waited on the counter. Great. The cult uniform. Just for him. He sighed and drew on the clothing.

"Yours are being washed." April reached for a linen sheath hanging on a hook and shrugged into it, turning around. "Zip me?"

He barely kept from rolling his eyes but zipped her up.

She smiled, the bounce back in her step. "This way. Isaac wants to meet you."

About time. Mal finger combed his too-long hair and followed her through the bedroom, through the big living room, and down to the end of a hallway. A woman was coming out, and Mal recognized Orchid, the informant. He gave her a nod, and she barely nodded back before continuing past him.

April knocked on the door.

"Enter," said a man's voice with a slight accent.

They entered.

Isaac leaned against his desk, looking pretty much unaged from the photos Mal had seen. A woman huddled by a brick fireplace with a boy of about six in her arms. Both had bruises on their faces.

Fire lashed through Malcolm and he pivoted, putting his body between Isaac and the terrified duo.

Isaac cleared his voice. "April, would you please take Mrs. Thomson and her son to the kitchen for food? They haven't eaten in a while."

Mal could take the guy out with one hand around the neck. Just squeeze until Isaac flopped like a fish on a hot dock. It was all he could do to let April escort the other two out of the room and shut the door. His fists clenched, but he couldn't help it.

"Detective West, please calm down. I didn't cause the bruises," Isaac said, gesturing toward one of two leather chairs flanking the desk.

Mal took a deep breath. "Then who did?" He sat.

Isaac took the other chair. This close, the guy looked taller than he had in pictures. The brown eyes were even more charismatic, and long-limbed muscles showed beneath his linen clothing. "I'm assuming her husband, considering we found her outside of a woman's shelter. We'll get her food and clothing and safety if she wants it."

That was one way to gain new members.

Mal tried to relax his jaw, remembering he'd supposedly been drunk outside a bar just a few hours ago. "Thank you for the food and shower. How do you know my name?"

"I'm Isaac Leon." He held out a hand to shake. "We checked you out the other night, after you met April. Can't be too careful who we invite home."

Mal looked around. "Yeah. This is a nice place." How long would the drugs take to leave his system? "Kind of seems like a touchy-feely type of group, though, and I'm really not into that." He tried to sound properly apologetic.

Isaac nodded. "I completely understand. But I was hoping, maybe in exchange for the food and shower, you'd spend a couple of hours teaching some frightened young women like Mrs. Thomson a little self-defense? Maybe take your experience as a cop and do some good?"

"Ex-cop," Mal said automatically. His weakness had been read instantly by an expert. Were those bruises on the woman and kid even real? Isaac had found the one thing that would've made him stick around.

If he was really being himself.

"Sure." He shifted his weight. "I could help out a little for a couple of hours."

Chapter Eighteen

Pippa couldn't shake the restless feeling that had plagued her all day. Sipping a nice glass of Riesling as it neared ten at night, she read Malcolm's second note to her. While she'd never admit it, she'd kept the first one in the file cabinet attached to her desk.

Pippa,

Sorry to leave so early, but I've been called to New York to deal with the shooting that just happened. I should only be gone for the day, and I'm sure the NYPD has found me a nice middle seat on a flight between two people who like to talk on planes. Which I do not. I'm digressing because I don't know what else to say. Thank you for letting me stay the night and hold you. There's a peace to be found around you that I haven't known in a long time, even when I can't sleep and the nightmares keep looming. Somehow, just having you there makes it better. I'll try to bring dessert this time.

> *Yours,*
> *M*

She trusted him. That quickly, she realized the truth. Could she tell him everything? He wasn't a cop any longer, but surely he believed in the law. Or could she just make this her truth? As far as she was concerned, she was Pippa Smith. The last two nights with Malcolm, that had been her. The real her. What did the past really matter?

Her phone buzzed, and she answered it. "Hey, Trixie. How are things?"

"They have a website," Trixie said, her voice panicky. "With our pictures."

Pippa dropped her glass and ran to the computer. She kept a continuous search going for her birth name as well as Trixie's, and nothing had dinged. "What is it?"

"AnTeaghlaigh dot com," Trixie said, her voice way too high.

"It's okay. Just hold on." Pippa typed the address and brought up the site. Nausea rolled through her. It was a pretty picture of a happy group of people "living off the land." She selected "About Us," and a full picture of Isaac came up on the screen.

Ice shot through her veins. Her skin itched. Bile rose in her throat, and she forced it back down. It was as if his eyes were looking directly at her like he used to. God. She clicked another link and was brought to a page talking about meditation, living off the land, and finding one's true purpose in life. "Crap."

"I know." Trixie's voice shook. "Click on 'Help Us.'"

Pippa tried to swallow and clicked on the link. Her picture scrolled up with Trixie's right under it. She read the caption out loud. "'Please help us find our lost family members. Mary and Tulip unfortunately started taking drugs and are lost to us. If you see them, please contact us immediately. We are offering a ten-thousand-dollar reward.'"

"Ten grand." Trixie chuckled, the sound full of pain.

"Well. I guess the good news is that they didn't turn us in to the cops. Yet."

Pippa forced her lungs to keep working. "This is new. Why are they suddenly on the internet and looking for us like this?"

"Because they haven't been able to find us any other way. You disappeared from Miami five years ago, and we've stayed off the grid since. They're desperate." Trixie's voice sounded just as desperate. "And you know why."

Yeah. Her birthday was in several days. Her twenty-fifth birthday—the special day foretold by the Bible that would elevate the family to the next plane. The ticking clock.

Trixie sniffed. "What's next? This is just one website. You know they've had detectives searching for years."

"Yes," Pippa said. "We need to find all the footage of the shooting the other day. Just to make sure we're not in there."

"I've watched every channel and looked at every online newspaper I could. No problems yet." Trixie audibly swallowed and then coughed. "Man. This stuff is strong straight out of the bottle." She sighed. "Have you ever thought that maybe Isaac is the real deal? That we're being punished for leaving the family? For our sins?"

Only in Pippa's darkest nightmares. "No. If he was the real deal, we wouldn't have been able to evade him for this long." How was it possible the bastard still wanted them?

Trixie's voice wavered even more. "Click on the link for 'Pray for Our Members.'"

Praying had been a big part of living with the family. Pippa clicked on the link and stopped breathing. "Mom." Fear burst through her chest. The picture was recent, and her mom had new lines at the sides of her pretty eyes. Pippa quickly read. "It says she has cancer."

"It's probably a lie," Trixie said. "Just to get you there. He'd do anything."

Pippa reached out and traced the screen. Tears pricked the back of her eyes. "I hope she's okay."

"Me too," Trixie said. "They're in West Virginia now. I thought at first they'd found us because they're so close, but then I saw their mansion, which was given over by a new member. Generosity first, remember?"

West Virginia? They were that close? Maybe fate had brought them full circle. "Should we head to California or something?" Pippa asked, her heart breaking at the thought. "They seem to be staying near the East Coast." Though members were from all over, there were numerous satellite recruiting areas, if she remembered right.

"Maybe. What about your hot ex-cop?" Trixie asked, her voice weary.

A knock sounded on the door outside. Pippa went from worried to breathless in a second. "He's here. I'll call you tomorrow." She clicked off and erased her browser before running into the other room and opening the door.

Malcolm stood in the bright porch light with a carton of ice cream in his hand. "I didn't know what kind you liked, so I brought vanilla with all sorts of toppings to choose from."

Her heart lifted into her throat. He was so big and strong and sweet standing there with his ripped jeans, dark shirt, and leather jacket. A fresh smell came from him. New detergent? "Come on in." She moved aside.

"Thanks." He strode past her to the kitchen.

"How was New York?" she asked, following him.

He set the groceries down, and his head dropped.

Oh crap. She moved up behind him, wrapping her arms around his strong torso and resting her cheek against his spine. "Forget it. You don't have to talk about work." Gently, she turned him around. His eyes were cloudy and his mouth tense. Must've been a bad day, talking about the shooting. "Shhh." Rising up, she pressed her mouth to his.

His large body shuddered. "Wait."

"No." She'd give anything to get lost with him again. Just for a night. "Please, Malcolm." She had to stand on her tiptoes to run her hands through his hair. Then she kissed him again.

Her soft touch was going to kill him. After a shitty day of being somebody else, standing here with Pippa, having her hands on him, was a blessing he didn't deserve. They needed to talk. He was tired of the lies.

Then she pressed her small body against him and bit his bottom lip.

He went from exhausted to ready in a nanosecond. His heart rate increased, and lava flowed through his veins. "Pippa," he murmured against her mouth.

"Yeah," she whispered back, sliding her hands down to grasp his whiskered cheeks. "It's just you and me tonight, Mal. No jobs, no worries, no outside world." On her tiptoes again, she licked along his bottom lip. "Please. I need this."

So did he. Right or wrong, so did he.

A low rumble rose from his chest and he ducked, lifting her into his arms. If they were going to get lost, he was going to treat her right this time. Gentle, and with a reverence she probably deserved.

Even if she was brainwashed and lying to him, he could forgive her after spending one day in that place with Isaac Leon. In fact, it was amazing she could even be here offering herself to him.

She nipped and sucked her way up his neck, biting gently into his earlobe.

Heat rushed down his torso to his balls, landing hard. Slow. He needed to go slow this time. Laying her on the bed, he divested her of clothing before tossing his shirt to the floor. Next, he kicked off his boots. "God, you're beautiful," he rumbled, gently caressing the smooth lines of her collarbone to her breasts. "So perfect." Her skin was the softest thing he'd ever felt.

"Malcolm." She planted her palms across his abs and traced each one. "I love these muscles." Then she traced along the knife wound on his hip and down to his scarred leg. "So much violence. You're a survivor." Her smile was the sweetest sight he'd ever seen.

She sat up, reached for his zipper, and released him, moaning softly as she stroked his length. His eyeballs almost rolled back in his head. "A true hero," she whispered, kissing his cock.

His balls bunched tight. "You can trust me, Pippa. You know that, right? I won't hurt you."

She licked along his length, and his legs trembled. "What if I hurt you?" she whispered, her breath hot on him. "I don't want to."

"You can tell me anything. I'll cover you." It probably wasn't smart to make that a real promise, but he meant every word. He tried to think of something else to say, but she closed her lips over him. Electricity zapped to his balls. He gasped air, and the blood roared through his ears. She sucked him like he was a treat, releasing him with a pleased smile. "I've never done that before."

The sweetness in her delight only spurred his need higher.

She grasped a condom out of his back pocket and bit the wrapper, spitting it out. Then she carefully rolled the rubber down, nearly killing him in the process. "I've never done that, either."

Her delight was going to end him.

He dropped his jeans and moved her up the bed, his mouth already seeking hers. Ferocious need rode him. One night with her hadn't been enough. Not nearly enough. What if he never got enough of her? Maybe he'd never be satisfied because the more he touched her, the more he wanted her.

The woman had somehow tunneled right into his blood.

He swept a hand down her body, memorizing her breasts. Her narrow rib cage. The contour of her hip. Was he being too rough? She kissed him back, her body arching against his. He licked her neck, right over her racing pulse.

Good. She wanted this. "Pippa," he murmured right before taking a nipple into his mouth and sucking.

Her hands tunneled into his hair as if to keep him in place. So he sucked harder. Her moan vibrated down his chest.

She arched against him, wet and ready. His dick throbbed at her entrance, and he pushed inside, feeling like he was finally where he was supposed to be. None of this made any sense, so he shut his eyes and just let himself feel.

Her scent, soft and wild, was all around him. Her body accepted him, vibrating along his length. He tried to go slower, tried to pause, but she scraped her nails down his back, and he was lost.

He pushed all the way home, lifting his head and kissing her again, taking anything and everything she wanted to give him. Every single sigh and second. Then he let her breathe, staring into her eyes. A deep and mysterious blue. Her body gripped him as if she'd never let him go. "Are you all right?" he asked, his arms quivering as he held himself back.

She rolled her body against him and widened her thighs. "Yes. All yours, Malcolm." She drew out his name with need in every syllable.

"Are you?" He pulled out and pushed back in, the feeling too delicious to stop. To even pause.

"Yes," she breathed, her voice softening. "Anything that matters in me is yours."

He stopped, balls deep inside her. If that wasn't a promise, he didn't know what was. Maybe they were two messed-up people who had found each other somehow. "Let me save you." Where the hell had those words come from?

She blinked. She caressed his back and shoulders, his face. "You already have. No matter what happens, you have." Tilting her pelvis, she took more of him. All of him.

A roaring filled his ears. Lightning jolted down his spine, sparking his balls. He groaned and pulled free, driving back inside her with a desperation he could almost taste. Harder and farther, he took her, galvanized by her little gasps urging him on.

She broke first, her body tightening, her nails scouring his butt. Her orgasm pushed him into his own, and he powered hard into her, shuddering as his entire body flared wide awake and on fire. Had he ever come that hard?

Finally, he came down, his chest panting.

Her mouth was formed in a small *o*. He brushed the hair back from her face, not missing the vulnerable glimmer in her eyes.

They were both lying to each other, and he knew that for sure. But in the moment, with her, this felt like the truth.

Chapter Nineteen

Pippa tried to slow her crazy heartbeat as Malcolm rolled off her and disposed of the condom in the other room. He returned, just a wide shadow in the darkness, and climbed into bed with her. Neatly flipping her on her side, he curled around her, his nose in her neck and his abdomen against her back.

"You okay?" he asked, his voice already sleepy.

She nodded, sinking into his warmth. "Yes." Then a huge yawn escaped her. "Are you?" Did he want to talk about his crappy day? She tried to keep her eyes open, but they closed anyway. Her body relaxed from head to toe. He was just so dang warm. "You can talk to me. You seemed stressed."

He chuckled lightly against her skin. "If I was stressed earlier, I'm sure not now."

She smiled into the darkness. "Glad I could help."

"If you helped any more, I'd be in a coma." He kissed the soft spot between her neck and shoulder.

She shivered, and her body warmed up some more. It felt so right to be in his arms. Bliss like this couldn't last. It wasn't possible. "Do you think the mistakes we make define us?"

"No." He nipped her earlobe. "I think the way we react after we screw up defines us. What do you want to talk about, Pippa?" His voice was a low rumble of pure heat and promise. In the darkness, all alone, he inspired trust.

She bit her lip. One night. Just one night to snuggle in and be Pippa Smith. Once she told him the truth, it might end. She so didn't want this to end. "Nothing." Not right now anyway. She cuddled closer and let herself drift off, safe for the first time in too long.

The music was always playing. In the house, out in the gardens, during meditation and school. Always the same beat, the same hum. They had moved to somewhere outside of Boston. New members of the family had generously offered their home and all the grounds to Isaac.

New members often did.

Her name was Mary now, but she still thought of herself as Pipsqueak. Even though she'd turned sixteen last week, she felt young. She knelt in morning meditation, her thoughts jumbled, her head hurting. A newer member had been punished the previous night because of untoward questions, which were never asked. She'd been ridiculed, and then she'd disappeared.

Probably into one of the thinking chambers. Oh, she'd be back. But she'd be exhausted and confused, and she probably wouldn't ask questions again.

Questions were bad.

The family was good.

"Mary," her mother whispered from the door. "Come."

Mary stood gracefully without using her hands, as she'd been taught. Her stomach churning, she followed her mother from the peaceful room where twenty other family members were still in meditation. "Yes?"

"Isaac wants to see you." Excitement flushed her mother's face as she smoothed the pure white silk scarf Mary wore

around her neck. Isaac had given it to her on her birthday, and she was to wear it at all times.

She hated that scarf. Completely. She'd thought of losing it in the garden the day before, but she didn't want to face Isaac's anger.

They passed several members cleaning the house, and her eye caught Tulip's. She was Mary's age and fairly new, with sparkling blue eyes and curly hair. She rolled her eyes.

Mary bit back a grin and kept walking, trying to quell the ache in her stomach. She always had to spend time with Isaac, but usually she just sat in the background as he conducted his meetings. It was a toss-up as to whether he'd be teasing, yelling, or touching whoever was in the room.

This time, he sat alone near the fireplace.

Mary stalled at the door.

Her mother gently nudged her inside. "Don't be difficult." She raised her voice. "Do you need me, Prophet?"

Isaac glanced up from the flames. "No, but thank you. I will require you tonight after supper."

"Of course." Her mother bowed out gracefully and shut the door.

"Come." Isaac gestured toward the chair across from him.

She tried to swallow, but the lump in her throat had gotten too large. Her legs stumbled a bit, but she made it to the chair and sat across from him.

He pointed to a stack of papers, numbers and charts, on the hearth. "Do you know what those are?"

She drew in a breath. "My natal chart. You showed it to me last week." Sometimes he forgot things. She wondered if it was the tea he drank, but maybe he just had so much in his head that things escaped.

"You know you're special, right?" he said, reaching out and touching her knee.

She kept perfectly still. "Because you have said so,

Isaac." She knew the right words to say. And she was always to use his name, when most people weren't allowed.

"Yes." He released her and sat back. He wore his usual light linen clothing, and his arm muscles clenched. He'd been working out a lot lately. *"On your eighteenth birthday, we will get married and then preparations will begin. I don't know yet which way the fates will flow, but on your twenty-fifth birthday, we shall do God's work."*

She frowned. *"How? How will we do God's work?"*

"That's up to the world. We'll either spread His love or His wrath." Isaac's eyes had an odd gleam to them. *"We will have children. Special ones. Do you like your scarf?"*

Presents weren't allowed in the family. Yet he'd given her one. One she had to wear around her neck always. *"Yes. Thank you."*

"This is how I want you to wear it." He looped it around once and let the ends trail down her breasts. His smile showed even teeth. *"And from now on, you shall only wear white. No other colors. Understand?"*

They mostly wore white anyway. But she did like the soft yellow she sometimes got to wear. *"Why?"*

He tilted his head.

"I mean, of course." Questions were bad. Her body flushed, and she eyed the door.

He grasped the ends of the scarf. *"The other day, I saw you talking to Eagle and Lake in the gardens when you were supposed to be picking tomatoes."*

Her body chilled. *"We were gardening and did pick tomatoes."*

He started pulling the scarf. *"You are to remain pure until your birthday. Until our wedding. Are you looking at other males?"*

"No," she croaked as he tightened the material across her throat. Her eyes started to water, and she couldn't breathe.

Unable to help herself, she clutched at the scarf and tried to jerk it away from her neck.

He was too strong. Her vision had gone black by the time he let her go.

She sank back in the chair, coughing and gasping, trying to breathe. Tears poured down her face.

"Robin," he called out, his face oddly calm.

A young woman hustled inside, her long brown hair swaying. She moved to his side, her attention solely on him. "Yes, Prophet."

He kept his gaze on Mary. "My bride has displeased me. Because she can't be touched until we wed, you'll take her punishment."

Robin looked at Mary and then back at Isaac, her face turning pale. "Of course."

Isaac grabbed Robin and threw her on the ground. Then he pulled up her skirt. "And you'll stay and watch, Mary. Rules must be obeyed."

Pippa bolted upright in bed, clutching at her neck and trying to breathe. She couldn't get any air into her lungs.

"Whoa." Malcolm sat up and put her right onto his lap, cradling her. "You're okay, baby. Keep breathing."

She shuddered against him, all but crawling into his warmth. Hard muscle and calm man held her, and she shut her eyes, allowing him to shield her. "Sorry," she croaked.

He chuckled, his breath stirring her hair. "Nightmares I understand. Live with them almost every night." Gently, he rocked her in the bed, the movement soothing. "Close your eyes and think of the cutest puppy or kitten you've ever seen. Then put yourself in a meadow with the sun shining down."

She did so, her chest moving as she breathed out. In and

out. Again. Her body stopped trembling, and she began to warm up. It was impossible not to in his arms.

"Better?" His big hand slid down her arm and back up. "I've got you."

He did. There was no question that Malcolm West had her. Completely. "Do you think of a puppy to calm yourself?" Her voice shook.

"No. I think of a pizza. A fully loaded one from Antonio's in New York."

She smiled, as no doubt he wanted her to. "A pizza. In a meadow."

"Yeah. No ants either. Just me and a big pie." He kissed her brow. "You better now?"

She nodded, her head moving against his chest. "Yes. Definitely."

"Do you want to talk about it? Rumor has it that talking about nightmares can help." He gently moved her back down under the covers and spooned around her, offering warmth and protection. Rain poured down outside, lending a sense of intimacy to the small room.

"Do you talk about yours?" She couldn't become dependent upon him, but nothing in the world would make her move away right now.

"No." He played with her hair, his arm extended up her torso. "There's a shrink with the new requisition unit who would love to dig into my head and discover all sorts of twisted emotions, but so far I've been able to evade her. Have you ever talked to anybody?"

"Yes. I saw somebody in person for a while who really helped, and now I have a counselor online. We Skype." In fact, she was due to meet with Dr. Valentine soon. "He's very good, if you want his number."

Mal chuckled again. "I don't think you and I should talk to the same shrink."

Yeah, neither did she. "It does help, though. I've worked through a lot." She didn't want to push him; it wasn't her place. "If you don't want to talk to your shrink, you could always talk to me." She held her breath.

"Like you talk to me?" he asked quietly.

She winced. He was smart and trained. Of course he knew she was keeping secrets. But a lot of people had bad childhoods, and hopefully, he was chalking her nightmares up to that. "I think my nightmares come from a less-than-ideal childhood. What about yours? Childhood with mean grandpa plus flying bullets?" She wanted to know everything she could about him.

He sighed. "Yeah. I guess. The bullets part is what has me hypervigilant. Checking locks, always looking over my shoulder, not trusting anybody. Standard PTSD without going too nuts on anybody. Yet anyway."

"You're trusting me." Maybe not completely, but he was naked in bed, talking about feelings. Guilt swept her. Well, she was talking about feelings, too. Just not facts. That had to count for something, right?

"Who hurt you, Pippa?" The question was soft, and his low tone took her by surprise.

The words invited trust. She wanted so badly to give all of herself to him. To let him work through some of the problems. She opened her mouth, not sure what she'd say.

Something dinged on the bedside table. She looked around.

"Damn it." He rolled over and reached for his phone. His body stiffened. "I have to go, sweetheart. Work calls."

She glanced at the clock on her side of the bed. "It's after midnight."

"Yeah." He slid away from her to stand, taking all his heat with him. He flicked on the lamp. "I'm not sure if I'll make it back tonight." Ducking, he grabbed his jeans off the floor.

She sat up, holding the sheet to her chest. What kind of midnight emergency could a guy in requisitions have? This was a man accustomed to going undercover. Was he undercover right now? What was going on?

He'd gone on full alert, his movements economical and sure. When he tucked his gun in the back of his waist, it looked like he'd done so a million times before. His jaw was firm, his focus already somewhere else.

There had been a gun on the table? She hadn't even noticed. "You need a weapon to fill out forms? What exactly are you working on?"

He didn't pause in drawing his shirt down over his flat stomach. "I'll always have a weapon."

That didn't really answer her question. "Malcolm? I really don't understand." Vulnerability swept her, and she drew up her knees.

He leaned over and pressed a hard kiss to her mouth. "We'll talk later. I have to go, sweetheart." Grabbing his boots, he headed out of the room, and soon the front door closed behind him.

She stared into the darkness. Something really wasn't right, and it wasn't just her brain misfiring. Her emotions were as well. Hurt. Pain burrowed deep, with a warning she'd learned the hard way to heed.

It was time to run.

Chapter Twenty

Malcolm shook out his wet hair as he nearly ran over Roscoe shoving his way onto the elevator next to Force. He had a Glock at his waist today, since the cult had kept his other gun. He pressed the Down button. "Why am I here?"

Force wiped his left eye. "From an anonymous tip, local authorities found the bodies of a man and a woman in a forested area outside Boston a week ago. One stabbed to death, one strangled. News just came through. The deaths have been dated to around the time the cult worked the area."

Anonymous tip? That was odd. "Were the victims listed as missing?" Mal asked.

Force nodded. "Yes, and we're trying to find a connection between either of them and the cult. So far, no luck." The elevator descended.

Who would've called? A former cult member? Or the cult itself? This wasn't making sense. Mal rubbed his aching temples as the elevator landed with a bounce and opened its doors.

Dr. Zhang was waiting, sitting on a desk in yoga pants, a tank top, and a pink sweatshirt. Her dark hair was piled high on her head, and her smooth face looked pissed. Oh.

The dog barked once and bounded to her. Her expression

softened just a little, and she leaned down to pet Roscoe's head. The dog made happy snuffling noises and sat, his tail wagging on the concrete. Then she reared back up as Force exited the elevator behind Mal. "Why are we here at this odd hour?"

"Sorry it's not the nine to five you're used to. Why don't you tell us why you're stuck here with us, and I'll try to be more considerate?" Angus strode by her toward his office, not bothering to look.

She slid from the desk to her feet, her mouth opening and her chin dropping. Red flushed across her high cheekbones.

Mal held up a hand. "Give us a second, Dr. Zhang. Please." He followed Angus into his office and shut the door, leaning back against it. "What the hell was that?"

Force moved around his desk and pulled out a chair. "What?" White lines cut along the sides of his mouth, and a muscle ticked visibly in his neck. His hands were steady, but fury glowed deep in his green eyes. "Have a seat." He gestured to one of two folding chairs facing his scarred wooden desk.

A dented file cabinet and several stacked evidence boxes were the only other furniture in the room.

Mal didn't move. "She's a shrink. Our shrink on this."

Force blinked. "I didn't ask her here. Even more disturbingly, I don't know why she's here. What's wrong with her?" Color filled his face.

Mal leaned his head back, amusement taking him by surprise. "Wrong with her? What? Anybody who'd want you for a friend must have something wrong with them?"

"Everybody here has issues." Force ground his back teeth together.

"You should probably apologize to her." Mal shrugged. "If there's something wrong with her, it'd be better if she trusted us." Man, he hated falling back on old habits, but trust was crucial in getting close.

"I know. You're right. I'll talk to her." Force glanced at his watch. "It's three in the morning. Why don't you take a look at the file we've just compiled about the bodies? The information might somehow come in handy when you go back in."

"I'm heading back to the cult in the morning," Mal said, his chest aching a little bit. "The family has made me feel all welcome and needed."

Force's eyes sharpened. "Have they, now?"

Mal nodded. "Yeah. I have pictures and an idea of the hierarchy. There are two men I'd like to take out. Clear a path in the upper echelons for a screwed-up ex-cop who knows how to shoot."

"Okay." Force stood. "Let's talk strategy the second Wolfe gets here. I called him when I called you. Where is he?"

Mal opened the door and let Force move past him. "Apologize to her," he whispered, sucking in air when Force elbowed him in the gut. "Butthead."

The elevator dinged, and they crossed the bull pen to where Nari was still petting a nearly purring Roscoe.

Mal looked up, expecting to see Wolfe. Instead, a man and a woman stepped off. He stilled. The guy was in his early thirties, with a dark jacket, a pressed shirt with tie, black hair, and perfect posture. The woman had wild reddish-blond hair, green eyes, and was wearing a peach-colored prison jumpsuit. Interesting.

Force moved forward. "It's about time." He nodded. "Special Agent Raider Tanaka and consultant Brigid Banaghan, please meet Dr. Nari Zhang and Special Agent Malcolm West."

Tanaka nodded his head.

The woman just looked around, her shoulders straight. "This isn't much better than a prison cell." Her soft voice held the faintest lilt of Ireland in it.

Force chuckled. "That's where you're wrong. Wait until you see the computer room."

Banaghan's eyes started to gleam. "Computer room?"

The dog turned around, viewed the duo, and then went nuts. He snarled and barked, leaping toward them, spittle flying from his mouth.

Tanaka shoved the woman behind him. "What the hell?" He reached for a weapon at his waist.

"Wait," Force snapped. "Roscoe. Down, damn it. Down." The agent jumped between the dog and Tanaka, blocking the other man with his body. "Your tie. Give me your tie."

Tanaka kept his gaze on the dog. "What?" he snapped.

"Your tie. Hand it over," Angus ordered urgently.

West came up on the other side in case the dog made a move on Nari. What was it with the tie? It was blue with a red crisscross design on it. Pretty boring.

Tanaka loosened his tie and jerked it over his head, tossing it at Force.

"Here." Force handed the tie to Roscoe. Snarling and growling, the dog took it over to the corner, where he started ripping it apart.

Tension edged with fear permeated the room. Adrenaline flowed freely.

Force eyed his calming dog. "I thought we were doing better with that. Hmm. Okay."

Banaghan angled her neck to look around Tanaka. "I thought dogs were color blind."

Force nodded. "Yeah. It isn't the color. No argyle prints for anybody. On shirts, on ties, and especially on sweater vests." He gave a shudder. "The last guy with a vest nearly lost his jugular."

Mal winced. "Maybe you should tell us all his quirks now. Just in case."

"We don't have that kind of time." Force grimaced. "Agent Tanaka, I apologize."

Tanaka held up a hand. "Raider. Please. Call me either Raider or Raid." His black eyes continued to track the dog.

"What happened to him? It obviously has something to do with the design."

"He got blown up by an enemy combatant with that criss-cross design on his tac vest," Angus said.

Mal scratched his head. "There are a lot of windows with that design."

Angus's face tightened. "I know. Roscoe goes right through those. It isn't pretty." He turned toward Nari. "Dr. Zhang, maybe you could work with him."

Her intelligent eyes widened. "You want me to counsel a canine?"

"Sure. If you're as good as they say, maybe you could help." Force's smile lacked charm.

Her gaze darkened. "Not a problem. I'll make you a deal: If I help the pooch, you come in for a session or two as well."

Force visibly retreated, his face losing all expression. "Let's not get ahead of ourselves."

"That's what I thought," Nari murmured. "And while we're getting informal, I wish everyone would call me Nari instead of doctor."

The pretty name fit her.

The elevator door dinged, and Wolfe stepped out, sprinkle-and-whipped-cream-topped coffees in his hands. He looked around. "I didn't buy enough."

Mal waved his hand. "Somebody can have mine." He couldn't deal with that much sugar right now.

"Me." Banaghan turned and made a beeline for Wolfe, taking the first cup he offered. She took a sip and hummed with pure happiness. Her eyes closed in bliss, and she drank several swallows. "No lattes in lockup."

Wolfe looked over her prison garb. "We're springing convicts now?"

Force nodded. "Miss Banaghan is our new computer

expert. Raider Tanaka is her handler and our chief investigator. He's also our liaison with the HDD in general."

Wolfe snorted. "What did you do wrong to get bounced to the basement?"

Raider winced. "Slept with my boss's wife."

Wolfe grinned. "That was stupid."

"No shit," Raider muttered. "Though I didn't know she was his wife when I took her home. Found out the next day."

"Right," Brigid Banaghan said. "And I didn't break any laws to end up in prison. Not a one. I was railroaded, man."

"Miss Banaghan," Force said, "you help us, you get the pardon. It's that simple."

She turned surprisingly clear green eyes toward Force. "Brigid. Informal, remember?"

"We're going informal?" Wolfe asked. "Cool. Call me Wolfe. First guy who calls me Clarence gets hit in the face."

Brigid chuckled, the sound lilting and somehow sweet. "Clarence? Like the angel?"

"Exactly," Wolfe said, craning his neck across the bull pen. "Why is the dog eating a tie?"

Mal leaned back against the far wall. Why did he feel like he was caught in the middle of the most macabre comedy ever? His head pounded and grit irritated his eyes. Maybe he *would* take a coffee. "We have to get serious, gang. Enough with the fun."

"None of this is fun," Force said quietly. "But your point is well made. We have work to do."

Malcolm studied the group. "Is this the entire team?" He pointed to the nearest desk, which was just as beat up as the rest of them but had all the knobs still in place on the drawers. "If so, I'll take that one."

"We have one additional member, but he's unavailable until later in the week," Force said.

"Another investigator?" Mal asked. They could use one more, probably.

Force shook his head. "No. Philosopher. Need his help with the serial killer case." He glanced at the sad walls. "All right. Two cases, so let's split up into two teams. Mal, Wolfe, and Brigid, you work on identifying the two guys Mal wants out of the cult. Come up with a plan by morning." He gestured toward the case rooms. "Raider and Nari, let's start the investigation into these bodies who might've been cult members. Then we'll all meet up in a few hours, before Mal has to leave."

Brigid stepped closer to Wolfe. "Is that a kitten in your pocket?"

Raider cut her a sharp look.

Mal sighed. There had to be a punch line in there somewhere, but he was too tired to worry about it.

Wolfe nodded. "Yeah. That's Kat."

Brigid sighed. "Oh, I love kittens. Can I hold him?"

"No." Wolfe turned and strode in his big boots toward the computer room.

"Huh." Brigid glared at his back. "Not nice." Then she brightened. "A wolf with a kitten. It is kind of cute."

Yeah. That was Wolfe. Cute. Mal caught Angus's eye. "I need a minute before we get to work." His mind wouldn't stop churning, so he let problems flash through in order. There were too many.

Force gestured toward his office and moved to walk into it. "You got it."

Mal followed and shut the door once inside.

Force held up a hand. "Don't give me a hard time about Brigid. She's a brilliant hacker, and we need her."

"Don't care." Mal faced him. "You can hire anybody you want. My concern is Pippa. She's not stupid, and I left in the middle of the night to go push papers. We have to think about my telling her the truth."

Force rubbed his chin. "You think you've gotten all you can from her undercover?"

All he could get from her? Like multiple orgasms and cuddling after nightmares? Mal kept his expression unreadable even as irritation clawed down his neck. "You're just fine with me nailing her, aren't you?"

Force lifted his chin. "Yeah. I'm absolutely fine with that." He waited expectantly.

"You're a prick," Mal said, heat flushing along his skin.

Force nodded. "I'm also fine with that fact. And you've gotten emotionally involved."

Mal lunged for him, standing an inch apart from the agent. "You can't go undercover without doing so. Trust me." Then he forced a smile. "Don't tell me for one second that you're not emotionally involved in the Lassiter case." Even if Lassiter was dead. A half-finished bottle of whiskey peeked out of the file cabinet.

"Again, I'm all about self-acceptance." Force's lip twisted. "You've stepped awfully close to me. Either kiss me or hit me, West. I have work to do."

Amusement grabbed him, and Mal barked out a laugh. "You're the last guy in the world I'd kiss." He took a step back.

"I'm genuinely relieved to hear that." Force tucked his thumbs in his jeans, his gaze remaining direct. "But here's the deal. If you bring Pippa in, you do it both literally and figuratively. I'll want to interrogate her, and I can't go easy. You understand how this works."

The memory of her shuddering body after her nightmare caught Mal. "She's innocent. I know it."

"She can be both innocent and planning an attack in the name of her lord." Force's voice remained reasonable and somehow gentle. "You know that, too."

Now the question remained, what would he do with that information?

Chapter Twenty-One

Pippa waited until first light to start packing. Everything in her hurt. Why had she let herself get emotionally involved with Mal? She'd known better. But she wouldn't trade the last couple of nights for anything. She called Trixie around five in the morning.

"What in the world?" Trixie answered the phone, her voice groggy.

"I'm taking off," Pippa said without preamble. She finished stuffing her socks into a large suitcase.

Trixie gasped. "Why? What happened?" Movement sounded across the line. "Do I need to run? I knew it. I've been followed. They have found us. This is terrible. Want to meet up?"

"Hold on. I don't think they've found us." Pippa sat next to the suitcase on the floor, her heart hurting.

"Oh." Trixie seemed to pause in her frantic movements. "Then why are you going?"

Pippa swallowed over a huge lump in her throat and told Trixie the whole story about Malcolm and his so-called job.

Trixie listened quietly until Pippa wound down. "All right. Let's look at this. He's definitely lied and isn't a governmental paper pusher."

Definitely. Pippa dropped her forehead to her knees. She had to get back to packing. "Right."

"And his job, before this one, was as an undercover cop."

Yeah. The guy lied for a living. Though she couldn't exactly throw stones there. "Yes."

"Chances are, he's undercover again. But isn't that supposed to be secret? I mean, he couldn't just tell his girlfriend all about a current case, right?" Trixie asked.

Pippa straightened enough to lean her head back against the wall. "Well, yes. I suppose so."

"What do you care if he's a current cop or an ex-cop? Either way, he'll probably want to enforce the law." Trixie coughed away from the phone and then returned. "But as far as I can tell, there's no crime for him to find out about. What we did? It was never reported. We don't even know what we did. Not really."

"That doesn't matter. The Prophet has me, and you know it." Pippa set a hand on her stomach as it started to ache. Isaac was a genius, and he'd set her up perfectly.

Trixie swallowed audibly. "I know," she whispered. "But Isaac is crazy, and he thinks he's in love with you. That you're soul mates. He won't really use that evidence and turn you in."

"He will if he can't have me." It was a fact Pippa had reconciled herself to years ago. If she could just make it to her twenty-fifth birthday, then maybe Isaac would give up on getting her back; his so-called prophecy would no longer be valid to him. In the meantime, he was obviously gearing up to find her with the new website. "I should run. If not for me, then for Malcolm. Even though he's good, Isaac has enough people doing his bidding that somebody could get a shot off if Isaac ever finds out I care about Mal."

"You do, don't you?" Trixie asked, her voice soft. "You care about him a lot."

Pippa's shoulders slumped. "Yeah. He's tough and sweet."

"Maybe you should just tell him the truth. If he cares about you, he'll believe you," Trixie said.

"I almost did last night. But even if he believes me, if Isaac turns me in, there's probably nothing Mal can do: Evidence is evidence, you know? And then Mal would probably go after Isaac." He would have no idea how evil Isaac could be or how strong his influence was over the family. "He's strong, but . . ."

Trixie coughed some more. "Do you ever think we have an inflated impression of Isaac? That he seemed invincible when we were kids, so we're making him out to be more than he is, even now?"

"No." Isaac had an army who'd do anything for him. "We see him as he is." Which was powerful and evil. A terrible combination. Pippa looked around her room. She loved this place. It would physically hurt her to leave it.

Trixie coughed again.

Pippa sat up. "Are you all right? You sound worse."

"I'll be fine. I went back to the clinic this morning for more antibiotics. Apparently, the last round only quelled the cough for a little while. These are stronger." Trixie was quiet for a moment. "I think you're at a crossroads. Either run or tell Malcolm the truth. You'll go crazy otherwise."

Crazier anyway. Pippa sighed. "I know." Enough about her and the problems she'd created for herself. Her friend didn't sound well. "Earlier, you said you'd been followed."

Trixie snorted. "I see shadows in shadows. Some guy said hi to me on the street the other day, and I yelped and ran in the other direction. Seriously. I'm nuttier than a fruitcake."

Pippa smiled. "Remember that year we made hundreds of those things and sold them in town?" She'd been twelve and hadn't yet realized how bad things were going to get with the family. She and Trixie had spent days baking fruitcakes during the holidays.

"Yes. I was so tired of nuts, I didn't eat any for three months." Trixie laughed. "Those days weren't terrible. The chores were okay, and who needs sleep at twelve?"

The terrible days came a couple of years later. Pippa sobered. "We're survivors, Trix."

"Hells ya," Trixie said quietly, her voice hoarse. "I sometimes wonder about my sister." Her older sister had been her guardian, and she'd brought Trixie to the family. "If she's still alive. If she's still with the family."

Pippa tried to roll tension out of her neck. "I wonder about my mom, too. And about some of the other people." Many had been nice to her, but they all followed Isaac. He was the law. How could so many people be so blind? She'd researched cults since leaving, so she kind of understood. But sometimes she could only shake her head and wonder why. "We have each other, Trixie."

"You could move in with me, if you wanted," Trixie said. "If you leave your place."

Pippa smiled, glad for her one friend. "Ditto." They'd lived together in Miami for a while, and it had been fun. But what bonded them also brought back horrible memories. The arrangement they had now seemed to work best for both of them.

"What are you going to do?" Trixie asked, coughing some more.

"I don't know. But I'll be in touch. Get some sleep." After saying good-bye, Pippa sat in her room and listened to the rain for several long moments. Maybe Trixie was right. Was it time to trust? Even so, it wouldn't hurt to pack her trunk, just in case. She carried the first suitcase to her car. Shoot. She needed gas. She usually got gas after seeing Trixie each month, but the shoot-out had changed her routine.

Sighing, she opened the garage door and slid into her car. Maybe she could make a decision while driving to get gas.

She had almost finished packing. She turned the key, and nothing happened. She tried again.

Her car wasn't working.

Malcolm sat in the passenger side of the van as April drove him from the fake crappy apartment to the mansion.

"You know, if you just stayed at the big house, it'd be easier," she said, her chipper manner back. Today she wore tan pants and a low-cut, white, see-through blouse. Her breasts bounced beneath it, and she thrust out her chest several times.

Was she supposed to try to seduce him again?

The music she played the entire time had a quick beat—close to a heartbeat. Hypnotic and rhythmic. The shrink had prepared him to listen for traps like that.

April turned down the heat. "It was really cool of you to teach us self-defense yesterday. A bunch of us practiced after you left."

He gave her a smile. "That's fantastic. What did you practice?"

She ran him through the different exercises, and he calculated the time spent. Feigning interest, he asked her what else she'd accomplished the night before.

Her list was impressive.

It also showed she'd only had an hour or so of sleep. Another classic cult trick: keep the members too busy to think and too tired to protest. But he had her alone for a little while, so he'd be an idiot not to take advantage of it. "I appreciate the ride," he murmured, looking out the window.

"You bet. But what about staying with us? With me?" she asked.

He watched the trees fly by. "You're sweet, but I've never seen myself settling down with one woman, you know?" His fingers tapped naturally with the rhythm from the iPod.

"I totally get it." She set her hand on his thigh. "Nobody is married in the family. The Prophet says marriage divides a family. Only being available to one person. That status is reserved only for him."

Mal turned his head. "The Prophet is married?"

Her smile showed dimples on either side of her generous mouth. "Not yet. Soon, though."

"Who is he marrying?" Mal asked.

She withdrew her hand. "That's personal family business."

Oh yeah. Asking questions was frowned upon. "No problem." He withdrew as well, turning to watch the trees outside.

She lasted about three minutes. "There's a special woman just for the Prophet. She's so very lucky."

"Hmmm." Mal didn't turn back. The special one had better not be a kid.

"I think we'd have fun together," she said, accelerating. "I like you." Her voice was wistful.

He turned slightly, pretending to warm to her. It was like manipulating a butterfly. "I like you, too. Are there guys you don't like?"

Her mouth tightened, and a flush spread across her girl-next-door face. "Of course not. I love everybody in the family." She said the words as if she was reminding herself. "I'm lucky to share any type of moment with the chosen few."

Any type of moment? "I assume refusing to share time or anything else with a family member is wrong." He tested his theory.

"Of course," she said, nodding emphatically. "We all belong to one another. People are just light and energy, you know."

How many others had the poor girl belonged to? Mal

searched for the right words. "You never told me how old you are." He still guessed around eighteen.

"Twenty." She pursed her lips. "Though age is just a number, right?"

He hated that saying. Some numbers mattered. "How long have you been in the family, April?" It was the first time he'd used her name, and he did it on purpose. Anything to throw her enough so she kept answering his questions.

"Forever. I don't remember a time I wasn't in the family." She turned and smiled at him, her eyes unfocused again. "You should join. I'd be there for you."

God, he was going to save this girl if it was the last thing he did. But for now, he had a job to do. "I'm kind of a take-charge guy. It seems like I wouldn't be welcome there."

She grasped his thigh again. "The Prophet really likes you. He wants you with us."

If Mal could get rid of a couple of the higher-ups, good old Isaac would want him even more. "Did he tell you that?"

She pressed her lips together and then, thinking it through, slowly nodded. "Yes."

"I don't know." He rubbed his eyes. "Ever since I was shot, I've been drinking a lot. It's hard for me to remember some things, and it seems like the family is big on, well, familyness. I don't think I could navigate that many people."

She squeezed. "You don't have to know everyone. That takes time."

"I'd hate to tick off the wrong person." He tilted away from her again. "Forget it. I deserve to be alone."

"No," she breathed. "You're not alone, Malcolm. I'll help you."

He turned fully toward her, patting her hand, feeling like the biggest ass in the world. "You will? You mean it?"

She nodded solemnly. "Of course. Okay. Besides the Prophet, there are three men basically in charge."

Mal listened and steered her in the right direction several

times as he gathered information. She had been perfectly groomed to manipulate, and for that, Isaac Leon would pay.

They finally reached the mansion, and as soon as April stopped the van, a tough-looking brunette of about thirty opened his door. "Malcolm. My name is Millicent, and the Prophet has asked me to show you around the gardens."

It hit him, then. He'd told April she was too young for him and not his type the day before. Apparently, she'd reported that back to the people in charge.

This woman was her opposite.

He stepped out and shut the door, waiting until April had made her way around the front. Then he winked at her. "I appreciated the ride, April. I hope we can meet up later."

The way her eyes lit up nearly made him snap. At the very least, if either woman reported to Isaac, they'd say he'd been appreciative and interested. Then nobody would punish April. Her happy hop as she bounced away made him want to kill somebody.

He smiled at Millicent, too easily playing his part. "Tell me about these gardens."

Chapter Twenty-Two

Pippa paced by her window, her mind reeling. The car wouldn't work. What she knew about cars could fit in a teacup. No, not a teacup. In a tiny little eyedropper. Yeah. Why would her car suddenly stop working? It was old, but she'd never had a problem with it before.

She called four mechanics before she found one who'd drive all the way out to her house, but the woman didn't have an opening for three days.

Three days.

Okay. Pippa gave her number in case there was a cancellation.

Maybe Malcolm knew something about cars. It seemed wrong to get his help and then take off without a word. Or perhaps he didn't know a thing about cars.

Who the hell knew?

But, she didn't want to leave. She wanted, for the first time, to stay and fight. To tell the truth to somebody. To Malcolm.

The flash of a truck caught her eye, and butterflies winged through her stomach. He was home. What should she do? Face him. That's what she should do. It was time to trust. If anybody could be trusted, it was Malcolm West.

The second she truly decided, a huge weight lifted from her shoulders.

She opened the door and walked out on the porch, making it to the end of her walkway before noticing that the black truck wasn't Malcolm's.

The dog she'd met before barked and rushed toward her, yipping happily around her feet. He brushed her legs, and she nearly went down.

The guy who worked with Malcolm slowly made his way over. What was his name? The cop at the diner after the shooting had said it. Angus Force. Yeah, that was right. She watched him carefully.

He moved like he could move much faster if necessary. "Roscoe? Don't knock the nice lady down." He kept coming, his boots spraying up water. His hair was cut above his ears, thick and kind of messy in a totally cool way. This close, his eyes were a deep green. Darker than Mal's. "You okay?"

She nodded, all words trapped in her throat. Ten steps. Ten steps backward and she'd be in the house. Away from this man.

He stopped a couple of feet away, his gaze searching. "I came to see Mal, but he's not home. Any idea when he'll be back?"

Wait a minute. This was Mal's boss. "I thought he was at work."

The guy blew out air. "He was, but then he said he had some errands to run. I told him I'd meet him at his house for pizza in about an hour, but I finished up early." He frowned and glanced up at the cloud cover and then back to her. "Oh. I'm Angus Force, by the way." He held out a hand.

Hers trembled, but she reached out and shook. This was one guy and not a crowd. He was Mal's boss, which had to mean he was okay. Yet when he released her, relief made her shake. "Pippa."

His grin made him look much younger. "I know. Mal's talked about you."

Her ears perked up. "He has?" Could she be any more of a dork?

"Yeah. Likes you a lot. Also says you're a great cook." Angus glanced at his watch. "I'm sorry to have bothered you. Roscoe and I can wait in my truck."

She'd be a total ass if she let them wait in the truck. If she was going to tell Mal the truth, demand truth from him, and start facing her fears, why not start now? "Um, would you like to wait inside? I have some biscuits and tea." The biscuits were a couple of days old, but they were homemade and would heat up nicely.

He paused, his eyes lighting up. "Are you sure?"

Was she? "Yes. Of course." She patted the dog's head again. "Roscoe can come, too." The dog wagged his tail happily.

Angus glanced back. "Why is your garage door open? Were you leaving?"

"No," she said. "My car stopped working, and I was trying to figure out why."

His eyebrows rose. "I know a bit about cars and could take a look, if you'd like."

The offer seemed genuine. And kind. "Would you?" she asked. "That would be fantastic. The soonest I can get a mechanic out here is in three days. Roscoe and I can go warm up the biscuits." The dog nuzzled against her knee, and she laughed. What a cutie.

"Sounds good." Angus turned toward the garage, whistling.

"Come on," she whispered to the sweet dog. He followed her happily into the house. "I'll slip you a biscuit or two before Angus gets back here." It was nice to have an animal in her home again. If she stayed, after telling Mal everything, then maybe she'd get another cat. Or even a dog. The backyard was fenced and had plenty of room.

She had just finished placing tea and biscuits in the front room when Angus knocked on the door. "Come in."

He walked in and wiped his boots on the mat before giving a look to his dog, who'd sprawled out in front of the fireplace. "You gave him a biscuit."

"I'll never tell. Please, sit." He was just too big standing here. As big as Mal, for sure.

He took a seat, and she poured him some tea. "Did you fix the car?" she asked.

He shook his head, accepting the warm cup. It looked tiny in his big hands. "No. I checked everything I knew, and I have no clue what's wrong with it. You said the mechanic could be here in a few days?"

She nodded, her blood chilling. Oh, she'd decided to stay, but not having any way to escape just in case gave her the willies. "Thank you for trying." Taking her tea, she sat in her bold, multicolored chair by the fireplace with the dog.

Angus overwhelmed the bright blue sofa with his sheer size. He took a sip of tea. "Delicious."

She rolled her eyes. "You don't seem like much of a tea drinker."

He smiled, and a surprising dimple winked in his left cheek. "You've converted me." He ate a couple of biscuits. "I was wondering why the two houses are so close and share a backyard."

She slowly started to relax in his presence. "Two sisters built the homes after they were widowed. Margie and Mertie Maloni. Margie passed on, and Mertie moved to Florida."

He nodded. "I figured it was something like that. Do you enjoy living so far away from town?"

"Yes. I'm not that great with crowds." The dog snuffled, and her heart warmed. This was nice. It was also an opportunity. "You and Mal work together, but I don't think I really understand what it is you do."

Angus sipped thoughtfully. "We're in requisitions."

Yeah. Right. "What exactly does that mean?" For some reason, questioning this man she barely knew was easier than pinning Malcolm down.

Angus's eyes lightened. "It means we acquire things for the government. You know. Paper, pens, clips." Amusement curved his lips.

She smiled, feeling like they shared a joke. "Right. I see."

He set his empty cup down on the table. "Mal is good at his job. Very. You don't have to worry about him."

The reassurance was sweet, considering they both knew Mal was doing something other than counting pens for some boring agency. "I appreciate that, but calls in the middle of the night mean that danger is near." She bent over and grasped the teapot, pouring him another cup.

"Does it?" He accepted the cup. "If it did, I couldn't tell you. But again, Mal's safe. Very."

This whole government secret stuff was kind of sexy. "If you say so," she murmured.

Angus nodded. "I do. What about you? Mal says you're a virtual assistant. That must keep you busy."

"It does." She sipped her favorite lavender tea.

"No need for adventure outside these walls?" Angus leaned forward slightly.

She shook her head. "No. I understand how that'd bother some people, but I like my home. It's cozy, warm, and safe."

He looked around, studied the several locks on the door, and then glanced at the sleeping dog. "It is at that."

The locks probably seemed like overkill. But for a woman living alone, it wasn't totally bizarre.

Angus chewed another biscuit and then swallowed. "I like your place. The colors are so vibrant and bold. It's energizing."

It was the direct opposite of the family's muted color scheme. She stiffened at the remembrance. "Thank you. I like it, too." They needed to talk about something other than her. "So, how did you get into government work?"

He sipped more. "My sister and I were in foster care most of our lives. It was always one official or another moving us around. They had the power and we didn't. City, county, state. All of them."

She tilted her head, studying him. Her heart hurt for the boy he must've been. "I see."

He nodded. "I wanted to be the one in charge. So I went to college and then started working for the government. Nobody would ever move me around again." His tone remained level, but his eyes were stark.

"What about your sister?" she asked.

He leaned back. His voice softened. "She passed away over five years ago." Then he shook his head. "I don't like to talk about it."

"I'm sorry." Her chest hitched.

He smiled, the sight a little sad. "You didn't know." He cleared his throat. "So. What about you? Any family?"

"No," she said instantly. "No family."

His eyebrows lifted. "Sounds . . . bad."

She forced a smile. The one she'd learned so long ago. "My dad was in the army, and he died in combat. I'm pretty sure. They never told us the details." She cleared her throat, unable to talk about her mother. The website said she had cancer. It would be a jinx to say it. "I left home at eighteen and haven't talked to my mother since. I don't even know where she is." Her gaze dropped to the sleeping dog. Oh, to be so peaceful.

Angus chuckled. "The two of us are just a barrel of fun, right?"

She looked up, startled. Humor glided through her. "Geez. No kidding." She glanced outside. It was starting to get dark. "Um, seen any good movies lately?"

Angus smiled. "Good topic. That or the weather."

They chatted then about good topics. Movies, spring flowers, birds. He had a surprising knowledge of the local bird population. Finally, his phone buzzed. He glanced down to read the screen and then sighed.

"Everything okay?" she asked.

He nodded, an apology in his gaze. "Yeah. Malcolm and I have both been called in." He held up a hand. "Nothing to worry about, I promise. Our job isn't dangerous, but I'm afraid he won't be home until late."

Disappointment felt like a pinprick to a balloon. She'd finally decided to level with the guy, and she couldn't get him in the room. She forced a smile. "I understand."

Angus stood. "Thank you for the tea and biscuits. It was nice to get a chance to talk."

Her smile felt genuine this time. "I agree. Thank you for staying." She meant every word.

The dog gave her a smile as he left, following Angus. They were both so disarming. Chatting with Angus had been like talking to an old friend.

Why that suddenly made her uneasy, she'd never know. She shook her head at herself. This being so paranoid had to stop.

It just had to.

Yeah. She could be a normal person with a maybe boyfriend next door. So she scrawled a quick note for him, saying that he should wake her no matter how late he got home. It was time they talked.

After leaving the note taped to his front door, she hustled back to her house to clean up. She could safely leave the door unlocked. If the family found her, locks wouldn't stop them. And it was silly to think a random burglar would find her house. So she stared at the locked door for a few minutes.

Her body wouldn't move.

Well, okay. Mal could knock. There was no reason she couldn't get up and unlock the door for him.

She sighed.

Maybe the locks she'd put on her life needed to be disengaged one at a time. She wasn't ready for that yet.

Hopefully, someday she would be.

Chapter Twenty-Three

Malcolm spent all day and long into the night being groomed by the family. First there was the tour through the gardens, where community health was emphasized. All the women were braless in linen and very friendly. Even the men—the ones he met—seemed kind and welcoming. A sense of acceptance was everywhere, and the members were of all ages, races, and nationalities.

He was made to feel needed and wanted.

Not once did he see Orchid, Angus's informant, but that wasn't a concern yet. He couldn't very well ask to see her because they'd never met.

After the gardens, he joined meditation for an hour. Rhythmic music, a short chant, and everyone saying the same words. It was as close to hypnotism as possible without being such. Nari had warned him of it, and damn, she was right.

Then he was asked to give self-defense classes. First to a bunch of really cute, earnest kids. Then teenagers. Then a group of young men.

Finally, women aged eighteen to forty. They were very touchy-feely and in awe of him. If he hadn't been a cynical ex-cop with control issues, he might've fallen right into the trap.

It felt good to be needed and admired.

They kept him so busy, it was around suppertime when he realized he hadn't eaten all day. Ah. Food and sleep. Those pesky things that altered brain chemistry.

During his tasks, he memorized the layout of the place and the scheduled comings and goings of people.

After self-defense classes, he attended another round of meditation. This time the music was louder and the chants more intense.

When he was finished, April met him at the door. "Hi." She ran her hand suggestively down his arm. Her hair was now up in the ponytail, making her look even younger than her twenty years. Her skin had pinkened from her time gardening. "I heard you've done a wonderful job today."

"It's a peaceful place." His head was a little light, and he had to concentrate to focus.

She grasped his hand and pulled him toward the outside patio. "We're about to have evening meal, and I was hoping you'd sit by me."

Millicent had disappeared earlier, after he'd rebuffed a couple of her not-so-subtle advances, so he'd figured he'd see April again. He feigned surprise. "Man, I am hungry. I forgot to eat all day."

She giggled, the sound tinkly and young. So young. "That happens all the time to me. It just means you're doing the Prophet's work. You're fulfilling yourself and being who you're meant to be." Approval was in her admiring gaze. "You're amazing, Malcolm."

Man, they poured it on thick. But the girl was earnest. Guilt caught him for a moment, but he had to play along to help her. This was a long game.

They walked outside to where a sprawling table ran beneath a wide awning protected from the weather. April sat him right smack-dab in the middle of a lot of smiling faces and linen clothing.

The food was plentiful, but nobody moved to fill their plates. So neither did Malcolm. Look at him, already conforming with the group. The tactics were effective, because he knew not to swipe a roll yet. Wouldn't even dream of it.

Isaac Leon strode out of a side door to the head of the table.

The energy around the table rose.

"My family." Isaac looked down each row, as if acknowledging each and every one of them. "It has been a worthy day for all of us. You are to be commended, and you are loved."

The guy all but dripped charisma. He wore white linen, slightly setting him apart from the rest. And his hair curled around his ears, making him seem earnest and caring. Mal looked around for the four guys he'd identified as Isaac's enforcers, but they were nowhere to be seen. They didn't seem to mix much with the rest of the group.

Unless they wanted to cleanse. He'd gotten that much out of April earlier. They were all in for sex, and a woman's refusing was frowned upon. The family was meant to serve each other, after all.

Isaac continued to speak, and although the group was no doubt hungry, nobody even glanced at the food. All eyes and attention remained on him.

Finally, he gave them sustenance. "My loves. Please eat." He sat and waited for a dark-haired woman next to him to dish him up a plate. She was stunning. Long, black, curly hair, deep brown eyes, a light smattering of freckles across her darker skin. She could be anywhere from eighteen to thirty, with no signs of age.

Mal looked around. April served him salad, a roll, and chicken casserole.

Where were the drugs? They could be in anything. So he ate the roll and worked on the chicken. His guess was the salad dressing. Or maybe in his glass of water. But he had to eat something, so he tried to be careful.

The meal was finished when Isaac stood up, whether people had cleaned their plates or not. The second he stood, so did everyone else.

Malcolm did so naturally. Wow. This unobvious cult shit was impressive. He'd automatically followed the group. Interesting. Then everyone bowed their heads. All righty. He did the same. His body relaxed, and a sense of euphoria wandered through his veins as Isaac said another blessing.

Mal swayed just a little. Damn it. Somehow, he'd gotten the drug. He should be pissed, but his body was too mellow. His mind too calm.

"Malcolm," Isaac said, his voice a low hum. "Would you please join me in my office? I would like to talk."

April patted his hand as if in support and excitement. She really was a sweetheart.

Mal moved away from the table and walked to meet Isaac. Okay. He'd been drugged. Knowing the fact gave him some power over the situation. And he'd taken just enough to be mellow and not pass out, so they didn't want him incapacitated.

Isaac led the way across the veranda and into the side door, which turned out to be his office. Mal studied the place again. Small table over by a bookshelf, sprawling desk flanked by a couple of leather chairs, and two bigger chairs and sofa over by a roaring fireplace. He let himself trip and almost went down, catching himself and grabbing the bug out of his sock.

"Whoa." Isaac grasped his arm and helped him get steady. "Are you all right, my brother?"

"Yes. Sorry about that. Just a little off balance." Mal slid the bug beneath the edge of the desk as they moved by it to take the chairs by the crackling fireplace.

Isaac also sat, leaning toward Mal. "Sometimes the pain in our lives can take away our mental acuity." His voice was soothing. Calm. "You've been drinking a lot. Trying to banish those demons from your time on the police force."

Mal nodded. "That would be the truth."

Isaac stood and moved to a cabinet in the wall, opening a slot to reveal a full bar. He poured two very generous glasses of Scotch and returned to hand one to Malcolm. "Alcohol isn't the problem. It's why we drink that matters."

So drugs plus booze. The hard sell was happening. Even so, Mal took a deep drink of the expensive elixir. It was like coming home.

The door opened, and three men strode inside. They wore the customary light-colored linen clothing, but two of them had guns strapped to their thighs.

Mal felt like he should tense, but his body was too relaxed. "Why are they armed?"

Isaac sighed, his brown eyes sorrowful. "We have to protect our family. There are people out there who threaten us and our way of life. Can you imagine that?"

Mal took another drink. "From the outside, you look like a cult."

Isaac's dark eyebrow arched, and his lips curved. "What do you think?"

Oh, definitely a cult. "It seems like a lot of people just trying to live, if you ask me," Mal said, sipping more of his drink. "I wasn't sure at first because of all the light clothing and everyone seeming so happy."

"Being happy is wrong?" Isaac asked.

"Just unusual," Mal said honestly.

"What changed your mind?" Isaac took a sip of his drink.

Mal partially turned to eye the guys with the guns. "The self-defense classes and the guns. Neither of those go with cults. People here are encouraged to take care of themselves, even if it means engaging in violence. That's not like a cult." He shrugged. "As far as I know."

Isaac studied him, his gaze shrewd. "Is that all?"

Mal met his gaze directly and then shrugged again. "I don't know. Part of me just doesn't give a shit anymore anyway. You know?"

"I truly do." Isaac nodded to the closest armed man. The guy was about six feet tall, bald, and scarred. "Leroy was a soldier for years and nearly got blown up. When he came to the family, he wanted to die."

Leroy nodded, not much expression in his dark eyes. "That's true. The family saved me."

Isaac smiled as if in approval. "Do you men need me?"

"No," Leroy said. "Just wanted to report in that we've scouted the entire acreage, and the fences are going up nicely. We should be better protected soon."

"Good. Let's meet in a couple of hours," Isaac said. "Before you go, Malcolm, please meet Eagle and George. These men help me protect the family."

Mal nodded as the other two did the same. Eagle and George? Who came up with the names around here? Something told him that Leroy and George had gotten to keep their original names. What kind of pain and baggage had come with them? Why didn't Leroy or George get new names and fresh beginnings? It seemed Isaac knew exactly how to push buttons with each member.

The men left.

Mal rubbed his eyes.

"You look tired. Would you like to stay the night tonight?" Isaac asked. "I know April would enjoy your company."

Mal kept his expression bland. "I would, but I have a teleconference with my old boss in the NYPD tomorrow about wrapping up my last case. If I missed it, he'd be on my doorstep in minutes." Yeah. No way would Isaac want that happening.

"Our duty always comes first." Isaac leaned forward. "After that discussion, are you finished with your case?"

"Yes. Everyone has pled out, and they just need my final

statement." Mal sighed, as if relieved. Which he kind of was. "Then I'm out. No more going undercover and pretending to be somebody I'm not. It's been so long, I'm not even sure who I really am."

"This could be a place for you to figure that out." The guy really did have a soothing voice.

Mal looked around. "I don't know. I'm not much for gardening and meditating all day."

"Meditation is important, but gardening, not so much." Isaac shared a smile. "I think with your background, you'd be vital in other areas."

Mal finished his drink. "Like what?"

"All in good time." Isaac stood, grasped the bottle, and returned to refill Mal's glass.

"Does my involvement come with April?" Mal let his voice slur just a little, as if his guard was coming down. It was easier than he thought. How drugged was he?

Isaac chuckled. "That's up to April. But she does seem to like you, and she can be very generous with her . . . time."

A timid knock barely sounded on the door.

"Enter," Isaac murmured.

A woman walked in, and it took a second for Malcolm to place her. He recognized Pippa's mother from those early photographs. Blond hair and the same blue eyes. His heart rate tried to speed up, but the drugs kept him nice and calm.

"I'm so sorry for interrupting." The woman had to be around forty-five. Beautiful and fragile-looking. Was she ill? "Mrs. Thomson is talking about returning to her husband, and I thought perhaps you'd like some time with her."

Isaac sadly shook his head. "Her husband beat them both so badly. Please keep her occupied for a little while. I shall speak with her when we're finished here."

The woman bowed out.

"She's pretty," Mal said, tilting his head. "Very."

"Angel is also available and very skilled in relaxing a man after a hard day's work," Isaac murmured. "In fact, I think she and April enjoy each other's company as well. Would you like me to ask them to have dessert with you later?"

The idea of sleeping with Pippa's mom nearly made him shudder. "No, but thank you. She seemed unwell to me."

"Sometimes God punishes us," Isaac said easily. "She will heal. I'm sure of it."

So Pippa's mom was sick? Did he have a duty to tell her that somehow? Or did she already know? He wiped a hand across his eyes.

"Headache?" Isaac asked.

"Yes." Mal's temples were starting to thrum as he came down from whatever they'd given him. At least it wasn't long-lasting.

Isaac moved forward on his chair. "Close your eyes. I can help."

This was weird. "All right." Mal closed his eyes and forced his body to relax.

Isaac pressed his fingers to Mal's temples and then placed his thumbs against Mal's closed eyelids. "Some of us are special, Malcolm. I've been given gifts I can't understand, but I want to help."

Lights flashed across Mal's closed eyes, and a sense of calm washed through him. Jesus. What the hell was that?

Isaac released him and sat back.

Mal opened his eyes. He blinked. "I feel better." What kind of experience had he just had?

Isaac smiled. "Of course. Now, before April takes you back to that apartment that's not worthy of you, would you please do me a couple of favors?"

Mal figured they'd tossed his fake apartment. No doubt

Angus had made sure everything inside stood up to scrutiny. "Yes." How could he say no after what had just happened?

Isaac laid out a list of things that needed to be accomplished, including a walk around several acres to check the perimeter. Only Mal could keep people safe. Yes, it would take many hours, but wasn't the safety of women and children of utmost importance?

Mal nodded. It was far easier for the cult to keep him from sleeping than he'd thought.

He was back undercover again. The thought sliced like a blade to the chest.

Chapter Twenty-Four

Pippa heard Mal's truck pull up around two in the morning, even through the wild storm going on. She'd been tossing and turning all night, trying to avoid nightmares. Sliding out of bed, she moved to the window to see him jump out of a truck. It wasn't his or Angus's truck. This one was a deep blue, almost black. She couldn't see the driver.

Mal looked at her house and then started up his own walkway.

She ran to unlock the doors and jump out on the porch. Rain and wind pummeled her, blowing her hair in every direction. "Malcolm?" she called.

He hesitated and then partially turned. She held her breath until he switched directions and walked toward her, stepping easily over the shrubs and then gracefully moving up her sidewalk through the rain. "Why are you up so late?" Water ran down the hard angles of his face.

"Couldn't sleep." Tension surrounded them, and not just from the storm.

Lightning flashed, and he frowned. "Does it ever stop raining here?"

She stepped back in the doorway. "Yes. This is a normal spring, though." What was wrong with him? His shoulders

were one tense line, and this close, she could see the vein
ticking in his neck. "Rough day?" she asked.

His scoff was more of a growl. "You could say that." He
scrubbed a rough hand through his already wet hair. The rain
molded his thin cotton shirt to cut muscles.

Energy seemed to ricochet off him. Dark and deep . . .
angry even. "Where's your jacket?" she asked, looking for
anything to say. Anything to gauge his mood.

He frowned and looked down the now silent road. "Left
it in the truck."

Her knees weakened just a little. Her hands trembled, and
every ounce of her wanted to take another step back. "Um,
do you want to tell me about your day?" Her lungs felt odd.

"No." That green gaze slashed back to hers, looking down
from an intimidating height. This was a part of him she
hadn't seen before. "I'm tired of being lied to. Tired of being
manipulated. Tired of being undercover."

Yeah, she'd figured he was undercover again. Hopefully,
he was talking about his job and not her right now. When
she'd been scared, he'd helped. "Would you like to come in
and cuddle?" Gathering her strength, she reached for his wet
shoulder, curling her fingers over the taut muscle. "I could
rub your shoulders."

"My shoulders aren't what I want you to rub." His voice
thickened.

She blinked. The crudeness caught her off guard, and yet
her body softened. Everywhere. "Come in, Malcolm."

"No." He shrugged off her hand. "Sorry. I shouldn't have
said that." The scent of whiskey drifted on the wind around
him. "This isn't good, Pippa. I'm not in a safe place right
now. For you."

What did that mean? She didn't know much, but she
knew he wouldn't hurt her. "It's okay."

His hands slid into his wet jean pockets, as if to keep

from touching her. "No, it really isn't. Not tonight. I can't be gentle like before. Let's talk tomorrow."

"That was you gentle?" she blurted out, more than a little intrigued.

His chuckle held a warning. "Yeah, baby. That was me gentle."

Heat bloomed in her abdomen, tugging low. She needed to talk to him, but not when he was in this mood. There was something so tortured about him, she wanted to help. To somehow soothe this beast of anger. "Then come inside and don't be gentle." She faced him, being as brave as she knew how to be.

"You don't know what you're saying." The dim light from inside played over his hard features, and his dark gaze trapped hers like a magnet. "Trust me on this. Go inside and go to bed."

"No." Her chin lifted. "I'm not afraid of you."

He moved closer to her, and enough heat poured off him that steam rose between them. "You're smarter than that. Get your ass back to bed."

A thrill zapped down her torso, flashing a surge of adrenaline through her veins. This was a challenge, a game she didn't know how to play. But if he thought the rough order would make her back down, he'd miscalculated. "Why?" she whispered, sliding toward him. She couldn't stop. Curiosity and an edgy need propelled her.

He looked down at her small bare feet against his thick boots. Tension ticked between them, harsh and full. "Last chance, Pippa. Go back to bed."

Even though the storm bellowed around them, she suddenly felt like she'd jumped into the path of a tornado. Might as well poke the tiger literally. She pressed her finger into his chest. "Make me."

His head snapped back up, a raw hunger in every line. "Okay." Faster than a gasp, he ducked a shoulder into her stomach and lifted her right off her feet. Her stomach hit his hard muscles, and the air blew out of her lungs. Shock kept her silent for a minute.

Her hair hung down, and suddenly, they were back in her house. She started to struggle.

"Stop it." She fisted her hand and nailed him in the right kidney.

His muffled oath was the only prelude to his hand descending on her butt. Hard. She yelped as pain radiated from his hand. Oh, it hurt. But it felt good, too. Warm and tingly. What the hell? She started twisting again, and he flipped her over, planting her on the kitchen counter.

Her breath panted out.

"I need to know." His voice went beyond rough to raw, the sound hoarse. "Do you have triggers?"

She blinked. "Triggers?" Like on a gun?

He snarled, his face moving closer. "Yes. Don't mess with me right now, Pippa. I heard the nightmare. Have you been abused? Touched? Do I need to back away right now? Tell me the truth. I will."

Oh. Her heart swelled right then, despite the rioting flash flood ripping through her body. "Abused? Probably, definitely emotionally. Psychologically. All of that." She'd worked through much of it with her counselors.

The sound he made was animalistic. "If they're not dead yet, they will be." His body was one rigid line of deadliness. Of promise. Of danger.

She gulped. "There was no touching as a kid. Nothing physical. No triggers. I'm okay." For the first time in way too long, she meant the words. Her body and mind concentrated only on him with a razor-sharp focus that made breathing nearly impossible.

The intense color of his eyes trapped hers, and his face came even closer. Within inches. "If I held you down, you'd be all right?"

A shocking thrill jolted through her. The mere idea sharpened her nipples into points so hard they hurt. "Yes." Her voice was hoarse this time. "Though you might not be."

His chin lifted at the challenge. "You ever been spanked?"

The spit in her mouth dried up. "No," she whispered, her skin becoming sensitized.

"You challenge me again, you will be."

It was a clear threat, and it made her wet. Wetter. She should be embarrassed or even concerned. But she wanted this. She wanted him, completely unleashed. The wildness she'd sensed in him, the primitive side that had drawn her from that first day . . . that she craved. She arched out and cupped his steel-hard erection. "I think you're full of shit, Malcolm."

He reared back, his shoulders seeming to broaden. "What did you say?" The words were mangled.

What was she doing? She couldn't seem to stop herself. He was trying so hard to stay in control. To treat her as something fragile he couldn't be himself with. This darkness? She wanted it. If it was part of him, she needed it. "All of this talk. You're the one who's scared." Her mouth just wouldn't quit.

Thunder bellowed outside, and the rain beat mercilessly against the windows.

He didn't move, but seemed to vibrate in place. It was as if the entire world held its breath. When he did finally move, it was with a deliberate control that caught her by surprise. One second she was facing him, the next he'd manacled her and flipped her around, facedown on the kitchen table. "I'd hate to be full of shit," he muttered, yanking her yoga pants down her legs.

She sucked in a harsh breath. Her feet dangled in the air. She'd dared him to do this. "Mal—"

The first smack on her bare ass stopped the words in her throat. She tried to lever herself up, and he planted one hand across her entire lower back, holding her in place. Then he brought his huge palm down on her ass a second time. The sound was a sharp crack, the sting a quick burn. Tears instantly filled her eyes. "I didn't mean—"

"Oh, you did mean." Four hard smacks punctuated his words.

More tears filled her eyes because he really wasn't holding back. He'd given her the out, and she'd challenged him. She could stop him. If she asked, he'd stop. But the raw, hot, pulsing ache between her legs kept her silent.

Pain and pleasure. She'd never explored this. He flipped on the light by the door, and she closed her eyes in protest.

"Now, that's better." The sound he made was full of hunger as he ran his palm over her heated butt. "So pretty and bright pink." He spanked her again.

She arched up, heat sliding from her butt to her clit. She whimpered.

He leaned down then, his broad hand pinning her to the table, his breath hot at her ear. "Here's the question, baby. You pushed me, you haven't really protested, your body is a nice little pink. Did you like your first spanking?" Dark and rough, his voice shivered over her.

She pressed her lips together. Even so, she couldn't give him everything. "No?"

His chuckle made her shiver. "You don't want to lie to me." He caressed down the small of her back, over her burning butt and between her legs. His fingers brushed her bare flesh, and a gasp escaped her from the electric shock. "And yet you did." He slid a finger through her slick folds and up across her engorged clit.

A low moan escaped her, and a tremble shook her entire body. Pleasure pierced her with a shocking intensity.

"Liars get punished." He palmed her sex while his other hand spanked her. Hard.

She cried out, thrown into an orgasm so sudden, she

didn't have time to tense her body. It bore down on her and she ground against him with a desperation that had her panting in time with the waves.

With a sob, she relaxed against the cool wood of the table, her heart thundering way too fast to be healthy.

"Do. Not. Move." He squeezed her butt, and the pain shot through her, blending into pleasure that shoved her closer to the brink again. The rasp of his belt unbuckling was thunderous in the quiet kitchen.

She stiffened.

He chuckled, the sound so dark it made her tremble more. Like a sapling caught in a tornado. His jeans zipper released. The feel of leather rubbing across her punished butt made her jolt and suck in a breath. "I told you not to move."

Her eyelids flashed open, and she shook, her body rioting.

He placed the belt by her head. "You haven't been that bad, baby." Amusement filtered from him. He leaned down again, sucking her earlobe into his mouth. Wet and hot and oh-so-firm. He released her with a soft plop. "Are you okay?"

The fact that he asked nearly made her cry. She blinked away tears and turned her head to see his shadowed face. "Yes. That all you got?" Her voice trembled, but she'd made her point.

"No. I've got a bit more. You haven't submitted completely yet." He rose up, and a condom wrapper crinkled. Then he pressed himself at her entrance and his hands lifted her hips straight up and off the table.

She took a deep breath to prepare like last time.

He shoved inside her with one incredibly strong stroke, all the way to the hilt. She tossed her head back, arching against the painful invasion. Deep and hard, he filled all of her. With his angle and control of her lower body, she couldn't move. She was helpless in his grip, his rough thighs against the back of hers.

The idea nearly threw her into an orgasm. She softened to the table, losing her tenseness.

"There you go," he murmured, his fingers tightening on her skin. "Next time I spank you, you'll submit instantly."

Next time? She wasn't sure she'd survive this time.

He didn't give her time to regroup. His thrusts were hard and powerful, moving her across the table before he yanked her back against him. The pain mixed with a sharp pleasure, keeping her on an edge that blurred the entire room.

The sound of his harsh breathing and the slap of flesh on flesh overwhelmed the thunder outside. He kept going, keeping her so close to falling over the edge, his stamina stronger than any animal's.

Without warning, he reached down and tapped her clit.

She exploded, crying out his name, her body shuddering uncontrollably. Stars flashed across her eyes, and her body fired in every direction. The orgasm was so powerful, she shut her eyes and let it take her over.

He planted himself hard inside her and stopped moving, his body jerking as he found his own release.

For several heartbeats, they remained in place. Then he withdrew and gently turned her around, lifting her against his chest. He leaned down and kissed her, his lips gentle. "Let's finish this in bed."

Chapter Twenty-Five

Mal's phone yanked him from the first peaceful sleep he'd had in too long. "What?" he muttered into the speaker, not opening his eyes, his back flat on the mattress.

"It's Angus. We caught something on the bug you planted in Isaac Leon's office. We waited to call, but we're ten minutes out now."

Mal forced his gritty eyes open. He'd been drugged before drinking way too much, and then he'd had the best sex of his life. He glanced at the clock on the phone. It was only four in the morning. "I can't sustain only getting one hour of sleep." Shit. Less than an hour. He and Pippa had gone at it for several rounds.

"Sorry. We need you. Get mentally prepared—we're on Op." Angus clicked off.

Mal breathed out, trying to wake his body. Pippa slept quietly, curled into him like a little kitten with her knees in his ribs and her head on his chest.

A surge of possessiveness grabbed him by the throat. A deep, dangerous, hungry possessiveness that was too feral to tame. They had crossed the line tonight—all sorts of lines.

She was his, whether either one of them was ready for that or not.

He gently extricated himself from her and slid from the bed, turning to make sure she was covered.

She murmured and then curled back onto her side. "Malcolm?" Her sleepy voice was sultry and sexy.

"It's okay. I have to go to work." Where were his jeans? He looked around at the dark floor but couldn't see anything. Wait a minute. He'd left all their clothing in the kitchen during round one—along with his gun. "Go back to sleep."

She rubbed her eyes. "I wanted to talk to you. We need to talk."

Yeah, they probably did. It was time to level with each other and figure out where to go from there. He leaned over and kissed her. "We'll talk when I get back. Enough with the secrets, Pippa. We go on together from here." Then to make sure she got him, he nipped her bottom lip. "For now, get some sleep."

She kissed him. "If you're hungry, there are some biscuits left from when Angus visited earlier. Take those." She snuggled back down with a soft sigh.

"Angus Force was here?" he asked, his entire body going cold and then hot. Way too hot.

She murmured something, already falling back to sleep.

What the holy hell? He found his jeans and shirt in the other room and had just finished buckling his belt when Wolfe's truck pulled up outside.

Tucking in his gun, he hustled out the door, making sure it was locked behind him. Then he strode toward the truck and yanked open the passenger side door. He jumped in, his hand fisting in Force's shirt. "What the fuck were you doing here earlier?"

Wolfe looked over from the driver's seat, his dark gaze observing. But he didn't make a move.

Raider cleared his throat from the backseat. "How about we talk about this as we drive? We don't have much time."

Force didn't try to dislodge Mal's hold. "I stopped by and had a nice chat with Pippa. Somebody who isn't screwing her needed to at least get a small read. A profile, if you will. She makes excellent biscuits and a nice lavender tea."

Asshole. Mal shoved him and then slammed the door before jumping into the backseat with Raider. His leather jacket was right where he'd left it, and he shrugged into it. "Leave her alone."

Wolfe backed the truck out and opened the throttle toward town.

Force sighed. "She's sweet, and I see why you like her. We didn't get a chance to talk world domination or mass killings, but I can tell you she had a messed-up childhood."

"No shit," Mal murmured, his gaze out the window at the darkness. "That's all you got?"

"No. She's head over heels for you, and she doesn't seem to be fighting it any. Makes me think maybe she's looking for a future, which would mean no suicide bomb. But again, I didn't have much time with her," Force said.

"I've had plenty. She's not involved with the cult," Mal said, his eyes aching with the need to sleep.

"Okay," Force said quietly. "But for the record, she did have me look at her car. Said it wasn't working."

Mal stiffened. "Where was she trying to go?"

"Didn't say."

Maybe she'd just wanted to visit her friend. It wasn't like she'd tried to get away the night before, and they hadn't had a chance to talk, so there was no reason she would've told him about her nonworking car. He should probably fix it. "She's not trying to run."

"Agreed," Force said.

Raider sighed. "Sorry to call you in. I was listening to the bug, and Isaac sent two of his guys to rob a pharmacy in Minuteville. The plan was decent, actually. It sounded like they've been working on it for at least a month. I have Brigid running searches all over the country for similar robberies."

"Drugs and money," Mal said. "Makes sense. What's the plan?"

"They're gonna get caught," Force said, settling back in his seat. "Loudly."

Raider grinned. "We have the local PD on stakeout, and I'm fairly certain they've already tipped off the media. If they haven't, I will as soon as we take them down."

"Whose arrest will it be?" Mal asked, putting the pieces together.

"Local cops, but then, because it's a drug issue, the federal government will step in. Those two will be in our custody within the hour, if all goes well." Angus turned and nodded at Raider. "You and I will represent the HDD. I'd like to keep Wolfe and West under wraps for now."

"Agreed," Raider said.

Angus partially turned around. "West and Wolfe, I want you guys on the perimeter, just in case one of the cult assholes gets loose. We have to take them down tonight. It's imperative."

"What's the urgency?" Raider asked.

Force shook his head. "Not sure. Orchid says they're gearing up for something in days—something big. She's not on the inside of whatever it is."

Mal rubbed his jaw, and scruff scratched his hand. He probably needed to shave at some point. "When tonight goes wrong, Isaac is going to look for a problem. He'll see one where you think you're covered. How good is Orchid?"

"Not great. We've arranged to meet up when she's out either peddling wares or recruiting members, and she's had to get away from the group several times. I don't think she's under suspicion, but who knows?" Angus flipped off the heat switch. "You have more undercover experience, and you've infiltrated the cult now. What's your recommendation?"

Mal ran his hands down his jeans. They'd dried overnight and felt rough. "Let me think about it. My gut feeling is that we need to pull her out. Soon."

Wolfe parked the truck outside a twenty-four-hour grocery store. The lights glimmered out into the parking lot, but nobody was shopping at this odd time. "The pharmacy is in a stand-alone building three blocks to the south."

Force handed back a tablet with the schematics of the neighborhood. He pointed to observation points. "West here, Raider, there."

West jumped out of the car. At least it had stopped raining. "Where are we taking them once we have them?"

"There are two interrogation rooms back at headquarters," Angus said as he slammed his door.

West paused. "Where?"

"Right off the elevator. Small door? Everyone thinks it's a closet." Angus checked his gun.

A siren split the night.

"Shit. Go," Force snapped, launching himself into a run.

Malcolm breathed in the fresh air and fell into step, staying in the shadows. They reached the scene quickly. Two uniformed police officers, one nearly hunched over with age, escorted two handcuffed guys away from a cheerful-looking pink building.

Force nodded at Raider. "Let's do this."

Mal paused and then kept to the side as Wolfe did the same. A newsman screeched to a stop in the lot. "Back," he whispered.

Silent as death, Wolfe retreated farther into the shadows. "This came together well."

Too well? Mal angled his neck to see Eagle and Leroy, two of Isaac's lieutenants. Apparently, George had gotten to stay home for the night.

"He might just shoot you the second you arrive," Wolfe said conversationally.

Mal watched as Force flashed his badge and started the dance with the local cops. Raider instantly moved to intercept the news camera, no doubt already pouring on the charm.

"I like it here. In the dark," Wolfe said.

Mal kept alert just in case. "Yeah, me too."

"I hope the cult people don't shoot you," Wolfe said. "If they do, don't worry. I'll hunt down each and every one of them and tear their heads off. Literally."

Mal cut his eyes to the soldier, who was barely visible near an old sycamore tree. "I'd appreciate that, Wolfe." Was the guy nuts or just dedicated? Or both? But he did have a point. Isaac Leon wasn't stupid. Mal was an ex-cop who'd shown up suddenly, and now two of the main family guys, men who'd been robbing and burglarizing across the country for years, get caught? "I'll need to retrieve that bug before Isaac starts looking."

"He might not know his guys were caught by the time you show up at the mansion. What's the plan?" Wolfe whispered.

"April is picking me up at the fake apartment around seven." Which left several hours for him to figure out how *not* to get his head blown off.

Wolfe straightened. "Here we go."

Mal watched as the local cops handed over the two prisoners, obviously with great irritation. A van pulled up, seemingly out of nowhere, and Force took the two guys toward it. "The van is a nice touch. You ever get the feeling Force has everything already planned? Every minute detail for the team?" Mal asked.

Wolfe shrugged. "Better him than anybody else, if you ask me. He just wants to catch the bad guys."

"At what cost?" Mal murmured quietly.

Wolfe took out and started unwrapping a piece of gum. "Any cost. You know?"

Mal exhaled slowly. Yeah, he did know. But for the first time in his entire life, he had something to lose. And Pippa was right smack-dab in the middle of this mess.

Chapter Twenty-Six

Pippa had just finished baking cookies when her phone rang. She moved to it, wincing at the tenderness in her rear end. Then she chuckled, feeling oddly light. Malcolm West as a wild man when unleashed. She clicked the button. "Hello?"

"Ms. Smith? This is Liliana at Wrenches Mechanics and More? You said to call if I had an opening to look at your car, and because my dumbass dickhead of a bastard boyfriend dumped me last night, it turns out my morning is free." The voice was strong, female, and sounded young. "You said you're about an hour out of Minuteville, and I can leave in just a few minutes. I've finished burning the clothes he left at my place."

Pippa sucked in air and tried to follow the conversation. "Um, okay." Wow. That was a lot.

"I need an address, lady," Liliana said easily.

Pippa shook herself into awareness. Giving her address went against everything she had inside her, but there wasn't a choice. She gave it, trying to sound sure, not tentative.

"Got it. I'll be there in an hour and will probably stop for a latte on the way. You want anything?" Liliana asked.

Pippa bit her lip. "No, but thanks." A latte would be cold by the time the woman arrived.

"Yep." Liliana hung up. Probably to go burn pictures or something.

Okay. The woman was a mechanic listed in the white pages on the internet with a good website. There were tons of reviews, and some of them went back five years. This wasn't some weird trap. If anybody from the family had found Pippa, they wouldn't have wasted time sabotaging her car. They would've taken her quickly.

She cleared her throat. If she was going to have any sort of life with Malcolm, she had to stop being so paranoid. Pressing Speed Dial, she tried to reach Trixie.

The phone rang, and the automated voice came on saying to leave a message. Pippa frowned and left a quick one. It wasn't like Trixie not to answer her phone, but maybe she'd ended up with a morning shift at the restaurant.

Pippa stretched her neck and set the phone down. Her body was all sorts of tingly. She glanced at the kitchen table, and heat splashed into her face.

The things he'd done to her. She'd challenged him to do each one. Her heart felt lighter somehow. Was this what love felt like for normal people? Was she in love with him? It had been such a short time they'd known each other.

Did that really matter?

More importantly, what did she want to do about it? She was tired of hiding and being scared. When he got home, she'd ply him with cookies until he hit a sugar high, and then she was going to tell him everything. Especially the bad parts that might put her in jail.

She'd already finished her work for the day. The construction company was expanding and wanted her to file paperwork on S Corp status. It was surprisingly easy. So, maybe she'd bake more cookies. Mal could always take some to work.

She baked happily for about an hour until a vehicle drove up outside. Curious, she moved to the window to peer out, seeing a gray van with the Wrenches Mechanics and More logo on the side. A woman about six feet tall jumped out, her hair curly and black, her bounce definitely energetic. Even wearing overalls and a slim tool belt, she looked like a runway model. All curvy and sleek. Within seconds, she was knocking on the door.

Pippa wiped her hands down her apron and opened it, her heartbeat ramping up. She was about to let a complete stranger into her home.

"Hi. You must be Pippa. I'm Liliana," the woman said, her brown eyes sparkling against her darker skin. "Where's the car?"

"In the garage." Feeling a bit subdued compared to so much energy, Pippa walked Liliana to the garage door and opened it. "I'm sorry about your boyfriend." Was that lame to say?

"I know, right?" Liliana shook her head. "What a dick. We've been dating for almost six months, and he's like, 'I'm not sure I'm ready for this.'" Her voice had lowered into a hick-sounding tone. "Duh." She moved forward and popped the hood. "Let's see what's going on here. In case I require it, is the owner's manual in the glove box?"

"Yes." Pippa stood there, uncertain. "If you don't need me, I have cookies in the oven. Just come on in."

"No prob." Liliana leaned over and started studying the engine, continuing to mimic the ex-boyfriend. "'I like you and all . . .'"

Pippa bit back a chuckle and walked up the sidewalk and inside, pausing after shutting the door. For the first time in five years, she didn't lock it. Liliana would need to come inside. It was time to start living a somewhat normal life. She'd need to with Mal.

Liliana knocked about fifteen minutes later, and Pippa called out for her to come in. Just like a sane person.

She finished setting some of the cookies on a plate and brought them into the living room, where Liliana was waiting by the front door. "Would you like to sit?"

Liliana's dark brows crinkled. "Um, okay." She moved to the chair by the fireplace, her tools clanking together. "Most people don't offer me cookies." But when Pippa set the plate down, she took one, her eyelids fluttering as she ate. "These are fantastic."

"Thanks." Pippa felt like a dork, but she sat. "So. How bad is the car?" She had some savings, but not nearly enough for another car.

Liliana finished chewing, her gaze seeking. "Well, not great. How's *your* boyfriend situation?"

A warning ticked through Pippa. "Um, good. Why?"

Liliana took a deep breath. "I couldn't see anything wrong under the hood, so I investigated a little more, checked out the owner's manual, and found the ignition fuse under the dash. Or rather, where the fuse should be."

Pippa clasped her hands together, relief overtaking her. "Oh. Good. It's just a burned-out fuse." Those had to be easy to find, right?

"No." Liliana shook her head. "There was no fuse. It was gone. Completely."

Pippa straightened. That didn't make sense. "Did it just fall out? Did you find it?"

Liliana's frown deepened, and she leaned forward, putting her hand on Pippa's knee. "You're not getting this. Somebody took the ignition fuse out of your car. On purpose. So it wouldn't run."

Pippa shook her head, panic coating her throat. "No. That's not possible."

"Okay. Deep breaths, Sister." Liliana leaned back. "Who has had access to your car?"

"Just me. And my, um, boyfriend." Pippa's throat hurt like she'd swallowed glass.

Liliana pressed her lips together. "Men are assholes. Why in the hell would he take your fuse? It's not like you can't call an Uber or taxi, even way out here."

Pippa tried to make sense of these facts. "Mal's friend was here yesterday, and he said he knew about cars. He looked at mine. Should he have discovered the problem?"

Liliana slowly nodded. "Yeah. If he was really looking, he would've found it. I did." She shook her head. "Dicks always stick together. If your jerk boyfriend lied, so did his buddy."

"Well, ah—" Pippa couldn't breathe. She stood, and the room tilted crazily around her. How did this make sense? Wait a minute. Why would Mal do such a thing? If not him, then who? There hadn't been anybody else around. What if the family had found her and just wanted her to stay in place? So they'd messed with her car.

That was crazy.

The family wouldn't have just taken a fuse. They would've taken her. She swallowed several times, really wanting to throw up. "Can you fix it?"

Liliana stood, her dark eyes concerned. "Let me go check in my van. I'm sure there are fuses in there somewhere that'll work. We'll get you taken care of." She swiped another cookie. "Are you in danger? I mean, do you want me to call the cops?"

"No," Pippa burst out. Then she calmed herself. "No, but thank you. My boyfriend, or rather ex-boyfriend, is just a little possessive. But this is the last straw."

"You go, girl." Liliana waved the cookie. "None of them are a damn bit good, I'm tellin' ya. A girl is better off with a cat for daytime companionship and a good vibrator for the night. Neither one will break your heart." She headed for the door, munching away. "I'll be back in a few."

"Thank you." Pippa forced herself to walk normally to the bedroom. She'd already partially packed, so she drew those suitcases out of the closet before heading to the office. Her records fit easily in a large bag, and her laptop packed up nicely. She'd have to leave the printer because it was so big.

A quick glance showed that nobody would know she'd moved on if they didn't open any drawers. Good.

Survival mode came back surprisingly easy.

"Pippa?" Liliana called from the other room.

"Coming." Pippa took her purse and walked into the other room, her head hurting almost as bad as her chest. "Did you fix it?"

"Yep. No problem." Liliana rocked back on her boots. "I'm really sorry, by the way. It sucks."

Pippa forced a smile. The serene one she'd learned to wear so long ago to survive. "It really does suck. How much do I owe you?"

Liliana waved a hand. "Nothing. It wasn't a big deal, and us gals have to stick together."

The kindness pricked tears into Pippa's eyes. "No. You had to drive quite a way, and you worked hard. Please let me pay you."

Liliana eyed the still-full plate of cookies. "Put those in a bag for me? We'll call it even."

Her throat clogging, Pippa moved into the kitchen for a bag. The table caught her eye, and she stilled, staring at it. Oh God. Anger finally punched through the fuzzy fog of shock. That total dick. Grasping a bag, she returned to the living room and packed the cookies for Liliana. "Thank you for everything," she whispered.

Liliana patted her awkwardly on the shoulder. "It's okay. He wasn't worth it, right?"

"Right." Pippa's chin lifted. "You're exactly right."

Liliana took her cookies and left.

Pippa stared at the closed door. The barrier that had protected her from the world until he'd moved in next door. Malcolm was an undercover cop currently working on an undercover operation. He'd sabotaged her car and wanted her to stay right where she was. Was he part of the family? If so, how did that make sense? Why not bring her in right away?

If not, then what was his case? If it was the family, then was he working her to get to them?

She didn't have any answers other than it had to have been Malcolm who'd messed with her car. Everything in her wanted to wait for him to get home and confront him. Maybe kick him in the balls. But what if he somehow had a good explanation?

Yeah, that was her ovaries talking.

She was so tired of being prey. So fracking tired. Turning, she grabbed keys out of her junk drawer and hustled through the back of the house and over to Mal's sliding back door. It was locked. Biting her lip, she used the key Mrs. Maloni had given her so long ago. Mal hadn't had time to change the locks, probably.

Nope. The door slid right open.

Feeling slightly victorious, she stepped inside and went through kitchen drawers, finding two hidden knives and another gun. The weapon was heavy in her hand, and she quickly returned it to its hiding place.

The living room was next. Nothing interesting.

His scent was all around her. Warm and wild. She moved into the bedroom and found another gun, as well as a manila file folder in the dresser by his bed.

Holding her breath, she slowly opened it to see pictures of herself as a kid.

When she'd lived with the family.

Betrayal snapped something inside her with an almost audible crunch.

Oh God. It was time to grab her hidden bag. She had to run. Now.

Chapter Twenty-Seven

"This thing probably has a weight limit," Raider observed, shifting his body as the elevator descended to their offices.

Malcolm winced. "You had to say that." The interior was way too jam-packed with the six of them. The two prisoners were cuffed and hooded, so they had no clue who was in the elevator with them. They were also oddly silent. Finally, they reached the basement and the doors opened. Raider escaped before Mal, but it was close.

When he'd gotten clear, he turned.

Force had Eagle by the arm while Wolfe had Leroy. "We'll be right back." Force pushed the guy he was holding toward the small doorway, which he opened with a key from his pocket. It swung inward.

Mal moved to his desk and yanked out his folding chair to sit. It was already around noon. The booking and then wrangling of the two burglars had taken a surprising amount of time. He wanted to call Pippa. Check on her, make sure she was all right.

Raider looked around. "Which desk should I take?"

Mal shrugged. "Whatever you want."

Brigid Banaghan strode out of the computer room with a

stack of paper in her hands. She'd ditched the prison jumpsuit for jeans and a sweatshirt. Her hair was in a ponytail, and her eyes were clear in the morning hour. "Angus sent me the prints on your two guys. I did a deep dive, and this is what I found." She handed the papers over to Raider and then waited, her feet shuffling.

Malcolm smiled and gestured toward the nearest desk. "Might as well claim your spot."

"I did." She tilted her head toward the computer room. "That place is all mine."

Raider flipped over a page. "So long as you follow the rules, you can stay. The second you don't . . ."

She glared at him. "You are such an uptight jackass."

Amusement took Mal, and he cleared his throat. "What did you find?"

Raider answered before Brigid could. "Both have priors, and their prints have been found at crime scenes, mainly burglaries, across the country. There was also an assault scene in Seattle and another in Dallas for the guy now called Eagle."

Raider tossed the papers to Mal, who quickly read up.

Force and Wolfe crossed into the room.

"Malcolm, I'd like to have a go at Eagle first. You interrogate and I'll observe," Force said. "I want to see his reaction to you. To finding out you're a cop."

Mal nodded. It'd be nice to know if Isaac was suspicious of him.

Wolfe whistled and headed to the computer room. "Where's Kat?"

"He's snuggling with Roscoe on a pillow I brought in. Under the desk over to the right," Brigid said. "He snores."

"Does not," Wolfe returned, disappearing into the computer room.

Mal stood and rolled back his shoulders, mentally preparing. It had been a long time since he'd interrogated somebody in an interview room. "Let's go." He kept the research with him and followed Angus through the small doorway.

A narrow hallway led to a cell at the far end. Two thick doors, the old wood kind, were set into the wall at even intervals. "Interesting," Mal said.

Force shrugged. "We have what we have." He pushed open the first door and Mal followed him inside.

A dinged-up table sat in the middle of a room with cement walls and floors. One can light had been set into the ceiling, directly above the table. Eagle sat across it, cuffed to a ring drilled into the table. His eyes widened when Malcolm walked in.

"Answers that," Force muttered, moving to lean against the far wall.

Yeah. Definite surprise. Mal slid out one of the two folding chairs to sit. "Hi, Eagle." He smiled. "Or should I say, Jackie Morose?"

"Eagle. That's my name." Eagle was in his early thirties with brown hair and eyes. His build was bulky with muscle, and he was a little twitchy. "God will punish you for this." He smiled, his teeth yellowed. "The Prophet will get you. He sees all."

Uh-huh. "Did he see you'd get caught tonight?" Mal asked.

"The Prophet has a plan," Eagle said, sniffing. "We don't have all the facts." His eyes were bloodshot, and he couldn't seem to sit still.

"What are you on, Eagle?" Malcolm asked.

"Nothing. Just life, man." Eagle looked around. "Where am I, anyway? This isn't a jail."

Mal flipped open the file folder. "No. You're at a dark ops site."

"I want a lawyer," Eagle said, his square chin jutting out.

"Too fucking bad," Mal said mildly. "You don't get one."

Eagle sputtered. "I have rights, man."

"No. You really don't," Force said with slight boredom in his voice, drawing attention away from Mal for a moment.

Eagle sat back, and his shoulders tensed. "You assholes are so stupid. You have no idea what you're doing. What is happening. What needs to happen." Spittle flew from his mouth. He shook his head almost in slow motion. "Fire and wrath are coming . . . soon. Real soon. You're gonna find out. Oh yeah, you are."

"When?" Mal asked.

Eagle shrugged.

Force snorted. "You're full of shit. Nothing is going to happen."

Eagle's eyes flashed. "The hail of hellfire is going to descend on nonbelievers. On holy day, the one we've waited so long for, sinners will burn." Absolute conviction colored his tone.

"What holy day?" Mal asked.

Eagle flexed his forearms. "This place looks secure. But not so much, huh?" In a shockingly quick movement, he jerked away from the table and pulled the ring right out of it. He bunched his legs and flew toward Mal, fists already punching.

Instinct took over. Mal came partially up, took the hit, grabbed Eagle by the shoulders, and pivoted, putting him down. The angle was wrong for full control, so Eagle's head hit the concrete before his body. He went limp.

Mal flipped him over and felt his pulse. Strong and steady. He stepped up, his fists clenched and adrenaline cutting a swath through his body. He needed to hit something. Now.

Force strode forward, looking down at the unconscious man. "Guess the table wasn't sturdy enough for the ring."

Mal slowly turned his head. Amusement shocked him, and he snorted. "Guess not."

Force opened the door. "You have to go. Sounds like you'd

better get into the inner circle sooner rather than later. Whatever this flash of fire is, it's happening soon."

Mal stepped into the hall. "We need to find out about the holy day. What, and more importantly, when."

Force locked the door, and they made it down the hallway into the elevator area.

Wolfe was waiting, slipping a Goldfish Cracker into his pocket. "Well?"

Force nodded. "Yeah. Take a harder line with the other guy. Do what you have to do."

Mal rolled his shoulders. "We have to have some rules." Even though they'd declared themselves a de facto dark site, at some point, they'd have to turn the prisoners over to the system. "Eagle wasn't wrong. The guy has rights."

"Not at the moment. I'll get him to talk. I promise." Wolfe pulled out Kat and handed him to Angus. The kitten was now a fluffy pure white with big blue eyes. Apparently, he'd had a bath. He meowed in protest. "Take my cat." Then Wolfe disappeared through the small doorway, ducking to keep from banging his head against the doorframe.

Mal looked at the cat and then Force, unease in his gut. "We can't just let him loose on somebody in our custody."

Force gingerly took the cat toward the bull pen. "Tell that to the people about to meet hellfire somewhere. Go to work, West. Get your head in the game."

Mal eyed the closed door. One thing at a time. "I'll report in."

"You want an earbud?" Force called back.

"No." There was a good chance they'd search him if they didn't just shoot him in the head on sight. "I'll be in touch when I can." He was already becoming somebody else when he stepped into the elevator.

Again.

* * *

Pippa was halfway to Trixie's when her phone buzzed. Her real phone. The burner was still in the pretty beach bag she'd bought somewhere in Florida last time she'd been on the move. She looked down, and her body jolted. Malcolm.

There was no reason not to answer him. She should be home working and staying under the radar. If she didn't answer, he'd wonder why.

"Hello," she said, trying to keep her voice light. Being out in the world gave her a stomachache, so it was more difficult than she'd hoped.

"Hi, beautiful," he said, his voice warm. "I wanted to check on you." A horn blared in the background. Oh no. Was he headed home for a late lunch or something?

She tried to give a small chuckle. "Good afternoon. I missed you." God, she was terrible at this. Her head started to hurt. "Are you headed my way? I'd be happy to make you an afternoon snack."

"No, I'm on the job."

Her fingers slowly loosened their painful hold on the steering wheel. Her lungs filled again. Good. "That's too bad. Maybe dinner tonight?"

"Maybe. It might be a really late night." He paused for a moment. "Where are you? I hear background noise."

"The television is on," she said lightly. He couldn't know she'd fixed the car and was on the move. That she'd found out what he'd done. "Nothing interesting."

"Oh." He was quiet for several beats. "Last night got a little intense. Are you sure you're fine?"

She bit her lip and tasted blood. "I enjoyed last night and you know it." When all else failed, stick with the truth. "Fun isn't quite the right word to use, but it's all I can think of." The lying, cheating, car-sabotaging bastard. Maybe she and Liliana the mechanic should form a club or something. Women who chose men badly. "Don't worry about me, Malcolm."

"I'll always worry about you, sweetheart." His voice had

that rich, dark tone that would've made her melt the day before. "We really do need a chance to talk."

"Right." She was so tempted to blurt out the truth, it hurt. But if he was undercover and investigating her, he'd have resources to find her. A lot of them. Oh, she'd call him when she was free, and she'd give him hell. But not now. Two could play at his little farce. Maybe she could even beat the big, bad, famous undercover cop at his own game. The righteous anger felt kind of comforting. "I would love to sit down and talk with you."

"It's a date." His voice lightened. "Hopefully tomorrow."

It did beg the question, though. If she was his case, or if her ties to the family were his case, where was he going? "Can you tell me anything about the case you're on?" she asked.

"No," he said flatly. "I'm on two cases right now, really. I can't talk about either one, though. Maybe someday."

Two cases. Did that mean two lovers? Was he working some other woman for information or whatever with that spectacular body of his? Anger roared through her, and it took a second to recognize the raw feeling of jealousy in there. Now, that was screwed up. Even though he couldn't see her, she let her eyelids flutter. "You're so brave, Malcolm." God. She almost gagged.

"No, I'm not. Just getting the job done so I can get home to you," he said quietly.

Good line. Definitely a good line. "It seems like you're awfully good at your job." Did bitterness creep in there? Damn it. "Just be careful. I'd hate to see anything happen to you."

"I know what I'm doing, Pippa. Don't worry."

Yeah. That's what she was afraid of. He'd really convinced her he cared about her. The guy probably had a wife somewhere. Maybe kids. The idea hurt deep in her chest. A part of her, one she didn't like at all, wanted to just confront him and get the truth. She wanted him to have feelings for her.

It was time to buck up. At the very least, he'd lied to her. He knew who she was and where she came from. Maybe she could mess with him a little. "It's nice to have you in my life. I miss having a family."

He didn't answer for a minute. Thinking that over, was he? "I'm sure you do. You've never told me much except that your folks have passed on. Tell me more about you."

That really wasn't a good idea. "I'd rather learn about you. All you've mentioned is your grandpa. Are you sure you don't have a wife and kids stashed somewhere?" Damn. Why had she said that?

He chuckled, hopefully taking it as a joke. "I think I would've remembered that fact. No. I'm all yours, Pippa."

All of a sudden, she didn't like him using her name. This name she'd created just for herself from a nickname her father had given her. The truest name she'd ever felt. The lying dickhead on the other end of the line didn't get to use it. "My cookies are burning, Mal. I should go."

"Me too. Work calls. I'll, ah, catch up with you later." His voice held a warmth she wanted to sink right in to—after she punched him in the face.

"I can't wait. Good-bye." She clicked off, finally reaching Trixie's apartment. The woman hadn't been answering all day, and even if she'd been at work, she would've gotten a message at some point.

Trixie lived on the ground floor of a weathered apartment building that had twelve units. Even though the place could use a can of paint, the grounds were lovingly tended with early spring flowers.

Pippa parked at the curb and looked around the quiet residential area. Trees swayed in the chilly wind, and the air hinted at oncoming rain. Nobody was around. Even so, she felt exposed being out in the world. Facing her fears sucked.

Her hair blew against her face and she pushed it back while walking up the sidewalk and turning at Trixie's door.

It was slightly ajar.

Everything in Pippa stopped short. Heart, breath, thoughts.

Trixie would never leave her door open.

Chapter Twenty-Eight

Malcolm barely made it to his fake apartment in time for April to pick him up in the same van she'd used the day before. He'd grabbed warm food and drink earlier just to keep himself going and felt a little better by the time she arrived. She was chipper again today, extolling the virtues of the family. She'd also handed him a lemonade the second he'd gotten into the van.

He set it aside, needing to stay clearheaded as long as possible. He couldn't risk being drugged so early. The fact that he'd had about an hour of sleep in days wasn't helping either.

He pumped her for information during the drive, but she either didn't know anything was amiss or she was a much better actress than he'd given her credit for. They reached the family mansion in no time, and he settled into his character.

His bloodshot eyes and raging headache from lack of sleep worked in his favor.

Tension blanketed the interior of the mansion as the members scurried around, cleaning frantically. "What's going on?" Mal asked.

Tree hurried in from outside. "Malcolm. The Prophet would like to see you immediately."

"Huh." Mal kept his expression mildly curious. "Okeydoke." He patted April on the arm. "Will I see you for lunch later?"

Happiness flushed her young face. "Definitely." Then she frowned, looking around. "What do you think is going on?"

"Dunno." Mal turned and made his way unescorted to the end of the hall, where he knocked and waited for Isaac to invite him in. The second he'd cleared the doorway, a gun cocked and a barrel was pressed to his temple. "I'm thinking you're not happy to see me," he murmured.

Isaac sat behind his desk, while George held the gun to Mal's head. He shut the door. "Ever seen brains splatter on a wall?" George asked.

"Yes. Have you?" Mal kept his gaze on Isaac, who watched impassively.

"Not yet, but I'm looking forward to it," George said grimly.

Enough of that shit. Malcolm dropped, punched George in the knee, and grabbed the gun as George fell. "It's a very ugly sight." He slipped the Glock into the front of his waistband for easy access and faced Isaac, tilting his head. "Want to tell me what the hell is going on?"

Isaac studied him, his eyes a darker amber than usual. "I don't believe in coincidences."

"Neither do I." Mal could barely see a silver gun held casually in Isaac's lap. He really didn't want to get shot again.

Both men ignored a groaning George, who had to use the wall to pull himself upright.

"Do you understand that ends very often justify means?" Isaac steepled his fingers together.

Mal scoffed. "You've probably seen my record. Of course I do. Always have."

Isaac nodded. "Can I trust you?"

Mal lifted an eyebrow. "As much as you can trust anybody, buddy." He kept an eye on George via his peripheral vision. "Listen. I don't need this crap. April is cute, and the meditation kind of helped with the headaches, if not the migraines, but seriously."

"Do you want to belong?" Isaac asked. "Do you want to protect abused women like Mrs. Thomson and scared kids like her son?"

"Of course." Mal leaned back against the door. "You know what I don't want? I don't want to walk into a room and have a gun pointed at my head."

A light flared in Isaac's eyes. "We need funds to keep this place safe for our family. Sometimes, we've robbed dens of inequity to make money and obtain necessary medication for some of our ill members."

Dens of inequity? Had the jerk really just used that term? Mal tried to nod.

Isaac continued. "For decades, we've taken from pharmacies. They're insured, and nobody has been hurt. We've had a couple of missteps, but last night, two of my best were captured. The police were waiting. Do you have an explanation for that?"

Mal lifted an eyebrow. "Were your guys any good?"

"The best." Isaac set his hand on the hilt of his gun but didn't lift it. "Don't you think that's a coincidence, considering you're an ex-cop and have just joined the family?"

Mal hadn't exactly joined the family. He frowned. "All right. I don't believe in coincidences. But the only person I've really hung out with is April. Are you telling me she's some sort of secret superspy who gave me information?"

Isaac leaned back. "No. Definitely not. Do you have an alternative explanation?"

Yeah. There was a bug two feet away from Mal. He had to get to it. "Well, approaching the issue like a detective, I'd ask if any of your members have acted funny lately. Used the phone without being authorized? Taken off by themselves when in town? Needed alone time to maybe talk to the cops?"

Isaac frowned. "George?"

George shuffled his feet. "Well, Beth has been on the phone a lot lately. And Orchid has disappeared several times while we've done outreach in the last few months. We've kind of joked about it. Like, 'where's Orchid off to now?'"

Isaac's nostrils flared. "Beth has been talking to her sister in Toledo, asking for funding. I okayed it. Get Orchid for me, please."

Malcolm moved so George could open the door. Fuck. The last thing he needed was Orchid losing it and giving him up. "What's your plan?"

"To get the truth," Isaac said shortly.

George returned with Orchid in record time. The woman's eyes were huge, and she shook visibly. She looked at Isaac, glanced at Mal, and then halted.

George shoved her into a seat.

Mal tensed. If he intervened, he'd blow his cover and lose any chance of finding out if and when the attack was going to happen.

Isaac stood and walked around the desk, gun in hand. He crouched by Orchid's chair. "You know the family means everything to me, right? That God has charged me with the protection and love of these people?"

Orchid slowly nodded. Her hair was in long braids down her back, and they seemed to jump to panicked attention.

"It has come to my attention that a member of my family, someone I love and trust, has betrayed me. Betrayed these wonderful souls who are just trying to do my work. To do God's work. What do you think I should do about that?" Isaac crooned, his gaze intense as he stared her in the eyes.

She gulped. "I-I don't know."

"I think you do." He set the gun on her leg, his hand over it.

She jerked, her breath panting. "I don't, Prophet. I really don't."

"Don't lie," he snapped, the sound harsh after his soft tone. "Give me the truth."

She looked frantically over her shoulder at Mal, who could only stare her down. If she gave him up, they were both dead. Maybe he could get her to play along. He lowered his chin. "Have you been talking to somebody outside the family?"

"No," she whispered.

He hardened his expression. "Maybe accidentally? Just someone you thought was nice?" First rule of any interrogation was to get the person to say something. Anything. Then one could take them down the path.

She slowly nodded. "Yes."

"What?" Isaac asked, falling into an interrogation style that was pretty damn good. "What did you say?"

Her voice shook. "I just told him about the family and what we do. That we love each other."

Malcolm moved in, standing at Isaac's side while he knelt. He hoped to God she followed his lead. "Who? Who is this guy?"

She visibly shrank back. "His name is Angus. I don't know his last name."

"But you know what he does, don't you?" Malcolm asked, keeping his tone congenial. If they were going to play at an interrogation, he might as well do it right. If he could just get to that bug . . . but Isaac was in the way. "It's okay, Orchid. Time to tell the truth."

She gulped down a swallow, the freckles standing out over her dark skin. "He's a cop," she whispered, the sound barely audible.

Excellent. She was following Mal's lead and playing along.

Isaac stood. "A cop. You've been talking to a cop about your family." He shook his head. "What did you tell him?"

"I told him about Stacy," Orchid burst out with surprising spirit. "She was just eighteen, and you made her sleep with your lieutenants. She wasn't ready for that. You can't just use women like that, Prophet."

Isaac's gaze hardened. "It is not your place to make that decision."

"She overdosed because of the pain and shame." Orchid lifted her face. "You were wrong."

George audibly gasped.

Mal stiffened. The woman was going to sacrifice herself for him. That couldn't happen. He had to keep her attention and not let her get too far away from what he needed to be said. "Watch your tone," he said.

Orchid glared at Isaac and ignored Malcolm. "Eagle hurt her, and you know it. I hope he's rotting in a cell somewhere right now."

Isaac struck, hitting her across the face. The slap echoed loudly around the room, and her head jerked to the left and then back.

Adrenaline poured through Mal's body, but he forced himself to remain still. "How did you even know about the planned robberies?"

She hung her head. "Leroy liked to talk after, well, you know."

Mal breathed out. Good. Blame the guy who wasn't there to counter the lie. "You told the cop about the robberies that were planned. Why? So you could get rid of Eagle? Or did you want to hurt the entire family?"

"Just to take Eagle away," she said, her shoulders slumping. "And I'm tired of being drugged. Sometimes I can't even remember whole days."

Isaac grabbed her braids and jerked her head back. "What else? What have you heard around here?"

"Nothing," she said, tears in her eyes.

Isaac frowned. "Did you tell the cop about the cleansing fire about to commence?"

Mal went on even higher alert.

Orchid blinked. "No, of course not. I don't know any details about that. I just wanted Eagle gone. From all of us."

The woman was a decent liar. Bone-deep fear would do that.

Isaac released her and stalked around the desk. "I don't believe you."

Mal moved to Orchid's side and dropped down, staring into her eyes. "How did the cop approach you? How did this come about?"

She dropped her gaze to her hands. "I was crying in the bathroom of the coffee shop in Minuteville. He said he was a cop and asked me what was wrong, and I don't know, I just kind of spilled everything about Eagle. About what he'd done, and about Stacy overdosing."

Mal looked over his shoulder at Isaac. "Is Stacy dead?" He kept his voice brisk.

"No," Isaac said. "When she poisoned herself, we took her to the hospital. Last I heard, she was in a coma there."

Yeah. That was right. Of course, the asshole was leaving out the rather important fact that they'd dropped Stacy off at the door and sped away. "So there's no body or crime." Mal stood and swiped the bug on his way up, shoving it into his pocket in one smooth motion. He looked at Isaac. "I'm not in charge, but if you ask me, you need to make an example here."

Orchid gasped and shrank back even more. She looked small and defenseless in the chair, and Mal had to fall back on skills he'd hoped to forget forever to stay in character. "I won't do it again," she croaked.

Isaac shook his head, the movement sad. "Malcolm? You have more experience with this than I do. What do you think?"

Mal sighed. "I don't know her as well as you do. In my line of work, once a snitch, always a snitch. But you may have insights here I lack."

George cleared his throat. "I say we make her an example. A good one."

Mal looked toward Isaac, as if waiting for guidance. "If so, it has to be quiet. Nothing obvious, but she has to disappear." Just how dedicated was Isaac's flock? Mal let the truth show in his eyes. "I've done things undercover, things I did for a mob family, that I'll never be free of."

Isaac's gaze sharpened. "Is that a fact? Are you offering to do the same for me?"

Mal made himself look around as if he was thinking it through. "I'm just searching for a place to belong. I like April, and I like that Millicent. This is a nice family. But if I stay, if I belong, then I call my own shots."

Isaac's eyes began to gleam.

Yeah. Challenge accepted. Mal was down and out, and killing Orchid would give Isaac something to hold over him. As a way of recruitment, it wasn't bad.

"You're special, Malcolm," Isaac said, his voice deepening. "Very. I would like for you to stay with the family. We could use your skills. We need you."

Nice. "I appreciate that," Malcolm said.

Isaac nodded. "If you take care of this problem for me, you can stay. Both April and Millicent shall keep you company as long as you wish. Angel as well, if you like."

Mal tried to look satisfied, but his gut churned with bile. "All right." He jerked Orchid to her feet. "I'll need to borrow the van." Somehow, he had to get her to safety.

Orchid whimpered, no doubt as scared as she was confused. But the woman was smart. She didn't say a word about him.

Mal pulled her toward the door.

"Wait," Isaac ordered.

Malcolm half-turned in time to see Isaac grasp a stun gun out of his desk and toss it to George. "George is going with you. In this family, we don't do anything alone. Especially the difficult parts."

Damn it. "I don't need help," Mal snapped.

"Too bad," George said, sounding downright gleeful.

Isaac motioned to Malcolm. "Please give me George's gun."

It hurt, but Mal handed over the weapon. They still had his gun. Well, one of his guns.

Orchid tried to pull free, but Mal held her arm tight. She hissed. "I've been with you for ten years, Prophet. How can you do this?"

Even after all this, she called him Prophet. Something ached in Mal.

Isaac's gaze was hard as rock. "You've betrayed me. You've betrayed God. You deserve this fate."

Mal gave the prophet a hard look. "You have any other weapons?"

"Yes, but bullets can be traced." Isaac shut his desk drawer. "You'll have to be resourceful."

"Fine." Mal let Orchid yank her arm free, and surprised, she fell onto the couch. He made a show of bending down to grab her. Twisting his shoulders, he attached the bug inside the fireplace, which had gone dead.

His smile even felt feral as he moved to open the door. He'd have to figure out what to do with George on the way. This was a mess, for sure. "Orchid, you'll walk with us through the house, and you'll say nothing. One word, and I'll knock your ass out."

The woman swallowed, her entire body trembling next to his.

He kept his expression hard. What the hell was he going to do with her?

Chapter Twenty-Nine

Pippa couldn't breathe. She looked frantically around the outside of Trixie's apartment building, but only the wind and pine trees stirred. Everything inside her wanted to turn and run back to her car. But if Trixie needed help, she had to go in.

She tugged a can of Mace out of her purse and nudged Trixie's door open.

Silence of the truly empty kind ticked like a bomb within. Pippa looked over her shoulder, saw no other people, and edged inside.

The living area was decorated in bold blues and purples, with a sofa and chair facing a television on the wall. The room was tidy, save for one bright pink throw pillow on the floor. Not unusual. The room led right into a sparkling-clean kitchen with a small round table. Mail and other papers were scattered across the table, as if Trixie had been working on finances.

Pippa kept up her Mace, ready to spray, as she looked into the bathroom to the left. It was the only one in the apartment. She held her breath as she whipped open the brightly colored shower curtain.

Nothing.

Okay. One room left. Exiting the bathroom, she moved

back toward the kitchen and swung into the room. The bed was unmade, but nothing seemed out of place.

Her shoulders went down. Glancing guiltily over her shoulder again, she moved toward the dresser and checked the false bottom beneath the lower left drawer. Trixie's go-bag was still in place. Pippa's chest constricted again. Why wasn't Trixie answering her phone?

Pippa put the bag back in place and hustled from the apartment, making sure she shut the door. The wind pushed against her as she made her way to the car and dialed Trixie again.

Only the answering machine. Igniting the engine, she pulled away from the curb, heading into Minuteville and the diner where Trixie worked.

Nothing could happen to her only friend. The skies opened up, as if in agreement, throwing rain down to splatter against the windshield. She clicked on the wipers, and their rhythmic swishing sound upped her concern. The window fogged, and she pressed the Defrost button.

Trixie had to survive.

That quickly, Pippa was seventeen again and being fitted for an all-white gown in Isaac's office. He sat by a wide window showing a mountain, his fingers steepled beneath his chin, his gaze hot on her.

She tried not to look at him as the two women inserted pins in various places.

"You look beautiful, Mary," Isaac said, his voice deep.

She tried not to shiver. Every time he looked at her like that, her stomach cramped. Her friend Trixie had already purified with Isaac, and she'd cried hard when telling Pippa all about it, saying it hurt. Bad. Those were their names now. Trixie and Pippa. Oh, they couldn't share those names with anybody else, and they might not be able to use them for a long time, but those were their names. That mattered. Choosing your own name.

One of the ladies finished the hem and stood, turning toward Isaac. "Prophet? I think we're finished for now." She was new to the family, and her name was some kind of plant. Pippa hadn't paid attention.

"Thank you, Fern," he murmured. "You and River can take the dress now so it's ready for tomorrow. I expect it to be perfect."

Pippa held absolutely still as they carefully removed the dress, leaving her in only a light white slip with no socks. They carried the dress out of the room as if it was made of gold.

"Come sit with me," Isaac ordered.

Her knees trembling, she walked toward the other chair by the window, looking around for a blanket. There wasn't one, of course. She crossed her arms over her breasts and sat, making sure the slip covered her thighs.

He looked her over. "You get lovelier every day. Are you looking forward to your birthday tomorrow?"

There was a correct answer for that. "Yes," she whispered, wanting to run.

"Numbers are important. Your turning eighteen on the seventh is very crucial to the way we live. Those numbers equal twenty-five, which is when you'll truly reach your destiny. It's a sign from God." Isaac leaned forward.

She tried not to shrink back. She tried really hard. His reliance on numbers didn't make any sense. Seven and eighteen and twenty-five? It was all just numbers. "Why don't you give anybody else names from the Bible?"

He set his hand on her knee. "Those names are for you and me only. We're special."

She tried to swallow, but her knee burned. Her being special had spared her the things that had happened to Trixie. So far. Tomorrow there would be a huge ceremony *with the whole family, and then Isaac was taking her somewhere for a week. He hadn't told her where.*

The idea made her want to throw up.

"Besides our holy union, your birthday starts the clock for seven years. Seven crucial years for the outside world to get its act together. To remake the family structure and find God." He squeezed her knee and released her. "I can only hope our leaders make good choices."

"Or what?" The closer she came to being forced to bond with him, the more she questioned everything he said. Often not out loud, though.

"Then we shall be the warriors for the Lord and teach them a lesson," Isaac said smoothly. "These have the power to shut up the sky, so that rain will not fall during the days of their prophesying; and they have power over the waters to turn them into blood, and to strike the earth with every plague, as often as they desire."

"Revelation 11:16," Pippa murmured. That was one of the passages Isaac made her read. The women in the family read the Bible almost every day. "I don't understand."

"There's a place that holds all the power in this country. If the world doesn't return to a state of proper peace, we will be God's vengeance. He will tell me what to do," Isaac said.

Why did he always talk in circles? What did any of that even mean? Pippa looked toward the door.

"You'll want to go prepare for tomorrow." He pinched her thigh, and she jumped. "If you're not smiling tomorrow, Mary, I will be greatly disappointed."

She nodded and stood, her head down as she walked as slowly as she could for the door. Managing to keep her hands from clenching into fists until she'd shut the door behind her was the hardest thing she'd ever done.

Trixie and their friend Tamarack were waiting, their faces pale. "You okay?" Trixie whispered.

Tears filled her eyes, and she shook her head.

"You will be." Trixie grasped her hand and pulled her away from the door. "I found a way out, and my friend will be waiting for us. The guy I met on outreach a month ago. Tonight. Meet me in the garden with the two lemon trees at midnight. Trust me. I'll get to the storage room first."

Where Isaac's money was hidden. So much money. Pippa shook her head. "Let's just go. We don't need their money."

"Yes, we do. It's the only way to get freedom," Trixie had whispered urgently. "You have to believe me."

Tamarack shook her head. "It's a mistake. You two will get caught and punished."

"Come with us," Trixie said urgently. "If we make it, he'll punish you."

Tamarack's green eyes darkened. At about six feet, she was tall for a girl, but her features were delicate. "If he does, then he does. I'll pray for you both." Then she ducked her head and hurried down the hall to the laundry.

Pippa needed to throw up. Bad. She'd seen Trixie's friend. The guy had gang tattoos all over his arms, his neck, even on his face. "Maybe we should just cut through the fence and run into the mountains. We don't need help."

"Yes, we do." Trixie snorted. "Say we get to the mountains. What then?"

Pippa couldn't answer. There wasn't an answer, really. "What about my mom and your sister?"

"We can't tell them. They won't come with us, and they'll tell Prophet. You know they will." Trixie peeled off to go pretend to do women's work in the laundry.

Pippa climbed the stairs to her bedroom, feeling around a thousand years old. She entered, stopping short at seeing her mother sitting on the white coverlet on the bed. "Mom." Hope burst through her so quickly her skin flushed.

Her mom had lost weight lately but still looked beautiful. "I wanted to check on you." For a quick moment, something familiar showed in her eyes.

"I don't want to marry him." Pippa shut the door. "It's not right."

Her mom stood and crossed to her, distress wrinkling her cheeks. "He's the Prophet, and he knows best. We're safe here, Pippa. With the family. We need them." She grasped Pippa's arms.

Pippa pulled away, her heart falling inside her chest. It hurt. "We don't need them. We never did." She wanted to be angry, so angry, but the sadness was eating her up.

Her mom didn't try to touch her again. "I love you, Mary."

Being called that was like a punch to the stomach, and Pippa nearly bent over. She spun around to face her mother. "Do you ever wonder what he'd think about this? What my father, the man you supposedly loved, would think about my being forced to marry a thirty-five-year-old man who thinks he talks to God?"

"He does talk to God." Her mother's face turned so pale her lips were blue.

She didn't have an answer for the other question, now did she? Pippa shook her head. "My father wouldn't let this happen."

"Your father is dead." Her mother's shoulders straightened, and her chin went up. "This is our family now, and we will follow the rules here. Someday, you'll understand." She left and quietly shut the door behind her.

Tears filled Pippa's eyes. How could her own mother do this?

What if, somehow, her mom was right? What if Isaac really did talk to God? Sometimes it did seem as if he knew things others didn't. And sometimes in his presence, she felt a peace she couldn't understand.

Trixie said it was drugs and tricks.

Was Trixie right?

Or did Isaac have gifts Pippa shouldn't deny? What if she

was going against God's will? Who was she to do something like that?

But sometimes, instincts mattered. Right? Or she wouldn't have any.

She'd been forced to spend enough time with Isaac to know and see that he liked hurting people. Especially women. He enjoyed their pain. He enjoyed making her witness their pain.

That had to be wrong.

Pippa swallowed and moved to the bed and her few meager possessions. She didn't know who was right or who was wrong. But it scared her to death to think of marrying Isaac the next day. Some of the things he'd done through the years, that he'd made her watch him do to other people, were horribly wrong.

Those things had to be wrong.

So she'd run. She'd pack and meet Trixie and then Trixie's guy friend. If that meant she would eventually go to hell, then so be it.

Hell couldn't be worse than this place.

Pippa jerked back to the present and pulled into the parking lot of the restaurant, not seeing Trixie's car. The old Buick hadn't been at the apartment either. It took her five minutes to push herself out of the car.

She ducked through the rain and opened the door, where the smell of bacon grease and cheeseburgers bombarded her. People were there. Too many of them.

She wanted to be back home. Safe by herself behind locked doors. Baking in her kitchen. Away from all these people, possible danger, and so many sights and sounds. Instead, she looked around for help.

A quick check with the nearest waitress confirmed that

Trixie wasn't at work for the dinner shift, and she was an hour late.

It was starting to get dark outside.

Pippa could barely breathe. She owed her entire life to Trixie. Something was very wrong. It wasn't like she could go to the police. There had to be something she could do, though. The walls felt like they were closing in.

Where was Trixie?

Chapter Thirty

Malcolm had driven about fifteen miles away from the mansion when George decided to climb in the back of the van with Orchid. "What are you doing?" Mal asked.

George paused. "I want to have some fun with her before we kill her. I mean, why not?" He pushed a couple of shovels to the side, and they clunked noisily. Then something crackled several times, and Orchid cried out.

Anger heated through Mal's chest. "You did not just tase her."

"Nope," George said cheerfully. "I just cracked it a bit in her direction."

Mal glanced over his shoulder. Orchid was pressed against the side of the van, her hands tied, tears flowing down her face. George was across from her, leaning in, the Taser precariously close to the woman's right breast.

The asshole.

Mal whipped the van into a turnoff against a bunch of trees, and George flew back to hit his side of the van with a loud thunk.

Before the man could protest, Mal was out of the vehicle. Cool evening air slapped his face, but at least it wasn't raining. He opened the back door.

George shook his head, as if trying to get his bearings. "What the hell did you do that for?"

Mal smiled. "You're not the only one who gets to have fun." He waited for George to relax. "Why don't you shock her a little? Just see what that thing can do?"

Orchid whimpered and drew her knees up toward her chest.

George's eyes gleamed. "Well, okay." He pressed a button, and the Taser charged.

"I want to be closer." Mal stepped up into the van, pretended to trip, and smoothly claimed the stun gun from George. He let out a fake gasp as he fell, pressing the weapon into Orchid's hand in a quick motion.

The woman lunged forward and tasered George in the chest. The man cried out, falling back, his eyes closing.

Mal leaped up and slammed George's head into the wall as hard as he could. The guy slumped down, out cold.

Orchid panted out several deep breaths. "Did I knock him out?"

"No." Mal lifted his knife from his boot and sliced the ropes off her hands. "A Taser won't knock somebody out. But a good bang to the head is always helpful."

She wiped tears off her face, her wrists obscenely raw from the rope. "Then he'll know you helped me."

Mal shook his head. "He won't. I waited until his eyes were closed. I'll tell him you attacked him and he hit his head." The jackass would probably be so embarrassed a woman had gotten the better of him, he wouldn't want to tell anybody. Hopefully. "I need him to stay knocked out. If he stirs, hit him with a shovel."

"Gladly," Orchid said, her eyes overly bright as the adrenaline no doubt drained from her system.

Mal hustled back to the driver's seat and quickly dialed Force. "I need a pickup and some sort of sedative that'll wear off in about three or four hours." He was more than two hours away from headquarters. "And a first aid kit. Can somebody meet me halfway?" He didn't want to continue hitting George in the head to keep him out. Not right now anyway.

"Affirmative," Force said. "In fact, Raider is in Minuteville right now dealing with the local cops. They've thrown up a bit of a hissy fit about our taking their collar, and he's smoothing over the issue. I'll have him drop by the local hospital, and he'll meet you in about thirty minutes."

"Affirmative." Mal hung up and turned the key, pulling the van back onto the road. "Orchid? Tell me everything I don't know."

The woman kept the Taser pointed at the unconscious George. "Like what?"

"This big attack. Is it still going to happen?" he asked.

"Yes. Prophet has been having a lot of closed-door meetings lately, and something is definitely up." Orchid wiped her nose on her sleeve. "I heard him say something about Friday being a holy day."

It was Wednesday night. "Do you have any idea what he wants to do?"

"No." Orchid sniffed. "I don't. Whenever something big happens, he calls an all-family meeting and announces it then. I think that's happening tomorrow. We've had extra food and drink brought in."

Mal had to get back inside. But he had George to deal with, and what about Pippa? "Do you know anything about Isaac's bride?"

"Not much."

"What about Pi—I mean, Mary. Do you know anything about the girl Mary besides what you already told Angus?" Just thinking about Pippa made his chest ache. How deep was she into this shit? Not at all, if he had to bet.

"I knew Mary," Orchid said. "She was one of the first to

leave. One day she was there, and the next, the Prophet said she was hiding in the world to create a way for us."

Mal's temples began to hurt. "Had you heard from her since?"

"I haven't, but that doesn't mean Prophet hasn't. I just don't know. I told Angus I didn't know." Orchid's voice rose.

Mal nodded. He'd have to find out about Pippa on his own. "Okay. Run me through everything you know again, and don't leave anything out. Even a small detail might help." Friday was too close. What if there wasn't enough time to get the salient details? How many people were in jeopardy right now?

Orchid told him everything she could think of, and soon Mal pulled the van into the parking lot of an abandoned fast-food joint at the edge of Minuteville. Raider was waiting in a nondescript white compact car. He slid out, looking way too big for the vehicle, his movements strong and sure. Definitely graceful.

Mal met him at the back door of the van. "What do you have?"

"Propofol," Raider said, taking out a syringe.

Mal paused. "Seriously?" No wonder Force had sent the guy to a hospital. It wasn't as if they could've gotten the sedative at a local pharmacy. "How did you get your hands on that?"

Raider shrugged. "We all have gifts." He filled the syringe. "Take off his shoe. We'll inject him between the toes."

Apparently, clean-cut Raider had some experiences Mal wouldn't have guessed. He followed instructions. "How long will he be out?"

"If he survives the concussion you gave him, you have about three to four hours," Raider said, tucking the drugs back into his pocket. "He'll be confused and probably not remember much, so you can create whatever memories you want. If he awakens."

"Do you have the first aid kit?" Mal asked.

"Yeah. Picked one up at the hospital." Raider jogged over to his car.

Mal helped Orchid from the back of the van and then shrugged off his shirt. He took his knife from his boot. "This is gonna hurt." He sliced his upper arm, above his shirt-sleeve. Blood flowed. Taking the knife, he dipped it, then swung it around the interior of the van.

"What are you doing?" Orchid gasped.

Damn, his shoulder hurt. "Creating a death scene." He flung more blood.

Raider jogged up. "Ah. Okay. You need more?"

Mal leaned over and let his blood pool on the ground. "Nope. That should do it. Just want to show a bit of a fight. I'll tell him I strangled her and she fought back pretty well." He accepted the bandage from Raider and slapped it into place. Then he turned toward the woman. "You're very brave. Thank you."

She shook her head. "I'm not."

"Oh, you are." He gently turned her toward Raider. "Go with my friend. He'll get you a safe place to stay and some help."

"What about you?" she asked, her lip trembling.

He looked at the deathly silent man on the bottom of the van floor. "I have to pretend to bury a body, and hopefully, wake this guy up. Then, back to the mansion."

God, he hated that place.

Pippa slowly drove around Trixie's neighborhood, look-ing for anything or anybody who seemed out of place. Her head hurt as bad as her heart. Mal had betrayed her, but

Trixie never would. Bone-deep fear made Pippa's hands shake.

After scouting the area for a couple of hours, she settled down in her car where she could see the entrance to Trixie's apartment, clearly lit by overhead lights. What else could she do? She'd called repeatedly, and there had been no answer.

Rain started to patter on her windshield. Good. Maybe it would fog up a little bit. Her phone rang, and she jumped. "Hello?"

"Hi," Malcolm said.

Her chest compressed. Why couldn't it have been Trixie? "Um, hi." Crap. Was he at his house, wondering where she was?

"I'm sorry I didn't make it home for dinner," he said, as if it were expected that they'd eat together. He sounded slightly out of breath. "This case is taking longer than I'd hoped."

"Which one? You said there were two," she reminded him, settling her head back against the seat.

He was quiet for a moment. "Both of them, actually."

"I imagine that's a hazard in your line of work." Her body felt as if she was trying to swim in Jell-O without oxygen. Was it possible Malcolm had Trixie? He'd met her at the shooting the other day, and surely he'd gotten her address.

Much as she hated to admit it, she'd prefer for Mal to have Trixie than Isaac. "Have you made any progress on either case?" she asked.

"Not nearly enough," he said grimly, sounding as if he was telling the truth. "But hearing your voice helps. I want you to know that I'm glad we met. The closest thing to peace I've felt in a long time has been with you."

Tears pricked her eyes. God, he was good. If only he were telling the truth. How much more would those words have meant to her yesterday? "You made me believe," she murmured.

"In what?" His voice deepened.

"That I could maybe have a normal life." It was wrong, of course. She'd never have a normal life. "With you, I thought that I could have a chance."

Rain could be heard over his phone, as well as windshield wipers. "Baby, you sound sad."

That tone shot right through her, spreading warmth. How screwed up was that? "I am. I've been calling my friend Trixie all day, and she hasn't answered. That's not like her."

Mal was quiet for a moment. "How not like her?"

"Not at all. Do you think maybe the feds wanted to talk to her about the shooting again?" Pippa gave him the perfect out. If he jumped on it, then he probably actually did know where Trixie was.

"No. There's no reason they'd talk to her without contacting me first," he said.

God. What did that mean? Was he so good undercover that he could second-guess what she was thinking? Or did that mean that he really didn't have Trixie? If she had run, she would've taken her go-bag. So that only left Isaac. Even so, Pippa couldn't help hoping Trixie had gone off for a weekend with a hot guy and forgotten to charge her phone.

Right. Just yeah . . . right.

Mal cleared his throat. "Pippa? What's going on?"

It was the soft tone that broke her. "I can't do it," she burst out. "I can't play this idiot game with you. I'm not good at it. It's over. We're done."

Silence ticked for two beats. "What are you talking about? I'm not playing games. This is real." He sounded pained.

"You dickhead," she spat, anger and hurt all but spewing out of her. "I know this isn't real."

Two more beats. "Where are you?" His voice changed

from warm to direct and commanding. Her body heated and then chilled. When she didn't answer, he continued. "Pippa? Enough with this. Let me come and get you. Trust me. Where are you?"

Trust him? Yeah right. It was shocking how much she still wanted to. She gripped the phone so tightly her knuckles hurt. "I'm at home, of course. Why wouldn't I be?"

"What's going on?" His tone softened just enough to make her want to cry.

"You know what I learned today, Malcolm?" she asked softly.

"No. What?" His voice sounded a little . . . wary? Yeah. Wary.

She dropped her chin. "I learned that an ignition fuse can be taken out of a car. I also learned that it's easy to replace. Great facts, right?"

The swish of the wipers came over loud and clear. "I don't understand what you're talking about."

Enough was enough. "Stop. Just stop." Her eyes were gritty, and her head was going to explode. "Can you tell me one honest thing? Just one? Please." Her voice thickened, but she couldn't stop it.

"Pippa, I really don't—"

"I have a key that still works in your sliding glass door. I saw the manila file about me as a child in the table by your bed." The anger slowly just flowed out of her, leaving her empty. Completely.

His silence was heavy. "Ah, baby. I'm sorry."

God. He was going to just shatter her heart, wasn't he? The asshole. "I don't care. Just give me one thing. Please." She was almost begging.

"Let me come and get you. We can talk about this," he said. "Please, Pippa. Let me explain in person."

Did he think she was crazy? Well, probably. She'd fallen right in bed with him, heart first. That was nuts. "I don't know what you wanted from me, but I'm sure you didn't get it. You could've just asked instead of sleeping with me." Tears slid down her face, but she didn't care. "Good-bye, Malcolm."

"No."

The sharp command in his voice had her instinctively pausing. She blinked, her body on full alert.

"Pippa? Right now, you tell me where you are."

She shivered. For the first time, he truly sounded just as dangerous as she knew him to be. "No," she said softly.

"Pippa." The low command sent her senses reeling.

Her body reacted to his voice, to that tone. It betrayed her by softening. Even her breath quickened. "You were great in bed, Malcolm," she admitted, her heart hurting as much as her body.

"I'm not messing around." The dominance in the words was punctuated by his deep voice. "Tell me where you are. Right fucking now."

"No," she snapped, her back straightening.

"You do not want me to have to hunt you down," he warned.

Tingles beat through her abdomen. She shivered. "You'll never find me. I'm a master at running."

He sputtered something, but she ended the call.

She ripped her phone apart and then threw all the pieces in the dirt outside the car. Trying to stop the tears, she started her engine and drove away from Trixie's neighborhood.

The problem was, she didn't have anywhere to go.

Chapter Thirty-One

"Damn it." Mal pounded his hand against the steering wheel. He dialed Force, who picked up immediately. "I need a trace on Pippa's cell phone. Now. She knows."

"Give me five minutes. Stay on Op." Force clicked off.

Mal glanced in the rearview mirror. George was still out cold, and the back of the van looked beyond creepy with all the blood. Stay on Op? How was he supposed to stay on Op when Pippa was out there by herself thinking he'd betrayed her?

Well, hadn't he?

His stomach rolled over and bile rose in his throat. He had to find her.

His phone buzzed. "Where is she?"

"No clue," Force said. "The GPS on her phone is disengaged. If she really knows the truth, then the phone isn't with her any longer, Malcolm. You know that as well as I do. It'll take time to ping where she's been all day. Where was she the last time you talked to her?"

"She didn't say." Hell. She could've been three states over by the time they talked tonight. "But she did mention that Trixie hadn't picked up her phone all day. Can you try to find her?" Mal asked.

"Of course. I'll have Brigid start a grid search for both of them. All traffic cams, street cams, facial recognition everywhere. Don't worry. We'll find them." Force shuffled some papers. "For now, stay on Op. There's nothing else for you to do."

He hated this. "Anything on the bug I planted in Isaac's office?"

"Not yet. He had sex with somebody and it was loud, but I can't tell you who. There wasn't a lot of talking." Disgust coated Force's voice. "Wolfe got information from the two guys we have here. The attack will take place on Friday, but that's all they know. Eagle's guess was New York, while the other guy thought Boston. I have Brigid looking for activities and large gatherings on Friday, but there are a lot. We need more info."

Mal breathed in, moving his chest. Focus. He had to focus, damn it. "Okay. I'll be in touch." He clicked off and slid his phone into his pocket.

He pulled the van over about a mile from the mansion and jumped back to shake George the hell up.

"What?" George sat up, his eyes blinking rapidly. He looked around, and his eyes widened at the blood spatter, as well as the dirt covering the shovel. Mal had dug into dirt for about two minutes to coat the stupid thing.

George gingerly touched the back of his head. "What happened?" he slurred.

"Orchid beat the crap out of you," Mal said without sympathy. "She tased you and then jumped on you, smashing your head into the side of the van. You've been unconscious for about four hours."

George turned even paler. "Did you tell Prophet?"

"Of course not. Why would I?" Mal helped the guy out of the back of the van and into the passenger seat, then slammed the door a little loudly. He crossed around and jumped into his seat, his hand on the key. "If you want, I can tell Prophet that you and I took care of Orchid together. We don't have to let him know she knocked you out."

George wiped his eyes. "Thank you, Brother."

"No problem." Mal started the ignition and pulled out onto the deserted road. "We wouldn't want you to miss out on the fun Friday, would we?"

"You know about Friday?" George asked.

Mal nodded. Part of running a successful cult was keeping members in the dark about who knew what. "Sure. Don't you know?"

"Just that it all happens Friday. I don't know where or when. Or exactly what." George kicked out his boots. "Just fire and cleansing. Do you know more than that?"

"No." Unfortunately. It looked like his good buddy George wasn't going to be much help.

George looked back at the carnage. "How did we kill her?"

"Ultimately, I strangled her," Mal said easily. "She put up a fight first, as you can see. We buried her in the forest near Minuteville. Her body will probably never be found."

George scratched his chin. "That sucks. I wanted to have her one more time." He sounded like a petulant child.

Mal's fingers folded into a fist. Rage caught him so sharply, he couldn't speak for a moment.

They reached the entrance to the mansion, and Malcolm parked the van. "I'll take care of cleanup after we report in to Isaac. My guess is you have a concussion."

George clapped him on the arm. "You're a good guy, Mal. Thanks."

It was all Malcom could do to keep from crushing the guy's larynx. His hands were shaking as he got out of the van, so he shoved them in his pockets and made his way through the front door and down to Isaac's office.

Isaac sat at his desk, pouring over what looked like a

map. He quickly covered it with his desk calendar. "How did it go?"

"Perfect," George said, his voice a little too high. "We took care of your problem."

Isaac studied George and then Malcolm. "Which one of you did?"

"We both did," George said, his smile not quite working right.

Mal stayed silent.

"I see." Isaac nodded. "It's almost midnight. Get some sleep, George. Malcolm, I'd like to speak with you."

George's sigh sounded relieved as he hustled out of the room.

Isaac gestured toward the chairs near the fireplace. "Sit with me." He walked gracefully to the bar and poured two generous glasses of Scotch before returning and handing one over. "Tell me. Does George have what it takes?"

Mal took the glass and sipped, almost humming in pleasure. "Yeah. George has no problem killing."

"Did he kill Orchid?" Isaac sat and took a drink.

"No. I did," Mal said, swirling the liquid in his glass. "Made a bit of a mess but will clean it up." He glanced around and then stood as if uncomfortable. "It's not who I want to be," he murmured.

"We're who we need to be," Isaac countered.

Mal moved toward the mantel, his eye caught by a picture of Pippa. He hadn't gotten close enough to see the pictures yet. She must've been around twelve years old. She looked innocent and young, and his heart hurt for her. "Your daughter?" Mal asked.

Isaac scoffed. "No. My bride. That was her as a child. She's an adult now."

"Oh." Mal turned and looked him over, then retook his

seat, his instincts humming. "I hadn't realized you were married."

"Sometimes the right woman captures your heart," Isaac said, lifting his glass. "To the right woman."

Mal lifted his glass, every primal instinct he had pushing him to snap this guy's neck. Now. "To your bride."

They both drank, and Isaac refilled their glasses.

"If you don't mind my asking, where is your wife? I haven't seen her," Mal said, the liquid starting to warm his stomach.

"She's not here right now," Isaac murmured. "But she's with me at heart. The woman is doing very important work. It matters, and so does she."

That was such a nonanswer. But it did sound like Pippa was in touch with Isaac, though the guy was a born liar. Mal mulled over the situation. He didn't want to give himself away, but he had to get more details about the attack coming on Friday. "It must be nice to be married." He looked around. "I feel like this place may be a little complacent for me."

"You just buried a body about two hours ago. How is that complacent?" Isaac asked.

Mal shrugged. "She was a threat to you. Threats go down." He took another drink of the potent brew. "But what do you stand for? Just peace and love and sex?" He rolled his shoulders.

"No. We're a guide for the rest of the world. And we're also God's wrath if necessary," Isaac said.

There it was. All right. "What does that mean?" Mal asked, trying for boredom.

"All in good time, my brother." Isaac sat back, his linen pants stretching over long legs.

There wasn't enough fucking time, damn it. Mal winced. "I'm not good at being in the dark, Prophet. Never have been." He scraped at dirt he'd put beneath his fingertips while pretending to dig a grave. "There's a tension in the air, in the people scurrying around, that I don't like. Something's up with your family, and it's not working for me."

Isaac nodded. "You are very astute, my friend. This is your family, too. Family comes with trust, no?"

Mal barked out a laugh. "No. Not in my experience. Definitely . . . no."

Isaac's eyes gleamed. "Trust goes both ways. Yet what you just said, I don't understand. Did you not have the gift of a family like this growing up?"

Mal's smile felt painful. "No. My folks died in a car crash when I was young, and I went to live with my grandfather, who was a steel worker in Detroit. The guy drank a lot." Mal rubbed the scar over his right eye. "A bottle to the head can knock a kid out for more than a day. Not many people know that fact." He tipped his head and finished his glass, the memories burning through him.

Isaac's expression formed in lines of what most people would mistake for sympathy. "I'm sorry that happened to you. When you became a cop, did you then find family?"

Mal hated this part of any undercover Op. To get, he had to give of himself, and what he gave had to hold the ring of truth. "Not really. I worked hard but didn't do well making connections. Then I started going undercover on different Ops, and you can't have connections to do that right." The closest he'd ever come to a brotherhood was right now, with Angus Force and his odd gang.

"Ah, my friend. I am so truly sorry." Isaac swirled his drink. "What about love? Women?"

The deepest feeling he'd ever had for a woman was with Pippa, and their relationship had been based on lies. From both of them. "I'm not sure what love feels like."

"For a woman? It's a burning obsession that you'd do anything for her," Isaac said.

Well, Mal would do anything for Pippa. Even if she was

guilty. "Then maybe I've felt love." The word seemed tame for what he was currently experiencing.

"As have I," Isaac said.

The irony that they were most likely talking about the same woman wasn't lost on Malcolm. "What about you? Did you have a family growing up?"

"Sort of. Basic folk with no big dreams. I knew I was meant for a large life. Serving God," Isaac said.

Right. Delusions of grandeur. "I need a mission. An Op at all times to feel useful." There was a little too much truth in that statement, but Mal went with it anyway. He had to get inside the organization.

"I understand." Isaac sighed. "In fact, because you mentioned it, while I hate to ask more of you tonight, is there any way you could track down Eagle and Leroy? Maybe use some of your contacts to find out where they are? I sent a lawyer to the local police station in Minuteville after the arrest at the pharmacy, and they said our men had been taken elsewhere."

Mal feigned a frown. Just how much did Isaac know? "By whom?"

"I don't know," Isaac said. "Would you help?"

Mal lifted his glass to his mouth and realized it was empty. He set it down on the table between the chairs. "Of course. After tonight, I'm all in, Prophet."

"You sure are. Welcome to the family." Isaac's eyes glittered. He reached into the drawer of the table between the chairs and drew out Mal's gun to hand over. "You should have this back. Would you please now go clean up the van you used tonight and find my missing men?"

"Yes." Mal stood and exited the room, tucking his gun at his waist. He leaned back against the closed door, his hands shaking with the need to punch right through Isaac's face. The man had no problem with murder. What kind of a hell had Pippa's childhood been?

Chapter Thirty-Two

Pippa had no clue where to drive. She couldn't just leave without knowing what had happened to Trixie, but she couldn't stay in the area either. Either the cult or the police had Trixie or none of this made sense.

One more time. She'd try one more time. Pippa pulled over on the side of the road and then remembered she'd thrown her phone out the window. She had the burner phone, but if she used it, the person who answered would have the number. If the cops had Trixie, then they'd be able to find Pippa.

Rain slashed down, and she wanted to cry. Never had she felt so alone.

The phone rang from the go-bag.

She gasped. Her heart raced. Only Trixie had that number. Thank God. Pippa scrambled to unzip the bag and slapped the phone to her ear. "Where have you been all day? I've been worried sick," she answered.

Silence ticked for a second. "That's so kind of you to say, my beautiful one," Isaac said, his voice deeper than she remembered.

The entire world narrowed around Pippa, and her vision blurred. "Isaac," she whispered. Her body shuddered and her stomach seemed to disappear. Bile rose so quickly up her throat that heartburn scalded her. "How did you get this number?" She already knew the answer.

"I believe she goes by Trixie now," Isaac said calmly. "Or at least she did until about thirty minutes ago."

Pippa let out a low sob. "If you've hurt her, I'll kill you."

"Oh, I've definitely hurt her," Isaac said. "I had no choice, and you know it." He chuckled, and icy fingers skittered down Pippa's spine. "I had to occupy myself with something until midnight. It had to be midnight when I called you. Exactly forty-eight hours from your birthday, my love."

She gagged. "Put Trixie on the phone. Now."

"You forget your place, Mary. You do not give orders." His voice sharpened like a razor, taking her instantly back to the time when she'd been a terrified, confused child in his home. "Who does give orders?"

She closed her eyes. Nausea rippled through her. "I am not playing your game. Ever again. Now tell me what you want."

"You. It has always been you," Isaac whispered. "I am with God. Did you really think you could do the devil's work for so long? That it wouldn't catch up with you?"

"I'm not entirely sure you aren't the devil." She'd given plenty of thought to the matter.

Isaac made a disappointed clucking sound that had made children quake in terror for years. "Are you trying to get Trixie and your mother killed?"

So Trixie was still alive. Pippa scrambled for something to say that wouldn't make him strike out at her friend. "How did you find her?"

"Picture in an online newspaper after the shooting the other day. One of my family members was a reporter with connections, and was able to track down her name and the fact that she worked as a waitress in the area. It was simple investigation from there." He chuckled, the sound ominous.

"I like the name Trixie. It was from those books you girls were caught reading, remember?"

She remembered the punishments. Isaac had no problem denying food or sleep to any of them. And manual labor was encouraged. "Did she tell you my name?"

"Pippa. It's an odd one. Where did you get it?" he asked.

"None of your business." Pippa's body chilled. For Trixie to have given up her name, she had to be hurt. Badly.

He sighed. "Yet she couldn't give us your address. I find that interesting. That she didn't know it."

Tears gathered in Pippa's eyes. "She wouldn't let me give it to her." They both knew Isaac wanted Pippa above all else. So Trixie had always refused to know Pippa's address in case she was ever caught. "She was protecting me."

"That's my job," Isaac said simply. "You have a destiny that God demands. I'm sorry we couldn't have these years together to prepare you, but you must repent and pay. Dearly."

She shivered. "What do you have in mind?"

"Come home and I'll tell you. It's your only safe recourse at this point," he said.

She blinked, exhaustion pounding through her temples. "What do you mean?"

"Authorities outside Boston have been alerted to a dead body, Mary. They'll identify your brother, and they'll be after you. Come home, and I promise they'll never find you."

"Mark wasn't my brother," she spat. "None of you are my family."

"Oh, you'll pay for that. For now, you have an hour to get here to prepare for the cleansing fire on Friday. I'll text you the address," he said, his voice so calm, they could've been talking about the weather.

She shook her head. "The cleansing fire? What exactly are you going to do?" She had hoped when he lost her that he'd find some other course of action.

"What needs to be done, and you're at the center of it. Come home. Now," he ordered.

There had to be time to figure out this mess. Her mind scrambled for something to hold him off. "I started driving west toward California the second the cops released me after the shooting. I'm at least twenty-four hours away, Isaac. You know I can't fly. No identification."

His suffering sigh was full of disappointment. "Get here as fast as you can. Every hour you make me wait, I cut off pieces of Trixie." He ended the call.

Pippa dropped the phone. Sobs racked her, and it took several sucking breaths to get herself under control. She had a gun. If there was a way to hide it on her, she could shoot Isaac in the head when she arrived. She'd go to hell, probably, but she'd be doing this world a favor.

Her hand shook so violently, it took several tries for her to turn the key and start the car.

She'd bought herself some time, but Isaac hadn't been joking about hurting Trixie. He'd enjoy it.

She remembered that fact well as she flashed back to the night that had changed everything. When she and Trixie had barely escaped.

Her backpack was heavy, but she didn't complain as Trixie led her toward the west, through trees with branches that kept grabbing her hair. The moon was bright in the sky and easily lit their way.

Was this an unholy mistake?

She hadn't lived in the outside world for nearly eight years and she didn't know what to do. The money in their packs would help them—that much she understood.

It was stolen, though. That was a sin.

Would God punish her? She probably deserved it.

Trixie slowed and gestured for Pippa to hurry up. "The back road is just up there," Trixie whispered, setting down her pack to retrieve wire cutters she'd stolen from one of the gardening sheds. "Jack will be waiting."

Pippa paused and tried to catch her breath. "Jack looks scary to me."

"Jack is scary," Trixie said, hitching her pack into place. "But he's on our side. The guy doesn't like cults."

"Isn't he in a gang?" Pippa asked, clutching her hands together.

Trixie nodded. "Yeah. He's a businessman. We've agreed on the price for our escape and for some really good fake licenses and passports. This is the only way to go."

A stick snapped in the forest, and Pippa jumped. She drew the large cutting knife she'd taken from the kitchen earlier. If they got caught, Isaac would punish them until they wished they were dead. So she'd fight.

Trixie showed the way through the trees, and they came to the chain-link fence. Rolls and rolls of barbed wire extended up from the top, making it impossible to climb over. On the other side, Jack waited on a narrow dirt road in a banged-up gray two-door car. He exited the car, looking big and scary.

"Hurry up," he hissed, his light brown eyes all but glowing through the darkness.

Trixie bent and started snipping the fence. The process seemed to take forever, but finally, she'd made a big enough hole so she could shove her pack through and then herself. "Come on, Mary. Let's go."

Mary. She'd never use that name again. Oh, she'd use a few different aliases, but when she was safe, when she could be herself, she'd be Pippa. Forever. She'd just started to move when strong arms grabbed her from behind.

She yelped.

"I've found them," Mark yelled. Men's voices roared through the forest.

Damn it. Mark was one of Isaac's top lieutenants, and he looked at Pippa like he wanted to both strangle and rape her. The guy was known to hurt the younger girls.

Pippa started to struggle. "Let go."

He pinched her breast. Hard. "Oops. That was an accident." His laugh was gleeful.

Pain and shock ripped through Pippa. She reacted without thinking, striking back with the knife. It slid shockingly easily into Mark's leg.

He bellowed and released her, falling back. Like an animal, she turned, stabbing repeatedly. His stomach, his hands, his arms as he tried to protect himself.

"Mary, come on," Trixie yelled. "We have to go. Now."

Sobbing, Pippa shoved Mark and dropped the knife on the ground. Turning, she ran for the hole in the fence and wriggled her way thorough, scraping her neck and arms in the process. It didn't matter. She was free.

Jack started the car, and Trixie jumped into the backseat.

"Mary." Isaac stood on the other side of the fence. "Come back here. Now."

She whirled around, her breath panting, her body freezing in place.

Mark shoved himself to his feet, hate in his gaze.

Isaac looked over Pippa's shoulder at the car. "If you come back, I'll let Tulip go. She can be free. Forever."

"No," Trixie shrieked from the car. "Get in here, now. We have to go."

Pippa hesitated.

Isaac reached down and grasped the knife. Was he wearing leather gloves? It wasn't that cold yet. "Mary. Obey me. Now."

"No," she gasped, backing away from the fence. The

opening wasn't large enough for any of the men, but they could probably make it bigger quickly. She had to run.

The moonlight seemed to surround Isaac in a way it didn't the others. That was her imagination. It had to be. He watched her, those eyes seeing everything. Then he grabbed Mark and pulled him to the side. "Look what you've made me do." Hard and fast, Isaac plunged the knife into Mark's back several times.

Mark's eyes widened, and he gasped. Blood bubbled from his mouth and dripped down his chin. He fell to his knees and then forward, his head hitting the ground and his legs kicking up.

Pippa gagged, her eyes wide on the dead man. "Wh-why?"

Isaac tossed the bloody knife, and it landed on Mark's butt. "Your prints are on the knife. You stabbed him repeatedly and then killed him. If the cops find out, they'll be looking for you almost as hard as I will."

Her mouth gaped open. What should she do?

Isaac moved toward the fence, and she started backing up. "Come back here, now, and I will take care of this problem. The cops will never know."

Tears pooled in her eyes. What should she do?

Isaac almost crooned. "You have no choice, Mary. You're not strong enough to hide from the police and me. Not to mention God. He will punish you for this."

Yeah, He probably would.

Pippa stared directly into Isaac's eyes. "We'll meet up again someday, I know." Her fate made that inevitable. "Next time? I'll be the one with the knife." She turned and ran around the car, jumping in the front seat and slamming the door shut. They peeled out.

The sound of Isaac bellowing her name followed them down the dirt road.

* * *

Pippa came back to the present, her entire face hurting from crying. She hadn't thought about that night in months. Why, she didn't know.

But here she was. So, the worst had happened. The absolute worst thing she could've imagined had just happened, and Trixie was back with the monster.

Pippa had nothing to lose. Hiding all these years and almost becoming a shut-in hadn't protected either one of them in the end.

She had promised him she'd have a knife next time they met.

Apparently, she'd lied. This time, she was taking a gun.

Chapter Thirty-Three

Angus Force kicked back in his office and listened to the conversation between Malcolm and Isaac at the mansion. Mal had placed the bug perfectly to pick up the entire room.

Malcolm was a genius at undercover Ops. No wonder he'd been able to take down one of the most powerful mob families in the world. But it did beg the question: just what kind of a toll did this duplicity take on the detective? Had he been ready to return to work?

Probably not.

Roscoe lay in the corner, munching contentedly on a red high-heeled shoe. He'd worn it for a while and now seemed to think it was a snack. Angus had no clue where he'd gotten it, but chances were, it was the shrink's.

The woman shouldn't leave her shoes where Roscoe could get them.

Raider Tanaka strode into the room, glanced at the dog, then slid out a seat. "He has somebody's shoe."

"Yep." Angus held up a finger as he listened to Malcolm leave Isaac's office. Then Angus turned down the volume but kept the tape running. "How did it go?"

"Good. We transferred Eagle and Leroy to a real HDD

dark site, and they can sit there until we figure out what the attack will be on Friday."

Brigid appeared at the doorway, her red hair pulled back and several pieces of paper in her hand.

Angus motioned her in. "Have a seat. Sorry to have you working all night so soon."

Raider pulled out the chair next to him. "Aren't hackers used to working into the wee hours?" Only slight sarcasm lowered his tone.

She took the seat and rolled her eyes. "Not as much as tight-ass feds."

Angus bit back a smile. Watching the straight arrow Raider deal with the wildcat hacker with the lilting Irish accent might be the only good thing going on in his life right now. "What did you find, Brigid?"

"Okay." She handed over the papers. "On Friday, we have an antiabortion rally in Boston, a women's rights rally in DC, and a diversity parade in New York. We also have multiple concerts in cities across the East Coast, business meetings, and international consortia. There are so many things going on, we need more information to narrow down the search parameters."

"What about the names and descriptions of women from the cult that Eagle and Leroy gave us?" Angus asked, pushing aside his qualms about how effective Wolfe had been in getting the information. The guy was brutal. After his interrogations, he'd headed home without speaking to anybody else.

Brigid shook her head. "I have searches running, but without actual photographs of these women, it's unlikely we'll find anybody. If we could just narrow it down to one city . . ."

Angus tried to think. "What about the photographs supplied by Orchid?" Who was now at a safe house.

"I'm trying with facial rec and the names they used way

back when, but no luck. We don't even know if the women in the pictures are really the ones who are out in the world now," Brigid said.

Damn it. Angus wanted to punch something. How could they narrow it down? Prophet Isaac had been too smart to give details to anybody, which was probably why the guy was still alive. It really was up to Malcolm to get the information somehow. "All right." Angus surveyed the bloodshot eyes of his two team members. "It's after midnight. Why don't you two get some sleep? None of us are any good if we can't function."

Raider stood and pulled out Brigid's chair so she could do the same. "What time do you want us back tomorrow?" he asked.

Angus glanced at the clock. "Seven? That should give you time to rest and time for the searches to run for Brigid."

"What about you?" Brigid asked quietly. "Shouldn't you rest?"

A nagging feeling wouldn't leave the back of Angus's neck, so he wasn't moving. "I will. Just a few more minutes and I'll head out."

Raider gave him the fish-eye but didn't contradict him. "I'll bring coffee tomorrow. Good stuff without all the sprinkles."

The two exited the office.

Silence reigned for about two seconds before heels clipped in the bull pen and Nari moved into the office.

Everything in Angus lit up. "Why are you still here? I told you to get some rest."

"You're still here," she returned, eyeing the dog in the corner. "Where did he get the shoe?"

"It isn't yours?" Angus asked, turning his head slightly.

She reared up, looking . . . affronted? "That cheap leather? Of course not."

"Huh." Angus was tempted to ask the dog where he'd gotten the shoe, but often Roscoe just ignored him. He was getting loopy from exhaustion, damn it. "Maybe one of the guys brought it in for him." Who knew? "Why are you still here?"

She leaned against the doorframe, looking young and tired. "I was working through profiles and the possible targets. There are too many. If Isaac wants to punish people who don't agree with him, he has a multitude of targets. There has to be a way to narrow things down." Tension and fear rode her words.

Angus could relate. "Malcolm is the best at what he does. He'll get the facts."

"Speaking of being the best, I still don't have a personnel file on Brigid Banaghan," Nari said. "I find it odd you let somebody out of prison to work here."

Angus leaned back in his chair. "I'll get you her file and you'll understand."

Nari lifted an eyebrow. "How so?"

"She's been in minor trouble her whole life but got caught hacking into a secured government site to expose a senator she thought was sexually harassing staffers." Angus could understand her motive, but breaking the law did matter.

"She thought?" Nari asked.

"Yeah. Turns out the asshole was part of a kiddie porn ring. Brigid exposed him, but to do so, she had to reveal herself. She got caught and took a plea." Angus tapped his fingers on the desk.

"That wasn't fair," Nari burst out.

Maybe, maybe not. "The law is the law." Angus turned back to his recording to see what Isaac had been up to with Malcolm out of the room. "And here, I'm the boss. So get yourself some sleep, Nari. That's an order."

Her lips tightened, but she didn't argue. Her clip-clopping sounded irritated as she turned and strode away.

Soon, Angus was the only person left in the basement.

The hum of the lights kept him company as he rewound the recording and started listening again.

The second Isaac made contact with Pippa, Angus's heart nearly stopped. He listened for a while, and then somebody started a fire, effectively killing the bug. So much for listening in on Isaac again. But Angus had heard enough.

He quickly dialed Mal's number.

"I'm in the middle of something here," Mal snapped, his voice hushed.

"We have a problem," Angus said, adrenaline taking over. That was the understatement of the century.

Chapter Thirty-Four

Pippa parked her car in a turnout about a mile away from the address Isaac had given her. The road was deserted, and forest blanketed each side. She stepped out of the car and shivered. The rain had ebbed to a mist that instantly coated her face.

The persistent wind continued its hold on the spring weather, making the trees sway and throw pine needles against her legs.

Dark clouds covered the moon. Save for the lack of light, the night was eerily similar to the one when Pippa had fled the family.

Maybe fate did always bring life full circle.

Chances were slim she'd make it back to the vehicle, but she left the keys beneath the driver's seat, just in case. Then she hid her gun in her boot and covered both with her jean pant leg. A knife went into her other sock, while her burner phone went into her back pocket. There was no reason to leave it.

Zipping her jacket, she strode down the road, keeping to the tree line in case a car came out of nowhere.

An owl hooted above her, and in the distance, a coyote howled.

The sound sent chills down her back. Her hands were freezing, as was her blood. She had hoped never to see Isaac again. The memories he brought back made her feel like a helpless child. But the heavy gun in her boot said otherwise.

The only way out of this was to kill him.

It was early enough Thursday morning that it was still dark, so there was time to stop whatever he'd planned for the following day. If anything. Knowing Isaac, he might just be spewing bullshit.

Or not. He was fine with killing, as she knew well.

She walked about ten minutes until a wide stone archway showed an entrance to a long drive. Isaac had outdone himself with this one.

She took a deep breath, steeled her shoulders, and started under the archway.

Strong arms banded around her waist from behind, and a hand clapped over her mouth. Her body seized. It took a second for her brain to catch up with reality.

She tried to scream, and the large male hand muffled the sound. The man lifted her right off her feet and turned, forcing her past the archway in the opposite direction from her car. Panic burst through her, and she started to struggle, fighting against him with all her strength.

His stride didn't shorten.

His hold didn't relent.

She struck back with both hands, hitting his thighs uselessly. Her lungs hiccuped and the blood rushed through her head, roaring in her ears. He was too strong. Whoever he was, he was too powerful to fight. She'd have to wait until he set her down.

She went limp.

"That's better," he said, low in her ear. It took her a

second. It really did. The moment she recognized Malcolm's voice, she lost it all over again. Her teeth snapped at the flesh of his palm, and she kicked wildly, her right heel catching his knee. She hit back as hard as she could, wiggling like a fish on a line.

"Stop." His order was harsh enough, she almost obeyed.

Then she fought harder. Stronger and fiercer than ever before, she battled him.

To no avail. Not a bit. He carried her in perfect control, as if he'd kidnapped her a thousand times before.

They reached a van parked in the darkness of a stand of trees. Still holding her, he yanked open the passenger side door, flipped her around, and deposited her butt on the seat. In an incredibly fast movement, he drew zip ties from his back pocket and secured her wrists together.

"Found these in the supply closet," he said, almost conversationally.

She blinked. Her mouth dropped open, and she shut it quickly. The man she thought she'd loved, the one who'd broken her heart, stood in the darkness, his face all but hidden by shadow. Wait a minute. He'd released her. She opened her mouth to scream.

He planted his hand over her lips again. "I'll gag you." Leaning in, he got close enough that she could see the different colors of green in his eyes, despite the darkness. "I don't want to, but you make one peep and I'll shove a rag in that pretty mouth until we're out of earshot. Got me?" He kept his hand in place until she slowly nodded.

"Good." He secured her seat belt over her arms and then searched her, taking her gun, knife, and the phone. Then he quietly shut the door. In seconds, he stretched into the driver's seat and started the engine, driving the van onto the road toward town.

So many feelings bombarded Pippa that it was impossible to grasp a single thought. She tested the ties on her wrists.

Like everything Malcolm seemed to do, they were perfectly secured. "I hate you."

"Probably," he said pleasantly, the lights from the dash caressing the hard angles of his handsome face. "I'm not so happy with you right now either." He flicked on the windshield wipers as the rain increased in strength. "But I'm going to save you, so I suggest you help me out."

She hated that reasonable voice of his. The bossy, arrogant, deep voice he used. "Fuck you."

The look he gave her shot alarming tingles through her abdomen. It wasn't just fear either. Desire, a reaction she really didn't appreciate, pumped through her blood.

He turned back to the road. "I'd be more than amenable to that, blue eyes. But first, we have some talking to do. This drive will take two hours, and by the time we arrive at our destination, I need all the info you have. Believe me. You want to talk to me and not a guy named Wolfe."

Was he threatening her? Even after everything that had occurred, she felt, deep down, that Malcolm wouldn't hurt her.

Yeah, she was a complete moron.

"I don't think you'd hurt me." Might as well throw it out there.

"You're right. And while Wolfe might scare you just by being Wolfe, I wouldn't let him hurt you either." Mal glanced sideways, his expression implacable. "You're safe."

What the heck was she supposed to do with that? She looked down at her bound hands. "Doesn't feel like it."

"Fair enough. But if you were unbound, you'd jump out of the van, and then I'd have to chase you. One of us could trip or fall, and we can't have that." He turned up the defrost. "Plus, my temper is very close to blowing, and *you* don't want that."

How could he make a threat, a genuine threat, in such a reasonable tone of voice?

She had to get free. Trixie's life depended on it. "I'll make you a deal. Stop the van and I'll answer any question you want. Then you let me go."

The muscle visibly ticking at the base of his neck only added to his bad-boy sexy looks. "Baby, I ain't ever letting you go."

Malcolm wanted to suck those words back into his mouth, but they'd already hit air. Until that very second, he hadn't realized his full intentions. Sure, he planned to protect Pippa from both the government and the cult, but he wanted more than that.

He wanted *her*.

Force would tell him he was thinking with his dick, like a teenager. Was he? Maybe. Even so, it didn't change his feelings. More importantly, it didn't change the fact that the woman needed cover. If she was brainwashed, she'd require help. If not, if she was being hunted, she needed a shield.

He could be that.

But first, no matter how much of an asshole he needed to be, he'd get the truth from her. "Why were you walking to the mansion instead of driving your car?" he asked.

She kind of huffed and looked straight ahead.

All right. New question. "What does Isaac have planned for Friday?"

Her shoulders hunched. "I don't know."

"Don't lie to me, Pippa." Mal's hands tightened on the steering wheel. "I'll get the truth out of you. The sooner you believe that, the easier this is going to go."

She partially turned toward him. "If you have any feelings for me whatsoever, you'll let me go back to the mansion. Right now."

"I have feelings for you," he said quietly. "A shitload of them."

She shook her head, and that gorgeous mass flew around her shoulders. "Let me go."

"No." The sooner she realized she had to work with him, the better. "I have a feeling a lot of people are going to die tomorrow if we don't stop it. I can't believe you're okay with that." He held his breath and then exhaled. Was she brainwashed or not? "Are you?"

"No," she blurted out. "Never. I'd never want people to be hurt."

"So tell me everything you know about Isaac's plan," Mal pressed, speeding up as they reached pavement.

The sound she made was a cross between a sigh and a groan. "I don't know, Mal. Okay? Until about an hour ago, I hadn't talked to Isaac in seven years. Whatever he has planned is beyond me. If you'd just let me go back there, I'll find out for you."

Wasn't that kind of her? Mal dug deep for restraint. "I've spent a lot of time the last week or so with the family. Infiltrating the place." How much did she believe about Isaac? "There's something magical about the guy, I know. When he pressed his hands to my head for a minute, I swear I saw stars."

She snorted. "That's an old trick. Push on the optic nerves and people see flashes of light behind their eyelids."

Yeah. Mal's research had brought up the same facts. "What else?"

"Constant rhythmic music, common goals, group meditation, and drugs. If you were feeling anything mystical or godlike when you were there, you've been drugged." Her voice was brittle. Pained. "I did plenty of research when I ran away at seventeen."

A part of him hurt for the little girl she must've been. "Why did you run away?"

"Isaac and I were to be married on my eighteenth birthday," she said bitterly. "I ran away the day before."

Mal's body ached, but he had to ask. "Did Isaac abuse you?"

She looked down at her knees. "Yes and no. I told you the truth when I said he'd never touched me. But he made me watch him with other people. Often when he was hurting them."

Mal's stomach revolted. Isaac should be put down like a rabid animal. He blinked to clear the fury. "I'm sorry, Pippa." He had to stay calm now that he was finally getting her to talk. "Speaking of which, is that your real name?"

She swallowed, silent for several seconds.

He let her work it through in her mind. At the moment, she had no other option but to cooperate with him.

"It feels like my real name," she whispered. "My dad called me Pipsqueak, so when I could actually choose a name for myself, that's what I chose. I started out as Jennifer."

Her sweetness flayed him. "Pippa fits you better," he offered.

She just nodded and turned more fully toward him this time. "Isaac has Trixie."

"I know," Mal said.

She reared back. "You know? You know?" Her voice rose. "Then why are we driving away from the family?" She gasped in air. "You work with the police still, right? You're a detective?"

"I'm with the Homeland Defense Department these days," he said. "We're investigating the cult."

She leaned toward him. "Then you're one of the good guys. Let's go get Trixie."

Extricating Trixie was going to be difficult, and Pippa only added more uncertainty to the situation. "As soon as I get you to a safe place, I'll go back and find Trixie." Hopefully. It made sense that Isaac would keep her alive to use as leverage with Pippa. "The second you arrive on scene, Trixie is probably dead." And most likely with Pippa watching, if Isaac's history was anything to go by.

Pippa shook her head. "That's not right. We have to go back."

"No." He couldn't be any clearer with her.

"Fine." The sound of her seat belt unlatching reached him just as she jerked her door open.

He slammed on the brakes to decrease her chance of injury.

She jumped and rolled twice on the dirt shoulder of the road, stumbling to her feet and running for the forest.

He set the van in Park and dove over the console and out her door, hitting the ground hard and rolling much the same way she had. Rocks and dirt cut into his neck, but his jacket protected him over all. Rain smashed down on his face.

Leaping to his feet, he started in pursuit, his eyes adjusting to the darkness quickly.

She thrashed down a trail, her hands bound in front of her. Had she hurt herself when she'd jumped from the van? He should've secured her better.

He didn't have time to chase her right now. Exasperation upped his blood pressure. The trees hid the very meager light from the cloud-covered moon, and darkness swallowed them from every direction. She ducked right and then left, going out of sight.

He increased his speed, his boots crashing into downed branches. Damn, it was dark.

Then, silence.

He paused. Ducking his chin to his chest, he listened. Only the sound of rain on trees caught his ear. The smell of dirt and wet pine filled his nose. He chose his path carefully, trying to follow the trail, hunting.

She'd turned left last, so he followed the barely there path.

Tension stopped him, the fear of prey holding its breath. He looked around, trying to see through the darkness. If he was running, hands bound, where would he hide?

A large downed tree partially blocked the path. He went left and followed it several feet. His heart kicked against his rib cage. He caught sight of the zipper on her jacket a second before she tried to bolt.

Chapter Thirty-Five

Pippa swung her arms and nailed Malcolm in the balls. He doubled over with a pained groan.

She leaped over the tree trunk and ran again, hoping her feet found steady ground. The rain cut against her, and the wind whipped into her, but she wouldn't give up. If she could just get free, she could find her way back to save Trixie.

She rounded a tree and smashed into Mal's hard body. Where had he come from?

This time, he was ready for her. He caught her easily and swung her up, placing her gently over his shoulder. "Did you hurt yourself when you jumped?" he asked.

She didn't answer and instead started fighting him, kicking and punching. Memories of the last time they'd been in this position ran through her mind, and her entire body heated from head to toe. The memory of what they'd done in her kitchen would stay with her forever

She kicked and struck him, and this time he just manacled her legs against his chest before she could really hurt him.

Definitely no fun this time.

"I'm not gonna ask you again," he snapped, striding effortlessly around a tree. "Did you hurt yourself?"

Pippa struggled uselessly and punched at his kidneys. Then she paused at the memory, going stiff. But the smack to her ass didn't come.

"I'm not going to hit you, Pippa." He ducked under prickly branches. "The night in your kitchen was consensual. This ain't. I know the difference."

"Then put me down," she gasped, her wet hair falling to his thighs.

For answer, he flipped her around until he could cradle her against his rock-hard chest. "Is this better?"

"No." She tried to punch up to his chin, and he tightened his hold, immobilizing her. "Let me go."

"Can't." They reached the open door of the van, and he set her on the seat. Again. He leaned in, his gaze deadly serious. "Stop for a minute and think. You told me Isaac liked for you to watch him hurt people, right?"

She drew air into her nose. If she punched him in the throat, could she get free? "Yes."

"You've supposedly escaped him for nearly seven years, and he has your co-conspirator in his control. What exactly do you think he'll do to her the second you show up?" Mal's face showed no give. Not an ounce.

Pippa swallowed. That made a horrible sick sense. "What's my alternative?"

"Me," he burst out as he threw his hands wide. Exasperation lifted both of his eyebrows. "*I'm* your alternative. I can go freely into the mansion without immediate risk to either you or Trixie."

She coughed out a shocked chuckle. His exasperation shouldn't be funny. "But—but you lied to me." Could she trust him? Did she have a choice?

His eyes, so close to hers, softened. "You lied to me, too."

"Well yeah." Her shoulders slumped. Where did that leave them? "I don't know what to do," she whispered.

"I do." He set the seat belt around her again and shut the

door, returning to his seat immediately. "The good news, if you take it as such, is that you don't really have a choice in what you do right now. So stop worrying about it."

She frowned, irritation tightening her chest. "That was such an asshole statement. Just in case you were wondering."

He pulled the still-running van out into the road again. "I wasn't wondering."

Life had just gotten way too confusing. Pippa set her feet on the dash and looked in the back of the van for the first time. Her heart stopped. "Is that blood?" Red was sprayed across the van wall and had pooled on the wooden floor, where a dirt-covered shovel lay.

"Yes, and before you freak out, it's my blood. I cut my arm and spread it around."

"Why?" she breathed.

Mal glanced at her and then focused back on the road. "To get Isaac to trust me, I convinced him I killed and buried a cult member. She's in a safe house, by the way."

Pippa's senses overloaded. Pure and simple. She went silent, even inside her head, for a couple of moments. She wanted to be angry at Mal for lying to her, but he'd been right that she'd lied, too. "So you and me. It was all an undercover Op." The words ripped into her heart.

"No, it wasn't." His jaw was so tight it had to hurt.

Right. "It was a coincidence you bought and moved into the house next to mine." She let sarcasm fill her throat.

"No. That was by design," he admitted. "Not mine—I had nothing to do with that. But the HDD pretty much manipulated me into buying my house. They made it the only acceptable available home submitted to me by my real estate agent."

"Then you just decided to fall into their plan? By getting close to me? Gaining my trust? Sabotaging my car? Coincidences?" Her voice went shrill and she winced.

He drummed his fingers on the steering wheel. "No. Those were on purpose as well."

Hurt flashed through her, pricking just beneath her skin. "Angus Force, your boss, coming by for tea and biscuits?"

Mal actually winced that time. "Part of the Op. He's a profiler, and he wanted to get a read on you."

Her head snapped up. Even her nostrils felt hot all of a sudden. "What was his take?"

"That you had a crappy childhood and might be innocent. Or maybe brainwashed. He needed more time to make a real determination." Mal turned off the quiet road and headed toward town.

Well, at least she was finally getting the truth from Malcolm. One more question, and then she'd stop asking. This one was going to hurt, but she needed to hear him admit the truth. "Sleeping with me was part of the job, right? To get me to trust you."

He sighed, his powerful chest moving. "Sleeping with you was definitely not part of my job. Hell. My job would be eons easier if I hadn't slept with you. Everything I said to you, everything you felt . . . that was real."

The thrill that ran through her should be taken out, shaken, and shot. "If I could think of words I'd want you to say, exactly, you just said them," she murmured.

He straightened just a little. "Well, good."

"No. It just shows how good you are at your job," she muttered. He had known exactly what to say to her from day one, now hadn't he? "Are you a profiler, too?"

"I'm just a good undercover operative," he said quietly.

Obviously. "You're no doubt the best, Malcolm." Bitterness burned her tongue. At that point, she had no choice but to help him so he could help Trixie. "What do you want to know?" she asked, her body beyond exhausted. "I'll tell you anything."

"What's so special about tomorrow?" Mal asked.

Oh. The answer hurt deep inside her. "It's my twenty-fifth birthday. The day the cleansing fire is supposed to occur."

Malcolm went on full alert the second he pulled the van into the HDD parking lot.

Pippa looked around, her face scrunching up. "This is the HDD office?"

"No." He twisted the key free. "We're a satellite office. One that's not exactly run by the books."

She turned to partially face him. "You're the rebels of the HDD?"

"Or the mismatched toys," he muttered, taking out his knife and slicing her hands free. He grasped her wrists, making sure he hadn't bruised her. Nope. Not even a red mark.

She glanced down. "You're awfully good at binding women."

He coughed. "If you ever forgive me and give me another chance, maybe I'll show you just how good." Yeah, it was a little flirty, but he'd do anything to see her smile again.

She rolled her eyes. "One thing about hating your guts is that I won't have to put up with your lame attempts at being smooth any longer."

"Ouch." He stepped out of the van and walked around to her side. He might not be a profiler, but even he could tell she didn't hate him. Oh, she was pissed off and really wanted to punch him in the face, but she trusted him at least a little or she would've tried to run again.

He opened her door and helped her out.

She looked around the mostly vacant parking lot. "It's two in the morning. What happens now?"

He took her by the arm and led her to the building, heading inside and pressing the elevator button. "Now we tell Angus everything you told me." Not much of it was helpful or had anything to do with what Isaac was planning. But Pippa had been able to put into words some of Isaac's philosophies and favorite Bible passages. Most had to do with fire and righteousness.

The dog met them at the basement entrance.

"Roscoe," Pippa cried out, relief in her voice. She bent down to hug the pooch.

He yipped and licked her face, sniffing out her pockets.

She snuggled into him as if searching for any comfort she could find. "I don't have any biscuits right now." His fur muffled her voice.

Mal looked up and met Force's gaze. "Pippa? We should tell your good buddy Angus everything."

Pippa stiffened and then stood, raising her head as she caught sight of Force. "Angus, you're as big a dickhead as this asshole next to me." Her eyes flashed fire, and she put her hands on her hips. "The only redeeming quality you have, and I mean *the only*, is your dog."

Force's lower lip twitched. "Oddly enough, you aren't the first woman to say that to me."

Mal gestured toward the conference room. "We can chat in there."

"No." Force moved toward them just as Wolfe exited the small doorway to the interrogation rooms. "Ms. Smith is going to chat with Wolfe and me in one of the rooms. You can type up your report in the meantime, and we'll compare notes." Force looked at the scarred desks. "We should probably get some computers. All right. Find a notepad and write things up."

Mal moved in front of Pippa. "No."

She pushed him aside. "I don't need your protection." Even so, she craned her neck to look at Wolfe around Mal.

Mal partially turned. Wolfe wore his usual ripped clothing and leather jacket, his facial scruff almost a beard, his eyes carefully blank. He'd scare the shit out of anybody with half a brain. "She isn't going in there with you," Mal snapped, fighting the urge to grab Pippa and run.

Wolfe tucked his thumbs into his jeans. "Why not? Is she lying about something?"

"No," Pippa said, partially turning to face the ex-soldier. "This is all so stupid. None of you gets to be mad about me lying. You all lie for a living."

She had a point.

Wolfe grinned. "I don't lie. These guys do, and they're good at it, but I never lie."

Pippa studied him. "Fine. Do you plan on torturing me?"

"Nope," Wolfe said. He scratched his ear. "Which would be good for you if I never lie. But you don't know if I was lying when I said I never lie. If I was, then I lie, and I might be lying now."

Pippa cut Mal a look. "Is he nuts?"

Mal wasn't quite sure how to answer that. "The jury is out on that question."

Pippa cleared her throat. "Is that a kitten in his pocket?"

"Yep," Mal said, staring down Force.

She audibly swallowed. "I don't guess you'd torture somebody with a kitten in your pocket," she mused.

"I give the kitten to somebody to hold if I'm going to hurt anybody," Wolfe said reasonably.

"Is the kitten coming with us?" Pippa asked.

Wolfe shoved the door open behind himself. "Yep. His name is Kat. You can hold him if you want while we ask you some questions."

She frowned and looked up at Mal. "Are you guys sure you're with Homeland?"

At the moment, he wasn't sure about anything. Except he wasn't letting her out of his sight.

Force strode toward him. They were about eye to eye in height and close in weight. It'd be a hell of a fight if it came to it. "You know we need to corroborate anything she might've said to you. It's the only way to clear her."

Mal bit back a threat.

Pippa looked from one to the other. Then she moved toward Wolfe, holding out her hands.

Wolfe gingerly removed Kat from his pocket and handed the furball over to Pippa.

Mal's shoulders relaxed just enough to be rock hard. Wolfe wouldn't have given her the animal if he intended any harm. Probably.

"Trust me," Force muttered, stalking past him and following the other two through the doorway, which he closed none too gently.

Mal stood there with the German shepherd by the elevator. Had he just made a huge mistake?

"Hey, Malcolm." Brigid exited the control room and gestured for him to come that way.

He paused and then strode toward her, the dog at his side. "What?"

She smiled, her green eyes sparkling. "We have video in the interrogation rooms now. Angus figured you'd want to watch."

Mal's chest settled. Force couldn't let Pippa know he was going to watch. "Trust, huh?" Mal followed Brigid into the computer room and took one of the three chairs. Maybe it was time to trust his team.

Even with the woman he was prepared to die for.

Chapter Thirty-Six

Angus Force finished the fourth hour of what could only be considered a grueling interrogation. Oh, not grueling for the sweet Pippa Smith.

For him. Between Pippa's flip remarks, Wolfe's growing adoration of her, and the meowing kitten, Angus wanted to put his own head into the wall by the time he'd learned everything he possibly could about Pippa. The woman had taken great pains to explain how well Malcolm could bring a woman to orgasm, because she'd promised to tell everything.

Angus could've gone his entire life without knowing how skilled Mal's tongue was or how large his dick.

Several times, Angus had glared at the camera Pippa didn't know existed. He could almost hear Malcolm laughing his ass off. Well, until she got to the part about his ball sac.

The woman had also been adamant that she had to go back into the family. That Isaac would tell her the truth.

She was probably right. There had to be a plan that would keep her safe, though. And Angus was convinced that she had had no contact with the cult the last seven years. In addition, her clients, even the construction company, weren't involved with Isaac in any way.

Finally, Angus stood. "We're done. It has to be breakfast time by now."

"I could use a coffee," Wolfe gave Pippa a shy smile while gently assisting her up. Then he put Kat back in his pocket. "There's a coffee shop just a few miles down the road that puts salty caramel on top of everything. I could get you one."

Angus shook his head. It was hard to believe this was the same guy who'd put Eagle into the wall. Several times. But his instincts with people seemed to be spot-on. If Pippa Smith was a terrorist, Angus was an astronaut. And he hated heights.

He stomped out of the room, figuring the other two could follow or not. Malcolm was already waiting in the bull pen. "Well?" Angus snapped.

"Same story. Repeatedly," Malcolm said, not looking nearly as happy as he should, considering he'd been declared the world's greatest lover at least twice by Pippa during the interrogation. His irritation served to cheer Angus up, however.

"I figured." Angus had asked the same questions a myriad of different ways, and Pippa's answers had been consistent. "I told you to trust me."

Mal paused. "She wouldn't have gone in there with you if I didn't trust you."

Well, now. That was true. Angus gave a short nod. His team was coming together. Excellent. Then he noticed the googly eyes between Malcolm and Pippa. Oh, she looked pissed and he looked determined, but close enough. Angus needed to separate those two to get shit done.

"Pippa, please go through all the photos Orchid got for us, as well as anything and anybody you remember from your time with the family. If Isaac calls on the burner phone, answer and say you're driving as fast as you can and will reach him sometime *after* midnight tonight. Maybe more toward tomorrow morning."

Pippa rocked back on her heels. "You want me to show up on my birthday."

"You're not showing up at all," Malcolm said, his face set hard.

Angus rubbed his chin and tried to focus. "Isaac will think there's something prophetic about you arriving on your birthday." He held up his hand before Malcolm could object. "*Supposedly* arriving on her birthday." Right now wasn't the time to argue about it.

"Wh-what about Trixie?" Pippa asked, her eyes a wide blue.

"She's fine as long as you're not there," Angus said. "She's leverage and he knows it." The key was Pippa's birthday. Isaac wanted her there for his plan. Oh, he'd probably go through with the attack without her, but she was the prize. He wanted her there, and he wanted her to pay. Right now, the bastard had to be kept off balance, whether anybody here wanted it that way or not.

Mal shoved his hands in his pockets, no doubt to keep from reaching for Pippa. "I have to go back in. It's our only chance of figuring out the location of this attack. He already has people in place."

Angus nodded. "Yeah. I know." He needed to get a bead on Malcolm to make sure his head was still in the game. The guy's feelings for Pippa might get him killed. "You call Isaac and let him know you have a lead on both Eagle and Leroy, and that you'll be in touch as soon as you can." That would appease the cult leader temporarily.

His phone buzzed, and he read the text. "A buddy with the Boston PD has agreed to meet with us in DC. He's there on some other case, and he has the file on the two bodies found outside Boston. Raider and Mal, you're with me."

Mal started to object.

Angus held up a hand. "I need everyone concentrating. You can deal with any shit between you and Pippa later."

Mal glowered but held his tongue. This time.

Angus ignored him and stepped onto the rickety elevator, wincing when Raider and Mal followed, and the entire car dropped several inches. A plan was starting to form in his brain that Malcolm wasn't going to like. At all. It'd help to have Nari's take on both Pippa and Mal. As a shrink, she was the best. So long as she was shrinking other people's heads and not his.

The elevator doors closed.

Raider leaned against the wall and cleared his throat. "We could just take out Isaac and bring in his entire family."

Angus shook his head. "He has women in place somewhere and has for years. If we take him, they might have orders to go through with the attack, and we don't know who or where." For now, he'd talk to the Boston detective.

He hated having his hands tied like this.

Pippa kept the panic attacks at bay by concentrating.

It was okay to be around these people. They were in a basement, protected by walls. They were good people, Malcolm's friends.

And, oddly enough, they were careful not to crowd her. That alone let her relax a little bit.

After hours of trying, she had been able to identify two of the women in the pictures, but so far, Brigid had been unsuccessful in tracking them down in the real world. They surely had false identifications, and apparently, facial recognition software wasn't as miraculous in reality as it was on television.

Figured.

It had to be late afternoon. She sat in Mal's chair in the depressing middle desk area of the HDD, petting Roscoe, who had his head in her lap. Wolfe worked over papers on his adjacent desk, keeping a close eye on her, his kitten sleeping peacefully near the stapler he'd found in a drawer.

"Do you really think Angus can protect me from being prosecuted for killing Mark?" she asked. "My prints are definitely on the knife." If all else failed, Isaac would definitely set her up. She'd told both Mal and Isaac the whole story, and shockingly, it seemed they had believed her.

"Yeah," Wolfe said. "Nobody has your prints on file, I don't think. Besides, I understand why you were scared about it all these years, but it's the least of your worries right now."

Those words probably weren't as comforting as Wolfe thought. "I should really get into place at the commune," she murmured, eyeing the elevator door.

"You won't make it, so don't try." Wolfe didn't bother looking up from the maps he was studying of a parade path in Boston.

Her burner phone buzzed again.

She stiffened, her body turning cold. "Should I answer it?"

Nari Zhang strode out of her office on kitten-heel pumps. With her black slacks and pink shirt, she looked like a lawyer about to head to court. "We've ignored the last three calls. I think you should answer this one."

Pippa drew in a deep breath. "All right." Her hand shaking, she lifted the phone to her ear. "Hello."

"Mary, why haven't you answered your phone?" Isaac snapped.

Just hearing his voice again made her want to puke. "I've been driving in and out of service, Isaac. I'm getting there as fast as I can." She didn't have to try to sound exhausted. She was already there.

"How much longer?" He sounded like a spoiled child.

"I don't know." She let the panic she was truly feeling enter her voice. "It'll be really late tonight or even early tomorrow morning. I promise I'm coming." And she was.

Whether Mal liked it or not. Then she swore. "There's a cop behind me. I don't think I can talk on the phone and drive here. 'Bye." She clicked off, her breath starting to pant.

"Good job," Wolfe said.

"You guys know I have to be there, right? If there's any chance to figure out where the attack will take place, it's with me." She looked at both Wolfe and Nari, but neither answered.

The elevator door dinged, and everything inside her grew still.

Malcolm, Angus, and Raider exited, all looking as if they'd been through a cement mixer. They'd been meeting with the Boston cops about the dead bodies.

"Bad scene?" she asked, her gaze staying with Mal.

Mal nodded. "We identified Mark Brookes and a woman— a girl really—named Louise Stratford. She had a notebook with the name Tamarack on it."

Sharp knives slashed into Pippa's chest. "She was a nice girl who helped me escape. But she didn't want to leave." And Isaac had killed her for that? Tears filled Pippa's eyes.

"We'll get him," Mal said grimly. "I promise."

"How did she die?" Pippa asked, trying not to puke

"Strangulation," Raider said, looking beyond them toward the computer room. "I hope my charge didn't escape today."

Nari's narrow nostrils flared. "Brigid isn't going anywhere. She likes working here already."

"Humph." Raider nodded at Pippa and then continued to the computer room. "We'll see about that."

Angus paused in front of Pippa's desk. "I know it sucks, but we need to concentrate right now. We'll mourn the dead later. Did you identify anybody in the pictures?"

"Yes, but we can't find them. Or rather, we haven't found them yet," Pippa said, trying to concentrate but only seeing Mal.

Angus studied them both. "Pippa? Mal? I need you in case room two."

The look Mal gave Angus did something funny to Pippa's stomach.

Wolfe looked up and studied the group. He turned to Pippa. "Do you want to take Kat?"

"No kitten," Angus snapped, sounding like a guy who'd reached the end of any patience he might've had. Stress lines cut into the sides of his mouth, and his pupils had narrowed, as if his head was pounding.

Pippa swallowed. "Angus, are you all right?" She couldn't help but ask the question.

"None of us are right now," he said tersely. "Come on. Let's get this over with." He'd almost reached his office when he called for Raider.

The guy stepped out of the computer room and followed them into case room two.

Angus shut the door and waited for everyone to sit. "Pippa. You've been living with this all day. Give me something."

She settled her body and tried to think. "Well, Isaac likes hurting women. He'll like the idea of using women to make the attack, especially if it's a suicide attack. And he'd love using women to hurt other women."

Angus nodded. "Okay. We'll do an analysis of that idea. For now, Raider is the strategic expert of the group, I'm the profiler, Mal is the operative, and Pippa is the wild card."

She blinked, sitting next to Mal. The heat from his body washed over her. She was the wild card?

"No," Mal said, pushing back his chair. "Absolutely not."

Pippa cringed at the venom in his voice. What was going on?

"Raider?" Angus asked.

Raider gave Mal a sympathetic look before standing and leaning against the wall. "Strategy-wise, the only way we're going to get a location is from Isaac. You both need to be on the inside."

"I'll go," Mal said. "It's too much of a risk for Pippa."

"She's the one thing that puts Isaac off-balance," Angus said. "She's the key, Mal. At the moment, you're more likely to be shot when you show up after failing to secure Eagle and Leroy. He won't kill Pippa, at least not at the home."

Pippa stilled. "What do you mean?" The guy spoke as if he knew what he was talking about.

Angus met her gaze directly, his eyes a slightly darker green than Malcolm's. "He wanted you pure and chaste for your wedding at eighteen. You've been gone for seven years, and chances are, he'll think you've betrayed him."

"So he'll kill me?" she breathed. Yeah. She actually hadn't considered that. For years, Isaac had treated her as if she really were set apart, even though he'd tortured her emotionally.

Angus lifted one muscled shoulder. "Could go either way. He's punishing the world with fire, and he might think you need punishment to be cleansed as well. Or he might see the others dying for your perceived sins the same way the Bible says Jesus died for our sins."

"Either way, you're not going," Malcolm said, crossing his arms.

She thought about the situation, her mother, and Trixie. About the brainwashed women about to not only kill themselves but potentially many other innocent people. "I don't have a choice, Malcolm." Her choices had been taken from her the second her mother had joined the family with Pippa in tow.

It was time to take those choices back.

Chapter Thirty-Seven

Malcolm drove the van past the city center of Cottage Grove with Pippa sleeping quietly in the passenger seat. It was an incredibly bad idea to let her go back into the family mansion. She'd been adamant.

Did he have a right to stop her? He understood her need to try to protect her friend and her mother. But what if she was killed in the process? If he stopped her from going, even though she'd probably hate him forever, at least she'd be alive to do so.

"Stop thinking so hard," she mumbled, sitting up in the seat.

"Can't help it." The clock on the dash showed it to be ten at night. Almost her birthday. Coordinating the Op for the next day had taken several more hours than he would've expected. Raider was a stickler for every detail. "I don't like this. Any of this," Mal muttered.

"Neither do I." She pushed unruly hair away from her face. "A part of me wishes we could just jump on a plane and go somewhere warm. Live on a beach and eat coconuts."

"Say the word and I'll make it happen. Right now."

She chuckled. "You can't turn away from this mess any more than I can."

No, but he could send her ahead to a beach and meet her when this was done. "You're clear on the plan?" He wanted to go over it one more time, just in case.

"We're both clear. Thank you for taking me back to my home one more time." Her voice was wistful. "I've been happy there. Mostly."

"You'll be back there tomorrow night," he said, hoping to God it was the truth.

She didn't reply.

"Pippa—" he started.

"No." She held up a hand. "We've hashed it out repeatedly, and the plan is in place. No more arguing, no more strategizing. We're there, Malcolm. On Op, as you would say."

He should never have agreed back at HDD, but yeah, the plan was in place. Angus had even arranged for somebody from the HDD to fetch Pippa's car and bring it back to her driveway.

Mal turned into his driveway and pressed the garage door button he'd taken from his truck. "We're not on Op for two hours. So we should probably talk."

She blinked. "Um, okay." Confusion blanketed her delicate features. "About what?"

"Us," he blurted out, his voice rough. There was a good chance one of them wasn't coming back from this. Every instinct he had bellowed for him to pull the van back out and drive away. Far away.

"Oh." She opened her door. "Well, okay. I have some cookies left over. Why don't you come over and we'll have dessert and um, talk?" They'd eaten pizza several hours before at the office.

He nodded. "Give me about fifteen minutes to clean out the back of the van and I'll be over after a quick shower." He only needed to ditch the shovel and wipe up the blood so it couldn't be seen. It didn't have to be a thorough cleaning job, just enough to please Isaac if he looked inside. The work would give him a chance to think about what to say to Pippa.

The words weren't coming easily.

Not with the threat of death hanging over their heads.

But this might be his last chance. He was taking it.

Chapter Thirty-Eight

Pippa walked through her beloved cottage, her heart aching. There was a chance she'd make it back home, but not a very good one. Even though she'd been alone for much of her time here, she'd been happy. Then even more so when she'd met Malcolm.

She took a fast shower and paused after brushing out her wet hair. Should she dress for her Op or for Malcolm? They had a couple more hours together, and even if things remained jumbled emotionally, she didn't want to miss the chance for another good memory. She slid pink lip gloss over her mouth.

Her heart thundering, she fetched a bright blue teddy set that showed off her eyes and then put it on. There was something empowering about making the first move. The silk top came to her midriff, and the matching panties were a thong. Slightly uncomfortable but definitely sexy.

She'd bought it on a whim and hadn't thought she'd ever actually wear it. The matching robe was in her closet, and she had to remove the price tag before sliding into it and securely tying the belt.

Should she put on high heels? Her one pair was black and shiny, so they'd kind of match.

His knock on the door stopped her musings. Heat burst into her face. What was she thinking? "Um, come in," she called, her feet frozen on her bedroom floor. Her bare feet.

The sound of the door opening came first, his footsteps second. "Pippa? Where are my cookies?"

She blanched. There was a good one-liner in there somewhere, but her mind was blank. Drawing on courage she hadn't realized she'd need, she strode into the doorway. "Why? Are you hungry?" she asked. Good line. Yeah, that was a good line. She'd nailed it.

He stopped near the colorful sofa, his chin dropping. His eyes flared a hot green as he looked his fill. Then he shook his head like a dog needing to sneeze. His still-damp hair curled around his collar. "Wow."

Her breath released. Okay. He hadn't rejected her outright. Her fingers fumbled, but she released the tie and let the barely there robe fall open.

The sound he made would stay with her for the rest of her life. Male and hungry. For her.

But he didn't move.

So she did. The guy had pulled her like a magnet from day one, and tonight was no different. Reaching him, she slid her hands over the hard planes of his chest and looked way up into his rugged face. "We have two hours, Malcolm. How do you want to spend them?"

His lip twisted. "I had planned on talking you out of the Op."

"No deal. What's plan B?" Her hands slid down his chest and over his ripped abdomen, pulling his shirt free of his jeans.

He swallowed audibly. His gaze darkening, he reached for her right shoulder and gently pushed the robe away. The silky material fell down to her elbow. He breathed out, the sound tortured. His gaze ran across her chest, and her nipples pebbled as if he'd used his hands. Heat poured from

him, overwhelming her as he pushed the other side of the
robe down.

The robe caught on her elbows, and she shrugged her
shoulders to free the material to fall to her feet, leaving her
in a teddy and thong.

His intense gaze traveled from her face down to her toes
before coming back up. "You're beautiful, Pippa."

He made her feel powerful. Very. "So are you." She reached
for the hem of his shirt and lifted it over his head. He had to
duck to let her, his movements slow and deliberate, as if he
was struggling to hold himself back.

She liked that. A lot. Then his bare and battle-scarred
chest stole her attention. So much strength and power there.

"We should probably talk," he murmured, settling his
palms on her upper chest, above her breasts. He watched as
his hands smoothed over her arms and caressed her wrists
and back up. He snagged one thin strap above her shoulder
and tugged it down her arm. Then he did the same with the
other side, baring her breasts. Cool air kissed her skin.

"Talk? Yeah," she whispered. Instinctively, she started to
cover her nudity, but the look in his eyes stopped her. Lust
and something softer. Need? Adoration? Pleasure. Yeah. It
was pleasure.

How she could feel both vulnerable and powerful in the
same second was beyond her. But she did. Because of Malcolm West.

He palmed her breasts, lightly rolling her nipples. Electricity zapped right to her core, which swelled against the
tight silk with a pulsing need. She moaned and reached for
his belt buckle, releasing it and pulling his belt free.

They'd had sex several times, but a new intimacy cocooned
them. She released his zipper.

That sound seemed to spur him on. He moved in, tangling
her hair in his fist and twisting. Her head went back and to
the side. Then, finally, he took her mouth.

Warm and firm and deep, he kissed her. Taking his time, sweeping his tongue in her mouth, tasting of mint and male. His scent surrounded her, his mouth took her, and his heat swelled across her, head to toe.

Every inch of her was somehow touched by him. And they were still partially clothed.

Both hands went to cup her face, and he tugged her up on her tiptoes while releasing her mouth. His determined gaze kept her as captive as the hold on her head. "I . . ." Frustration crossed his face as he obviously struggled for the right words.

"I love you," she blurted out. Geez. Talk about smooth. She winced. "I know it's really fast and we've only known each other through lies, but now we know the truth, and feelings are feelings even if they don't make any sense." Shut up. She had to stop her mouth right here and now. Nothing could interfere with the excellent sex she was about to have. It might be her last time ever.

"I love you, too," he murmured, his gaze hot. "I worry that I'm taking advantage because you've been on the run so long, but you have my heart."

The words slid into her and settled, warming everything she'd ever be. She leaned up to kiss him, but his strong hold prevented her. "Malcolm?"

"Tell me you're mine." His hold tightened on her face. "Right now. Say it."

Her mouth partially opened, but she held the words back. The raw emotion glittering in his eyes gave her pause. Those words meant something to him. Something big. Realization dawned on her, and she pressed her lips together. He wanted license to keep her away from the cult. To protect her whether she wanted it or not. "I'll give you whatever words you want . . . on Saturday," she whispered.

The sound that rumbled up from his chest could only be called a growl.

She tried to shake her head but couldn't move. "I have to do this, Malcolm." Not only for her friend and her mother, but for herself. She couldn't live with the regret if she didn't try to stop Isaac.

The anger in Mal's eyes was almost her undoing.

Then he kissed her again, releasing her face to grasp her hips and lift her off the ground. She grabbed his shoulders to keep from falling and then wrapped her legs around his waist.

The kiss was feral and deep, pouring into her with anger, need, hunger, and a desperate promise. He started to move and soon set her gently on her feet in her bedroom. "Then I'm enjoying myself tonight," he murmured, starting to walk around her. "Stay put."

A smile tickled her lips as she obeyed. As he moved, he ran a finger along her collar bone, over her shoulder, and then across her upper back. "Mal—"

"Shhh." He stayed behind her and traced a line down her spine to her buttocks and then back up. The cami was still pooled at her waist, and he gently slid it down, leaving her only in the bright blue thong. "This is nice." He caressed one bare buttock. "If I remember right, these turn an enticing shade of pink." He squeezed.

She gasped, and heat flowed right from his hand through her abdomen and between her legs. She remembered just as well that he hadn't exactly held back last time. The thought alternatively thrilled and warned her.

He traced his hands over her thighs and down her legs to her ankles and then back up. "Are you wet for me, Pippa?"

She could only give a short nod. Words were trapped in her throat; her body was wide awake and busy shutting down her brain.

"I asked you a question." He tapped her ass, none too gently.

She jumped. Nerves flared to wild life, and her breasts ached heavy and ready for him. "Yes," she whispered.

He stepped into her, his chest to her back, his mouth leaning down, his breath hot on her ear. "Yes, what?" Those words, low and dangerous, licked through her somehow. Even now, even here, there was an edge to Malcolm West that called to a primal part of her she hadn't known existed.

"Yes, I'm wet. For you," she added before he could ask. "Though you could check, if you want." She couldn't help throwing down the challenge.

"That's kind of you." He slipped a finger under the back of the thong and traced its path, spreading her butt cheeks slightly.

She stiffened.

His chuckle in her ear threw tingles down her entire body. "You're not ready for that. Yet."

She shivered, caught in his spell.

He continued, between her legs, and brushed across her labia.

Her knees trembled, and she almost fell.

"You're right. Wet." He slid his hand free and wrapped an arm around her waist, pulling her back into an obvious erection. "Very." Then he pushed his hand inside the front of her panties, two fingers working her clit.

Pleasure burst across her sex, and she lost her balance.

He held her upright with one arm, his strength stealing what was left of her breath. "I don't have a lot of time, so let's get you primed now." He pinched, and an orgasm exploded through her, making her whimper and press back against him.

Her body rioted as he flipped her around and tore off the panties. A second later, his jeans hit the floor, and he rolled a condom over his straining and impossibly engorged penis.

She reached for him and quickly found herself flat on her back.

He covered her, and she reached for him again, pulling

him down. "Now, Malcolm," she ordered, needing him inside her more than she needed her next breath.

He kissed her again, going deep, and shoved himself inside her with one hard push.

Finally.

Mal paused, balls deep in so much heat he could barely breathe. He wanted to be gentle, but his body was fighting him. Every instinct he owned bellowed for him to make Pippa his. She already lived in his heart. If this was love, it sure as shit wasn't the smooth, happy, dance-in-the-tulips feeling he'd always figured it would be.

He'd also never figured to find it.

But here she was. Beneath him, holding him tight, trusting him to keep her safe. The fact that she wouldn't actually let him do that made the beast inside him want to break its chains. The civilized beast he'd had to create to survive in this world.

That part of him wanted to claim her forever.

She scratched her nails down his arm, avoiding the bandage over the cut he'd given himself. Then she arched against him, tracing his chest and digging those nails in.

The sharp bite propelled him to move. He slid out of her warm body and back in. Her internal walls clamped down on him, gripping every nerve he had and threatening to steal the small amount of control he'd been able to retain.

He'd try to manipulate her right now, but if she tried the same, she'd definitely win. The woman owned him, body, heart, and soul.

The idea of her being harmed cut through him, and he powered back inside her, going as deep as possible. She moaned and spurred him on, her legs widening to give him more room.

He planted one hand on the mattress by her shoulder for leverage.

She looked up at him, those sapphire eyes full of trust . . . and need. Her dark hair was sprayed across the pillow, soft and silky.

He'd never had a family. Even with his grandfather, that hadn't been family. In fact, he'd never had anyone who was his. Truly his. Until now.

He tangled his free hand in her soft hair, brushing his knuckles across her face. Her bones were so delicate.

Breakable, vulnerable, and fragile.

His.

Desire coiled harsh and tight inside him, bringing out a possessiveness in him that was nearly feral. He drew back and then pushed in again, going harder and faster.

She shuddered around him, her gaze wide and direct. *Beautiful.* The word didn't come close to describing her. He wanted to lose himself in her gaze as much as he was losing himself in her tight body.

Her gasps as he powered into her increased his speed. Relentless pleasure threatened to shred him, but he couldn't stop. Close. He was so damn close. So he tilted his hips, brushing across her clit, and then ground against her.

She dug her nails into his chest and convulsed around him, her eyelids closing and a flush washing across her delicate features. Her interior walls clamped down on him.

He let himself go completely, hammering hard and deep into her, his breathing rough. The pleasure threatened to blind him, so he shut his eyes and let it take him over. His orgasm was stronger than a round of bullets, and he finally paused, barely keeping himself from falling on top of her.

She panted against him as he rolled to the side.

The alarm buzzed on his phone. That quickly, he went from warm and cozy to stone cold.

It was time.

Chapter Thirty-Nine

It took Malcolm about two hours to drive the van to the mansion. He stopped a mile down the road and called Angus. "I'm a mile out," he said without preamble.

"Good. I have forces preparing to infiltrate the mansion, but we don't want to bring attention to ourselves by driving through that small town to get there. The second you give the order, it'll take about fifteen minutes to raid the compound," Force said. "Call it in the moment you have a location of the attack, or if you've been compromised."

"Force—"

"Nope. Not discussing it any longer," Force said. "We're on Op, Agent."

Mal's neck ached. Agent. Not detective. Did it matter? The feeling was the same. Pride mingled with anxiety. "Angus, listen to me. If Isaac tries to put a bullet in me the second I get there, if he's successful, you have to cancel the Op. Give me your word you won't send her in if I'm not there to protect her."

Silence ticked over the line. "All right. I give you my word."

The weight lifted very slightly off Mal's chest. "Thank you. It's a bad idea anyway."

Force sighed. "I've read your file. Did you ever confront

your jerk of a grandfather about beating the shit out of you as a kid?"

Memories flashed back, bright and sharp. Blood and anger and a hell of a lot of pain. "I beat him in a fight when I was sixteen and never looked back."

"She needs that, too," Force said. "Pippa needs to face Isaac if she's ever going to be able to stop running and have a normal life."

Mal really didn't like that logic, although he understood Force's reasoning. "Don't let her head here too early. I want her to arrive during the daylight, so Isaac doesn't get any ideas of a last night together before he does whatever he's going to do."

"Agreed," Force said. "Try to call in with a status if you find Trixie. I'd like for her to be alive."

"Me too." Mal checked his watch. It was about three in the morning. "I have to go. Hey, Force? Thanks for looking me up."

"Thanks for saying yes. See you on the other side." Force ended the call.

Mal pulled back onto the road and before long was aiming down the driveway for the mansion. It was odd that the place didn't have any guards on duty. Isaac truly didn't fear the authorities. Either he believed he was covered by God, or he figured his people were all there willingly and were nicely brainwashed.

Or both.

Mal parked the van and stepped out. Several vehicles were parked in front of the house, no doubt ready to take family members wherever the attack would take place. They were close enough to drive to several cities within the day. For once, the clouds had cleared, leaving the moon high and bright. It shone down on the deserted front lawn. Even the wind was silent finally. Shaking off the willies, he stalked up the stairs and entered the quiet mansion.

George was waiting by himself in the dim light, on a settee inside the foyer. He looked behind Mal. "Where are Leroy and Eagle?"

"Couldn't get them," Mal said, sounding just as weary as he felt. "In fact, we have a huge-assed problem. Where's Prophet?"

George sat back down. "He said if you were the one to get here first to send you up to his room. It's on the second floor, farthest from the left. Wake him up if he's asleep."

Mal's blood started to hum. "Who else is coming tonight?"

George shook his head. "The chosen one, man. You'll meet her."

Mal was already wearing her scent all over his body. He looked George over and didn't see any weapons. "All right. You sure you don't want to go wake the Prophet up?"

"Nope. Orders are orders." George settled back down.

Wonderful. Mal's gun was heavy in his boot, as was the knife in his other boot. If he had to take off his shoes, he was screwed. He memorized the layout as he jogged up the stairs and took a sharp left, knocking on the farthest door.

Nothing.

He knocked harder.

Bedclothes rustled. "Enter," Isaac said.

Mal walked inside just as Isaac flipped on the bedside table lamp. He lay in a monstrous bed with two obviously naked women. One of them was Pippa's mother.

Isaac's eyes narrowed. Was that disappointment? Oh. The sick bastard had wanted Pippa to see her mother with him.

Mal stiffened. Deep inside him, in a place he rarely visited, he grew very still. "We have a problem."

The other woman rolled over, and his gut clenched when he saw it was April. Bruises marred her neck and chest, and her vibrant eyes were downcast. God, he was going to kill Isaac. Mal turned away. "See you downstairs." Without waiting for a response, he turned on his heel and jogged down the stairs to the office before he could rip Isaac apart piece by piece.

The leader joined him in about fifteen minutes wearing pressed white linen pants and a matching loose shirt. "I wasn't sure if I'd see you again."

Mal turned and crossed his arms. "Why not?"

"You kind of disappeared." Isaac moved to the bar and poured two tumblers. "I thought maybe what you did to Orchid sent you over the edge or something."

"I told you I'd track down your men. I did." Mal accepted the offered drink.

Isaac cocked his head to the side, his eyes alert even though he'd just been awakened. "Yet they are not here with you."

"No. They aren't." Mal swirled the liquid in the glass. "I tracked them through the Minuteville cops to DC, where I spent the entire day and most of the night calling in every favor I have with pretty much anybody I could connect with."

"And . . . ?" Isaac took a deep drink, his attention absolute.

Malcolm didn't have to pretend to be angry. The emotion boiled just beneath the surface of his control, threatening to detonate. But he was damn good at using genuine emotions while remaining in character. "The good old FBI has them. To be more specific, the Counterterrorism unit of the FBI has your two family members."

Isaac stopped moving. Completely. He might have stopped breathing. "Why?"

"Well now." Mal forced sarcasm into his tone. "Surprisingly enough, they wouldn't tell an ex-detective from New York. I exhausted every friendship I might've had just finding those two guys."

"Fuck." Isaac strode to one of the two chairs flanking the fireplace and sat.

It was the first time Mal had heard the Prophet swear. Interesting. "Listen. I realize you don't know me all that well, but what is going on?" He moved around the free chair and sat. "I can't help if you don't tell me, and I've proven to you that I can be trusted."

Isaac leaned over, lit a long match, and set fire to the paper and logs already in place. "Do you believe in justice, Malcolm?"

Hopefully, the bug Mal had planted was buried in soot in the corner. "Sometimes," he answered.

"What about sins? Can they be cleansed?" Isaac sat back, his gaze on the flames.

"Cleansed?" Mal tried to listen for any other noises in the house, but it was silent at this early morning hour. "Not really. Punished, sure." He shrugged. "But I ain't the expert on the Bible you seem to be."

Isaac partially turned to study Mal. "You're not a believer. In the Good Book or in me."

Mal exhaled as if thinking it over. "Man, I don't know. You have a nice place here, and the folks are kind. And you can get two women to sleep with you at once, so you must be doing something right."

Isaac chuckled. "Yet you haven't availed yourself of April or anybody else."

"When?" Mal kicked back in the chair, his head jerking. "It's not like I've had time to avail myself." He shook his head. "I've been tying up loose ends in not only my life but yours." Which was the absolute truth.

Somebody knocked on the door.

"Enter," Isaac said.

George strode inside and walked toward the chairs facing the fireplace, his gaze down. "The first of the chosen has arrived." He stopped behind the chairs.

"Ah, good." Isaac leaned forward and patted Mal on the knee. "It's going to start soon. And by the way, Malcolm?"

He waited for Mal to lift an eyebrow. "We've been drugging Orchid periodically during meditation time, questioning her afterward, and we knew she'd talked to the police. The woman didn't remember being drugged, and she certainly didn't remember telling us about the cops. Then you showed up. Even so, I'd hoped you were legitimate. That you could be family. Yesterday we found the bug you planted."

Something steel hard and hammerlike came down on Mal's head before he could move. Lights exploded behind his eyes, and he crashed immediately into darkness. His very last thought, if it could be considered such, was of Pippa.

Isaac turned to see George looking at the bloody hammer in his hand. "Search him."

George shook himself and set the weapon on the table before turning around and bending down. He found a gun, a knife, and a phone.

Isaac took the phone and scrolled through. No contacts, calls, pictures, or apps. Mal had apparently wiped the device before entering the home. Smart. "Is he dead?" Isaac frowned and peered down at the very still ex-cop bleeding all over his floor. He wanted some time with the betrayer before he went to hell.

George felt for a pulse. "No, but he isn't going to move for a while."

"Good. Take him to the basement," Isaac ordered, moving to his desk and the battle plans hidden beneath the calendar.

George hesitated. "He's a cop, and he must've taken Leroy and Eagle. We have to get out of here. They'll know about our plans."

Isaac lifted an eyebrow. "What are the plans?"

George faltered, his eyes remaining down. "I, um, don't know. Just that today is a big day. An important day."

Exactly. Nobody knew the plans. Which was why Malcolm had come back to the family. Obviously, the government feared Isaac had plans, but they had no clue what they were, and Mal was to find out more. By the time they discovered the truth, it would be too late.

Nobody, not even George, knew of the new home for the family. Isaac had been quietly sending people away for the last month, and he'd sent the remainder of his family the day before. He would meet up with them the second the cleansing was in motion.

Only those who were no longer useful to him would remain here, where no doubt the government would raid soon. Once the fire started. Those left behind knew nothing. Not one thing.

Oh, hellfire would consume sinners today. He'd known for years that Mary's twenty-fifth birthday would be the day God called him to do his duty, and he'd been planning just as long. There had been a chance—not a good one, but a chance nonetheless—that humanity would turn to good. Would be righteous.

It hadn't happened.

"I'll be right back," George said, his voice shaking. "I'll need help carrying him."

The cop was a big guy; that was for sure. Isaac stood and crossed over to stare down at the sinner who'd dared to infiltrate the family. Anger rushed through him, sharp in its intensity. He kicked Malcolm in the ribs. Once, and then again. The sound of one breaking calmed him. That was nice.

When he'd discovered the bug, Isaac had been so furious he'd nearly ripped the skin off April's nubile body. It had been her job to get close to the cop, and she'd failed.

But in the end, he hadn't been able to kill her. It had been much more satisfying to teach her a lesson she'd never forget, one she'd screamed through. A woman's screams could be so cleansing, truly. Then he'd decided to use her for the higher purpose of today. She was fortunate he was so forgiving.

God had taught him that.

George returned with an older man named Hector who had lost his usefulness and started questioning Isaac months before. They hefted Malcolm off the floor, both groaning with the effort.

Hector cleared his throat right before leaving. "Two more of the chosen have arrived."

"Good. Keep them in the kitchen until I call for them." Isaac glanced at George. "It's a good thing Leroy finished with the preparations before being foolish enough to get caught." Of course, that was probably Malcolm's fault, really.

George nodded, his face pale.

Isaac lost interest and sat down to review his map. The locations he'd chosen were prime for destruction. He'd been planning this for so long, it was hard to imagine today was the day. God had tested him, and he'd risen to the occasion.

He double-checked the plan from every angle for hours.

Finally, a knock sounded on the door again. He looked up. "Yes?"

George opened the door. "She is here, Prophet. Mary has arrived."

Finally.

Chapter Forty

An invisible iron band constricted Pippa's chest. This mansion was new to her, but it smelled the same as the old one. Meditation oils, cleansers, and an unidentifiable scent of hopeful fear. She let the man lead her down a long hall-way lined with expensive oil paintings. He must've joined in the last decade; she didn't recognize him.

He opened the door, and she walked inside a sprawling home office complete with a crackling fireplace.

"Mary." Isaac sat behind a gleaming mahogany desk with maps spread across it. He leaned back and studied her.

The door closed behind her. Even though it hurt to breathe, she studied him right back. The decade had been good to him. Now in his early forties, he still had thick, light brown hair, and his eyes were the same gleaming amber she remembered. He wore a neatly trimmed mustache and goatee, which made him look younger than his years. Not a strand of gray showed. Did he dye it? Or was he just genetically blessed?

The charisma she remembered poured from him, but it was tinged with evil. That might just be her interpretation. "Where's Trixie?" Pippa asked without preamble.

He didn't react. Not one facial tic showed he'd even heard her. "You are dressed improperly for the family."

She glanced down at her multicolored skirt and bright blue top. Colorful bangles jangled at her wrist, and her boots were a red brown that gleamed in the soft light of morning falling through the wide windows. She tilted her head to the side and looked at him. "Did anyone ever tell you that linen makes a guy look like a wimp?"

He abruptly stood.

She took a step back before she could stop herself. Feelings rushed into her with a force that weakened her knees. Helplessness and fear. For a moment, she returned to being that terrified and confused kid facing a grown-up she'd been groomed to trust.

Trust, her ass.

Wearing the skirt instead of jeans had been difficult, but it allowed her to hide the gun nestled between her thighs. It was attached to her right leg, and she needed to tug the holder around so it wasn't so uncomfortable. But it had escaped the quick search from the guy at the door because nobody would have the courage to touch her there. Not Mary.

She tried to steel her shoulders, but fear made her muscles feel like mush. "I'm here, as demanded. What do you want from me, Isaac?"

He strode around the desk and moved toward her like a graceful cat. "You've grown more beautiful through the years." Reaching out, he brushed a strand of hair away from her face.

Her stomach revolted, and she tried to think clearly. She stood five-foot-four in her boots, and he only had about five inches on her now. She'd remembered him being taller. Bigger. Malcolm was at least seven inches taller than Isaac.

That thought, more than any other, calmed her. He was here somewhere. And outside the gates, she had backup waiting. She had more than that. She had Malcolm. "Touch me again and I'll rip your arm off."

Isaac instantly grabbed her by the neck and yanked her forward. She lifted her right arm to stop him, and he slapped it down. Her eyes bugged out, and adrenaline poured down her body, beneath her skin, with nearly painful pricks.

"You will remember how to behave in my house," he said, his nostrils flaring.

Her vision narrowed from the edges. She didn't know how to do this. She wanted to fight him, to hurt him. To kick him in the balls and prove he didn't frighten her. But she had a mission. She had to find out the truth about the attack. How had Malcolm been undercover for so long? She tried to swallow, but Isaac's hold made it difficult. "I'm sorry," she croaked.

His hold relaxed slightly. "That is better." He caressed her neck, ending at her heart. "It's prophetic that you should return today of all days."

"That was your intent, wasn't it?" She swallowed easily this time, her entire body needing to step away from him.

He sighed. "I had hoped Trixie, as she's been calling herself recently, would help us find you."

Yet she hadn't.

"All we could get from her was your phone number." Isaac smiled, showing perfectly white teeth. "And here you are."

"Where is she?" Pippa asked. "I'd like to see her."

"You will." Isaac finally removed his hand and turned to look at a clock on the mantel. "We shall prepare in about an hour."

Pippa followed his gaze, her heart lurching at the sight of the pictures of her next to the clock. The guy was seriously nuts. Then something caught her eye. Blood had pooled on the floor by the fireplace. "Who did you hurt?" she whispered.

He shrugged. "Nobody important. Why? Did you want to watch me cleanse somebody? I think your mother is available."

"Is she really sick?" Pippa asked, the fresh adrenaline rush giving her a headache.

"So, you did see our website." Isaac's lips turned down in a way that used to make Pippa want to run away. "How pathetic you wouldn't make contact for your ill mother."

"She made her choice," Pippa said, the guilt still feeling like hot pokers in her chest. "What's the truth?"

Isaac tilted his head. "George? Send Angel in."

Pippa gasped and partially turned as the door opened and her mother walked in. She was pale and wan. "Mom." Her feet were frozen in place.

"Mary." Angel rushed forward and drew her up in a hug.

Tears threatened Pippa's eyes, and she returned the hug, losing herself in her mother's still-familiar scent for a moment. Then she released her. "How are you?"

"Well. So glad you're back home." Tears of real joy filled her mom's eyes. "I knew you'd come home to us. I just knew you'd find the right path."

Disappointment crashed into Pippa so quickly she swayed. Her mother hadn't changed. Even after all this time, she was blindly following Isaac. For the first time, pity replaced the anger in Pippa's breast. "Are you healthy?"

Her mom shook her head. "No, but I will be. The Prophet protects us all." Gray liberally streaked her blond hair now, and fine lines extended from her eyes. The light-colored linen clothing washed out her coloring, but she was still beautiful. Her sparkling eyes met Isaac's over Pippa's head. "Thank you for bringing my daughter home."

Isaac slid an arm around Pippa's shoulders and pulled her into the side of his body, facing Angel. "Mary is my one true love. Of course she'd be here for this. For the cleansing."

His hold tightened. "I do have to know. Have you been pure for me, Mary?"

What was the right answer? The urge to punch him in the gut and tell him she'd found love nearly overwhelmed her. "Does it matter?" she asked, trying to remember the tricks Mal had taught her about getting information from a source.

"Yes." Isaac turned her to face him. "It does matter, very much."

"Why?" Which answer would get her what she wanted?

His chin lifted. "You always were full of questions. All right. If you've betrayed me, you will need to be cleansed in the fire if you're to have any chance of redemption."

"And if I haven't?" The idea of where this was going cramped her stomach.

"Then we have more work to do here. I'll put you somewhere safe while I do God's work." He planted his hands on her shoulders. "As God flows through me, you cannot lie. It's impossible."

The hell she couldn't. She looked him directly in the eye. If he put her away somewhere safe, then she wouldn't be able to find out what was happening. But his punishment for the truth might be more than she could bear. "Isaac—"

"I will confirm your claim of innocence, Mary. Quickly." He lowered his face. "God demands you tell the truth."

Isaac really believed his own bullshit, didn't he? An iron fist grasped her heart and squeezed. The only way to find out about the attack was, apparently, to become part of it. Her legs trembled so hard, her skirt rustled. "I-I can't lie. I have not been true to you."

His chest fell. "Ah, Jennifer. I am so sorry to hear that." He smiled as if somehow pleased.

Her mom's voice quavered. "Jennifer? Why not Mary?"

Isaac slowly shook his head and released Pippa. "This isn't the true Mary. I shall have to start seeking her now. This woman is an imposter. Put here by the devil to distract me."

Right. Pippa clasped her hands together to keep from punching him in the nose. She was probably too old for the nutjob now, considering she was in her twenties. Where was Malcolm anyway? "You promised if I came back I could see Trixie, Isaac. Even God keeps His promises."

"The assumption was that you were still Mary," he said, glancing at his watch. Then he lifted his head and called out, his voice echoing around the room. "George? Please bring in the chosen ones."

Pippa angled herself more toward her mother. If she had to get to her gun, it was going to be awkward with the skirt, but there hadn't been another way to conceal the weapon.

She held her breath, hoping Malcolm was coming.

Women filed inside the room, and Pippa recognized one from her time with the family years ago, and one from . . . the television? She tilted her head and studied a woman of about thirty with long red hair, freckles, and intense blue eyes. "You're Sylvia Newtonburg," Pippa said slowly. Wait a minute.

Sylvia nodded. "I am publicly anyway. My true name is Faustyna."

"The Apostle of Divine Mercy," Pippa murmured, remembering her lessons well. She'd seen the woman on the news lately. What had it been about? She wracked her brain, and it finally came to her. "The woman's march in DC later today. You're one of the organizers?" Her mind spun.

"Yes," Isaac said. "Faustyna has been in place for five years, owning and working in a store in DC. She had infiltrated many organizations until she was in position to help plan this rally, along with the date and parade route. She has truly done God's work."

The dawning realization of the true reach of Isaac's plan nearly dropped Pippa to her knees. She looked at the five other women in the room. One was her mother, another was a pretty and very bruised blonde. The woman Pippa recognized from a decade ago had been named Lilac. "Lilac?" she asked, remembering the now fiftysomething woman's kindness when she'd once been stung by a bee.

Lilac's dark gaze hardened. "I work as a waitress on the parade route Faustyna so carefully set up. No one will question my being there."

Heat scorched Pippa's throat. "What are you planning?"

"The backpacks are in the cabinet by the sliding glass door," Isaac said to George. "Fetch them."

George faltered and then moved toward the cabinet, opening it and ducking down to retrieve seven very different colored backpacks. From a light beige pack to a designer pack to an obvious student pack, he hefted them out carefully, setting them down as if they weighed a significant amount. "What's in the packs, Prophet?" he asked, finally standing.

"God's wrath," Isaac replied. "Suit up, ladies." He nodded toward a muted white bag near the door. "Bring that one over for my dear Mary." He coughed. "Old habits die hard, don't they? Oh well. We can call you Mary for the day."

She jerked away from him, fully intending to go for her gun. The sight of a shiny silver pistol in his hand stopped her. He'd been quick to grab it from his pocket. "I will not be used to harm anybody else, Isaac," she hissed.

He turned the gun on her mother. "Put on the backpack, Mary."

Pippa watched in disbelief as the other women chose backpacks, slipping their hands through the straps. "Are you people crazy? Do you understand what's probably in those? Do you realize you're about to hurt a lot of people?"

They moved woodenly and yet somehow with purpose.

Her mother chose the designer bag, oddly enough. She slipped her arms into it and secured it across her chest. "Mary. This is the only way."

They were lost. They were all so damn lost. The only

good news here was that the police had the road covered. No cars would make it out of the forested area to get anywhere near DC.

George settled the heavy backpack over Pippa's shoulders. She fought him, but he yanked her arms through the straps and secured them. The weight almost pulled her backward, and she had to shift her hips to keep her balance. "At the very least, you can tell me what's in here," she muttered.

Isaac smiled. "Presents in a pressure cooker. Nails, ball bearings, fireworks, gas, and powder."

She shut her eyes and swayed, quickly regaining her balance. "The same type of bombs as those used at the Boston Marathon years ago."

He nodded. "That's where I got the idea. Except these will detonate at chest level and hit abdomens, heads, and torsos. Not legs."

Oh God. He really was crazy. Even if Pippa died, these things couldn't make it to DC.

Isaac smiled and reached for a box. "I have your detonators here and will give them to you once we're in DC. I'd hate for one of you to accidentally press the button." He laughed.

Pippa turned, shock coursing through her. He really was that insane.

He looked at George. "Burn the mansion down. Use all the gasoline we have in the kitchen pantry."

George's eyes widened. "What about Malcolm and Trixie? They're locked downstairs."

Pippa jerked hard. Malcolm was locked down there, too? Had Isaac figured out he was a cop? "Let me go. Please let me get them."

"No. Burn them all, George." Isaac gestured toward the sliding glass door. "It's time to go." The women began to file out.

Pippa tried to fight him. Why would they go into the backyard?

Isaac grabbed her arm in a painful grip and propelled her toward the door. "You didn't think we were taking the front road, did you?"

She struggled against his hold, but with the bomb on her back, she couldn't gain leverage. "There's a back road?" The cops would have that covered, right? They'd get to Mal before George could start the fire, too.

"Probably. But for this? We have a helicopter."

Chapter Forty-One

Malcolm slowly came to, his head pounding and his torso feeling as if he'd been bashed with a wrecking ball. He was lying on a concrete floor. Wine racks surrounded him. "What the hell?" He forced himself to sit up, and the room spun crazily around him.

"You were hit in the head," said a soft voice over by the door. "You've finally stopped bleeding."

He turned to see Trixie sitting on the floor with her arms wrapped around her knees. Bruises mottled her face, and purple marks in the perfect shape of a man's fingers stood out on her delicate neck. "You okay?" he asked.

She nodded, looking small and defenseless. Her red hair only emphasized the raw purple markings and her pale skin. "Wasn't my first beating from the Prophet."

Mal tried to breathe and stopped as pain blasted through his rib cage. He pulled up his shirt to see a horribly red bruise. "Bastard broke my rib." He gingerly felt along the damaged area and lost his breath at the pain.

Trixie wiped dirt off her chin. "He likes to kick people when they're on the ground. Should we bind it or something?"

"No." Mal grasped a rack and pulled himself up, ignoring

the pain exploding behind his eyelids. "I take it we're locked in?"

She nodded.

"How long have I been here?" he asked, bending his arm over his waist to keep the pain at bay. Was Pippa already in the mansion?

"I don't know. I was knocked out, too," Trixie said. Then she sniffed the air. "I smell smoke." Panic widened her eyes.

Mal grasped her arm and pulled her to the side. His head aching, he moved to the door. Solid, with an old-fashioned keyhole. There was only one way through. "Stand back."

He kicked as hard as he could near the lock, and the door shimmied. Pain rippled up his leg.

Then again.

A third time.

Finally, on the fourth kick, the door crashed in.

Mal scouted the family room outside the wine cellar, looking frantically for the stairs. They were at the end of a long hallway, and smoke was pouring down. "Trixie? Get outside, now," he bellowed, turning into the smoke and rushing upstairs and down the hall toward the burning office.

Damn it.

He ducked low and tried to cover his mouth. The fire was already consuming the chairs by the fireplace as well as the curtains, and it had spread across the floor to the desk. The smell of gasoline was as overpowering as the stench of burning fabric.

Where the hell was Pippa?

Isaac had obviously deserted the mansion. Good. There were roadblocks in both directions, so the asshole would be caught any minute. The only worry was if there were already family members in place for an attack.

Mal leaped over a burning chair, and the second he landed, pain lashed through his rib cage. He caught his breath and fell against the desk, coughing. Pain exploded in his palms, and he yanked his hands back. The desk was burning hot. Papers were already curling across it, and he grabbed up what he could and ran from the room, slamming the door.

Trixie met him in the hallway, soot already in her hair. "I checked upstairs; nobody is here." She coughed. "I think we're clear."

"Outside." He coughed, and agony blew apart his side.

She crouched low, beneath the smoke, and rushed for the door. Mal kept on her heels, stumbling down the stairs toward the van.

George sat against one tire, his phone in his hands. "I don't think he's gonna call me," he said, a snot bubble popping out of his nose.

"What?" Trixie screamed, her hair a wild mess around her head.

Mal skidded to a stop across the expensive bricks. The same cars were in place as when he'd arrived. He whirled around, looking at the mansion. Smoke poured from broken windows. "What the hell? They didn't drive?"

George sniffed loudly. "No. There was a helicopter hidden beneath some tarps in the far back. They flew. Without me."

Mal grabbed the moron by the collar and yanked him to his feet, ignoring the rush of agony in his rib cage. "Was Pippa with them?"

"Pippa?" George frowned, his eyes glazed.

"Mary. Was Mary with Isaac? With the Prophet?" Mal shook George violently.

"Yes. He took her with him." George shuddered. "She doesn't even like him. Why would Prophet take her and not me?"

"Where? Where were they going?" Mal slammed George back against the vehicle, no longer feeling the pain. "Tell me."

"I don't know." George sobbed. "The Prophet didn't tell me. I helped put the backpacks on them, and then they left.

I would've worn a backpack. I'm a believer, you know?" He wiped his nose on his sleeve. "Why? Just why?"

Mal punched George across the jaw with his good arm, seeing red at the word *backpack*. "What was in the backpacks?"

"Prophet said something about pressure cookers," George said, his voice defeated.

Oh God. Mal grabbed the phone out of George's hand and dropped the papers to the bricks, spreading them out. Parts were burned, and some ink had run. He quickly dialed the phone.

"Force here." Thank God Force had answered the call, despite the unknown number. "Who are you?"

"Angus, it's Malcolm." Mal pored over the different maps. "Send in everyone—the mansion is on fire. Isaac is gone. So is Pippa." Just saying her name was like a kick to the balls. He looked up at George, who was crying against the van. "When did they leave? How long ago?"

George shrugged. "I don't know. Maybe an hour?"

They could've already landed. Mal shoved the first sheet over and then paused. He recognized a street corner and peered closer, his blood humming. "They're in DC, Angus. They've probably already landed."

"Okay. I'll be right there to extract you," Force said, his voice calm. "I have a helicopter on standby ten minutes away, just in case."

Malcolm glanced at the different diagrams on the map. "I think I can determine where the bombers are planning to stand." Then he glanced at the clock on the phone. "What time is the parade in DC? The women's march planned for today?"

"Let me check." The phone was silent. Then Angus returned, his voice dark. "It starts in thirty minutes."

Chapter Forty-Two

Pippa continued arguing with the other women as a plain white van drove them toward Washington, DC. They'd ignored her on the helicopter and had continued doing so in the van. A man she didn't know drove it, while Isaac sat in the back, on the floor with them.

"Mom—" Pippa started.

Isaac unsnapped her backpack and shoved it to the side. She blinked. That could only be good.

Then he grabbed her and yanked her over onto his lap. She struggled, panic infusing her, but he held tight. He even locked one of his legs over hers to keep her still. "I've had enough. Oliver, did you bring me what I requested?"

"Yep." Oliver handed something back.

"Mom, help me," Pippa begged, shoving against Isaac as hard as she could. He was surprisingly strong. She'd forgotten how often he worked out.

"Hold her," Isaac ordered.

The two nearest women grabbed on to Pippa's shoulders and pushed them back against Isaac.

He released his hold. "Extend her arm."

Pippa's eyes widened. Her chest heated. "No." She tried to struggle, but the three of them were too strong.

Without any care, Isaac plunged a needle above her inner elbow and depressed the plunger.

Heat and pain instantly sparked beneath her skin. "Wh-what?" she asked, her breath panting out so quickly her vision fuzzed. "What did you just inject me with?"

"Release her," Isaac ordered.

The women moved back to their places along the sides of the van. The floor was wood, and one woman's pants tore along the knee.

Dizziness and euphoria swamped Pippa, and she swayed. Her muscles started to relax one by one.

"Interesting." Isaac removed his leg and settled her back against his chest. "I aimed for a muscle, which would take around five minutes to have an effect. Looks like I hit your vein instead."

What? She tried to blink. The interior of the van was warm and cozy. She didn't feel any pain. What was happening? "Drugs?" she managed to gasp.

"Heroin," Isaac said, his mouth close to her ear.

She chilled. He wasn't like Malcolm. Mal was better. Much. Where was he? "Let-let me go." She couldn't move. Her body felt like dead weight, and her head lolled on her neck.

"No." Isaac opened his knees, and she fell down onto the floor, still enfolded by him. But now he could see over her head. "My beautiful creatures sent from God, I love you all so much." He nodded. "April, please hand out the sustenance."

April opened a mint tin and took a pill before passing it on to the next woman.

"What is that?" Pippa slurred.

"Courage, and something to help us all relax," Isaac said, his voice deepening in the way she remembered from childhood. "You don't need any." He chuckled at his own joke.

"What you do today is in God's name. You're fighting His fight, and you will be rewarded in Heaven."

Her mother smiled, but the happiness didn't quite reach her eyes.

The van hit a pothole and jostled everyone inside. Pippa's mom fell sideways and quickly righted herself.

"You are my greatest accomplishments, and before the day is through, you will be angels," Isaac said.

Pippa couldn't think. Thoughts moved in slow motion through her brain, and she could almost see them go. But she couldn't grasp one. She tried harder. "This isn't right." Her voice sounded very far away.

The van pulled over.

Isaac nodded. "You all know where to go. Faustyna?"

The beautiful redhead drew a cigar box off her lap and handed out what looked like garage door openers. She read the sticker on each carefully before handing it to one of the women. "These are the buttons to heaven."

Buttons to heaven? Pippa snorted. Talk about crazy. Her eyelids closed, and she had to fight to reopen them.

The door opened, and the women all climbed out. Her mother paused at the last moment and turned to her. "Mary, I hope you understand. You were made for this. Always." She smiled and shut the door. Then quiet. Just Pippa and Isaac and the driver.

"Go," Isaac said.

The van pulled out into what sounded like a busy street.

Pippa shook her head against his chest. He sighed and pushed her off him. She struggled to sit and then barely was able to balance herself, her skirt lifting to her knees. She tried to pull it down, and he grasped her hands.

"Let go," she slurred, swaying with the effort.

"No." He slapped her face, and the echo repeated through her head several times. A pain in the far distance pricked her face, but she couldn't quite grasp it. "Concentrate, Mary."

She blinked, staring into those amber eyes that had haunted her for so long. "You're just a man," she murmured.

He smiled. "We both know I'm more than that."

"I don't like your smile," she blurted out in slow motion. "Never have." She waved her hand, and then dropped it to the floor. Not like Malcolm. He had a great smile. So handsome. But she shouldn't say his name. She knew she shouldn't. Why? Huh. Why was that?

Isaac slapped her again, and this time her face hurt.

She tried to focus on him.

"I made you. Everything you are right now, I made," he said, leaning toward her.

His claim struck her as funny, and she laughed. Oh, it might be the drugs, but who cared? "You've never meant anything to me," she whispered, knowing there was no way that could be the full truth. But she'd never give him the satisfaction of knowing that for years she'd feared the sound of branches against windows was him coming to find her. "You don't matter, Isaac. You never have and you never will."

He punched her in the mouth this time, and her head rocked back. Pain flared for just a second and then was forgotten. Score one for the drugs. She tasted blood. "Why me?" She'd never understood.

"You know why," he said, his smile a tad lopsided. "You've always known why."

She shook her head. "No. I haven't. Blue eyes and brown hair? That's what Mary is to you? And the numbers? Those silly numbers of seven, eighteen, and twenty-five? They don't mean anything."

"I hope my face is the last thing you remember," he muttered, retrieving the backpack and forcing her arms through it. When he attached the front this time, he clicked a lock into a ring. "I had this made especially for you. There's no taking it off."

Man, it was heavy. She tried to shrug out of it, her mind spinning again.

He held a garage door opener in front of her eyes. "I can't wait to push this. What a disappointment you've been. I've been searching for you for almost seven years. For what?"

She smiled and felt blood dribble down her chin. "I didn't think of you once. Not once." Her head lolled forward again.

"I'm making the sacrifice of you to God." His grip on her arm hurt. "You're dying in hellfire today, Mary." He dragged her across the wooden floor, and the gun at her thigh scraped her. Oh yeah. The gun. She had to get to it. "And you're going to take a lot of sinners with you."

Chapter Forty-Three

Mal hit the ground the second the police car lurched to a stop. They'd landed the helicopter outside of DC and had instantly been picked up. He spread the map over the hood of the car and pointed out potential bomb locations.

Force spoke into a radio, sending directions for HDD teams and bomb squads while also pointing out positions for the team. "Wolfe go here, Raider go here," he ordered. "I'll go to this one, and West? I'm assuming you want the big intersection right here?"

Malcolm nodded. "That's my guess. He'll want something big and special for Pippa." The intersection was right in the middle of the parade route, covered on both sides by storefronts. There was nowhere to run or hide.

"Be careful, and try for containment as much as possible," Force ordered. "We don't know anything about these bombs. There could be a dead man's trigger, so if you shoot the person holding the remote, the bomb may explode. Use extreme caution." He zipped his jacket to hide his gun.

Mal did the same and pressed harder on his earbud so it wouldn't fall out. "The schematics show the triggers are remote, but you're right about the dead man's switch." He gave Force a look. "Keep tight." Then he turned and jogged as discreetly as possible through the milling crowd that was making its way up the avenue toward the Capitol, a mile away.

Every time his right foot hit pavement, his ribs jarred in a way that stole his breath. Shoving all feeling away was the hardest thing he'd ever done.

But this was for Pippa.

The paradegoers moved up the street, chanting and singing. The jovial mood extended to the crowds on the sidewalks, many of whom were holding signs or milling around with food in their hands.

Mal cut left and then turned down the route toward the spot Isaac had marked on the map. Then he took another right at the end of the block.

He saw Isaac before Pippa. The cult leader was about three yards from the street corner he'd designated. Mal eyed the area. Everything inside him bellowed that Isaac didn't want to die. He was fine letting his followers die, but he wanted to live.

Mal could use that.

He came up on their left, his vision narrowing for the tiniest of seconds on Pippa. She stumbled next to Isaac, trying to say something, her voice drowned out by the crowd. A large white backpack covered her entire lower back.

Mal's chest compressed.

His blood pumped faster, and he looked wildly around for a solution. There was only one. Timing his movements exactly right, he pivoted and shoved both of them into the open doorway of a coffee shop.

A lady yelped and fell against the wall.

"Get out!" he yelled, holding up his badge. "Everyone get out now!" People scrambled for the doorway.

Isaac partially turned, fury darkening his face. He held up a small garage door button.

"You push it, you die, too," Malcolm said as the door

closed behind him and the place grew quiet. Shouts could be heard from outside, but inside, only the hum of a coffee machine pierced the tension. "Are you prepared to die, Isaac?"

Isaac tried to move away from Pippa, and she grabbed his arm, staying with him.

Smart girl.

Isaac shook his head. "How are you even here?"

"God wants me here," Mal shot back. "Do you think He wants you dead?"

Pippa swayed on her feet.

Mal nearly reached for her and then stopped himself. "What did you give her?"

Isaac looked around, his gaze oddly serene.

Pippa coughed. "Malcolm? You should get out of here. Trust me." Her voice was slurred.

Isaac stilled and then focused on her. His jaw went slack. "You know him." He shook his head and stared at Mal. "How? How in the hell?"

"I love him," Pippa said, grasping the back of a chair for balance. Her eyelids were half-closed, and the bomb on her back seemed to be pulling her.

Betrayal flashed through Isaac's eyes. "You can't. You love me. I'm sacrificing everything here."

"No." She coughed. "You can't sacrifice what you don't have."

"But I do. Just like God sacrificed his only son." He smiled, the sight chilling.

She blinked. Once and then again. Her face turned even paler. "No. You're wrong."

"I've been hinting at the truth forever." He shoved her, hard, and scrambled toward the door.

Mal stepped in his way and drew out his gun.

Isaac paused and held his hand higher. "I will push this button."

Pippa fumbled with her skirt, but Mal kept his gaze on the crazy guy. "If you push it, we all die." He smiled. "I've been ready to die since my first assignment. What about you, Isaac? You sure you're ready? Have you done everything you planned?" God, he had to get that remote. Now. He had to figure out a way to save Pippa.

"Say the words," Pippa murmured, a gun suddenly in her hands. "I want to hear you say them, even though you're so wrong."

Mal eyed her. What was she talking about?

Isaac lowered his chin, his focus on her. "You already know. Always have. Your mother and I were together, right before she met your father. It's destiny. You can feel it."

Whoa. Was he saying—

"You are not my father." Her hands shook.

"Oh, but I am," Isaac said. "First Corinthians is more than clear. *So then both he who gives his own virgin daughter in marriage does well, and he who does not give her in marriage will do better.*"

"Your interpretation is wrong," Pippa said slowly, her words slurred. "So wrong. You really are a nutjob of classic proportions. You wanted to marry your own daughter?"

Isaac's chest puffed out. "Think of the purity of our line. The blessed children."

Pippa gagged.

Mal's earbud crackled. "Got one," Force said tersely. "Have isolated, removed the backpack, and am clearing the area. Bomb squad move in."

Wolfe's voice came next over the line. "We've isolated, but she won't take off the pack."

"Ditto here," Raider said quietly. "Working on it."

"Retreat if necessary," Force ordered. "Don't let them take you out as well."

Mal shut off all the outside noise and concentrated. The second Isaac got out the door, he'd press that button. "Pippa? Can you take off the backpack?"

"It's locks, I mean locked," Pippa said. "Leave, Malcolm. Please get out of here."

If she thought he was leaving her, she was nuts. "Can't. You're my heart," he murmured.

An explosion rocked the city.

"No!" Pippa cried out. She tried to move forward and then had to catch herself with a chair.

Isaac lifted his head to listen, delight crossing his expression.

Another explosion detonated.

Mal's stomach dropped. God. How many people had just died?

Glee had Isaac dancing in an odd parody of celebration. "That's two. How lovely. *But because of your hard and impenitent heart you are storing up wrath for yourself on the day of wrath when God's righteous judgment will be revealed.*"

"Romans 2:5," Pippa murmured. "You know, Isaac. I don't think you really understand the Bible." Her head lolled a little on her neck, and her gun shook wildly.

Mal tried to keep his head. "Pippa? Put down the gun, honey." If she shot Isaac, there was a good chance the bomb would trigger.

She sighed. "I love you, Malcolm. Please leave."

"Love?" Isaac spat. "What are you saying?"

Her eyes widened even as her head bobbed. "We've had sex. Lots and lots of sex, Isaac. Tell Malcolm to leave, and I'll tell you all about it. We can die together. See God together. Wouldn't you like to see me punished?"

Isaac turned beet red. "Malcolm doesn't get to live on.

We will all die. I have done my duty for my God." His body tensed.

Force's voice crackled over the line. "Bomb squad here. Have confirmed there is not a dead man's switch. Repeat. No dead man's switch."

Mal fired instantly, hitting Isaac between the eyes. Then he slid forward on his knees and caught the garage door opener before it could hit the floor. Jesus. He froze in place. Pippa still had a bomb on her chest. "Bomb squad to Sam's Coffee Shop. Now," he whispered, his voice hoarse.

Then he stood and moved toward her.

Force ran inside, out of breath, wire cutters in his hands. "Two of the vests were locked." He approached Pippa slowly and then snapped the lock.

He and Mal gently slid it free of her arms just as she went down, her eyelids fluttering, her body going still in unconsciousness. Mal caught her, and her gun dropped to the floor.

"Run," Force ordered, grabbing the door.

Mal tucked her tight and ran as fast as he could away from the backpack.

Chapter Forty-Four

Pippa awoke to the beep of monitors and the vague feeling of aches and pains in her face. She opened her eyes to see a private hospital room with a huge bouquet of vibrant red roses on the counter. Malcolm slept in a chair, his whiskered chin on his chest, his large body hunched. "Mal?" she croaked, her throat dry.

He jerked and opened his stunning green eyes. One side of his lip lifted in a lopsided smile. "Hey, beautiful."

She blinked several times and tried to remember everything that had happened. Vulnerability swamped her, and she felt exposed. Way too far out in the world. Then she frowned. "My skin itches. Bad."

He leaned forward and pushed the hair away from her eyes. His touch was gentle and comforting, and this close, his scent of man and forest eased her. "It's a side effect of heroin. The docs checked your blood, and Isaac shot you up but good."

"Isaac," she said, her head aching. "Dead?"

"Very much so." Mal's eyes darkened. "So are your mother and the redheaded woman who planned the march. I'm so very sorry, Pippa."

The words were a blow but not unexpected. "How many people did they kill?" she asked, tears clogging her throat.

Mal shook his head. "None. We had them contained and were working to get them to remove the backpacks. They both decided to detonate instead." He sighed. "There were some injuries outside the blast area, a couple serious, but everyone is going to live."

There was at least that. "I wish I could've helped her somehow." Pippa's chest hurt.

Mal smoothed his knuckles across her cheek. "You were a kid, baby. Nothin' you could've done."

Maybe not. But she'd always wonder. "What about Trixie?" She held her breath.

"She's fine. In a room down the hall, actually. I'll bring her in later to see you." He smiled.

Relief filled her so quickly, her body itched more. Then she looked around, noting the door was shut and the room very quiet. Okay. She could relax here a little bit. "Private room?"

He nodded. "Figured you wouldn't be up to a lot of people or noise."

Her heart warmed. "I'm not going to be a shut-in any longer." Though it was nice to have time to make baby steps. Very small steps.

Raider Tanaka moved into the room, a bright green plant in his hands. Scrapes and bruises covered his face, and his dark eyes were somber. "How's our patient?"

Pippa smiled, surprised that she felt okay having him there. "Alive. I'm glad you are, too." She hadn't had a chance yet to get to know this coworker of Mal's, but he had an air that inspired confidence. He was somebody you could trust. "Thank you."

He set down the plant, placing it gently on the counter. The green brightened the place up. "You bet." His hand landed on Mal's shoulder. "How's the rib?"

"Broken." Mal grimaced. "I've had worse."

Wolfe poked his head in. "Just got yelled at by a really pretty nurse about Kat being in my pocket here." Then he moved fully inside and handed over a big orange balloon that said *Happy Birthday*. "They were out of get-well ones."

Amusement took Pippa. It felt okay having Wolfe there, too. Somehow, even though there were three large men in the room, she felt safe. "It's perfect. Thanks."

Wolfe glanced down at Mal. "How are you?"

"Busted up but will survive. Where's the rest of the gang?" Mal asked.

Raider rubbed a scratch across his cheekbone. "Force and Nari are interviewing the cult women we managed to save. Once we get information, we'll try to find help for them. Especially that April you were worried about."

Mal's shoulders seemed to relax. Pippa smiled.

Raider continued. "Brigid is conducting computer searches to trace all movements of other cult members. We found the new family home in Kansas City. We have work to do."

Pippa bit her lip. "Find anything else?"

"Yeah. We're handling the killing of Mark and the young woman right now. It's no problem." Raider's face softened. "You don't have to worry about that. Even if your prints are on the knife, we have you covered between your statement and Trixie's. So no worrying."

She nodded. She and Trixie could take a lie detector test if necessary, but she didn't think it'd get to that point. The Requisition folks had her covered. So this was what real safety felt like. "Thank you," she said.

Raider clapped Wolfe on the back. "I'll drive you and Kat back before you get us kicked out of the hospital."

Wolfe nodded. "See you at the office." With a wink, he was gone.

Pippa straightened beneath the blankets. "You have a nice group. At your office. Good people."

"Yeah." He took her hand in his. "So."

"So." Tingles wandered down her torso. What now?

Mal was thoughtful for a moment. "What Isaac said. About you—"

She shook her head. "No. It doesn't matter. My dad was a hero in the army, and he died when I was six." She believed that in her heart, and that's where it mattered.

"Understood." Mal's gaze softened.

"Thank you for saving my life." It was the least she could say.

"Always." The way he said the word, it sounded like he had plans. "Here's the deal." His gaze cut away.

Was he nervous? The idea warmed her with a soft delight. "We're making a deal?"

He nodded and focused those amazing green eyes back on her. "Yeah. We haven't known each other very long, so this is the plan. We're going to date for a while. Get to know each other. Get you used to the outside world in your own time."

"My own time," she murmured.

"Yeah. Then maybe we'll move in together. Test the waters." He cleared his throat. "After an acceptable time, I'll ask you to marry me in some crazy way, and then you'll say yes."

Her heart lurched. Even the monitor buzzed.

"Do you want kids?" he asked.

"Yes," she whispered.

"Okay. We'll have a boy and then a girl, and then maybe a couple more. I'll keep working with Force for a while, and then I'll figure out what I want to do. I mean, we'll figure it out." He swallowed, and that foresty gaze seemed to bore right into her heart. "Okay?" Then he seemed to hold his breath.

Delight burst through her, brighter than any color she could imagine. "I'm not sure you can plan all of that, especially the order of kids."

"I can try." His eyebrows lifted.

"I have a counter proposal," she murmured, so warm she couldn't believe it. "How about you move in right now? I'm tired of not living. So let's live together."

His grin held a sweetness he rarely showed. "Good line."

Yeah, it was. It really was.

"I accept your proposal," he murmured, leaning in to gently kiss her lips. "In case I forgot during all that planning, I love you. Always will, no matter what."

Her breath caught. Was it possible to be this happy? "I love you, too."

"It's gonna be a good life, Pippa. That I promise." He kissed her nose and leaned back.

She nodded. Yeah. He was right. She'd make sure of it.

Epilogue

Malcolm West walked into the bull pen of the HDD and stopped short. A tarp covered the desks, which had been shoved to the middle of the room. Bon Jovi blared from a speaker pod in the corner, and Roscoe was dancing near it, shaking his furry ass like his life depended on it.

"The dog has issues," Wolfe said, not looking away from the wall he was painting a soothing beige. Kat peeked out of his pocket, looked around, meowed loudly, and then snuggled back down.

Pippa laughed next to Mal, and the sound filled his chest. She'd been released from the hospital two weeks earlier, and anything that made her happy was a good thing as far as he was concerned.

Angus stood on a ladder and painted the top of the far wall while Raider painted along the base; there was a strip of paint down the back of his dark T-shirt. Apparently, there had already been a paint fight.

Brigid walked in from the computer room, paint all over her T-shirt and even on her chin.

Mal grinned. "Did you paint the wall or yourself?"

She snorted and rolled her eyes, grabbing a couple of

paintbrushes off the tarp and heading his way. "I hope you're here to work."

He nodded and accepted a brush before handing one to Pippa. They'd both worn old clothing, and she looked adorable with her hair in twin braids. He couldn't help but tug one.

She playfully slapped his hand and took her brush over to Raider to paint where she could reach.

Malcolm watched her, wondering when he'd lose the hypervigilance he always experienced with her. Ever since he'd seen her with a bomb on her back, he hadn't been able to let her get far from his sight. The good news was that she seemed to like spending time with him.

The bad news was that he'd probably need to talk to the shrink for a while. He rubbed his aching ribs. It had been two weeks, and his torso still hurt.

Brigid rocked back on her heels. "Still in pain?" Her slight accent warmed her words.

"It's better." He studied the area. "The new paint on the walls makes the ceiling look horrible." Dingy and old.

Nari Zhang stepped out of her office, her feet in dark running shoes. "I've ordered new lights, and we'll paint the ceiling next. We have screens coming for the walls that'll make it look like we have windows, and then we can do something with the concrete floor." Her painting clothes were dark jeans and a red-checked shirt. Not a drop of paint was on her yet. She moved past Roscoe, petted him, and then crossed into Force's office. "We'll do this office next," she called out, her voice thoughtful.

Brigid watched Nari and then sighed, turning back to Mal. "That's a good plan." Her eyes darkened.

Mal frowned. "What's wrong?"

"Nothing." Brigid shrugged her shoulders and tried to tug down her paint-riddled shirt. When Malcolm just stared at her, she rolled her eyes. "It's just that she's so, well, so put together? You know?" Her voice lowered to a whisper.

Mal eyed Nari in the far doorway as she studied the doorframe. "Yeah. So?"

"Nothing." Brigid turned to go paint.

Mal grasped her arm. "Hey. You can be anybody you want to be, you know?" He'd never had a sister, but this team was turning into a family, so what the hell. "Brigid?"

"Right," she scoffed. "No problem."

"Yeah." He released her. "Believe me. You can become anybody you want to be. You want to look like a put-together nosy shrink? I can help you."

She bit her lip. "I don't want to look like a shrink, but I wouldn't mind looking like a professional." Her gaze slid to Raider and then back, while pink flushed across her cheeks. "And not an escaped convict."

Mal grinned. "You don't look like an escaped convict."

"Huh. Tell him that." She jerked her head toward Raider and then visibly shook herself out of it. "I'll take the help, Malcolm. After we paint." She patted his arm and left a paint mark before heading over to work near Pippa.

Mal sighed.

Wolfe glanced at him. "I'm thinking of painting my house next. You in?"

Mal blinked. He'd moved in with Pippa, and Wolfe had instantly claimed the house next door. "I didn't even paint it when I was there."

"You weren't there very long," Wolfe said reasonably. "I'm getting something called slipcovers for the furniture, too. Pippa showed me how to find them on the internet. Maybe I should have a housewarming party." He reached up and ran a strip of paint above his head. "People have to bring gifts to those, right?"

"I think so," Malcolm said. He'd never been to a housewarming party. "What kind of gift would you like?"

Wolfe thought it over. "I could use a new SIG."

Pippa walked their way, her hips swaying beneath the old jeans. "Are you going to just stand there or help?" Her smile made her pretty blue eyes sparkle.

He wiped a smattering of paint off her chin, enjoying the feeling of her soft skin. "Wolfe is going to have a house-warming party."

"That's a great idea." She nearly hopped. "You need some plants, Wolfe. And probably wineglasses and a painting or two."

So much for the SIG.

Wolfe nodded, like he knew what she was talking about. "Yeah. That's what I was thinking."

Mal shook his head. "All right. Where should I start painting?"

Pippa looked up at him, peace on her face. "Next to me. Always."

Now that was a plan.

Read on for an excerpt from
Rebecca Zanetti's next Requisition novel,

FALLEN,

coming soon!

The damn man took up all the space in the dilapidated elevator as it descended. All the oxygen as well. Brigid studied the six-foot-two government agent from beneath her lashes, trying once again to figure Raider Tanaka out.

Jet-black hair, thick and a bit wavy, showcased a hard-looking and symmetrical face. His eyes were somehow even darker than his hair, and they often seemed to look right through her. His lean physique was muscular, and he moved with the grace of a swimmer. A swimmer who could kick your ass if necessary. The guy probably had an exercise regimen he practiced religiously. He seemed like the type.

He returned the survey, *not* beneath his lashes. The man had no problem keeping an eye on her.

That was part of his job, of course.

"Stop looking at me," she murmured.

"You're looking at me," he returned easily as the elevator stopped abruptly and jumped twice. The door didn't open. He frowned. "This thing can't be safe."

No doubt. Brigid pushed her unruly hair away from her face and forced thoughts of small spaces out of her head. Kind of. "Why were we called in on a Saturday?"

Raider shrugged. "We finished painting the offices last

weekend, so I figured we'd have some time off. Guess not." His tone remained unconcerned, and he appeared relaxed. Yet a tension, a promise that he would leap into action in a nanosecond, always emanated from him. It both fascinated and irritated the heck out of her.

Brigid bit her lip and stared at the closed elevator door. "Shouldn't this be opening about now?"

"Yes," he said, leaning back against the scarred faux wood wall. On his day off, he wore faded jeans and a dark leather jacket instead of his normal suit. In the casual wear, he somehow appeared even deadlier than usual. "The door will open soon. Probably. Who knows? It's ancient."

Wonderful. Being stuck in a rickety elevator with Raider was the last place on earth she wanted to be. Well, the second to last place. Prison had sucked—royally. "You didn't have to come with me today, you know. Angus called me in. Not you."

Angus Force led the small unit of the Homeland Defense Department that was hidden in the basement of this crappy building.

Raider didn't answer.

Irritation clawed up Brigid's neck. "I said you're not needed."

He lowered his chin, his gaze more than a little direct. Oddly so. "I'm your handler. Where you go, I go."

Handler. The way he said it, or maybe the way she heard it, sent sparkling tingles through her that she so did not need. Not at all. It was crazy, insane actually, to look at Raider as anything other than another government drone put on earth to make her life more difficult.

Yet there was something about him, a respect or just politeness when he dealt with her that she simply couldn't figure out. She was a former con—at least he thought she was—and he was an HDD agent. But never once had he been unkind. Not once. She could tell, though. He didn't appreciate convicts being free, and he really didn't like being her handler. No doubt it was a huge step down for him. "Why are you here?" she whispered.

He looked at the closed door, as if contemplating what to do with it. The elevator was so old that there wasn't even a phone inside. Or an emergency button. "I told you."

"No." The walls were starting to close in on her, and she took a deep breath. "Come on, Raider. I can tell you're used to action." Even when relaxed, he was way too alert. Sure, she'd heard he'd gotten into trouble by sleeping with his boss's wife without knowing who she was, but something told Brigid that Raider could've fought being demoted. "Why are you stuck babysitting me?"

"You're a threat." He said the words simply, his gaze meeting hers again. "Your ability with computers, with hacking and coding, make you incredibly dangerous to this country and everything I believe in. Watching you, making sure you don't create a disaster, is an important job." He scrubbed a hand through his thick hair. "Keeping you safe is just as important."

Her eyebrows lifted of their own accord. "Keeping me safe? I'm not in danger."

He gave her that look then. The one she'd seen more than a dozen times in the last two weeks since they'd met. The look that said he thought she was slightly nuts. "You're one of the best. You've been able to hack into systems that are unhackable."

"Nothing, no system, is ever unhackable," she returned without thinking.

"Exactly. You're known now. After being arrested and incarcerated, your name is known worldwide. Do you have any idea what a foreign enemy would do to get their hands on you?" he asked, his voice soft.

Yeah. That was the whole point, actually. "You're overestimating me."

"Not even close, Irish."

She blinked. He'd started calling her by that nickname the first day they'd met, and every time she heard the sobriquet in his deep voice, something warmed deep inside her. "My accent isn't strong enough to warrant the nickname," she muttered. Her mother had been Irish, her father Bostonian, and her speech pattern held slight, very slight, hints of both. That was all. She grew up on a farm in the USA, for Pete's sake.

"I think it does." Raider moved toward the doors and placed his hand in the middle, digging his fingers between them. Or rather, he tried to do so.

Nothing happened.

Brigid's breath quickened. That quickly, she was back in a cell. Her lungs hurt. Her vision narrowed from the outside, making her eyes sting. Were they even on the basement level? Or did they have farther to fall? God, she had to get out of there. She sucked in air.

He turned then, narrowing his focus on her again. "Whoa." Stepping in, he grasped her chin and lifted her face enough to meet his eyes. "Take a deep breath."

She couldn't breathe.

"Now, Brigid." The command in his voice shot through her panicked mind.

She instinctively heeded it and pulled in air, filling her lungs.

"Now let it out. Slowly." He waited until she did so. "Again."

She obeyed his order, and her heart rate slowed down. Then she started to notice something other than the suffocatingly small space. His size. His scent of male and musk. His nearness and warmth.

Her heart kicked back in along with her libido. Heat flushed through her, igniting nerves, softening something deep inside her. His grip remained gentle yet firm on her chin. If he lowered his head, his mouth could be on hers.

Where the heck had that thought come from? Heat burst into her face, no doubt turning her a very unappealing crimson.

"It's okay," he murmured, his tone deep and reassuring. "The door will open."

The door? What door? She coughed. "You don't like me." The words blurted out. Was she reminding him or herself?

Both of his dark eyebrows rose. "That's not true." He released her and stepped back.

"Yes, it is." She wanted to cross her arms but forced herself to remain still and in control.

"No. I just haven't figured you out." He turned to the door again.

She frowned at his broad back. "So?"

"I figure everyone out." He smacked his palm against the door. "Open, darn it."

The door hitched open.

Humor bubbled through the unwelcome desire in Brigid. "You're magic."

He looked over his shoulder. "You have no idea, Irish." Then he crossed into the small and dimly lit vestibule of the basement offices.

Had he just flirted with her? For Pete's sake. She moved out of the too-small space on wobbly legs. Enough of that silliness. Reaching the wide-open room, she sighed. The fresh paint had brightened the office a bit, but the myriad of desks was still old and scarred, the overhead lights old, yellow, and buzzing.

Raider looked down at the cracked concrete floor and grimaced.

"We're supposed to paint that next," Brigid said, coming up on his side. Wasn't that the plan? "And I think there's art coming, or screens that show outside scenes." The basement headquarters were a step down from depressing, even with the fresh paint. The big room was eerily silent as well.

Three doors led to an office and two conference rooms, while one more door, a closet for the shrink, was over to the west.

A German shepherd padded out of the far office, munching contentedly on something bright red. It coated his mouth and stained the lighter fur around his chin.

"Roscoe," Brigid breathed, her entire body finally relaxing. Animals and computer code, she knew. It was people who threw her.

The dog seemed to grin and bounded toward her, his tail wagging wildly. She ducked to pet him. "What in the world do you have?" This close she could see that the stuff was thick and matted in his fur. She frowned and tried to force open his mouth. "Roscoe?"

As if on cue, Angus Force stepped out of the second conference room, also known as case room two. "Hey, you two. Thanks for coming in."

Brigid looked up. "Roscoe has something."

"Damn it." Angus made it through the desks in record time. "Is it Jack Daniel's?"

Brigid smiled. "No. It's red." The dog had a drinking problem?

Angus glared at his dog. "Drop it. Now." The command in his voice would've made Brigid drop anything she was carrying.

The dog sighed and spit out a gold-plated lipstick.

Brigid winced. "That looks expensive."

The dog licked his lips.

Angus sighed. "I told everyone not to leave makeup around. He likes the taste."

"No, you didn't," Brigid countered.

Angus pierced her with a look. "Well, I meant to. Roscoe, get back to the office. Now."

The dog gave her a what-a-butthead type of look and turned to slink back to Angus's office.

"You two, come with me." Angus turned and headed back to the case room, no doubt expecting them to follow.

Raider motioned her ahead of him. Yeah. Like she'd return to that death trap of an elevator. Though it was preferable to dealing with Angus Force. The former FBI profiler now headed up this division of the HDD, and he seemed almost able to read people's minds. Was he reading hers? Did he have one clue that she wasn't who she was supposed to be? How much had he guessed?

She crossed into the case room to face a whiteboard across from a conference table. Several pictures of men, some older and some quite young, were taped evenly across the expanse. "New case?" she asked.

"Yes." Angus gestured for them to sit.

She was the computer expert in the small unit, so she was involved in every case. Her fingers actually itched to get back to her keyboard. The last case they'd worked on had involved a cult planting bombs at a rally. They'd saved hundreds of people that day. Curiosity took her as she sat down, with Raider sitting next to her.

Angus moved around to the board. "New case kicked to us by the HDD. They think it's crap, and I think it has merit. Either that, or somebody is messing with us."

Raider stiffened just enough that Brigid could feel his tension. "How so?"

"While the Irish mob no longer exists in Boston, there are criminals, past associates of the mob that have risen in the ranks and become threats recently," Angus said, standing big and broad on the other side of the table.

Brigid settled more comfortably in her seat. She had no problem hacking into criminal affairs.

"How so?" Raider asked, all business.

"Instead of working within the usual, or rather former, hierarchy of the mob, these guys are outsourcing work to incredibly skilled computer criminals," Angus said.

"Like me," Brigid said quietly.

Angus nodded. "Exactly. We have a line on a group using a site on the dark web. We think they're running drugs for sure, but we don't know what else."

The dark web was nearly impossible to hack. "I can't find a site without knowing where it is," Brigid said. "The key to bringing down somebody on the dark web is—"

"Getting them to meet you in person," Raider said. "Guess that's my part of this Op."

"Partially," Angus said, eyeing them both. "There's more."

Warning ticked through Brigid. Why, she didn't know. But her instincts rose instantly, and she stiffened. "What?"

"We think this might be one of the key players." Angus turned and taped one more picture to the board.

Brigid stopped breathing. She stared at the picture. He had aged. His skin was leathery, his nose broken more than once, and his hair now all gray.

Raider glanced at her. "Who is that?"

"My father," she whispered. The man she hadn't seen or talked to in nearly eight years. She coughed. "You're crazy. He's a farmer. Always has been."

Angus winced. "No. He was involved with the mob for years. Formative ones. Then he supposedly got out, but now we think he's back in."

That couldn't be true. No way. Brigid rapidly shook her head. "You're wrong."

"Prove it," Angus said mildly. "You and Raider go talk to him and prove I'm wrong. But be prepared to be incorrect about this."

Brigid shook her head. "You want me to take an obvious government agent to my father's farm and what? Just ask him if he's involved in cybercrime?" No way. "Believe me. My dad wouldn't talk to a fed if he was dying."

Angus's smile didn't provide reassurance. "No. You're going home to reconcile with your father because you've finally found your way in life with the upstanding, calm, and boring man next to you. Who you want to introduce to your father before you marry."

"Marry?" Brigid blurted out, her mind spinning wildly. "Are you nuts?" She turned to the straitlaced hottie next to her. "Tell him this won't work."

Raider hadn't moved. "This is important, Force?"

"Crucial," Angus affirmed. "There's more going on here than drugs. I just know it."

Raider turned and studied her with those deep and way too dark eyes. "Well, Irish. Looks like we're engaged." His smile sent butterflies winging through her abdomen. "This is going to be interesting. Now that you're mine, I'll finally figure you out."